YOU WILL TURN
WORLDS UPSIDE DOWN.

TRICKY
PRINCESS

L.L. CAMPBELL

TRICKY MAGIC SERIES
BOOK TWO

TRICKY PRINCESS

TRICKY MAGIC SERIES

BOOK TWO

Tricky Princess
Book Two of The Tricky Magic Series
Copyright © 2022 L.L. Campbell

ISBN 979-8-9854622-8-9
Publication Date: September 13, 2022

The characters and events portrayed in this book are fictitious or are used fictitiously. The settings are inspired by real locations. Specifically where I grew up in New England. Any similarity to real persons, living or dead, is purely coincidental and not intended.

Cover Design | Elizianna@elizianna.the.one
Internal Design | L.L. Campbell
Page Formatting| Books n' Moods
Published by L.L. Campbell @readsbylexi
Copy Editing: Lavender Prose

Full TW can be found mid-way down the linked page.

DON'T START READING YET...

There are graphic sex scenes, somnophilia, FFFM,
talk of emotionalabuse, hint at sexual assault,
killing, parental loss, and a shit ton of swearing.

Emotional abuse is written throughout the story.
There are several graphic sex scenes. Somnophilia
is in one scene and is FFFM.

Groping and cornering can be found
throughout. Once published I will have exact
chapters and locations.

www.llcampbell.com

If you have any questions or concerns with my
work, please feel free to contact me:
booksby@llcampbell.com

I hope you enjoy the characters and the world
they live in.
xo L.L.

To Ash, for all the texts and late nights. To my readers, for giving me a chance. And to my gaggle of fickle smut sluts, I love you more than you know!

al an

portsmouth

rosier's lake

glenover

sea

gela point

halifax

mortal terr

southern territory

supernatural te

ruler: Belizbub
dwellers: the malevolent
description: enless waste,
the pits, fire, and pain

ruler: Leviathan
dwellers: supernaturals only

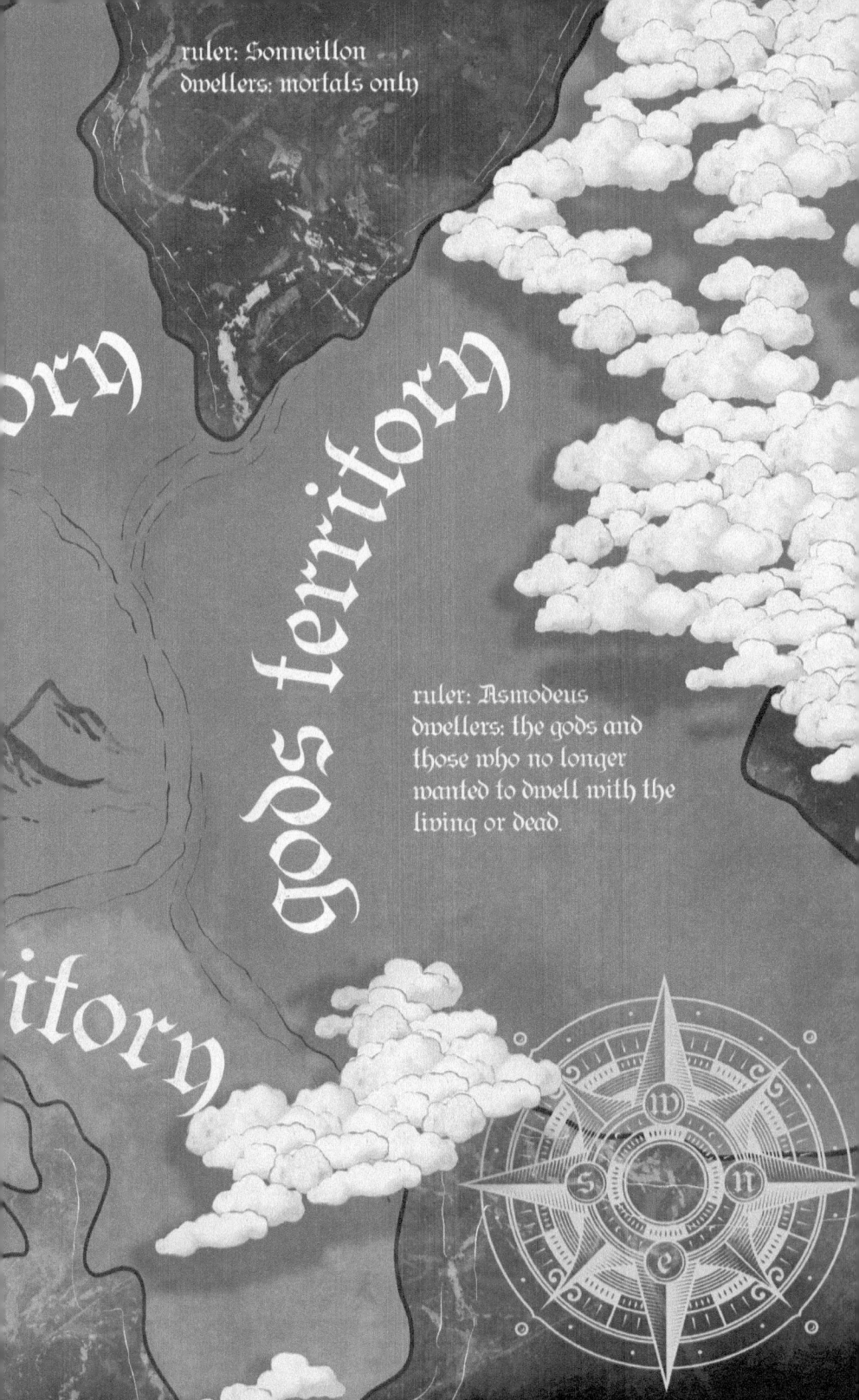

ruler: Sonneillon
dwellers: mortals only

ory

gods territory

ruler: Asmodeus
dwellers: the gods and
those who no longer
wanted to dwell with the
living or dead.

itory

Playlist

Carry on Wayward Son - Kansas
all the good girls go to hell - Billie Eilish
NBK - E Niykee Heaton
Bow - Slowed - E Reyn Hartley
Nightmares - Ellise
Neon Moon - Brooks & Dunn, Kacey Musgraves
Not Enough - Elvis Drew, Avivian
Play with Fire (feat. Yacht Money) - Sam Tinnesz, Yacht Money
Lilith - Ellise
Power - Isak Danielson
Put It on Me - Matt Maeson
The Curse - Agnes Obel
July - Noah Cyrus
Lady Like - Ingrid Andress
Start A Riot - BEGINNERS, Night Panda
Goddess - ME Jaira Burns
Far From Home (The Raven) - Sam Tinnesz
Where Are You? - Elvis Drew, Avivian
Devil - E Nivkee Heaton
Don't Blame Me - Taylor Swift
And more!

GLOSSARY

I'm an ass and picked more weird names:

Ellea: EHL-iyAH
Jadis: JHEY-DihS
Rosier: ROH-zee-ur
Belias: BEL-iy AS
Asmodeus: az-mo-DEE-uhs
Duhne: doon
Sonneillon: s-aw-n-eh-l-ee-oh-n
Leviathan: luh·vai·uh·thn
Mhairi: MahHHAARiy
Macaria: m-aa-k-aa-r-EE-aa
Esmeray: es-mer-ay
Beelzebub: bee·el·zuh·buhb

Part One

My soul will find yours.

1

Rosier

One Week without Ellea

"How do I get to her?" The question was a growl as he sank the blade further into the demon's chest. Blood gushed from its mouth. "How do I save her?"

Each stab became more desperate, more feral, as he slipped further and further into the depths of his dark soul. He would live in the pits of shadows and death if it meant he got the answers he needed.

"I can't..." It was a pained groan as it tried to get the words out. Ros ripped the blade from him only to plunge it in again. "I told you—"

The demon's words were cut off by his own sobs, tears mixing with the blood that coated his face. They always got to this point, losing all their vile pride, their disgusting comments turning into cries for mercy. Soon, he would beg for his life, but it didn't matter. This one had nothing more to give; even if Ros got the answers he sought, it would end up dead in the end.

Slowly, Ros sunk his obsidian dagger into the commander's chin, its sharp point breaking through bone and tissue with a sickening crunch. The sound mixed with the demon's final rattling gurgles. Then there were only the heavy breaths that heaved through Ros' chest as visions of Ellea's frightened face flashed before his eyes.

An empty glass dangled from his hand as Ros glared out the window of Ellea's library, the too-small chair biting into his tired muscles. Muscles that had hunted and killed for the past seven days.

Seven fucking days without her.

He brought the glass to his lips for another sip, but growled when no amber liquid was there to wash away the taste of rage that coated his mouth. He stood only to stumble a few shuffling steps before he caught the wall by the fireplace, the rough-cut stone grating on his hand. He steadied himself but couldn't help the urge to throw something. The house intervened—probably tired of the messes he'd made in his countless fits of rage—and filled his glass.

"Good house." He blinked slowly as he brought the glass to his lips. His mouth instantly watered. The drink had a light, earthy taste with a hint of citrus and lime. "A fucking margarita?"

His lip curled, and the emptiness of the cabin washed over him. His powers answered with a splintering rage. Ellea was in Hel, alone, and only the Gods knew what she was going through. Shadows crept up the walls as he relived each of the last seven days and his failed attempts to save her. His shadows curled around him, trying to hide him as his eyes burned with shame and frustration. All of this power, and he couldn't get to her.

He whirled and threw the drink into the fireplace. It was her favorite drink, and that was enough to set him on yet another spiral. The flames erupted as a roar came from deep in his chest, and the house shook around him. He forced a breath down; demolishing the house wouldn't help. Another breath, and the lights stopped their shuddering. A *tink* sounded in the empty room as a glass appeared before him.

"This better be bourbon."

Silence answered as he hesitantly brought the glass to his lips. A deep oak flavor exploded in his mouth and warmed his still heaving chest. "Better."

Ros had been throwing things all week, more so since Felix and Jadis left two days ago. They'd been brought here as soon as Ellea was taken. Well, as soon as Ros had realized he couldn't portal directly to Hel to save her from his father. Ros had gone straight to her family with help from Billy. He was able to portal to Halifax, but not to Hel. It should have been easy; that dark realm was a constant pull on his soul. With a single thought, he should have been able to step into his shadows and out into the castle he knew too well. The connection now felt severed, its edges frayed and impossible to piece back together. If his father wanted him home so desperately, he was making it hard.

Jadis and Felix surprisingly didn't blame him. They were upset, beyond upset, and had stayed as long as possible while planning and learning all they could about Hel. Like most witches, they hadn't been paying attention to the old ways or any other supernaturals. The council eventually called them back to meet about the situation, not that it would help. He was the only one who could do anything about it, or so he thought. Ros shifted his shoulders as more rage washed down his back. He finished his drink in an angry gulp, and the home instantly filled it before he could put it down.

Taking a smaller sip, he paced. There had to be another way, a spell or a demon he hadn't thought about, one he hadn't killed. Garm was no use either, his own abilities blocked. He internally cursed the hound even if it wasn't his fault.

A door slammed open. "Speaking of the bastard." Ros readied his glare as the sleek black body of his oldest friend crossed the threshold, his lover trotting close behind.

Fucking Hel, Billy cursed inside his head.

Both beasts slowly walked into the library, matching Ros' glare with their own as they sniffed the air. Garm grimaced, his large sharp teeth showing as his lips curled.

Who did you kill now? Garm asked. *And when was the last time you showered?*

Ros looked down at himself, wondering why Garm sounded so judgmental. His hands were clean, but everywhere else was splattered with black blood.

"I summoned one of Beelzebub's lower commanders." He paused to shake his empty glass in the air. It slowly filled, and he gulped most of the contents before continuing on to explain what his uncle's commander had had to say. "Questioned him for a bit, tortured him for a bit longer, and he finally spilled some minor details."

They watched him drink down the rest of his glass. He swayed where he stood, and Billy rushed to push a chair under him before he fell.

Enough! Garm commanded, and the house listened, refusing to fill his glass. Ros glared. *Get on with it, boy. What did the bastard say?*

Ros rubbed his face. He had been drinking for the past hour to try and forget what the vile piece of shit had said. His laughter still rang in his head, along with the sound of his final moments. It was the only demon out of the twenty or more he'd hunted that had news or a whisper of Ellea.

"Ellea is still alive, but she won't be able to evade them for much longer. The fucker said something about the demons in my father's court keeping her preoccupied."

Billy's snarl shook the frames that lined the walls. Her wild anger answered his own.

Did he say anything about our powers? Garm growled.

"No, he only laughed and said, 'Good luck getting to the princess.' Then I stabbed him so couldn't utter another word."

The princess? Garm questioned. *Why would he call her that?*

"He was probably trying to piss me off," Ros growled. "Using my nickname for her."

Billy gave Garm a look before walking closer to Ros.

We have an idea. She nudged him, forcing his hand away from his face.

"If it's killing more demons"—he looked down into her amber eyes that glinted at his comment—"I'm in."

She had hunted beside him a few times. Not only did her anger match his, but she was utterly bloodthirsty. He had come to realize that she could be ridiculous as much as she could be deadly.

No, she scolded. *Well, we can always kill more demons. I'm talking about the road to Hel.*

"The road to Hel is fucking blocked." What did they think he'd been doing this whole time? "Garm and I cannot enter Hel."

You can't enter your usual way. I'm talking about a literal road to Hel, Billy said.

Ros stared down at the beautiful beast; she looked so serious. All he could do was laugh, a deep, hoarse laugh. "That's a myth," he choked out. "If there was a road to Hel, why wouldn't people hop into their cars and try to visit those they lost?"

"Try" being the key word. You couldn't disturb a soul who had found peace.

You ignorant idiot, Billy snarled.

She's right. Garm stepped in before Billy could snap at him again. *The road is as old as time and as old as the Gods. It's a journey, one you can't drive, and at the end there is a gate to Hel.*

Ros stared at the two beasts. He had heard about the road but never thought it was real. Why would he? Until now, he hadn't needed any other way to get into Hel.

"How hard could it be?" Ros asked.

Hard, Garm answered.

"Why?" Ros shook his head. "We were born in Hel. We should be able to get in easily."

This road doesn't follow the same rules.

I've taken it many times, Billy said with a distant look in her eyes. *It won't be fun, but we can do it.*

"Let's go!" Ros yelled, trying to stand. "What are we waiting for?"

Garm rushed to him, but it was too late. As Ros stood, his long legs tripped over themselves, and his large body crashed to the ground. He groaned into the wooden floors and burped unceremoniously.

"How about you sober up first?" came a gruff voice from the door frame. Sam slowly walked up to Ros with his nose pinched between two fingers. His sharp features and angular eyes softened as he took him in. "And shower."

Devon leaned against the door frame; he and Sam had walked in with no one noticing. Devon looked as rough as Ros, cleaner, but he still had that hollowed look in his eyes. His usually bright blue eyes were cloudy, and his rich skin was pale. They were all looking and feeling rough since his father had walked out of the shadows and taken someone they cared about. Devon had been reading day and night, trying to find ways to get to Ellea. He'd even gone as far as contacting his family to see if they had any idea on what to do. They didn't, and neither did the books he read. Ellea was in Hel, and it seemed the only way to get to her was this road Garm and Billy spoke of.

Devon cleared his throat and pushed off the wall. "Sam, take Ros up to shower."

Sam looked up at his boyfriend, appearing slightly shocked by the sternness his voice carried. "And what are you going to do?"

"Billy, Garm, and I will talk about the plan to get to this road," Devon said, walking toward the desk and crossing his arms. "And then to get to Ellea."

"How much did you overhear?" Ros mumbled into the floor.

"Enough," Sam and Devon said together.

Billy seemed ready to protest, but Devon gave her a stern look. She returned it with a smirk.

Yes, Billy said. *Take the princeling and hose him off. We will begin planning and talking when he's more sober.*

Sam easily gathered Ros under his arm and steered him toward the door. The sound of running water could be heard from the upstairs bathroom thanks to the magic of the house.

"Come on, Ros," Sam said. "Let's get you cleaned up, and then we can plan the snacks for the road trip."

The two men navigated through the lower level of the cabin. Their large bodies melded together, and Ros took up so much more room as he stumbled under his friend's care.

"We need to get her, Sam," Ros grumbled.

"I know, buddy." He squeezed him a little tighter. "We'll get her."

"We will," he agreed and began carrying more of his own weight. "Then I'm going to burn my father's kingdom to the ground."

2
Ellea
One Day in Hel

Ellea trailed a finger over the smooth obsidian throne. It sloped elegantly from the sharp crest at its center to its furthest peak that ended in a jagged point. Each of the sharp crests could easily slice through skin. As she rounded the throne, Ros' father, Asmodeus, a king of Hel, stood before her. She looked down at the floor where claw marks sat deep in the stone, and the vision flashed before her eyes again. The dream she'd had of someone she didn't want to admit was Ros. It seemed her dreams were visions, ones that always led to him.

Ellea stood where Ros had in that dream; she could still feel the pebbled skin and feathers of the demons she'd trudged through.

Asmodeus cleared his throat, snapping Ellea out of her memory.

"I know this is a lot to take in."

He wasn't wrong, but there was more going on than being dragged to Hel by her boyfriend's father.

"You said Ros left his legacy," Ellea said with a voice much calmer than she felt. "What makes you think he wants it, or that he will even come back?"

He chuckled softly, his voice deep like Ros'. She'd expected him to be menacing, but it didn't feel that way. "I'm not dumb, Ellea. I know Rosier doesn't want this, but he has no choice."

"We all have choices."

"No, we don't; we all have responsibilities, and this is my son's."

Ros had never spoken of having to take over his father's domain in Hel. She had never asked either, but why would she?

Gods, she was ignorant.

He was a prince, of course his father was a king. Why wouldn't this be his legacy? He didn't have any siblings (that she knew of). She scoffed loudly, and Asmodeus arched a brow at her.

Steps sounded from the far end of the room, but Asmodeus didn't seem worried about the man who came out of the darkness. He walked with his hands clasped behind his back and gave Ellea a bored look before turning toward the king and bowing.

"Lord Dale, this is Ellea, my son's..."

He trailed off, glancing at her in question.

"I'm a lot of things," she answered with a smirk.

Dale. What a funny name for a demon.

Dale was broad in a pressed black suit. His magnificent ginger beard glinted in the low light. It was such a stark contrast to the sparse hair on his head.

"Right." His look was dismissive. He turned sharply to Asmodeus.

"I have a message for you from Sonneillon."

"She can wait," he answered harshly.

"I'm sure she can." Dale's eyes flickered to Ellea. "It's about... her wards."

Asmodeus surveyed the demon before him, but Dale didn't balk under the king's heavy gaze; if anything, he only looked more bored.

"Fine." Asmodeus bowed shallowly toward Ellea. "Please excuse me; it will only be a moment."

As their steps faded, the silence pressed in on her, and anxiety quickly crept up her chest. She was in Hel, a different realm, surrounded by the dead and demons. Ellea steadied herself and gripped the side of the throne. She inhaled deeply, held it, and released the breath before her powers could begin to crackle under her skin. Her spine stiffened as a pretentious voice came from the other side of the room.

"You look good here, Ellea," Belias said, strolling toward her from the darkness.

She forced her voice to be calm; it wanted to shake in the presence of the man who had broken her trust. "What are you doing here?" she asked. He had stood by while her parents tortured her and her friends. They had attacked those she cared about because they wanted her. Belias was working with them, and she had a funny feeling that he had been for a long time. He was still in the same black clothes she'd glimpsed in the field with her parents.

My parents. Are they here?

More panic pressed in on her. She had to move, and something was telling her she had to put distance between them. Ellea circled the throne, but he was quicker and pinned her against the hard obsidian backrest. He grasped her face with his icy hand, forcing her to look into his eyes that were so much darker. They matched the stone around them and seemed bottomless. No light and no happiness shone in them. She could kick herself for not seeing it sooner. "Where are my parents?" The pressure of his fingers gripping her made it hard to speak.

He chuckled softly and loosened his grip. "Busy, but not here, if that's what you're worried about."

"This isn't you," she said, trying to make herself believe it more than him.

A finger traced the shape of her lips, and she pressed them together, fighting to not react, to not snap and bite him.

"There is a lot you still need to learn about me." His breath washed over her face, and the battle to fight or curl in on herself raged. When he continued, bile rose up in her throat. "How often I found myself staring at these lips, wondering how they felt."

He seemed to be speaking to himself, but her powers didn't know that. She begged them to calm down, to form a blade instead of bringing the castle down around them. She needed something, anything, to protect herself. He would bleed for what he had done and what he was planning to do. The heft of cool stone weighed in her hand, and she let out a shaking breath.

Belias caressed her again, trailing a finger along her jaw before grasping the back of her hair. She curled her lip as he tugged at it, and when he brought his lips to hers, she struck. Bringing her newly made obsidian dagger under his chin, she halted his lips that had barely brushed hers. He didn't shy away from it, only pressed into her and the dagger.

Ellea snarled and pressed the dagger harder into his chin. He smiled and grabbed the dagger by its blade, removing it from his chin. The smell of iron hit the air as blood ran from his hands down the hilt to where Ellea still grasped it.

"Nice try, witch." He smiled wider. "You can't create obsidian with your tricky magic."

In a flash, his smile faltered as the sound of sizzling blood sounded through the room. He hissed and let go of the blade, looking down at his hands.

"That's not possible," he whispered.

His blood wasn't enough; she would carve out his heart for siding with her parents, for using her and putting her friends and Ros in danger. She pictured it, the dagger ramming into his chest, but a booming voice interrupted her.

"Step away from her, nephew."

It was a king's voice, and the pride and authority of it rattled her knees.

Belias frowned at his uncle. Before he could utter a word, flames and shadows opened under his feet. He yelled as he fell, and the floor closed around him, shutting out his screams.

"Good luck crawling out of the pits by dinnertime," Asmodeus snarled before turning back to Ellea, searching her from head to toe. "Did he hurt you?"

Ellea shook her head and tried to shake the feeling that was always left behind when a boy thought he could get the upper hand. She swallowed hard and straightened her shoulders. "It's his blood, not mine."

"Good. You could have made him bleed more." He pulled a green handkerchief from his suit pocket and placed it in her bloodied hand. "Let me show you to your room."

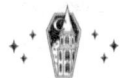

As they left the throne room, Asmodeus turned left and brought her through a grand archway that was built of the same black rock.

Power seemed to zing across her skin before they headed down a wide hallway. The sound of his powerful steps was muffled by the thick, dark carpet that ran along the passage. Ellea stopped, needing to take in the magnificent structure before her. It was vastly more decorated than the first hallway they'd taken. Those walls were endless obsidian, these were a black marble with veins of gold and some kind of crystal running through them. Her eyes traveled up the solid walls, taking in the ornate molding that connected the walls to the rounded ceiling. Solid gold chandeliers were spread along the high ceiling, and each held about fifty black candles. As her gaze came back down, she met the eyes of the king. She hadn't realized he had also stopped; instead of gawking at the decor, he was staring at Ellea.

"It is hard sometimes to realize that not everyone will ever come here."

"To Hel?" she asked, confused with his unprovoked statement. Then she remembered that everyone comes here in the end. She had learned that for the first time after her conversation with Ros, Sam, and Devon. "I thought everyone comes here?"

"They do," he said. "But not here. These are our—I mean my— living quarters. This hallway, along with the one I'm bringing you to, are mine alone. Well, they used to be Ros' too." He paused, seeming to catch himself. Clearing his throat, he continued, "No one comes to these quarters without my knowledge."

Ellea slowly closed the distance between herself and the king, someone she had never really thought of, and the few times she did, it was nothing like this. Her eyes continued to take in the intricate details that surrounded them as she tried to figure out what she was feeling. It felt dark, but warm, with glints of light. It was marvelous and magical, but there wasn't time to drool over the prettiness that Hel was presenting to her. There were so many questions raging in her head, along with fear, anxiety, and defiance. She was brought here against her will, so why wasn't she putting up more of a fight? Not once had she felt threatened by Asmodeus. Her magic wasn't even reacting to him, not like it had in the presence of Belias. That didn't mean she shouldn't take a little revenge for being plucked out of what was turning out to be a decent day, especially after the shit show she'd endured. She met Asmodeus' eyes under lowered brows, but before she could try to scare him, before she could try to conjure a whisper of her magic, he let out a soft chuckle.

"I will not hurt you," he said kindly. "Even if you attempt to fight, I will do you no harm. But know this, it will be a waste of your brilliant magic."

"Why would it be a waste?"

"You're going to need your strength," he said. "I will do my best to protect you, but seeing you, and realizing what you are down to your core, I can only do so much."

"What does that mean?" How he could even gauge an ounce of who or what she was? "You don't know me. I've been here for less than an hour."

"Oh, darling…" He stood taller. "I am no mere king, holed up in a castle, blind to the comings and goings. You are a troublemaker, a powerful trickster, and I fear more for my subjects than your safety."

Ellea didn't know how to respond. She wasn't truly a troublemaker. The occasional trick or scare couldn't cause such a permanent label on her soul, especially from someone she had never met. She rolled her eyes, knowing she would cause trouble anyway. Defiance was quickly overtaking anxiety and fear, but not the sadness that clung to her throat. It couldn't stop the crumpling in her chest as she remembered the look on Ros' face before she'd disappeared. What would he think? What was he doing right now?

"Don't worry." Stepping closer, Asmodeus grasped her still bloodied hand in his warm one. He turned it over, quickly cleaning it before a small cloud of shadows shimmered between their palms, the bloodied cloth disappearing. He gave her a small smile before continuing, "He will be here in no time. I'm planning on it."

"You seem too intuitive. Are you a seer *and* a demon king?" It was barely audible, but she needed to know. Maybe that was why she felt so comforted by him.

"Not a seer, but I can feel your emotions, know your lies and fears. Most demons would use it to be vicious and cruel. I find it to be more useful in other ways besides torture."

"So you really aren't going to harm me?"

Asmodeus gave her a searching look before shaking his head. She believed him. It didn't make her any less angry, but he squeezed her hands and turned gracefully, heading back down the hall. Ellea glanced down at her clean hand as another pain splintered quietly in her heart. She hoped Ros would hurry the fuck up. She continued walking down the hall after Asmodeus, her heels snagging the thick carpet. It had been a month since she last wore heels; it had always been boots or running shoes while she was in Glenover.

The vast ceilings and dark marble with glints of gold continued, and she wondered if there were no windows in this part of the castle. The only one she'd seen so far was in the room she'd arrived in. Maybe it was good there weren't many windows, hiding the horrors that would be Hel. She picked up her pace to match the long strides of the king as he rounded the corner. She was about to ask him one of the many questions whirling around her head, but she was blinded by radiating light. As her eyes adjusted, she found Asmodeus standing in front of massive windows that were like the ones in a library or office. Whatever this room was, it added to her questions. Ellea also wondered if she could call him something else. Asmodeus was so long, and referring to him as *the king* seemed like too much, especially with how he looked at this moment.

The gold light made him look so much younger, chasing away the harsh lines and angles the shadows and darkness gave him. She was able to fully take in his features and realized he wasn't graying as much as she'd originally thought. His thick black hair had neater curls than Ros', but he probably didn't run his hand angrily through it like his son constantly did. He looked so composed, a king looking over his land. *A king, not* the *king,* she remembered. There were multiple rulers of Hel. She had so much to learn. She also noted a tattoo poking out from his crisp collar, one she couldn't identify. It was all intricate lines and swirls. He turned his head slightly toward her, and the light glinted in his hazel eyes. They were more green than gold, she realized. He jerked his head lightly to the left, beckoning her to join him.

She passed two large, ornate doors before standing next to him and tearing her gaze away from his features that reminded her so much of Ros. His nose, the heavy brow, the coloring of his skin… Holding her breath, she readied herself to look upon Hel, a place she never dreamed of existing or going to. She closed her eyes and tried to calm her breath as she turned her face toward the warm light. A gasp escaped her as her eyes opened and she glimpsed scenery she would have never expected. The sprawling landscape was full of light and colors.

"Not what you expected?" Asmodeus asked.

Where flames and shadow should be, there were vast mountains and valleys. Green, blue, and gold shimmered all around the landscape. A clear blue river flowed down the middle of the deep valley, two massive peaks framing it. Her eyes widened as she took in the larger than normal sun that was setting to her right. Its rays sparkled off the jagged, snow-capped peaks that glittered with frost. The snow descended in rivulets that met with the greenest grass Ellea had ever seen.

"No, Asmond." The nickname felt funny, and she decided she hated it. "This is not what I expected."

"Asmond?" His nose wrinkled, and she rolled her eyes at her own mistake.

"I was trying something."

He shrugged and turned his attention back to the window. "What did you expect?"

Ros hadn't told her much about it, only mentioning a dark castle, brats running about, and how he hated the place.

"Fire, pits, demons running about," she said with a wave of her hand.

"Ah." He nodded in agreement. "I'll show you that part another day. This is where the Gods sleep. It's where I mainly rule over."

"Mainly?" Ellea asked.

"Yes, mainly," he said coyly, not giving anything else away.

"Where are we exactly? Besides in Hel. Are we someplace else or under something? I'm very confused about the logistics of all of this… amongst other things."

He chuckled softly and turned toward her.

"We are just here." Ellea huffed a breath at his flat answer. "Our universe isn't up or down, east or west. It has vast layers, pockets, and worlds. We are simply here."

He raised a hand, and a small hole of shadow formed above him. Reaching in, his hand disappeared as if it was behind an invisible door. He plucked out the dark green handkerchief Ellea had used to clean the blood off her hand.

"Things don't disappear in my shadows." The handkerchief disappeared again. "They go someplace else."

Ellea's ears began to buzz as endless possibilities ran through her head. "And Belias? Is he floating around with your discarded items?"

He gave her a wicked smile. "I like the way you think." He shook his head. "That was a pocket between places. I simply opened a door for him to fall through."

"Simply!" Ellea scoffed. "Easy for you to say. It took every ounce of willpower just to form a dagger."

"I doubt you were in a state of mind to conjure something made of an element you aren't familiar with. It will get better—easier, actually. The longer you're here, we will work on things; and you might find your magic will like its surroundings."

Why would her magic like its surroundings? And why had it conjured obsidian? She'd only asked for something pointy to stab out Belias' stupid eyes. Maybe it did because they were surrounded by it? So many questions whirled around her head. Why wasn't she angry? Asmodeus' kind words and his hopeful expression put her more at ease than they should.

He kidnapped you, don't let Stockholm syndrome set in this soon.

"Well, hopefully, I won't be here that long," she said, making her tone harsh.

"Yes, well…" He paused as if searching for the words. "Regardless, we will work on it."

"We? You took me from my home. Why would I ask for your help?"

"Why wouldn't you ask the King of Gods for help with your godly gifts?" Asmodeus said in his stern king's voice.

"Gifts? Gods?" She shook her head. "I'm a witch, that is all."

He stepped toward her and grasped both her shoulders. She didn't shy away from the embrace and looked up into his eyes. "You are so much more."

3
Ellea
Second Day in Hel

Ellea felt languid in a soft bed, its silken sheets caressing her body, so different from Ros' rough bites against her skin and the harsh snap of his hips. Each desperate thrust pushed her up the pillowy bed. He was desperate in his fucking, chasing her release as much as his own.

Everything became fuzzy before she was able to beg for more. Anxiety overtook the bliss that was crashing against her. She blinked in the darkness, trying to remember why she was scared, what she should be worried about. The answer was so close she could taste it, but it slipped away as her stomach fluttered and her legs clamped around Ros' strong body. She searched for his mouth, needing it on hers to swallow the pain and her cries of pleasure. Yanking him by the hair, she pried him from her breast that he was so focused on. He moaned into her kiss as her fingers raked up his strong back.

"More, I need more." She broke from his mouth, lifting her hips so he could go harder, deeper.

He growled against her throat and became more erratic with his movements. "I need you."

"You have me."

She could barely get the words out as she clamped around his hardness, so close to oblivion, then there was nothing. Her body felt hollow, and sadness replaced the euphoria that was Ros and his cock.

"Fuck," she grumbled into the soft pillow.

Ellea closed her eyes tighter, trying to get rid of the sliver of light dragging her from her dream. She searched for Ros' large arm to hold her tighter and bring her back to it or wake him and demand he finish what his fake self started. The comforter under her hand was ornate and silky, nothing like the comforter they shared. Opening her eyes, she groaned, realizing the spot behind her was empty—and then it hit her. She was in Hel, in Ros' room, and very alone.

She didn't remember falling asleep, only that she'd fought it off as she waited for Ros to step out of the shadows and bring her home. Boredom eventually took hold, and she'd busied herself with searching through every drawer, every cabinet, and the closets despite Asmodeus giving her the grand tour before he left her for the night. He'd even shown her how to work the bathroom, worried that her realm wasn't as advanced with their plumbing. It was strange for a king to do such a thing, at least she thought it was. She had even voiced her opinion on the matter, and he'd answered with, "I didn't want the staff or subjects to overwhelm you on your first day." Someone cleared their throat behind the closed double doors.

"She might not be awake yet," a female voice said in a failed whisper.

Ellea's heart began to race as she froze in bed. There were people outside of her doors. Were these the staff Asmodeus had worried about overwhelming her? What did they look like? The only demons she knew of were Ros, Belias, and the one she'd killed. Oh, and Dale.

"Florence," came a familiar, harsh voice. "It's almost eleven; she has to wake up."

"She doesn't have to do anything," Florence shot back.

The sound of their voices faded as they seemed to move away from the doors. Ellea scrambled out of bed and crossed the room on silent feet. She cracked the door open and caught a glimpse of a young female shooing Dale out of the entryway. The door closed behind them, and Ellea was left alone. She closed her door and pressed her back against it, taking in the dark room and steadying her heart. She moved to the window and slowly pulled back the curtains. A large, bright sun hung above the mountain tops outside her window. If there were creatures or people out there, it didn't show. Even this room held no life, no smell of Ros, only a familiarity in small details. A few posters hung around his room in addition to small and ancient artwork. They weren't posters like the ones she'd grown up with; they were stitched on faded cloth. One read:

Farquha

THE DEMONIC   TROUBADOUR

The landscape in the poster was faded, and she wondered if the troubadour was from Hel since the drawing depicted a bat playing some sort of fiddle. Or had Ros traveled to another realm as a young lad to listen to music? The idea made her laugh as she moved on to the next poster.

The Living Banshees - A Magical Trio

Ellea wished she had her phone to look these names up and learn their history—or call Ros and see where the fuck he was. She paused for a moment, steadying her breath, and tried reaching for him with her magic, to feel any inkling that they had some sort of supernatural connection. Her powers always seemed to find him, pull her toward him, but now she felt only emptiness. She fought the burn in her eyes and headed to the attached bathroom. After relieving herself, brushing her teeth, and glaring at herself in the mirror, she walked back to the empty room. She turned in a circle, taking in the room, and sighed.

Where was Ros?

She missed him, and this room wasn't helping. There was no comfort in the many books and trinkets or the massive suit of armor in an alcove. The shirt she'd found in the chest didn't even help. It wasn't his, only meant for him; it didn't smell like him. Asmodeus had said that everything had been refreshed and brought in recently, "Ready for their arrival." It was as if he had been planning this for a while. When she'd explored the night before, she only gave the clothes meant for her a quick glance before moving on—it was all too much. She also preferred sleeping naked, but it didn't seem right, considering where she was. Gods knew who might barge in. She'd settled for a shirt meant for Ros. If only she could figure out how to pluck the shirt she'd swapped for the dress when she arrived, like Asmodeus did with his handkerchief.

Ellea walked up to the armor that was once Ros'. Asmodeus had avoided it yesterday when she'd asked about it. It was massive, and stood as tall as Ros on its stand. She ran her palm across the breastplate to the teeth of a snarling wolf that decorated the middle. Two swords crossed behind the well-detailed head, and some phrase was embossed in a circle around it. It was in a language she couldn't understand. A large greatsword was sheathed at the armor's side. Its black handle swallowed up the light as if it was made from night, and a glint of gold sparkled when she removed it partially from its sheath.

Sheath? Scabbard? Ew, no, that can't be right.

She thought about hunting down a book on the anatomy of a sword as she pulled the handle. It hissed as she freed it fully from its holder, then the loudest and most embarrassing clunk sounded through the silent room as she dropped it to the floor. It was so much heavier than she'd thought it would be.

Her heart beat aggressively and her ears rang as she looked around the room. She expected Dale or the king to barge in and scold her for being a silly girl. Ellea chuckled softly at the thought before turning back to the gold sword that glinted from the dark carpet. She took a steadying breath as she crouched closer to it. It wasn't just gold, it had black veins of rock swirling through the blade.

"Obsidian," she whispered to herself as she traced the veins with her finger.

It was beautiful, sharp, and very heavy. She tried her best to lift it without slicing her foot off. Carefully, she used two hands to guide it back into its sheath.

"Fucking Hel," she cursed, wiping her sweaty hands against her shirt.

How could she ever wield such a weapon?

Why would I need to wield such a weapon?

She shook her head, ridding herself of the thought. She was in Hel in nothing but a t-shirt—proof that anything was possible. At least she wasn't in the presence of a king. Her stomach growled, interrupting her thoughts.

"Pants, then coffee," she said to herself.

Ellea could conjure leggings, the dress wasn't that hard yesterday. She would need to since the only thing in the chest and closet were dresses and clothing she wouldn't want to wear while trying to figure out what to do next. Stilling her thoughts, she went to work. Snug, soft fabric hugged her curvy legs and formed around her lower stomach. She smiled at the familiar feeling of stretch and support. Now a sweater; it wasn't cold here, but she missed the comfort of her favorite sweaters from the cabin.

After a few minutes of summoning, she was in a thin gray sweater, leggings, and a replica of her favorite boots. Now food. It had always been hard for her to summon, and she didn't usually work on cooked food. She'd never tried to summon coffee; she actually loved the steps it took to make her favorite lattes. Grinding specific beans and the smell surrounding her in the kitchen was all part of the magic, so to speak. She didn't have much of a choice now; she could either summon coffee or leave her room and walk through a castle that held demons and people she didn't know.

Ellea looked around the room and found two glass cups on a tray near one of the windows. She brought one over and sat back on the couch. She planted her feet firmly on the ground and held the cup between her hands. She took a shuddering breath and envisioned her favorite coffee: espresso, milk, and she could go without the sugar if she had to.

45

Closing her eyes, she thought of the smells she loved so much, their richness and earthiness. The warmth of a cup in her hand surprised her. When she opened her eyes, she cursed, "Fuck."

It looked like warm mud water. Sniffing it, she scrunched her face and brought it to the bathroom to dump out. It seemed she would have to leave the room after all. She *could* wait for Dale or the woman, Florence, to come back, but her stomach groaned at the thought of waiting any longer. She crept out of the bedroom and headed toward the ornate double doors. Holding her breath, she slowly opened the door and peeked through the opening.

Looking to her left and right, there wasn't a soul in sight. She stepped into the hallway and released a sigh, unsure if she was happy or worried about the lack of people. She retraced her steps, heading the same way she and Asmodeus had come from the night before, past the large windows with their beautiful landscape, around the corner, and to the doors. She cracked them open and crept in. She was once again greeted with no sound, so she continued into the throne room.

Ellea paused for a few breaths after the door gave an ominous click behind her, waiting to see if anyone was there. The room was massive and she couldn't see into any of the shadows, but she didn't hear anything. It was deathly quiet and dark, the only light coming from above the main throne. She wondered why there was one separate from the other three, a question she filed away for later as she quickly walked past it. She didn't let the thought of Belias cross her mind, trying to not wonder if he made it back from wherever his uncle had sent him.

Ellea went through the door, leaving the foreboding room that held too much history behind. Only one more door until she was in the room Asmodeus had originally brought her to. Ellea crept down the obsidian hallway and paused outside the doors. She thought about knocking, but instead she barged through and stepped inside. She turned toward the desk, ready to greet the king.

But no one was there. She frowned. How had she made it all this way without running into anyone? Placing her hands on her hips, she walked the perimeter of the room. She peeked curiously at the books crammed into their shelves and stopped at his massive desk. She turned toward the windows where similar scenery of valleys and hills greeted her. To the left, the mountains and valleys transitioned into a coastal landscape. She could see a hint of what could be a beach or a large body of water. She pressed her forehead against the glass, trying to get a better look, but it wasn't easy to see.

Ellea headed toward the unknown door to her left. It was shrouded in shadows. Beyond it lay rooms and halls she hadn't visited yet. Holding her breath, she reached out a hand and grasped the wolf-shaped doorknob.

"What are you doing?" came a whisper in her ear.

4

Rosier

Eight Days without Ellea

R os' nose twitched as Ellea's hair tickled his face. He held her tighter. Waking up to someone was a feeling he never knew he needed. It was as though the world was where it needed to be. There was no one to hunt, nothing to avoid, and no fears, only the comfort of lying with someone whose heart beat with his. He didn't mind her worse-than-usual morning breath, only thought of what they would do today.

Yesss, a voice hissed in his head.

His eyes popped open, and all he could see was a blurry version of Billy's blazing amber irises and the smirk on her wide muzzle. Ros' heart dropped as he looked down to see Garm's large head on his chest. He groaned and rolled away. His heart continued dropping, but he pushed the anger away and reminded himself that he would get to her soon.

No! Billy protested. *I was about to join you two.*

"Gross, Billy." He got out of bed and headed toward the bathroom.

Their mumbling was barely audible as he splashed cold water on his face. A shower was tempting even though he'd already showered the night before with help from Sam. The shower and his rage had quickly sobered him up, but they hadn't been able to stop the twinge of a headache behind his eyes.

Last night, Devon had quickly briefed them as Ros dried off and batted Sam away from drying his hair.

"You'll catch a cold if you go to bed with your hair wet," Sam had said.

Ros had ignored him and crawled into Ellea's bed, laying his wet head on the pillow. He'd grabbed the one she usually used and hugged it to his chest.

How did Garm slide into bed without me knowing?

He shook his head and thought about what the day would bring. They would portal to where Billy said the last known entrance to the road to Hel was. It had been a few thousand years since she had been there, and no one was sure how different the area would be since life had changed vastly since then. That was the easy part. Next, they would begin the journey. Based on Billy's calculations, it would take about five days on foot if they traveled by day and only rested at night.

Sam would be here soon with supplies from the farm—tents, food, water canteens—and Ros would pack a few weapons. They would have to try and reserve as much of their magic and strength as they could for when they crossed into his father's kingdom. No one knew what type of battle would ensue once they got to the castle, but Ros was more concerned about what would happen on the road. Billy had said that the last leg of their trip would be the hardest. Leftover powers from the Gods would do their best to stop them from reaching the end.

Ros wasn't sure how she'd done it by herself so many times or why she, a familiar, would go to Hel at all. Apparently, she and Garm were keeping a big secret about Billy's past, but he would worry about that later. Right now, he just wanted to get to Ellea.

He still hated that Sam and Devon were coming along, but lucky for them, he had been a little too drunk to argue. They loved Ellea and wanted to help in any way they could, so he understood—still hated it, but he got it. In Sam's absence, three of his betas were going to oversee the pack and town while they were gone. He'd even given a heads-up to a couple packs on the west coast that he trusted. They were going to travel closer to be on standby if something happened while they were out of reach.

Billy had visited Felix and Jadis at some point in the night and let them know some of the plan, but not all of it. She only wanted to make sure the council was aware that Glenover would be left without its strongest. Unsurprisingly, they hadn't been concerned.

Ros ran his fingers through his hair, pushing it away from his face. It quickly fell forward, and he growled, pushing it back again. He didn't have time or patience for his hair to be uncooperative. There was enough to deal with, like tight-lipped demons and beasts encouraging a threesome. Looking to the right of the vanity, he saw one of Ellea's hair ties. There were a few of them scattered across his cabin, and about a hundred scattered across this one. The thought of her thick hair wrapped around his hand caused such a pang in his chest. Swallowing past the lump in his throat, he roughly grabbed the black band and rolled it between his fingers. It had been a few decades since he pulled his hair back regularly.

Ros placed the hair tie between his lips and teeth, careful not to tear it with his sharp canines. Gathering his hair the best he could, he grabbed the band and tied his locks up into a rough knot. One strand fell forward, and some hair still fell on the back of his neck, but it was better than nothing. A small cough came from behind him, and Ros looked into the mirror to see Sam leaning against the doorframe.

"I can cut it if you want."

"It took three months to grow it out of that horrendous haircut you gave me last time," Ros grumbled.

"Yea, well, I tried my best."

Sam assessed Ros, his gaze drifting from his hair to his bare ass. It took too much strength to not turn around and throw a hairbrush at his friend's head.

"Stop ogling me." He felt self-conscious enough as it was, failing at every turn, drinking like he was a young demon who had just lost his mother.

"The tattoo came out good."

"I would hope so, you picked it out."

He had. When Ros was drunk (again) on the third or fourth night without Ellea, Sam had convinced Ros and Devon to go to a local tattoo parlor. The whole night was a blur, and the next morning, Ros had woken up with a snarling wolf on his left butt cheek. Thankfully, it was right under his waistline and his pants hid it.

"I meant the one you got while you were sober."

Sam walked into the bathroom and gripped Ros by the shoulder. He studied the intricate design that started at the base of his neck, a crescent moon whose tips pointed and flowed like his shadows up into his hairline. Flowing from there, down his spine, was the design that matched his mother's sword, the sister sword to his own. Each sword forged by the Gods had its own look and none were the same. They were similar, but the veins of power that ran through the chosen metal created a path on its own. He had gone back to the tattoo artist after the drunken night, and every night that came after another day of failing Ellea.

Sam slapped Ros on his bare ass, jerking him from his thoughts. He suppressed his yelp with an angry growl.

"Put your pants on. We can't have Billy distracted."

"You're the one that put me to bed naked," Ros snapped.

"You always sleep naked." Sam shook his head as he walked away.

Ros was sure Billy had glimpsed plenty over their time together as a weird, mismatched group that didn't understand boundaries. Devon was the only one who hadn't seen Ros fully naked—yet.

Ros headed to the bedroom and grabbed his favorite jeans from the chair in the corner. The house had worked through the night cleaning clothes, weapons, and for some reason, stacking about ten romance novels next to his daggers. Nine daggers in total lined up neatly in a row, all silver except for one. The black obsidian dagger was his favorite and oldest weapon. Spinning it once in his hand, it disappeared with a whisper of his shadows. He did the same with four more and then packed one in each boot. The last two would go downstairs for Devon and Sam to use. Grabbing his bag, he shoved his clothes, a few hair ties, and toiletries in the dark canvas sack. The sound of his friends bickering was quickly becoming louder, and he mumbled a prayer for strength.

Soon, they would be back, and the cabin would no longer feel so empty. Even with his friends circling around him, it had never felt right. A warm breeze tickled his neck, and he turned before crossing the threshold. The stack of books caught his eye, and something tugged at his chest, causing his shadows to shudder around his hands as he rubbed at the painful pull. He headed toward the books and grabbed the top three, flipped each over, and then let them disappear into the shadows with his daggers. They would be available for him when he needed them.

As he headed down the stairs, both Garm and Billy's voices sounded louder than usual. As if...

"Can you stop ogling her?" Devon whispered.

"He can ogle me all he wants." Billy was smirking as Ros stomped into the kitchen.

The deep tone of Garm's growl shook the small window above the sink. His presence in his human form was startling, and Ros felt the need to back down. Even in his basic jeans, long-sleeve cotton top, and boots, his oldest friend was breathtaking and scary. His massive amount of muscle was intimidating, and he was so tall that his dark curls almost brushed the ceiling. Ros wasn't surprised Devon looked ready to wet himself. Sam stood there with his mouth gaping open, his eyes bouncing between Garm and Billy. It was only the second time Ros had seen Billy in her human form, and it was still a shock. The two beasts made a magnificent pair. Her canvas pants, boots, and simple sweater did nothing to dull her beauty. Amber eyes glowed wickedly as she baited Devon and Sam to say something, to poke the beast who was vibrating in front of her, blocking her view from the friends who didn't know how to function with her in this form. She poked her head around Garm's towering frame, causing her dark hair to sway.

"That's enough," Ros bellowed.

Sam's mouth closed with a snap as he blinked rapidly, and Billy only smirked more. Garm still shot daggers at Sam, whose eyes were now trying to look anywhere else. Ros glared at all of them and paused on Devon who was shrinking further behind Sam. There wasn't time for bickering or getting used to Billy and Garm being on two legs.

"Please," Ros said, pinching the bridge of his nose as his headache gave a painful pound. "We don't have time for this."

Garm glared a little more before Billy rested a hand on his crossed arms. His shoulders instantly relaxed as his eyes met hers. He searched her face quickly before grumbling and crossing the room to lean against the wall.

"A little warning would have been appreciated," Ros said to Billy. She had to choose today to show herself to Sam and Devon. "Is there a reason you're in your human form?"

"Since we don't know what the town is like, I figured this form would make it easier to blend in." She shrugged.

Billy had a point. The five of them would portal to the town that was on the coast of their destination without investigating first. They didn't want to waste the energy to portal all the way there, back, and then there again. Billy made it seem simple; you stepped over the entrance and you were *moved* to the edge of the road to Hel. Ros was still skeptical, but after his numerous failed attempts, he was desperate.

"Easier to blend in? You look like a dressed-down queen, and Garm over there looks like a Norse god. How big are you, anyway? Do we have time to measure you?"

"Do you mean his height or his dick?" Billy's sharp teeth glinted as she gave them a full smile.

"Both," Sam and Devon said together.

"How about no?" Ros groaned. "Is everyone packed? Do we all know the plan?"

Billy whined, a tone she used regularly in her beast form, probably sad that everyone wasn't about to whip out her favorite body part. But then she said, "Yes, grumpy shadow daddy, we are all ready to go save our girl."

A spark of possessiveness crept in his mind. Ellea was his. But he needed to realize that she was also theirs. They were all about to risk themselves on a dangerous journey, and he would need to leave his brutish tendencies behind. Billy gave him a look like she knew the thoughts running through his mind. Probably because she did; even in her human form, she could read his mind.

"Grab your bags. Let's get out of here before we get into a dick-measuring contest." Ros headed toward the table to grab the small bag Sam had packed for him and shoved it into his own.

Billy stepped toward Ros, grabbing him by the arm and forcing him to look at her. He had expected judgment and teasing, but Ros saw his own feelings mirrored in her eyes.

"This will work," she said softly.

"It has to."

Everyone stepped in close, exchanging glances before they each grasped someone's hand or shoulder. Ros and Garm would work together to take them to their destination. Their shadows shimmered and stirred together, and as one, they stepped through the opening they created.

The world was cast in darkness as their single step paused and their world moved around them. In a second, darkness turned to cobblestones and silence greeted them. Ros quickly looked around to find so many people looking at them, dumbfounded. They had arrived in the middle of a celebration.

"Fuck," Ros cursed as the shouts started and Devon began dry heaving.

"Shit," Billy added. "Let me find a phone and we can call the council to take care of this."

"And say what?" Sam huffed a laugh while he rubbed his boyfriend's back. "We were some surprise magic show who appeared at the wrong spot?"

"That's not half bad." Billy looked hopeful as she headed toward a nearby store.

"I don't feel good." Devon groaned before throwing up more of his breakfast.

"You'll get used to it, Dev." Sam continued to comfort him through his wave of nausea.

Ros knew Devon would feel better in time; your first time stepping through the folds of the world was always hard. Even for him, a jump across the water to another continent took a bit of his own powers. But he could feel his magic slowly regenerating, like a well being refilled. Creating portals, using his shadows, and a bit of flame didn't cost him much of his power, if any. If he was using magic in a battle and got injured, then he would worry about losing his strength. It was the same for Garm, but the beast always seemed to hold on to a bit more power. It was annoying.

The crowd around them had thinned by the time Billy came out of the store.

"The council has been notified, and they will take care of any issues."

"Imagine if mortals didn't know we existed," Sam said with a laugh.

"Yeah, the council would have something more to do than scold Ellea." Billy glared off in the distance for a moment.

Devon clearly held the same contemptment. "It's the same here," he said. "This area is more interested in controlling who marries whom and what strong line of supernatural will continue. It's gross."

"Well, let's leave before the council comes and scolds us," Sam said. "What's next?"

Billy pointed across the road to the sea. Beyond it was a small island, and built on top of it was a massive stone structure.

"It seems the road to Hel is now covered by a prison," Billy said.

"Not a prison." Devon came up behind them and wiped his mouth.

"It's a monastery. You know, for worship."

"Worshiping what?" Sam asked.

"Some saint or savior. It's called St. Patrick's Purgatory."

"Fitting name," Garm remarked gruffly.

"How do we get across?" Ros asked.

"Ferry," Billy and Devon said together. Then Billy added, "Probably not the same type of ferry I had to take back in the day."

Devon smiled, probably thinking about all the history and magic in this place that Billy had been able to experience. "No, this one has cocktails and chips. Did yours?"

She laughed. "No, mine had a creepy old man in a smelly robe."

5

Ellea
Second Day in Hel

Ellea cursed and twisted at the voice she didn't recognize. Her magic zinged across her skin, and another obsidian dagger weighed heavy in her hand. She was surprised by how swiftly her magic took over. She tried to swipe to the left to create distance, but instantly bumped into one of the many bookcases.

"Shit," she cursed before steadying her stance.

A warm laugh answered as the man who had scared her stepped back a few paces. He was massive, and as the light hit him, she was able to see him fully. His palms were facing toward her, hovering by his stomach and level with her gaze. She felt her eyes widen as they slowly raked up his chest, past the light brown scruff, and stopped at the deep green eyes that glinted in Hel's rising sun.

"Woah," she whispered.

"Hi." He had a slight accent. "You're as tiny as a bauchan."

"Who the fuck are you? And what is a *bauchan?*"

Ellea tried mimicking the way he said the "chan" with a deep gruff, like he was trying to clear his throat. She had only met one or two people in her life with an accent like his.

"Why are you whispering?" he asked, mirroring her lowered tone.

Why was she whispering? Oh right, she was currently sneaking through the halls of a castle in Hel. His eyes lowered to her raised hand that still held the obsidian dagger.

"Ah," he said with an even broader smile, showing off his oversized, sharp canines. *Demon,* she guessed. He reached out a finger to tap the tip of the dagger. "So you can create obsidian? Wicked."

"Wicked?"

"You're whispering again." He chuckled. "Let's put the weapons away, little one."

Ellea squinted at him. There wasn't much a tiny dagger would do with this guy, demon, or whatever he was. All she knew was he was huge, taller and broader than any male she had ever met—even the brute who was taking way too long to get there. Ellea shook her head and glared up at him. His short brown hair had a soft wave to it, and his freckled face offset the green of his eyes. They glinted as he studied her the same way she was studying him. She noticed an intricate tattoo poking from his simple black shirt, but didn't get a chance to inspect it as he reached his large hand toward her. She pulled her hand back, unwilling to let him take the dagger.

"I'm Duhne." He held out his massive hand. "You must be the princess the staff has been going on about."

"Staff?" She hadn't seen any staff yet, only Lord Dale. "How? I haven't seen anyone."

He cocked a brow at her and retracted his un-shaken hand.

"Well, besides Modeus." She made a face at the attempted nickname, and Duhne's eyebrows rose, his eyes crinkling with amusement. She cleared her throat and continued, "Asmodeus, Lord Dale, and Belias."

He leaned in close and whispered, "The walls have ears, eyes, and teeth."

Teeth? Well, it is Hel.

"I'm Ellea." She waved the dagger, chasing away her thoughts of being eaten by a wall. His green eyes warily tracked the movement. Rolling her own, she conjured a black leather thigh strap and placed the dagger in the sheath.

"So," he said, straightening and growing an extra foot. "Why are you in my uncle Modeus' office?"

"Let's not tell him I tried Modeus." She gagged on the name. "And I was trying to find coffee."

It shouldn't be this hard to get the only source that helped her function at a somewhat normal level. A pain was forming behind her eyes from the little magic she'd been able to do and all the conjuring she'd attempted. She suppressed a groan. Maybe if she could find coffee, she could…

"Please tell me you have coffee in Hel." Ellea rubbed at the spot between her brows. She may have to burn this place to the ground if they didn't have it.

Duhne chuckled and walked over to a tasseled rope hanging by a door she hadn't noticed. As soon as he pulled it, someone walked out of a nearby bookcase as if he had been standing with the shelves just waiting to be summoned. He was dressed in an all-black uniform, buttoned to his wrists and throat. He clasped his pale hands in front of his waist, and his eyes widened when he saw Ellea. All the blood drained from his pallid face. Besides him visibly shaking in her presence, she couldn't help but love how cute his horns were. They jutted out from his temples and curled around his ears. They were bone white and had a faint opalescent sheen to them. His golden hair curled in tight ringlets that seemed feather-soft next to the rough edges of his horns.

"Reaver," Duhne addressed the demon. "I'm sure you've heard about our visiting princess—"

"I'm not a princess," Ellea cut in. She barely liked it when Ros called her that. Well, she kind of didn't like it.

"Ri—" The demon, Reaver, stuttered a few times before finally saying. "Yes, I've heard a few things about our, er, visitor."

He seemed unable to tear his gaze from Ellea, and with each second of his gawking, she found herself wanting to tease and provoke him. Duhne stepped forward and blocked Ellea from his view.

"Reaver," Duhne said in a deep, commanding voice. "I called for a reason."

The demon peeked around Duhne's body, barely coming up to his chest. Reaver seemed to be a little taller than Ellea but very spindly. She didn't feel threatened by him, only curious about what type of demon he was. Did he have specific magic or powers? He tore his eyes away from Ellea and looked up at Duhne, straining his neck to meet his gaze.

"Yes, Prince Duhne. You called?"

"Ellea and I would like coffee in the west library," Duhne said, and Ellea's stomach grumbled in response. "And an assortment of breakfast pastries and sandwiches."

Reaver looked very confused and then said, "Breakfast and lunch?"

"It's called brunch," Duhne said with a smirk.

"You know what brunch is?"

"Of course, I know what brunch is." Duhne glowered at her over his shoulder.

Ellea snapped her mouth closed, not wanting to say the wrong thing. She once again had so much to learn.

Reaver bowed to both of them before walking through the door Ellea had tried to open earlier. "Right away."

"Why didn't he come back the way he came?"

He laughed. "Through the bookcase? How ridiculous."

Ellea blinked at him a few times. He only winked and turned toward the same door.

"Come, princess, let's go sit and wait for brunch," he said over his shoulder.

"I'm not a princess, for fuck's sake."

She came to a skittering halt as soon as she crossed the threshold into the massive hallway. It was bustling with mostly human-looking people and some not, all rushing around. Some were talking to companions, while others mingled near a window or corner. There was a group of females giggling to one another in hushed tones, and a scaly green creature walked by her, holding a stack of dark linens. Snapping her mouth shut, she hurried after Duhne. She tried to ignore the side glances and gawking directed at her by taking in the detail of the hallway. It was tall and lit by giant windows on either end. White marble mixed with the black and gold colors Ellea was used to from Azzy's side of the castle. It was so much brighter and open, and it made her feel vulnerable. She slowly reached toward her thigh and lightly stroked the solid handle of her dagger. Knowing it was there brought her a shred of comfort. Her powers lightly crackled at her fingertips, and the sound of a sharp squeak drew her attention to a demon at the height of her hip. It had seen the movement and was now shuffling away with steam wafting off the tendrils of its hair, holding a jack-o'-lantern almost the same size as its small body.

"Are those Halloween decorations?" She couldn't help the high-pitched tone that came out.

Duhne turned, walking backwards and looking at her as though she had three heads. "We aren't barbarians; of course, those are Halloween decorations."

Ellea's eyes roamed the halls again; people were taking down wicked and adorable Halloween decor. It made her homesick, remembering how spectacularly Glenover had been decorated before she was taken away.

"Why are there so many more people here?" she asked, running to catch up with Duhne.

"Only a few venture into my uncle's wing."

"Why?"

"Because." It was said with such finality, but she didn't care.

"Because why?" She came to a quick stop as he whirled toward her.

"Because that is the way it is," he said with a hint of annoyance. He shifted his shoulders and gave her a small smile. "Things tend to be what they are here. They don't need an explanation."

"That's stupid." He arched a brow in response. "Everything has a reason for being a certain way."

"Well..." He paused and chewed on his response. "I don't have an answer for you."

He turned away and continued down the massive hallway. She cursed her short legs and tried to compose her rushed stride. Her stomach fluttered when she couldn't ignore the countless looks and whispers. Duhne had turned sharply down a narrow hallway, and she was about to tell him to slow down when she was shoved against the wall. No, not against it, into it. A shadowy mist surrounded her as something pushed her through what should have been a solid surface.

It wasn't painful, but strange.

"Don't speak, little one," he whispered before turning away from her. The misty wall somehow held his weight as he leaned against it.

Ellea took a deep breath, trying to ignore her fear of being in a dark and enclosed space. Swallowing past the lump in her throat, she pressed against the wall, but it wouldn't budge.

"Duhne…" It was a weak whine, but he picked at his nails with mock boredom as two people slowly crept toward him.

"Cousins." He didn't bother looking at them. "What are you doing on my side of the castle?"

They were beautiful in a scary sort of way, two red-headed twins. The woman was lean and elegant with sharp features and bright green eyes. They were almost neon compared to Duhne's, which were the color of a field in the summertime. Her brother was slightly broader but equally sharp. His eyes were the same. With the mist and marble obscuring her vision, even the pattern of their freckles looked the same.

"Are you hiding something, Duhne?" they said together.

"What would I be hiding?" She could sense the roll of his eyes.

"Maybe a little witch?" the man suggested.

"The staff can't keep their mouth shut about her," the woman added as both of them peeked around him, studying the wall.

The man's eyes glinted wickedly, as if he could see her through the marble. She covered her mouth and hid behind Duhne's broad back.

"I will ask again," he said, growing taller. "What are you doing on my side of the castle?"

"You and Rosier are the only ones who can't share," the woman said. "This is our family's castle. No one has their own side."

"Right. I'll keep that in mind as I run around your wing naked."

The woman's features flashed, changing to something wicked as she bared her teeth at her cousin.

"Keep your manhood away from my wing."

"That's what I thought," Duhne said with a devilish chuckle.

"You and Asmodeus cannot hide the witch forever," the man said.

"Who said we were hiding her?"

"We haven't had a witch here since—"

"Don't you dare speak her name," Duhne cut him off.

"She wasn't only your aunt, Duhne," the woman said, her tone softer than it had been a moment ago.

Duhne's shoulders seemed to cave the slightest before he righted himself. Ellea shifted to the left, trying to gauge his reaction. Were they speaking of Ros' mother?

"Well, if you would excuse me, I have to go rub my dick on all your doorknobs, Cara," he said, and the woman paled. Her brother only chuckled and walked past Duhne.

Once they were gone, Ellea pressed against the wall, trying to free herself. Claustrophobia had quickly crept up her back once she was no longer distracted by their interesting conversation. Her breaths came in quick, short pants, and she could hear her mother's cackle in the back of her mind.

"Duhne," she whimpered.

He reached through the mist and marble, wrapping his large hand around her wrist and tugging her free. It felt as if she was moving through sand, not a marble wall. She quickly checked herself, but she didn't have a mark on her, nothing to show she'd been shoved through a hard surface. Taking a steadying breath, she looked up at Duhne.

"Could you warn me next time?"

"Like I had the time." He rolled his eyes and continued toward the west library. She grasped him by the bicep, stopping his retreat.

"How did you do that, and who were those two?" Her thoughts were under a mountain of questions.

"My creepy cousins, and demon magic," he said with a bored wave of his hand.

"So you're a demon too?"

"What did you think I was?"

"I didn't want to assume." She let a nervous laugh escape.

"I'm half human, half demon."

"Okay, and them? What are they, and are they dangerous?"

"They are full demons. Their mother is like Asmodeus and their father was some incubus or succubus or something. A sperm donor."

"Lovely." She shivered. "They seemed creepy."

"Creepy, yes." He thought for a breath. "Dangerous? No. They probably want to get to you before anyone has influence over you."

"Influence? Why would they have influence over me? I don't plan on staying here any longer than I need to."

"Right," he said slowly. It grated on one of her last nerves. "Let's go before our coffees get cold."

Duhne turned and stepped away, but then paused to look back at her. He waited for her to step beside him and bent his elbow toward her.

"Is this you trying to influence me?" she asked, linking her arm through the crook of his elbow.

"I don't think anyone could influence you."

They walked in comfortable silence down the hall as Ellea's thoughts were carried away toward Ros' mom. He hadn't spoken of her that much, and Belias had only mentioned her that one time. It seemed two out of the four rulers were single parents.

"Who were you raised by?" she asked, curious if he was raised by both parents.

"My father, Leviathan." His love for his father was easy to see in the warmth of this voice and light in his eyes.

"And your mother?"

"She passed away during birth." He fidgeted, looking much smaller than he was. "She was a mortal human. It was too much for her."

"I'm sorry, Duhne," she said, looking up at him.

He dismissed her pity with a wave of his massive hand. "It was eons ago." He turned her toward a set of massive double doors.

They opened swiftly, and on the other side was Reaver, looking a little flustered.

"I was beginning to think—"

"Fucking cheese and rice!" She roughly pushed past Duhne.

Before her was an endless library with ceilings that went on forever. Each shelf rose well beyond thirty feet, and every section of books had a ladder. There had to be thousands of rows of books. Ellea took a shuddering breath and squeezed her eyes shut for a moment, muttering a silent plea. She opened one eye, and the library was still there. Her chest ached at the thought of all of these books. She wouldn't want to read all of them—she would bet an espresso machine that most of these shelves held mundane books on rules and how women need to be kept quiet—but the sight of so many books still took her breath away.

The distant muttering of Duhne and Reaver pulled her out of her stunned silence and thoughts. She hadn't realized her feet had moved her down about twenty sections of books. It wasn't like a library in the city where you would find students or professionals studying and working. There were no tables, only various statues and glass enclosures scattered throughout the space. She could see some small tables sitting outside on balconies.

"Are any of these good books, or just history and boring old man shit?" Ellea called over her shoulder while inspecting a row of books that were in a language she didn't recognize.

"Well, aren't you a rude little demon?" said a translucent woman poking her head out of the books right in front of Ellea's face.

Ellea yelped and shuffled back so fast she crashed into the case behind her.

"My books!" the woman yelled.

Ellea looked up to see a few heavy volumes teetering on the edge of the top shelves. Her heart dropped into her stomach, and she braced her hands over her head, attempting to protect herself. Heavy steps sounded, and Duhne's boots appeared in her line of sight. She flinched, waiting to be hit, but nothing came. Looking up, she saw Duhne's misty shadows spread above her like a small portal. She stepped away from it and saw the books that had been aimed at her dropping into a neat pile a few feet away.

"Careless." The woman fretted over the books on the floor. "All you demons are careless. I don't know why I stay here."

"You could leave, Viatrix," Duhne grabbed the books and magicked them back to their place.

"Leave?" She choked on her words. "And who would care for this endless library? Not that anyone bothers with it anymore. I swear, you all go about doing evil things and forget about me."

Ellea blinked a few times, trying to follow the direction of the woman's outburst. Did she want to be left alone or did she feel alone?

"She's a Draugr," said Reaver, sidling up to Ellea.

"A what?"

"I think you would know her as a ghost or spirit."

"Are all the dead here ghosts?" Ellea whispered, not wanting to insult the very angry ghost librarian.

"Only a few. Most of the dead you will see here are as solid as you or I."

Ellea smirked a little as the demon became paler the longer they spoke. "Do I scare you, Reaver?"

Reaver leaned his head back and gaped at her. He audibly swallowed and seemed to choke on a response. She blinked at him, leaning in to an uncomfortable proximity, testing her bravery on this little demon who seemed so perplexed by her existence.

"Leave the poor beast alone." Duhne chuckled, slapping an arm around Ellea's shoulders.

Reaver stepped back and straightened, pulling at his high-buttoned shirt.

"If you won't be needing anything," Reaver said with a curt bow. "Call if you need me, Duhne, princess—"

Ellea cut him off with an arch of her brow.

"Ellea," Reaver corrected and turned toward the doors.

"Come, little one." Duhne steered her toward a table full of food and cups of what looked like coffee. "Let's go eat, and then I'll show you a section of books you may like."

6
Ellea
Second Day in Hel

A slight breeze swept over her skin as they walked out to a table on a small balcony. She wasn't sure what the weather would be like from the views on her tour, but the crisp air reminded her of early autumn. The smells of turning leaves, nutmeg, and clove and the chance of a chilly night made her feel at home. Almost *too* at home. How could a place surrounded by beasts and the dead smell so comforting?

"You called Reaver a beast. I thought he was a demon?"

"He is, but aren't we all beasts?"

She slowly smiled as she took her seat. The faintest smell of salt and brine passed under her nose. Peering over the wall of their sitting area, she could only glimpse the valleys and mountains she had already seen. She leaned further, squinting to her left. There seemed to be a divide at the edge of one of the hills. A slight ripple of magic danced across the scenery. Beyond it, the hill turned to rough rock and sand, a glimpse of the beach she could only smell from here.

"What is that?" She pointed to the ripple of magic.

"A divide."

He poured her water and didn't seem as concerned as she was about a magical wall dividing the land.

"What kind of divide?" She tried to lean over the wall and get a better look. "Dividing what?"

"Do you want sugar in your coffee?" he asked, opening a gold sugar bowl. "Reaver put steamed milk in it but said something about you probably not liking sweet things."

"Of course, I like sweet things," She snapped her head toward him, snatching the sugar from his hand.

It looked like regular brown sugar. She pinched some and placed it on her tongue; it tasted like sugar too.

"What are you doing?" His eyes crinkled at the edges.

"Well"—she paused to sniff the coffee that smelled like coffee and pure bliss—"we're in Hel, so I thought the food would be different."

"There are a lot of things that are different, but the food is mostly the same."

"And the divide?"

She suppressed a moan as the richness of her first sip of coffee hit her tongue. Her shoulders instantly relaxed, and she took another sip, savoring the taste of her favorite drink.

"Is your coffee okay?" He seemed eager to abate her question yet again.

"Why won't you tell me about it?"

He grumbled under his breath. "I have a feeling that once you learn

76

what it's for, I'm going to have to spend my time making sure you don't get into trouble or hurt."

Ellea's eyes went wide as the words rushed out of his mouth. It had to be something good. First he wouldn't tell her about the twins, and now he wouldn't tell her about a simple ripple of magic dividing something. How bad could it be? She was already in Hel. And why was he so worried about her?

"Tell me anyway." She smirked over her cup. "And then tell me why you and the king think I'm some kind of troublemaker."

He squinted at her and slowly sipped his own drink.

"It's your nature, the energy you give off."

"Don't tell me you're reading my 'aura.'" She made air quotes with her free hand.

"No and yes," he said, scratching at his short beard. "Consciously or not, your magic naturally gives off the energy of a troublemaker."

Ellea thought about it. He wasn't wrong, but he wasn't a hundred percent right either.

"I don't go around playing tricks on people," she said with a shake of her head.

"What about that moment with Reaver?"

"He seemed like he was scared of me." She paused, blinking a few times and then rolling her eyes. "So I wanted to see if I could push him."

"And when I tell you that divide is there to separate mortals from the resting Gods, what is the first thing you want to do?"

Ellea pressed her lips into a thin line. Her first thought was to go to it, feel the magic, and push it. She had spent her whole life suppressing her magic, and now that it was free and she was in a place where she was scared and unsure, she didn't want to hold back.

"Wait." Something clicked. "You said mortals. Where are the

supernaturals?"

His lips pressed into a thin line before he blew out an aggressive breath.

"They are to the east of the Gods' territory," he said with a clipped tone.

Ellea's eyes unfocused as the realization of what he was saying fully formed in her mind. Mortals were separate from supernaturals. She skipped past the Gods completely, saving that for another time. Mortals and supernaturals were kept separate.

"Why?" she blurted out. "Why would they be separate?"

"Because that is how it is and how it always has been," he said with a sigh. He seemed unhappily resigned to it.

"That makes zero sense." She placed her coffee down as it turned sour in her stomach. "Is this the fucking seventeen hundreds? Is time different here?"

"No," he said. "Your time is our time, but these ways were set before the Gods retired. It's how it always has been."

Ellea pushed around a small sandwich on her plate. What if a supernatural was friends with a mortal? Were they in two different parts of Hel, unable to visit each other? She looked up at Duhne, who already looked defeated. This was only her second day in Hel, and she didn't want to push away the only person who had talked to her. She took a small bite of her sandwich and let the information she'd been given wash over her. The sandwich settled poorly as she glanced toward the divide.

"What kind of books do you like?" Duhne asked after he finished his food.

"Fantasy, romance, or anything with dragons and monsters." She smiled sadly, thinking of the book she'd dropped before she was taken here.

"Are you done eating?" he asked. With a glance toward the food she'd barely picked at, he stood.

"Yeah." She stood too, waiting for him to dictate what came next.

"Follow me." He walked toward the double doors. "Viatrix has a collection of books you may like."

Ellea followed him into the library, down a few sections of books, and took a right at a very crude and beautiful statue of a man seated on another man's lap. They both wore extremely pleased looks on their faces.

"Here." He gestured toward a wall of books.

"What are these?" she asked, getting in closer to read some of the names.

"Viatrix has been here for ages," Duhne said with a chuckle. "Every book in the world of the living dies here, and she cares for them. Her afterlife has been spent organizing and researching every book that has ever existed—even the smutty ones."

"You mean…" Ellea couldn't help her dramatic gasp as she clutched her chest.

"Any book you could ever want is probably here," he said with a warm smile. "It may not be shelved yet, but it's somewhere in this realm."

Ellea looked back at the countless books in front of her, taking in the names. Some were in other languages, but others she could make out. She was utterly overwhelmed by the sheer amount of books. Remembering how quickly she intended to leave Hel altogether, she grabbed the first one she could comprehend. Would she have time to finish it before Ros showed up? Duhne looked over her shoulder.

"*Dracula and His Consort.*" He gave her a devilish smirk.

She quickly flipped through it, searching for words that would help her determine the filth level without giving away too much of the story. She smiled widely and looked up at Duhne.

"This will do."

Ellea had grabbed a few more books before Duhne said he would take her back to her room. She slowly followed him out, flipping through the pages and savoring the feeling of having something to read. A thought popped into her head as she noticed Reaver at the end of the library.

"Duhne," she said, stepping toward the balcony where they'd eaten. "I'll meet you by the end of the library. I want to bring some snacks to my room. I didn't eat enough."

He gave her a worried look, but nodded before walking toward an eager Reaver. Ellea waited a moment before whispering, "Viatrix?"

The woman appeared at her elbow, and Ellea muffled her shocked gasp. "Fucking Hel."

"You called?" she said with a bored tone, glancing at her opaque nails.

"What are the chances of you getting me any book I can read on the history of Hel?" Ellea asked, keeping her tone low.

Viatrix's pale eyes seemed to glint at her request.

"It will take some time, but I can get a few delivered to your room later today," she said, keeping her voice low as well.

"Do you know where I'm staying?" Ellea asked, her brows coming together.

"Of course, I do, you silly monster," she scolded. Ellea rolled her eyes at the insult that actually felt warming.

"I will be forever grateful for any help you can give me," she said sweetly, stepping toward the table and grabbing a few scones and pastries. She didn't want Duhne to get suspicious.

"Doubtful," Viatrix said as she floated away, scanning volumes of books on her way.

"Thank you," Ellea said under her breath and headed for the door as her plan fully formed in her mind.

7

Rosier

Eight Days without Ellea

I t was a short fifteen-minute ride on the ferry to the small island, but Sam still managed to eat three bags of chips and drink a breakfast margarita. "Might as well enjoy it while I can," he had said to a grumbling Ros. He wasn't wrong. This was going to be the easiest part of their journey.

Billy had spent the whole trip trying to shoo away his negative thoughts. "Save it for the last two parts of the journey," she had said.

The deckhand led them up a path as he droned on about the history of the island and the monastery on top of it. Ros blocked it out and calculated how long it would take before he would see Ellea. The answer: too long. He rubbed at his chest to try to ease the ache that had settled there when she was taken. Billy grabbed their attention, and they slowly crept away from the tourists and headed toward the intricate garden at the back of the massive building.

The garden had a maze of ferns and bushes as tall as Ros. The five of them followed it to its center, passing rose bushes along the way.

"Hey, it's you." Devon pointed to a giant bush of thorny roses.

Ros only grunted and walked past him.

"What do you mean?" Sam asked.

"Rosier, it means 'rose bush' in some languages," Devon explained, catching up with them.

"Pretty and prickly," Sam said with a small laugh. "It's perfect."

"I'm not pretty, you annoying pup," Ros grumbled, but he couldn't help the smile pulling at the corner of his mouth.

They rounded another hedge when a wave of magic weaved around his ankles, making it feel like he was trudging through sand. Ahead of him, Billy stood at a fork in the maze. To the left was a clear and easy opening filled with the morning sunshine; to the right, the shadows surrounded a turn Ros couldn't make out.

"Last turn." She pointed to the right. "In the past, the entrance was just a divide in the path. You could feel the magic as you got close, and each time you went through, it got easier. It seems, over time, nature and those who care for this island have stepped in."

All five of them stood there looking at one another.

"Ready?" Garm asked.

"This is the easy part," Billy said. "It will feel like stepping through a shadow portal. When we arrive, be ready. I never had issues as I entered, but it's been so long."

Devon and Sam both checked their weapons at their hips. Ros knew where his were when he needed them, and Billy's claws slowly elongated.

"Ready," Ros stated.

They all headed toward the darkness. It welcomed them.

Ros felt stripped bare as his foot hit a grassy floor. He quickly took in the area, making sure no one was going to jump and attack them. When it was clear, he felt for his weapons. Everything was still there, but it felt as though something was missing. The rest were doing the same, and he wondered if they felt as shaken as he did.

"Is everyone okay?" Ros asked, looking at his friends.

Everyone but Devon nodded, patting themselves down and checking their bags. Devon was hunched over again, dry heaving from the trip. Billy turned slowly in her spot. She sniffed once and then met eyes with Ros.

"It's the same. Even smells the same."

"Then lead the way," he said to her. "I want to get as far as we can before night falls."

Devon tightened the straps on his bag as Sam gave him a quick kiss on the cheek, avoiding his mouth. The hollow feeling in Ros' chest grew, but he had hope. He was in the same realm as Ellea, or as close to it as he had been for the past eight days.

Ros tore his eyes away from his friends' exchange and took in the surroundings again. They were at the base of a vast mountain that reminded him of the ones outside his window in his bedroom at the castle. To the right, there was a small wooden bridge hugging the rocky wall. Billy nodded toward it, and they headed that way.

It took them two hours to climb the mountain with its wooden bridge. Then another five hours by foot to get through a sparse forest. Hills and valleys took up most of their journey, and they settled for the night a hundred feet outside a dense forest.

"Well, that was easy," Sam said, throwing his bag on the ground.

"Sam," Billy and Devon said.

"What?"

"Don't jinx us, pup," Billy scolded.

Ros shook his head at his friend's blatant disregard for superstition. It didn't matter how many times he told him not to speak ill of something or not to kill a spider because it would rain.

"But it was!"

"You say that now." She shook her head and grabbed a tent from her pack. "The next leg will be equally easy. It's the last two we need to save our energy for."

"How did you manage alone all those years?" Ros asked.

"It's easier to sneak around when you're alone. I also didn't stop much."

"Are you going to tell us why you had to visit Hel so much?" Sam asked with a raised brow.

"No."

Ros pressed his lips together. He knew Billy was hiding something, but she would come out with it when she was ready. Or he would pry it out of Garm after things were settled. Four more nights until he would be at his father's castle. Four more sleepless nights until he would get to Ellea. He wondered when they would be able to rest. It would be a battle to get her out, and he didn't know if they would come back this way or if his ability to portal would be fixed. Either way, he only wanted to touch her, kiss her, see her. To make sure she was whole and safe—his.

A day in Hel was enough to change her, let alone almost two weeks. He worried for her mental state more than her physical. She was strong and powerful, but after her parents' encounter and almost losing Sam, he was worried about how much she could take.

They would get through this; he knew they would. He could feel it in his bones and the depths of his depraved soul. There wasn't any other choice, and this was only the beginning of the battles they would face together. Then came the ones she would face without him…

"Rosier," Garm called, pulling him from his thoughts.

"Sorry, what?"

"Can you help start the fire?" he said, looking at him warily. "We are going to eat and then take shifts throughout the night."

Ros nodded before looking back at the large setting sun. How many more days did he have with her?

8

Ellea

Second Day in Hel

uhne walked her to her door and said he would be back in the morning for breakfast. He had matters to attend to on his side of the castle and mentioned something about messing with his cousin. Ellea laughed to herself as she strode through the sitting room. Duhne was so different, and she found herself liking him. If she could meld Ros, Devon, and Sam into one person, it would be him…with some added benefits. She didn't know if she was going to poke the beast, mess with him some for all he said about her *energy* coming off as trouble. She could prove him wrong, or torture him and show how much trouble she could get into. A wicked smile graced her face as she opened the door to her room, then stopped quickly. The bed was made and the curtains drawn fully open. Wrapping her arms around herself, she tried not to worry that someone was in here. Was that even possible? When she saw the king, she would ask him.

Ellea placed the small stack of romance novels on the bedside table and brought one with her to a chaise near the floor-to-ceiling window. The breathtaking view of mountains and valleys made it hard to be worried. How could an evil place be so open and bright? She ignored the endless questions floating in her head and opened the book. She'd only read the chapter title before a swoosh and thud sounded next to her. It was so loud that she screamed and jumped out of her seat. A stack of books appeared out of nowhere, and she hurried to steady them before they toppled off the table. Cursing the ancient librarian, she organized them into a neat pile, taking in the titles.

Some were basic history books and journaled accounts. Others were rules and patriarchy outlines. History seemed like a good place to start with her need to understand why things were separated. The patriarchy outlines would probably only make her mad. Ellea thought it would be best to hide the remaining books in the massive chest she'd been given to store things in. The massive skirts of an obscene dress seemed like a good place to hide them; there was no way she would be seen in something like that, but it should still serve *some* purpose.

It took forever to get through the first few chapters. It was so much harder than her typical spicy read and she found herself reading passages over again to better understand the history and stories the book presented to her. If only she had highlighters and paper to mark the areas and her thoughts. She felt there were things hidden in half-truths and metaphors. A giggle escaped as she envisioned the look on Viatrix's face if she turned a book back to her all marked up. Her laugh was stopped when a knock sounded at the door. Standing quickly, she tried looking less suspicious. She changed the cover of the book to match one of the romance novels in her unhidden stack.

"Come in," she called, heading toward the sitting room.

A woman waltzed into the room, her beautiful black dress swishing with each step she took. The detail was fascinating; gold thread twined from her elegant wrists and blended into the black cap sleeves. A crown of braids criss-crossed throughout her golden hair, pulling it from her beautiful face. Every part of her was petite, except her large golden eyes that glinted with mischief. It only added to her devilish smirk as she appraised Ellea.

She gave a shallow bow. "Ellea, I'm Florence."

"Please don't bow; I have no idea how to respond to it."

"A simple nod will do." Her voice was light and sharp like a dagger. "I will not stop bowing, and you will find many in the castle and realm will do the same."

Ellea breathed out, rolling her eyes, and Florence chuckled softly before righting herself.

"Before I steal you away, I wanted to make sure you knew you could call me for anything you may need. I'm here to help guide you and serve in any way I can."

"I don't need a maid."

"I am not a maid. I serve only the king because it is my will. That now extends to you and Prince Rosier—when he comes home."

Ellea sucked in a breath at the mention of Ros. "Do you know him? I...I mean, did you know him?" She reached toward the woman, regretting this first encounter. "I'm sorry, this is a lot, and I haven't had a chance to learn or understand anything. I didn't mean to assume anything."

"First, I was too young when Rosier was running around these halls to know him. As for the rest, that is why I'm here." She brushed past her, heading to the bedroom. "The king would like you to join him for dinner so he may make sure you are comfortable and answer any of your questions. But I will always be here if you need to discuss anything."

Florence opened up the chest where the books were hidden, pulling out a skirt and beaded top.

"If you're not a maid, why are you choosing clothes for me?"

"Because I can, and I want to dress your curves." She didn't look back, only reached for shoes to match. "I'm quite jealous of them."

Ellea was a little lost for words as she glanced at the outfit Florence had picked out. The skirt was paneled like the ones she had worn before. The sleeveless beaded top was something else, with gold and black beads twisted and whirled into beautiful detail. But it would leave her barely covered. The small woman came up behind her with a bralette to match; it had an excessive amount of straps.

"Perfect," she said, reaching to pull Ellea's sweater off.

She tried swatting her away, but before she knew it, she was topless and Florence was pulling at her leggings.

"Cheese and rice." Ellea covered herself with her hands.

Florence stepped back, boldly examining her with the eyes of someone appraising unbruised herbs at the market.

"Stop covering yourself and turn around."

Ellea stood taller, rolling her eyes and giving in to the demon. She had to be a demon with *that* attitude.

"I thought you would be softer." She poked her ass with no restraint. "You're as fit as some of the men in the army."

"No, I'm not." She scowled and looked down at her stomach. She brushed her hand against it, wondering how she could compare her to strong men with abs and muscles poking out in various places.

"You're soft in places that matter. Gods, I'm jealous."

She turned and grabbed the skirt, holding it out so Ellea could step into it. Then she handed her the bralette and let her put it on.

"Let me put your hair up," she said. "It will catch on the top if you wear it down."

Ellea cocked her head, thinking how weird it was to have someone waltz into your room, dress you, then demand to do your hair. Florence gestured toward the bathroom vanity where Ellea could sit and pulled a brush and a few pins out of the shadows.

"I'll have your bathroom stocked while you're at dinner," she said, brushing Ellea's hair back.

She worked quickly, braiding the crown of her head in a thick plait and swooping it around. She conjured a simple gold and black crown with a single, small peak at the center. She was about to protest, but Florence's eyes glared at her before she could get it out.

"Don't waste your breath on silly things," she said, fitting the crown behind her braid. "You have a lot to discover, so save your energy for the right questions and actions."

Florence seemed so much older than she presented. She placed her hands on either shoulder and gazed back at her in the mirror.

"One more thing," she said and then smothered Ellea's face in shadows.

Her own magic rumbled to the quick beat of her heart, but the shadows were gone in a second. When she glared at Florences's reflection, she saw perfect liner and a bit of blush on her face.

"Perfect." Florence grinned back. "Let's get you in that top and to dinner. I can hear your stomach growling."

Ellea glanced at herself one last time. When was the last time she looked put together like this? She liked it, but it had her longing for loose hair and bare feet walking around a cabin in the woods.

Ellea and Florence strolled down the hallway. A book was clutched under her free elbow and her new demon friend had hers looped through her right. Florence slowly led her to their destination, giving curt nods to those who passed by. The windows flared with a dim red light as Hel's sun set. People walked down the halls, lighting candles in wall sconces. They didn't speak as they walked; the only sound came from the swish of their skirts or the beading on Ellea's top. Florence had squealed with delight when she'd finished lacing her into it. They turned sharply and walked through two black doors that opened on their own. The room before them was quaint and warm. Ellea had expected some vast dining hall like the ballroom at her family's manor. A few lounging chairs took up the walls. A bar cart stood near the fire where Asmodeus stood, alone. He turned, and Florence quickly bowed. She gave Ellea a look when she didn't follow, but the king only nodded his head with a warm smile spread across his handsome face. He wore a black suit similar to the one that Ellea had seen the day before, but there was no tie, and he seemed more comfortable with a couple of the buttons undone.

"Hello, darling," he said, walking up to Ellea with both hands stretched out in front of him.

Ellea paused, not sure what to do at his gesture. She glanced at Florence, who looked as lost as she felt.

"Florence, thank you for delivering our princess," he said, grasping Ellea's free hand with both of his in a warm squeeze.

"First off—"

"Choose your battles," Florence mumbled, cutting her off.

Ellea pursed her lips and gave the king a nod. "Thank you for inviting me to dinner."

"Florence," he said with a nod as she backed out of the room. "I'll see you in the morning with a report."

"Yes, my king." She bowed again, grasping each door handle. "Enjoy your evening."

She left with a wink, and Ellea didn't have time to object.

"She's not staying?" She suddenly felt abandoned. She'd been enjoying her company, even with its crass nature.

"Florence has some work to do." He led her to the table and pulled out a chair for her. "I'm sure you will see her tomorrow."

Asmodeus took the seat to her left at the head of the table. It could seat at least ten people, and it was covered in different foods, candle sticks, drinks, and elaborate decoration, all black and gold like his wing of the castle. The fire behind him was large, bathing the cozy room in warm light. He looked so at ease tonight, a small smile stuck on his face.

"How was your day?" he asked, pouring her some wine.

"Boring," she said, bringing the cup to her nose and sniffing it. It smelled like normal red wine. Taking a sip, she was instantly warmed by notes of cinnamon, berries, and a rich chocolate flavor.

He chuckled and sipped his wine. "I heard you got to see the library after your self-driven tour of the castle?"

"I'm surprised I got as far as I did." She smirked at him and leaned back in her chair.

Ellea surveyed him over the rim of her goblet, waiting for a scolding. He only mimicked her, leaning back in his own chair. He tapped on his cup, seeming thoughtful as he surveyed her.

"I hope you spend more time with Florence."

"Why, so she can keep an eye on me?"

"Yes, but I think you can learn from her. I think you could learn from each other, and you will find that she is more than she seems."

"More than a meddling demon with no boundaries?"

"Yes, more than that."

Ellea liked Florence a lot from their short encounter. The only girls she had ever spent any time with were her grandmother and Billy. Her chest hurt thinking about her familiar. They had never been this far apart. Their recent separation had only been because they were too busy with the men in their lives, and not by something so vast as being in different realms.

"Ellea?" Asmodeus asked, pulling her out of her thoughts.

"Sorry, I was thinking about someone," she said, leaning forward to survey the food.

What would Billy think of this place? She wondered if she would bound the halls, snapping at little demons and drooling over Duhne and the king. Or would Ellea get to see her human form? They could play dress-up together. Ellea's heart felt heavy, but she couldn't help but smile at the thought.

"Rosier?" he guessed. "I'm quite disappointed in my heir. I thought he would have stormed the castle by now."

"No, my familiar," she said, poking at what looked like a cooked turkey as she tried to dampen down how worried she was. She was sure Ros was doing everything he could to get to her. But what was taking him so long? "Your son may be mine and all-consuming, but I have room in my thoughts for others."

Asmodeus chuckled again. He seemed to laugh a lot in her presence.

"Do I entertain you?"

"Yes," he said, cutting a piece of meat and offering it to her.

"You're welcome?" She was a little put off by his direct answer.

"It gets lonely as a king." His eyes were so warm and almost sad as he held her gaze. "Especially when your only heir runs off."

"It must be hard as a widower as well." She was curious about why he hadn't mentioned his wife.

"Yes," he said, tearing his eyes away. "So when a young woman comes into my realm—"

"You mean is dragged to your realm…by you?"

"—one who is crude and doesn't hold anything back," he continued, smiling at her, "I find myself enjoying the company."

"Maybe you should kidnap young women more often."

"My subjects may start to talk if I start welcoming others so frequently."

"Welcoming?" Ellea snorted. "And they aren't talking already?"

"Oh, they are," he said, sipping his wine. "Haven't I been welcoming? The clothes, the quarters?"

"It's been a day, Azzy; my heart hasn't warmed to the situation yet."

Azzy, she repeated, liking that nickname.

"Azzy?" he questioned with a raised brow.

"Azzy." She raised her glass.

He clinked his with hers, and they began to eat the meal he'd plated for both of them.

"Why don't you talk about Ros' mother?"

They had finished eating and were now seated in two wingback armchairs by the warm fire. Their conversation was light besides Azzy trying to talk her into training with him after breakfast. He seemed to have some insight on her magic and wanted to see if it was as powerful and adaptable as he remembered from other witches. Or if she had more than what he remembered.

He let out a long sigh. "What is there to say?"

"Anything. Ros never spoke of her. Duhne ignored it and bit off the head of the creepy redhead we met when she brought her up."

"Her loss is something we all still feel, even after a thousand years."

His eyes grew distant, and she worried she'd brought up something too sad, too painful, but he continued.

"I'm sure you've noticed that us kings don't have any spouses."

Ellea nodded.

"Esmeray lasted the longest. We almost thought she wouldn't be plagued by the curse whose darkness hangs over this castle. My wife was the mother figure for all of the heirs. And with all the love she had, none of them went without feeling important. She was also as fierce as she was caring. Before I whisked her away to this realm, she was a powerful witch in your realm, one of the very first and last chaos witches."

Ellea's heart felt so heavy from the love pouring into his words. He continued, telling amazing stories of how she'd fought in the earlier wars and times she'd battled for supernatural rights well before her time. With each tale, it was easy to see how magnificent and strong she'd been. No wonder he was still mourning the loss. Poor sweet and broody Ros.

"Wait." He had finished one passionate tale, but Ellea had questions before he started another. "If everyone comes to Hel, why can't she be back here? Why are you mourning her?"

"It doesn't work like that. Hel has its rules, and those who come here are at peace and resting. Even I, a king, cannot disturb that."

"That's dumb."

He barked a laugh. "There is a lot you need to learn, which brings me back to helping you learn more about your power."

"Can't this be a vacation while I wait for my knight in shining armor to save me?" She didn't actually mean it. With the little she had already learned and read, she knew there would be no rest. She was eager for knowledge and to understand everything about Hel and the Gods. Maybe she even wanted to learn about her powers from the King of the Gods while she waited for her savior.

Azzy gave her a long look as if he could read her weighing the options in her mind. So she rolled her eyes and gave in.

"When do we start?"

9

Ellea

Third Day in Hel

This was awkward. Or that's what she thought it should be as Azzy twirled her around his sitting room. She did her best not to trip on her feet yet again. When they had talked about training, she had expected the Rosier version with swords and daggers, forcing her to control and use her magic while exhausted and her hands were full. Her hands were full now, her right placed in Azzy's hand and her left gripping his shoulder. He was practically holding her up.

"Focus. I can see your mind working."

She grumbled at herself, trying to remember to slide her left foot back as he made a half turn. "Why—" Her toe caught the rug, and she let out a hiss.

"Don't stop, keep trying."

"What kind of sick training is this?" She winced as she stepped on his foot for the tenth time. He didn't show a hint that it bothered him, only continued guiding her through the movements. "The King of the Gods is giving me dancing lessons? I expected magic and fighting—anything but this."

"This isn't magical?"

She snorted and shook her head. It was something, but she wouldn't use the word magical to describe it.

"Florence can help you with fighting. I need you ready to take on the rest of the kings and their courts."

"By dancing?"

"If I took you to a ball, what would you do?"

She thought of the only dancing she usually did and winced. It involved some type of fire, limited clothing, and being under the stars.

"Okay, sure, but what about my powers?" She wasn't going to have much time with him, and she wanted to learn what he knew. He was ancient, and it seemed a bit easier to learn from someone you weren't fucking.

He paused and then smirked. "Turn my pocket square into anything you can think of."

Ellea glanced down to the satin square. As soon as she thought about turning it blue instead of green, she tripped so hard she almost fell on her ass. Azzy held her and laughed. "How about you learn the steps, then we can work on magic while moving?"

So they continued, turning and striding around chairs and tables. She half expected her powers to churn and be erratic. But they were peaceful, almost lulled by the music playing quietly from a small record player. It was an ancient melody that seemed endless and breathy. There was no singer, only instruments Ellea couldn't place, and Azzy hummed with it. They only spoke of trivial things as he continued to be graceful for such a large man. And he was so very patient despite the amount of times she'd messed up or almost tripped him. But she was slowly picking up the movements and had finally stopped stepping on his toes.

"Is there anything else you plan on teaching me?"

What else would she need to learn to deal with all that she hadn't seen yet? She didn't want to be left out blinded to reality ever again. She wasn't an ignorant child.

"I would like you to learn the old language, the layout of our realm, politics, and magic specific to Hel and its rulers. You seem to have history covered with the book you snuck to dinner last night."

Ellea cocked her eyebrow, not able to find the words.

How does he know?

"I know your lies, even your magicked ones."

"That must have been annoying for Ros while he was growing up." She couldn't help but smile, and Azzy answered with his own. "Did I do something wrong with the books? Borrowing them, I mean."

He shook his head and guided her through one final rotation. "I need you to learn as much as you can. We'll go over things while you're here. Train with Florence when you can and meet me for lunch or tea, then we can work through things together."

"Why?" Why did he want her to learn so much outside of magic? Why the history, the politics? She knew her reasons for it, but what were his?

They stopped in the middle of the room, and he searched her face. It felt like they stood that way forever, and she wondered if he'd forgotten what she asked.

"You need to have access to as much information and power as you can if you expect to survive this place." She was about to interrupt him, reminding him she would be home soon, but he didn't let her. "Don't. I know I took you from your home, from my son. But you should trust me on this and utilize what I'm giving you."

She shouldn't, but it was hard to find a reason not to. Ros had ruined demons for her, and she was becoming too trusting. Looking at him, this powerful being and demon that had stolen her away, there was only trust and a feeling of comfort. It was strange, but she would go with it...for now.

"Okay, Azzy. What's next?"

"Tea and talking." He guided her toward a small table, and Reaver walked through one of the walls, a tray of drinks and snacks in his pale hands.

"Princess Ellea prefers coffee, my king."

Ellea gifted the little demon a grin, one that had him almost dropping the tray.

Azzy pressed his lips together. "Thank you, Reaver."

"Yes, thank you, Reaver," Ellea said a bit too sweetly.

The demon slowly backed out of the room while they both fixed their drinks.

"Politics, history, or kings?" Azzy asked.

She leaned back in her chair, one too large but very cozy. Looking out the window, she took a moment to think it over. What would she need to learn first?

"Kings."

Ellea's brain hurt. She'd left Azzy's sitting room a few hours ago, but her head was still swimming with all she'd learned. He'd told her about the rules, how the kings were appointed, and how the dead lived—well, how they spent their days. The one thing she couldn't wrap her head around was how Hel had four kings, but Azzy had the final say in everything. The other three had their own domains, but the Gods had given him the most power. Before the heirs were born, there had been several attempts to overthrow him, mostly by Beelzebub and once by Sonneillon, the twins' mother. But old age seemed to have settled things.

Azzy barely looked forty, with only a small amount of gray hair and just a hint of wrinkles arounds his hazel eyes. Even he could die, though, or retire as the Gods had. How long would it be until Ros had to take his father's place? Five hundred years? A thousand? Gods, her head hurt. She hadn't slept well either, which wasn't helpful. Back in her room, she'd found a note from Florence. It said to be ready to leave during the witching hour. That was all. She had no idea what she needed to be ready for, but she dressed in a black shirt, leggings, boots, and tucked a dagger into her waistband. Nothing good could come from a three-in-the-morning meeting, so simple clothing seemed best. Unless she was taking her to some orgy, but she doubted that.

Ellea peeked up from her book as the door opened silently. A whisper of shadow beckoned her to come out. They were soft and silent, unlike Duhne's storm-cloud shadows, or Ros' strong, solid ones. She stopped her thoughts as they started drifting toward the wicked things they did. She crept toward the door and poked her head out. Florence was leaning against the opposite wall, waiting.

Ellea shrugged at her and whispered, "Why are you being creepy?"

Florence only gave her a smirk and a nod, gesturing for her to follow. *Demons.*

Ellea shook her head but followed, doing her best to mimic the demon's silent feet. She was jealous of how gracefully she slunk around the halls, her shadows opening doors. These halls were less decorated than the others she'd seen, as though they were going through the servants' quarters. And they were endless. She was about to ask what the plan was when Florence opened a door to a room instead of another hallway.

"Florence," Ellea hissed.

She only shushed her and led them to a balcony shrouded in shadows. Florence pulled her down behind the ornate railing, and they both crouched there. Ellea was about to protest when she heard slurping and sucking sounds coming from the neighboring room. She glared, and Florence rolled her eyes. She brought her delicate hand to her ear. *Listen.*

Ellea mouthed *gross,* and Florence gave her a wicked grin, but agreed with a nod of her head.

"You like sucking a prince's prick?"

Bile crept up Ellea's throat. Not only was that the dumbest thing she'd ever heard, it was fucking Belias getting a blow job.

Fucking Belias.

An even more horrendous, muffled giggle sounded as the ass-hat came to a sad finish. Someone knocked on the door. Had Belias even given the girl a moment to clean up? She shot Florence a look, and they both seemed to think the same thing.

Sad and gross.

Florence perked up when the visitor began talking.

"Belias, I got your message. I do not know how many times I need to tell you in a day, but your spell is holding."

"So we won't get any visitors?"

"Yes, as I told you hours ago."

Someone strode across the room with loud, clipped steps. "But how long will it hold?"

Belias' voice grated on her skin, and she had to hold back the urge to jump onto his balcony and stab him in the face.

The visitor huffed a sigh. "As long as it needs to. And before you ask, no one else is getting in or out."

"Good. You're dismissed."

She shooed her blood lust to the side and tried to understand what they were talking about. Spell? No one getting in or out? But the visitor cut in.

"Learn some respect, Belias, I will only play your games for so long."

"You will play my games as long as I say so. It won't take long before—"

"They are games; don't think I believe your crusade will be fruitful."

Before Belias could snark back, the visitor left the room. The door slamming shut made Ellea jump, and Florence grabbed her by the wrist, dragging her from the room and back to the servants' hallway.

The trip back to her room went by quickly as one thought after another went through her mind. Florence came in after her, shutting the door quietly and guiding her to the bedroom before closing those doors as well.

"Why?" Ellea asked, unable to find the right question to start with.

"Which part?"

Ellea climbed into bed, leaning up against the headboard and clutching a pillow in her lap. "All of it? Why bring me? What do you do? What is going on?"

"Besides my courtly duties, I spy for the king."

Ellea stopped her eyes from rolling at the obvious statement. "Are you part of one of the families or...?"

Azzy had explained to her that most of the court was made up of old families or gentry, ones whose lineages had started at the beginning. Their lands or titles were passed down through the generations.

"Gods, no." She shook her head. "Asmodeus caught me stealing—or attempting to steal. I was so young then and didn't have a family. I was also a bit too ambitious."

Florence smiled deviously, and Ellea could picture it. She could see a smaller, younger-looking version of Florence sneaking through the castle and dodging guards.

"You didn't try to steal from a king, did you?" No, she couldn't be that ambitious.

"Oh, yes." Florence took a spot across from her, grabbing her own pillow to lean against. "I was dumb and young. I didn't care what happened to me, and I wanted to push things, see how far I could go. I tried joining the guards since I had nothing, but they wouldn't take some low-born demon who was too small and weak."

Her eyes became a bit glassy as she stared at nothing. Ellea recognized the look; Florence was going someplace else, lost in a distant memory or vision. Clearing her throat, Florence continued.

"Long story short, I was a little mad about the whole situation, so I attempted to steal something big, something that would put me up for a while—"

"Wait, why didn't you go to the other realm? Start over in the land of the living?"

"It's not that easy, and this place was all I knew. Young and dumb, remember?"

Ellea knew the feeling. Living your regular life, not reaching or trying something different. "So who caught you?"

"The king himself." She smiled wide, and a hint of mischief sparkled in her gold eyes. "I expected a guard or some court member. Instead of throwing me in the dungeons, he recruited me. He seemed quite impressed that I'd gotten into his quarters unseen by anyone but him."

She brushed off her shirt, smugness seeping from her.

Ellea shook her head and laughed. "How long ago?"

"Two hundred years or so."

It was amazing how long some lived for. Florence's smooth, perfect skin showed no age. "And now you…?"

"Do what I can, keep an eye on things."

"Like spying on a prince?"

Florence straightened. "He has been up to something for years, and I think we are finally getting to the end point."

Ellea chewed on her lip, unsure of how much the demon knew or how much she wanted her to know.

We are doing things differently.

No more hiding, no more shoving things in a closet and ignoring them. She glanced at the chest where she'd hidden the books from Viatrix.

"So you know about him and my parents?"

"Pieces of it from Asmodeus and news that travels here. But what Belias is up to with them is hard to say. He always speaks in code or is vague when meeting with people. There has never been enough evidence to pin something on him."

So Ellea knew as much as Florence. That made her feel a little better.

"Do you spy on anyone else?"

"Not lately, not as much as I did when I first started. Things have been quiet this decade—well, until now."

Until her parents.

She needed in. She would not sit out on whatever was going on. "What's the plan?"

"Have fun, spy, learn all you can."

"More training." Ellea groaned, but she didn't mean it. "Do you know what the king wants with me?"

Florence huffed a laugh. "Isn't it obvious?" Ellea shook her head. "He wants you to rule with his son."

Ellea choked a sputtering laugh. "Why? Did he say that to you? Those exact words?"

Florence cocked her head. "No, but why not?"

Why not? Ellea shook her head, thinking of how mere months ago she was in her small city, reading a romance and avoiding dumb boys and clients. "I'm only a witch, one who spent her days reading and avoiding people besides reading fortunes." Also avoiding the council, her fears, and a vision of a future that had haunted her since she was young. But she didn't voice that to Florence. "Now I'm in Hel, and you're telling me the king expects me to rule with his son one day? We only met and decided to date, like, a month ago."

Florence was quiet for a moment before she laughed, a loud cackle that shook her small frame. She laughed until Ellea hit her with her pillow. The demon wiped at the tears that had escaped her eyes.

"You are a powerful supernatural. You are not meant to be a lowly fortune teller." She shook her head again, looking more serious. "My Gods, girl. What were you thinking?

Ellea threw herself down on the bed, looking up at the ornate ceiling.

What was she thinking?

"That I could read, make a ton of money, and not be bothered."

Florence threw herself down next to her and sighed. "Isn't that the dream?"

10

Rosier
Nine Days without Ellea

Ros was both trying to forget and hold on to the dream that had been plaguing him for a few nights. He and his friends were on a trip to Hel, it wasn't the time to have visions of Ellea moving under him. They had been trekking through the dense forest for a few hours. Billy and Garm were fine in comfortable silence, while Sam had done nothing but complain. Devon was actually using his time wisely.

He was taking deep, steadying breaths with each step, and shadows flickered around his skin. They weren't like Ros', witches held a different type of shadow magic, but creating them was a similar process. The shadows disappeared, but Devon—ever the patient and centered one—didn't grow frustrated. He looked toward Ros, ready for the next instruction.

"Now that you can find them, you need to understand them." Shadows lived in the darkest part of the soul. "You need to learn to understand them, why they are there and how to care for them. It's not like an element you can control—"

"What if you don't have any darkness?" Sam cut in to ask.

Garm snorted. "We all have darkness, even lap dogs like you, Sam."

Sam grumbled something under his breath and went back to kicking pine cones.

"As I was saying, you pull them from the darkest part of you, accept and care for them, and then you can utilize them."

Devon nodded and went back to concentrating on Ros' instructions. Shadows began to seep and flicker around him again, and he smiled. Devon was so smart and such a fast learner.

"I remember a time when that was considered dark magic," Billy said.

Ros huffed a breath, trying to forget his vision of witches burning on a pyre and the endless war between mortals and supernaturals. "No magic is dark or bad. It's the people who wield it for their evil reasons."

Like Ellea's parents.

"You should save your energy," Billy said to Devon.

He held on to the shadows for a few seconds longer before letting them disappear around him. "I've been working on deepening my power; this is only surface stuff."

"Well, we have about another five hours of walking before we rest for the night. Tomorrow is going to be a battle."

"You keep saying that," Sam whined, "but I feel like I'm on a nature hike."

"I thought wolves loved running through the woods," Billy said.

"We do, but it's more fun when you're chasing a tasty boyfriend under the moonlight."

Devon's eyes went wide, and he dipped his chin, probably trying to hide the dimple that was trying to appear.

Ros bumped him with his shoulder. "Could be worse, he could be like Billy, trying to get sandwiched between you and Garm."

Devon smiled and bumped him back. "I probably wouldn't say no to that." They both laughed as Billy began fanning herself.

It would never happen, but they could joke and be too close for most people's comfort. He couldn't wait to have Ellea back in the mix of their weird group.

The snap of a stick had Ros awake instantly. He didn't open his eyes but reached under his pillow for his dagger as his tent flap opened. It could be a friend, or it could be something else. This part of the realm was messing with his ability to sense those around him. He had taken the first watch, no one should have been waking him up yet. Before they could speak, Ros turned and grabbed them by the shirt and pressed the dagger under their chin.

"It's Devon."

Ros instantly dropped the dagger and inhaled Devon's scent. *Lemons, vanilla, and rosemary.*

Devon's pulse was a flurry of fear, and Ros got to his feet instantly. "What is it?"

"Sam, h-he never came back from watch."

Ros pushed through his tent and sent a stream of shadows and thoughts to wake Billy and Garm. He stormed around their site, looking for any sign of struggle. The sun was barely up, but Ros could see a small area where the leaves and dirt had been disturbed. He rushed through the trees, following a groove left in the dirt. It looked like something had been dragged. It lasted about thirty feet before there was nothing.

"They could have two to four hours on us depending on when they took him," Garm said, pulling a shirt over his head as he made it to where Ros stood.

Fuck.

Gods only knew what had taken him. He sniffed the air; the smells of pine and cedar mixed the rancid smells of dead flesh and moldy earth. Any creature imaginable could be responsible. Ros turned back to the campsite, where Billy was consoling a worried Devon. It was time for a plan, not to crumble. This was simply one bad step on a hard journey; all missions had them.

"Shift, follow the scent, and report back," Ros ordered. "We'll pack up and be ready to hunt them down by the time you get back."

Garm nodded once and looked to Billy, who was already shifting to her beast form. They both bolted in the direction of Sam's fading scent. Ros walked to Devon and grasped him by the shoulders, forcing his light eyes upward.

"We'll get him back."

"I should have taken watch with him."

"No, we aren't blaming ourselves for this. Let's pack up and be ready to get him back."

Devon searched his face before finally dipping his head in agreement. They got to work, packing and clearing any trace they'd been there. Ros hoped they wouldn't be too late. He shook the thought from his mind. He wouldn't think the worst; they would get him back.

Ros was helping Devon with his pack when Billy and Garm came bounding back through the clearing. The search had only taken them fifteen minutes in their beast forms; it would take them longer on foot.

Ten of them, Garm said. *They look like hags, but they aren't. It's hard to explain, but he's still alive.*

"Lead the way. We will find a place to drop the packs along the way and get him out."

"What do they want with him?" Devon's voice was pure ice, and his features had turned sharp and vicious.

Garm shook his large head while Billy's eyes glanced between the both of them. Ros could only imagine what was going through Devon's mind; it was probably the darkest thing he could think of.

We're wasting time, Billy said, and that snapped Devon into action. He left them all behind and began running in the direction Garm and Billy had come from.

Fuck. Fuck. Fuck.

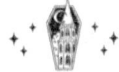

They had dropped their packs behind a large bush and now spied on a group of creatures around a large fire. There were ten, like Garm had said, but they didn't look like the old, pudgy hags he knew. These creatures looked deadly with their inky green skin, elongated fingers, and sharp claws. Their noses and ears were pointy, and it looked like none of them knew what a hairbrush was. Excitement radiated off of them as they spoke in a language Ros couldn't understand. Sam was still alive. He looked furious, tied to a tree and gagged with a pine cone. They'd left him in his pickle print boxers, and he looked...shiny?

They want to eat him.

Ros' powers cracked under his skin as the scents of fear and bloodlust wafted around him. He took a deep breath and then grabbed Devon, who was ready to bolt for Sam. They had a plan and needed to stick to it. Garm and Billy were already getting into position, creeping around the camp on opposite sides. Ros sent his shadows along the forest floor. They coiled around the ankles of four of the creatures and yanked them into the waiting maws of his friends. They both got to work, snapping and ripping heads and body parts. Ros and Devon only had a moment of surprise to attack the six that were left. They put themselves between Sam and the others. The hair on the back of Ros' neck stood when their screams and howls shook the trees around them as they witnessed their ilk being killed. They didn't have time to free Sam as they pounced. Claws and black teeth slashed and bit. Both men threw magic and wielded their daggers, fighting, blocking, and never allowing them near their next meal. They'd gotten three down by the time Billy and Garm joined them.

One hissed to Devon in that ancient and wild language. He snarled a "fuck you" back before jumping on it. He caught the creature's neck in his free hand, and before it could claw and fight back, Devon rammed his dagger into the side of its skull. He yanked it out and stabbed it over and over again.

It was well beyond dead by the time the others were finished. Billy pried Devon back; he was still screaming and snarling like a beast himself.

It's over, rang through Ros' mind as Billy tried to calm him down.

Devon snapped out of it. After one last glance at the bloodied beast at his feet, he turned to a wide-eyed Sam. Ros hurried to cut down the rope they used to bind him to the tree. Devon went to his boyfriend, and with a gentleness he wasn't showing moments ago, pulled the pine cone from Sam's mouth.

"Did they hurt you?" Devon asked, searching Sam from head to toe.

He didn't answer, only flung his arms around Devon and kissed him. Kissed him so hard and soundly that Ros and the others turned away to give them a moment. Ros couldn't help the smile that spread across his face. Even after the short and brutal fight, warmth spread through him to see how happy his friend was. He was whole and with the person he loved. Both of his friends had found love—well, if you could call what Garm and Billy had love.

"How did they get you?" Garm asked, now in his human form.

Sam shivered before he could answer. "I'm not sure, but I was circling our site after hearing something, and the next thing I knew, I was hit over the head. I woke up when they tied me to that tree. They were rubbing something all over me."

"Is that why you're so greasy?" Devon asked.

Billy, also now on two legs, sniffed and grimaced. "Animal fat." Sam looked like he was about to be sick. "If you weren't such a damn snack, maybe you wouldn't get kidnapped."

"I think I'm well-seasoned too." Sam tried to brush off the herbs that clung to his lard-covered body. "What were those things?"

Ros didn't know; they weren't anything he had witnessed in his long life. He looked toward Garm, but Billy answered.

"We don't have a name for them, but they lived in this realm before the Gods arrived. They were left to haunt these woods."

Sam shivered, and Ros glanced down at the dead creatures around them. Beasts older than the Gods? He had a lot to learn.

"Let's go," Garm said. "There is a stream ahead where you can wash off, and then we need to move before more creatures come for us."

They all looked at each other. Ros swallowed hard, realizing that what came next would be the hardest part of their journey.

11

Ellea

Six Days in Hel

Ellea left Azzy's study and headed toward the library. After almost a week of being in Hel, she was navigating the castle fairly well for someone with horrible direction. The demons and creatures had stopped scurrying around like they were afraid of her, and not a moment too soon; it had reminded her too much of being in Halifax. Each step into the hallway during those earlier days would have her stomach dropping to her feet and her magic roaring to scare them all. But now, she was finding a routine and some comfort. She was mostly left alone on her usual route from her room to the study and then to the library. Sometimes Duhne or Florence escorted her, but her "handlers" hadn't picked her up today. So she opened her book and let her feet guide her from memory. She was on a mission to bug Viatrix for some more books. The one she was reading now was an ancient journal from one of the first dukes in Azzy's court. He had passed away almost a thousand years ago, and his accounts were fascinating. It was a good distraction. Yes, she loved what she was learning, and all of her training had her feeling stronger than ever, but she couldn't stop thinking about Ros, her friends, and her family.

She was getting through a passage on a time when Beelzebub had tried overthrowing Azzy when her magic zinged under her skin. It was a warning. She kept her stride steady and eyes on the pages, but let the sounds around her and any flicker of movement wash in. Under her lashes, she eyed an alcove about ten feet away. The shadows inside moved slightly, as though someone was hiding there.

With her eyes still trained on her book, she reached one hand down and feigned that she was fixing her billowy skirt. The closer she got to the alcove, the more her magic buzzed and her blood roared in her ears.

We aren't afraid.

Her powers answered with a wicked caress. *No, we are ready,* they seemed to say, and Ellea smirked as her hand curled around the dagger that was hidden in the fabric of her skirt. A large scaly hand reached for her, curling around her upper arm and pulling her into the shadows. She didn't even think. She didn't take a second to worry that it was a friend. Her dagger thrust into armor-like skin. It would have held strong against a regular weapon, but hers was made of obsidian. A loud howl answered as she sliced through what she thought would be his groin area, and blood sizzled as the demon crumpled to the floor.

She yanked the dagger away and held it to its chin. "Who sent you?"

It only hissed and tried swiping her hand away, but she was so much stronger than most realized. It was hard to see any features in the darkness, but it didn't matter. The demon faded into shadow and disappeared. "Fuck."

She was actually surprised it had taken this long for something to attack her. Had Duhne or Florence been shielding her from them? She poked her head out of the alcove to see if anyone had seen the altercation, but the few people she'd seen before seemed to have vanished. Hiding the dagger back in her skirt, she slid into the hall and continued on her way. She kept her book tucked under her arm as her powers continued to churn under her skin. She took a steadying breath. "We are fine, this is fine," she kept mumbling to herself. There were only two more turns until she would be near the library. She rounded the corner and ran right into someone.

"Fucking Belias," she hissed.

"Hello, Ellea."

She felt the color drain from her face and her lip curl. He was all pasty sharp features and boring black clothes. She had been able to avoid him this whole time, only seeing him when spying with Florence at night. But here he was, smirking and standing in front of her. Could she stab him? Was that allowed? What she'd witnessed in her spying seemed to be enough to allow it. He was shady, up to no good, and a horrible lover. The fact that the females put up with him was astounding. They still hadn't figured out what he was up to exactly, but he was always meeting with someone, speaking in code, and arranging for things to happen.

He reached for her, and she stepped back. "You have been very hard to get a hold of."

So he had been trying. What a creep. Two guards wearing Duhne's emblem turned around a corner in the distance, and the sight of them settled her a little.

"Take a hint, Bel, and stay out of my way." She said it loud enough that the guards lengthened their strides, heading straight for them.

The ass-hat eyed the two men, then gave her a shallow bow. "Until next time."

She walked away without another look. The guards eyed her as she got closer. "I'm fine and I'm going to the library." She figured they would relay the message to Duhne or someone who didn't want to attack her and continued on her way.

But when she turned the last corner, she saw the twins standing outside the library doors.

"Fucking shit balls." She escaped through the nearest door. She wasn't frightened of them, but she was in no mood for heirs and their games. They had cornered her once before and offered to give her a tour of their side of the castle, even inviting her to dinner. Duhne had swept in and said something obscene that had Cara hissing like a cat before he led her away.

Taking in her current surroundings of simple marble walls and floors, no decor, and basic lighting, she realized these were servants quarters. She could probably make her way back to her suite without being seen. Or she hoped.

She was lost. There was no way her suite was this low in the castle. None of the windows she peeked out looked like the same scenery she saw from her room. The few demons she passed hadn't helped either; any time she thought about asking for help, they would scurry off through the walls, doors she hadn't seen, or puff into shadows and smoke. She *could* go back the way she came, but she was too stubborn to turn back now. If only she could step into the shadows like Ros and Azzy. She stopped in the middle of the hall with her hands on her hips and glared at the ceiling.

"Of all the things you could give me, you couldn't let me portal."

She wasn't sure who she was talking to, but she needed to blame someone for her situation. But maybe someone was listening; she heard a shout a few doors down. Could it be a savior?

She went straight to the door and yanked it open without a thought to worry about what was on the other side. What she found wasn't something she'd expected.

Three demons sat around a small worn table, each with cards in their hands. Two of them had claws, but there was a set of humanoid hands. Drinks, coins, and trinkets were scattered around the table. The two demons snarled at the sight of her standing in the doorway, but the human-looking demon stood and bowed. He wore gold armor with Azzy's emblem on his chest. She was both relieved and frustrated to see him; he would probably take her right back to her room and tell Azzy that she'd been found wandering the halls unattended. But they looked like they were having fun, and she wanted in. She'd only ever played cards with her nana and uncle. The thought sent a small wave of sadness through her, so to stamp it out, she stepped into the room and shut the door.

"Princess—"

Ellea raised her hand, stopping him. "I want in."

The demon looked amused and intrigued by new blood. She could have some fun and possibly get answers from a different sort of castle dweller.

"I don't think that's a good idea."

One of the demons said something she didn't understand, and the guard shot it a look. She didn't want to be dragged back to her room, and she wanted to interact with demons outside of the three she saw regularly. "I said"—she stepped further into the room and grabbed a grungy chair that was against the wall—"I want in, and I would like a drink."

The guard grumbled under his breath before pointing to the two demons. "I'm Mythis, that is Midgy, and the ugly one is Kas."

12

Rosier

Eleven Days without Ellea

R osier knew two things as he chopped the head off of a crazed Wolven.

One, that everything up until this point had been too easy.

And two, he hated the Gods for putting a purgatory full of evil beasts in the way of saving his girlfriend.

"On your left!" Sam called from where he was taking down a vampire crossbreed with his claws.

Ros feigned right and cut the other vampire's legs. Sam, Billy, and Garm were all in various forms of being half-shifted. Their claws and teeth were already coated in blood from their day-long battle. They'd only just gotten Sam cleaned up when they were attacked again.

"We're close," she yelled after clawing down another vampire. "They're trying to stop us from getting across the territory line."

"Please tell me the next part has less assholes," Devon called as he enclosed another beast into a hole he'd created in the earth.

Devon had used every bit of magic in this battle, elemental, telekinetic, and even the bit of shadow magic he'd picked up yesterday. Ros added a mental note to work on it with him when they got through all of this—whenever that would be.

"It's worse," Billy answered, and all of them glared at her. "Less bloody, but it will be worse…for some of us."

Fuck.

A line of beasts held strong about fifty feet in front of them. It appeared they couldn't go any further. They snarled and kicked the ground, waiting their turn to take down the intruders. Ros glanced at Billy, and she gave him a knowing nod. *That's the border.*

Ros pulled at the well of magic in the depths of his soul, skimming his charred fingers through the black surface and pulling it up past all the agony he had felt over his long life. Taking all of the inky blackness, he directed it at the thirty snarling beasts that were trying to stop him from getting to Ellea. He thought of her gray eyes and tracing the freckles across her face and her body with his fingers. He thought of how her heart beat with his and how much he missed her. He growled, guttural and inhuman, and the beasts didn't have time to show a glimmer of shock; they all burst into shadow and black mist.

His roar continued to echo through the otherworldly forest as white-hot rage washed away from him and his breaths came in quick pants.

"Woah," Sam said, his voice breaking through the ringing in his ears.

Ros whirled around to see only his friends gathering around him, no longer battling beasts.

"What?" Ros asked, dumbfounded as he searched the area around them.

Had he managed to finish all of them?

He glanced down at his hands. His veins were black and red with a fading glow, a sight he hadn't seen in a very long time.

Fuck.

"That was hot," Billy said, fanning herself. "Does Ellea hold on to those horns when she's riding your face?"

"Billy," Devon scolded.

Ros reached up but only found air. Feeling his face, it felt normal.

"It was only for a second," Garm said to him.

Ros swallowed once and nodded at his hound. His demon had been bound to show itself sooner or later; every step closer to Hel had it clawing to be free. The years outside his father's realm had made it easier to hold on to his human side, but as soon as he stepped onto Hel's soil…it would be a lot harder. He wondered if Ellea would react like Billy had. He doubted it. Who would embrace horns, a tail, and skin that was charred and cracked because it could barely hold the beast and power beneath it.

She will take you anyway, Billy said telepathically. It wasn't her teasing tone, but a kind and gentle one.

Ros let out a breath and led his friends near the border, where the beasts no longer stood snarling.

"We are going to have to travel through the night," Billy said, toeing the invisible line. "We can rest for a few hours, clean up and eat. But we can't stop and sleep here."

"But when we get to Hel, I won't be able to stop," Ros added.

"We will be tired," Billy answered. "But we will be whole—physically, at least."

"What do you mean?" Devon asked, forcing water into Sam's hands.

"The next part will mess with us mentally, pull up our deepest fears or worst memories. We will be able to walk, mostly, but you won't even know that something has crawled into the darkest parts of your mind and nested there until it's too late."

"Then why can't we sleep?" Sam asked.

"It will make it worse. You won't know what is a dream and what's reality."

"Well..." Ros said, crossing the line first. He turned back to his friends. "Let's get going, then."

It took three hours of walking before he really understood what Billy had said. Each step brought him closer to a memory he'd buried deep. He could feel himself swaying, feeling almost drunk on wine and sex. It brought him back to that night.

The walls of his father's wing glimmered in the low candle light as he stepped out of the musty room of moving bodies. Taking a steadying breath, he shook off some young lord with curling horns and an eager smile who gripped his arm. He begged Rosier to stay and go another round with him—and anyone else who reveled in sleeping with the crowned prince. Rosier wiped his hands down his linen shirt. They felt sticky with wine... and other fluids. Grasping the wall, he headed toward his room.

Ros' hand brushed along the rough bark of a wide and ancient tree. He growled low, fighting off the memory. He kept reminding himself that it wasn't real.

Ros' hand brushed rough obsidian. He blinked rapidly, trying to focus. How did he end up in the throne room? He swayed again, but caught the wall and turned, looking for the way back to his room. The spinning was relentless, but the main door came into a blurry focus. He reached forward, trying to steady himself, and noticed that his hands were coated in blood.

"No," Ros groaned, looking down at his hands. They were clean. He blinked once, and then there it was, the blood he could never wash away. The forest spun around him before he fell on his back.

He fell and something warm and wet seeped through his shirt. He rolled to his side, trying to steady himself, trying to find purchase on anything, but his drunken mind kept slipping. Slowly, he looked up, trying to find his bearings. A shape blurred in front of him—a crown. Feeling the top of his head, he felt the simple gold ringlet in place behind his horns, where it stayed no matter the circumstance. Blinking again, he saw a hand reaching toward him, unmoving. A body lay in front of his father's throne. Her long black hair fanned around her, bones and flowers strung throughout it.

The children in the castle would decorate his mother's hair in anything pretty and dark. She had her favorite chair in the library where she would read, and they would sit behind her, braiding in their little trinkets.

His mother.

Ros' chest burned with power.

His mother.

Flames covered his hands, illuminating the throne room. The heat burned out any drunkenness left as it crawled up his arms.

His mother. She lay there crumpled, her hand reaching out. A single finger pointed toward the last throne to the left.

"Mother?" Ros croaked.

He crawled to her, dragging her into his lap where flames touched her but did no harm. They would never harm someone he loved so much.

"Mother?" *he whispered.*

Her head lolled back, and across her neck was a vicious slash, cutting through skin and bone.

"MOTHER!" *he bellowed, and his powers erupted.*

Flame and shadow engulfed the room as he curled his mother toward his face, sobbing into her chest. Her many necklaces scratched at his face, and her smell broke through the tinge of iron, of her blood. Her electric smell of thunderstorms clung to him.

"Rosier?" *The deep sound of his father's voice broke through the sobs and magic.*

"Rosier!"

Ros sobbed again as hands grabbed his shoulders and shook him. Opening his eyes, it was not his mother he saw, but his legs as he knelt on the forest floor.

"Fucking Gods," Ros cursed.

Wiping at his nose, he stood, taking in the surroundings. He felt exhausted, and his friends looked equally exhausted as they looked back at him. Sam was the palest, and he stood furthest from them.

"We have to keep going," Billy said softly.

Ros turned, and he could almost see the wastes in the distance. A newfound need to get there burned in his chest. He would get Ellea, and he would burn the rest.

After another five hours of walking and fighting old memories, the gates were in sight. Sam still hadn't recovered like the rest of them, but Ros wouldn't call his current state recovered either. He could still see his mother's blank blue eyes and her sage dress. He could see the splattered blood mixing with her freckles and the pained look in his father's eyes as he took down anyone who came near her body. They'd lost hundreds of people the week following her death, either by Ros' hands or his father's. When they never found her killer, Ros left for good.

He looked toward Sam again, worried. He'd thought he would be the least affected by their horrible trip down memory lane.

Sometimes those with the best mask in place suffer the worst, Garm said to him telepathically.

He grunted in response, turning back to their destination. In the distance, he could make out the massive castle where birds and beasts circled the peaks. But closer was a set of massive black gates. Ancient skulls lined each post, and a solemn male stood in front of them.

"Garren?" Ros asked loudly. He couldn't help the smile that crossed his face even after their journey.

Garren was one of his oldest friends, regardless of his hatred for the kingdom. They used to spar, drink, and revel in any way young males would in the court.

"Rosier D—"

"Don't even start with that," Ros cut him off, grabbing him by the forearm.

"It's been ages, prince," he said. "And you've brought friends?"

"Yes. This is Billy, Devon, Sam, and you know Garm."

"Fenrir," Garren said with a deep bow. "Welcome home, Garm of hounds. Nice to see you on two legs; you know I like my men tall."

Billy smirked devilishly, catching his attention.

"Wilhelmina?" he exclaimed. "You little fox, how long has it been?"

Garm growled before she could answer, and Garren stepped back with a chuckle. Ros really needed to figure out their story.

"Well, this has been fun. If you could open the gates, we will be on our way," Ros said, stepping toward them.

"It's been almost fifty years since I've had a visitor, and even more since I've had someone come through the front door," he said with a nod toward Billy.

"Open the gates, Garren."

"All right," he said with his hands up. "It gets lonely out here, I'm sorry I wanted to talk with some old and new friends. Especially Wilhelmina—"

Garm and Ros growled again.

Was he stalling?

No, he had known him for ages and remembered him to be quite chatty.

"Please open the gates, and I'll make sure my father invites you to the feast I'm sure he will throw once I get *home*," Ros said, gritting out the last word.

"Oh, that would be grand," he said, turning toward the gates. With a wave of his hand, they opened on a silent wind.

"I'll see you soon, Garren," Ros said with a pat on his shoulder.

"See you then!" he called after their retreating forms, waving enthusiastically.

13

Ellea

Seventh Day in Hel

"**P**ay up, bastards," Ellea said, slamming her cards down on the rickety table.

The three demons around her cursed, throwing their losing hands down. Ellea smirked over her cup, eyeing all of them to make sure they didn't cheat her out of her money. They mumbled words in languages she couldn't understand. A lot of it sounded close to "bitch" or "cheater," but Ellea didn't mind. She had been wiping the dusty floor with their beastly faces for the past two hours. It had only taken her a few games to pick up on the rules and on how to cheat them out of money and answers.

Mythis, the general to her left, was rubbing the back of his neck.

He mumbled, "I owe you." She liked him; she liked all of them, even though they'd tried stabbing her yesterday. Well, only Kas and Midgy had tried pulling a fast one on her. They'd quickly scrambled away when Ellea threw a dagger at Midgy, landing in his scaled thigh, and held another under Kas' chin. Kas wasn't actually ugly like Mythis said. He had a pudgy face, pointed ears, and the eyes of a goat. Midgy, on the other hand, looked like an ancient male whose body was half-shifted into some scaled beast. "Now that's over, can we play cards?" Mythis had said, yanking the dagger out of Midgy's thigh and handing it back to Ellea, who let it disappear with a whisper of her powers. The demons had gawked at her in wonder. By the end of their game, they'd all been laughing and heavily buzzed. Well, they had been while Ellea kept turning her wine to juice. Yesterday had been a day for stabbing, it seemed. And today was one for winning and answers. Mythis was a high-ranked general, and after about two drinks, he would answer any question she asked.

"I was thinking about your question about getting in and out of Hel, the one you asked yesterday," Mythis said, leaning in to whisper.

Ellea cocked a brow at him while she gathered her prize. Before she could ask for more, Duhne barreled through the locked door, splitting wood and stone. She could have sworn lightning crackled behind his eyes as the males jumped around her.

She leaned back in her chair. "Couldn't you have teleported in?" Ellea asked him with a bored tone.

"I could have," he grumbled. "If someone hadn't magicked the room against it."

Ellea smirked at him, and he glared back. It had actually worked. Every morning before Duhne arrived, she had been practicing summoning, creating, and even sword work, using a light sword she had created with her magic. All of that didn't include what Azzy was

140

also teaching her at their designated tea times or before dinner. The barrier spell was new and had been a bit harder to master.

"I have no idea what you're talking about."

"Right," he said, crossing his arms. He gestured toward the door. "Your Highness."

Ellea rolled her eyes. "I'll see you boys tomorrow."

"No, you won't," Duhne said angrily. "Mythis, I would have expected better of you."

Ellea looked back at the general, who was now pale. Kas and Midgy had their heads bowed, shuffling cards and trying to look invisible.

Ellea pursed her lips. "It was only a bit of cards."

He didn't answer, only forced her to walk ahead of him.

"How'd you find me?" She crossed her arms over her chest and didn't bother to hide her pout.

"After we lost you yesterday, I had you followed without you knowing about it. Mythis I don't mind; I don't trust the other two."

"I was fine." She stopped to glare up at him. "I took care of it the first time."

"What do you mean 'took care of it?'" He paled. "If anything happens to you, my uncle will string me up by my balls."

She hid her smile at the vision. "They got mad. I kept winning, and they tried to jump me." Duhne dramatically brought his hand to his chest. "It was fine, I had it handled. I stabbed Midgy in the leg and was *this* close to slicing Kas' neck. They haven't tried anything after that."

"Ellea," he said, pinching the bridge of his nose.

"It was fine, easier than the demon that tried jumping me in the hall."

Duhne looked like he was about to be sick. "I'm going to have to tell my uncle about this."

"I'm sure Daddy Azzy already knows," she said with a wave

of her hand.

"What? You know what, never mind. Let's go. You have a dinner to get ready for, and it's not just going to be *Azzy*," he said with a disgusted shiver.

"What?" It was her turn to look shocked.

"Some of the courts and kings are tired of my uncle keeping you hidden. So, we are having a full banquet tonight. Dancing, debauchery, everything."

Ellea found it hard to swallow. This must be why Azzy had been working with her on so many non-magical skills.

"I need Florence," she said, quickly walking down the hall.

"She is already in your room and would like to know how you snuck past the wards."

"Is she mad too?"

"No, she wants to know how so she can figure it out."

Ellea hid her smile. Of course, she would want to know.

Duhne threw Ellea's doors open and then threw himself on a chaise, grabbing one of the romance novels from the small table next to it.

"Finally," Florence said, rushing out of Ellea's bedroom. "Oh my Gods, you smell like a tavern."

Ellea sniffed her arm and didn't smell anything. "Wait, you have taverns?"

Florence ignored her, pushing her toward the bathroom that had steam billowing out of the shower. "Go shower, we're running out of time."

"Don't you two need to get ready?"

"We happen to be clean and don't smell of wine and kitchen demons"

Ellea stuck her tongue out at the small woman who was quickly becoming a friend and headed into the scalding shower. She thought they were both being dramatic, but quickly washed and stepped into the towel Florence held up for her. She had changed into a billowing ball gown while Ellea was getting washed up. Florence used magic that Ellea was extremely jealous of to quickly dry and style her hair. It would have taken her ages to dry and straighten her hair without it. Her makeup was made up of harsh eyeliner, dramatic blush that made her round cheeks look sharp, and a plum lipstick that was practically black.

The whole process was a rush of delicate hands, grumbling from both women, and then a rude shove to the bedroom where a deep purple gown hung from her dresser. It was as beautiful as it was different; one long sleeve was covered in gold beads and the other stopped at the shoulder. It also had a dramatic slit in the left side of its heavy skirt. But Ellea was more excited by the two gold daggers glimmering on the bed. She rushed for them, passing her doors, causing Duhne to curse and hide his face from her nakedness. Ellea didn't care, but magicked the doors shut with barely a thought as she took in the amazing detail.

Florence sidled up next to her and picked up the other dagger. "I figured you could create a comfortable holster to match."

"These are gorgeous," Ellea whispered, caressing the sharp edge.

They were a simple shape, but the intricate designs swirling in the middle made up for that. It reminded her of Ros' great sword. Buttery black leather wrapped around the hilt.

"I've noticed you've only been carrying steel and obsidian." Florence smiled warmly before reaching to grab the dress off the hanger.

"That's all I can conjure."

Using her powers, she fitted herself with a slim black holster on her left thigh to hold both daggers. It fit neatly along her waist and wouldn't show under the dress—but the daggers would. It seemed fitting for her first dinner with the whole court. Florence had the gown unbuttoned and held it open for her to step into. Ellea was careful as she slid her arm through the embellished sleeve. Surprisingly, it was comfortable and allowed her to move freely. Florence buttoned her in before handing her each dagger.

"Perfect," she said, brushing Ellea's hair over her back.

"No crown tonight?"

"Not from me." She pressed her lips together, almost hiding her smile, and helped Ellea step into a pair of strappy gold heels.

She summoned several gold, amethyst, and obsidian rings and handed them to Ellea. Just as she started to slip them on, there was a knock on the main door. The women entered the sitting room to find Duhne, pale and bent at his hip, bowing to the king. Ellea found herself feeling pity for Duhne until Azzy gave her a wink. Florence bowed next to her.

"Nephew," he said, "can you and Florence please step outside while I have a word with Ellea?"

Duhne audibly swallowed before heading out to the hall, Florence by his side. The doors closed quietly, and Ellea raised her chin to the king.

"Asmodeus," she said, noting his pocket square that matched the purple of her dress. He also wore a grand black and gold crown with emeralds throughout the whole piece. It was a king's crown, an ancient and wild one. The green and gold were bright against his black horns. They swept away from the sides of his head before turning back in sharp points, reminding her of a scorpion's tail. He'd hidden them from her the first few days, so she was still getting used to them. She wondered if Ros would show her his.

"Oh, now, now darling," he said, walking up to her. "Keep the formalities for when we are surrounded by the beasts and monsters."

"Should I be worried?" She searched his face for any hint of what to expect.

"A little," he said before his hands dipped into shadow.

When they reappeared, he held a beautiful crown of black and gold. The base was the body of a snake, and in its center, surrounded by two black birds with emerald eyes, was a hound. The hound's teeth held a beautiful amethyst. He placed it on top of her head, and it fit snugly, not moving and not too heavy. She found she was standing a bit taller than before. Cocking her head a little, she tested its stability, and Azzy chuckled.

"You will still be able to look at people sideways tonight with this crown," he said, grabbing her chin gently and straightening her head.

"Thank you," she said, looking into his hazel eyes. "If it wasn't for this week, I'm not sure I would be ready for tonight."

Even though he was the reason she was here. She shooed away that thought.

"I couldn't hide you away any longer; the vultures are circling. Tonight, you will need to figure out what kind of beast you're going to be."

She searched his face; it had gone cold, something she had only seen glimpses of before.

What kind of beast was she?

Perhaps a blackbird, bringing death and shrouded in mystery. A hound, vigilant and strong, with sharp teeth and claws? Or was she a snake, cunning and seeking answers no matter the cost?

"What if I want to be all of them?" she whispered.

Azzy sucked in a breath and gave her a wicked smile. "Then be all of them, darling."

Ellea was even more thankful for Azzy's lessons the past several days as she sat in the grand dining hall. It was like it had been pulled from a romance novel. For there to be an artist out there who could chisel out the delicate whorls and lines seemed impossible; she had to assume someone had used magic to create all of it. She couldn't help but look up in wonder every so often, if only to save her from Belias and Beelzebub, who were both glaring at her from their end of the room. Azzy had warned her on their walk over that they would be here, and she was glad the tables were separated as they were.

Four long tables sat in a square with room on the ends to enter the dance floor or for servants to move through to fill their drinks and plates. Azzy sat in the center seat at the table furthest from the door with Ellea to his right and Lord Dale to his left. Florence was thankfully on Ellea's other side since Duhne had to sit at his own table with his father, Leviathan.

The dynamics were so interesting. Belias and Sonneillon's tables were full of preening court members. Sonneillon was female, but identified as a king of Hel; she was the mother of Cara and Carver. They kept passing devilish looks to one another and Ellea. She knew she could only avoid them for so long. Her table, and Duhne's, were practically empty. Leviathan only had one demon to his left, and to the right of Duhne was another male demon Ellea hadn't seen yet.

"Do you and your son have something to say?" Azzy bellowed to Beelzebub.

The slight snarl in his voice brought up memories of Ros that made her chest ache. It was almost impossible to think of him in this setting, but not too impossible to imagine him leaning back in a chair and snarling at anyone who thought of looking his way.

"You've been keeping that witch cooped up all week, all to yourself and out of sight," Beelzebub sneered.

The way he said "witch" had her seeing red and thinking of a way to make sure he knew and feared her name. Then his spawn spoke, and she deserved a medal for keeping her cool.

"She hasn't been cooped up at all, actually, and has been wandering the halls unchaperoned."

"Not creepy at all, Bel," Ellea said. "Was that your demon who jumped me the other afternoon? Did his balls grow back? I was so very curious about the regenerative magic with some of your beasts creeping along the castle."

Florence covered her choked laugh with a sip of wine and nudged Ellea under the table with her knee.

"Wandering alone, spending time with soldiers and lowly kitchen demons," Beelzebub added. "Now you're parading her around in your late queen's crown? What's next, are you going to steal her away from your son to have a powerful trickster sit beside you?"

"What if I wanted to share?" Ellea cut in, leaning back in her chair and enjoying the horrified look on Beelzebub's face.

It was a joke, of course—Asmodeus was every bit the father she'd never had, but the look on the asshole's face was worth it.

"I will never tire of your jokes, Ellea," Azzy cut in, patting her hand that was sparking with power. "And as for her crown, it would pass to her no matter the circumstances."

Ellea forced herself not to look at Azzy, hiding her shock the best she could.

"If you're done throwing insults," Azzy said, "I think it's time we danced."

Azzy clapped his hands once and stood, and everyone followed, even Ellea. A show was being put on and she had a part to play. The sneers from Bel and his father couldn't be missed as she reached for the king's outstretched hand and let him guide her to the dance floor.

"Did you enjoy your meal?" Azzy asked as he guided her around the room with a dance they had practiced many times.

"They accused you of trying to seduce me and you're going to ask if I enjoyed the steak?"

"I have been accused of far worse," he said and then spun her slowly. "They are jealous and worried about an exchange of power. They see you in my son's court and know that when you two are joined, our part of Hel will be even more untouchable."

"Asmodeus—" she started, but he cut her off.

"You can tell me a million times that you are not meant to be here. That as soon as you're allowed, you're going to leave," he said kindly. "But I know the truth, and you will see it too."

An answer or a denial didn't surface as she searched his hazel eyes that reminded her so much of Ros.

"I want you to explore the lands tomorrow," he said, cutting into her thoughts.

"Would you like Florence or Duhne to accompany me?"

"I want you to go and explore on your own," he said with a wicked grin. "Cause some trouble, and bring something sharp."

"You're serious?"

Ellea gaped at him. Was he really going to let her explore the lands on her own? She hadn't gotten farther than the gardens before she'd been stopped by Duhne, Florence, or Reaver.

"If you aren't back by the time the torches on the keep are lit, I'll send Duhne to find you."

14

Ellea

Eight Days in Hel

Ellea hadn't been on a horse since her mid-teens. Her grandmother owned two, and they used to go riding around the manor's property after school or tutoring. Sometimes they'd even take long rides along the coast on the weekends. After both horses aged to their thirties, it was time for them to enjoy the sun in the green pastures, and Ellea brought them treats any time she was there. The horse beneath her was the very opposite of her old, fat gelding. This mare, Mhairi, felt more like a small dragon as it snorted around every corner, probably attempting to scare off any beasts that may be lurking.

Duhne had brought her to the royal stables that morning and

introduced her to the stablehand who managed the many stalls and beasts. Some of them looked more demon than horse with varied coats, eyes, and even wings. Ellea had eyed a winged horse closely, but when she grinned up at Duhne, about to open the stall door, he shook his head and brought her to this one instead.

"Easy, girl," Ellea cooed. "You aren't in a battle anymore, you're only taking me for a tour."

The mare tossed her head.

"How about we go for a gallop once I get my sea legs and visit more of Hel?"

Fire-red ears perked up, and she whinnied in response. Ellea chuckled and patted her large neck.

"They keep you well-fed and fit for being retired."

The horse stomped once, like it was insulted by the term "retired."

"I think I've seen you in a vision before," she said, caressing her neck. "You wore gold and black armor and looked magnificent with a very handsome male atop you."

The horse huffed in agreement.

"I will bet you ten apples you were deadly," she said.

The horse raised her head high and bounced it up and down, lips flapping. Ellea gathered up the reins again and directed the mare around the next bend. The horse was actually leading, but they were both too proud to admit who was in charge. She had a feeling that the beast knew where to take her.

After an hour on their higher-up trail, they made their way to flatter ground. There was a sea to her left and a valley to her right. She was close to the divide she had been studying for some time. Breathing in deeply, she relished the fresh air that filled her lungs. The sun warmed her upturned face, and she felt peaceful. The sound of lapping waves reminded her of the water crashing outside the manor. *Waves?* the thought broke through her bliss. She hadn't seen waves on their trek down, only smooth, calm water.

Ellea looked toward the splashing and saw a young woman trying to find a grip on the rock wall, but her dark hands kept slipping. She looked utterly human, mortal, and in her thirties. Ellea kicked Mhairi, urging her toward the beach and to the woman.

The horse traveled up the small cliff that was about ten feet high, and Ellea hopped off when they got close. The mare stayed in place. Ellea threw herself on her stomach, reaching for the woman.

"Here!" Ellea yelled at her.

"Fuck," the woman cursed.

Why wasn't the woman happy to see her?

"Let me help you," she said, reaching further.

A vice-like grip clamped onto her booted foot and she was thrown closer to the woman. Mhairi was helping. The woman reluctantly grabbed onto Ellea's hand, and the horse pulled them back up. Ellea stood before helping the woman.

"Are you okay?"

"Yes," the woman grumbled. "You found me, I'll go back on my own."

She began to stalk off without another word.

"Wait!" Ellea ran a few steps toward her. "I didn't try to find you. Where are you going to go back to?"

The woman looked her up and down and over at the horse that was a step behind, following Ellea wherever she went.

"Aren't you a guard?" she asked.

A giggle escaped from her throat.

"Do I look like I guard the walls of Hel?"

"Maybe," the woman said, crossing her arms. "If you aren't a guard, then who are you?"

Ellea thought quickly. "A visitor." She didn't want to say princess, and honestly, she didn't know what she was while she was here.

The woman eyed her again before she sidestepped and tried to swipe her legs. Ellea was quicker and dodged it.

"What the fuck?" Ellea called after the retreating woman.

Putting her hands on her hips, she saw the woman run up the valley. She realized they were at the divide.

Oh.

Ellea was brushing grass and sand off of her clothes when a large head bumped into her back.

"We'll catch up, let's give her time," she said, patting her warm neck. The horse stooped down on one knee, helping her climb into the saddle since.

"Thanks, girl. Now let's go; I have questions."

Ellea and Mhairi trotted up next to the breathless woman, who was moving pretty fast for a mortal. Well, a dead one.

"You're a human," Ellea called down to her.

"Clearly." She was huffing as she continued to run.

"And you're going…?"

"To my husband and son." Admitting that made her move a bit faster.

"They aren't with you?"

"Clearly, or I wouldn't be running away."

The woman stopped and placed her hands above her head.

"If you aren't going to stop me, can you just leave me alone? You and your horse are going to bring attention, and this is the closest I've gotten."

"Where are they?"

The woman glared up at her. "They are wolven and with the other supernaturals."

"But…" Ellea paused.

The woman arched a brow at her. "You don't know?"

"Oh, I know, but I thought they would at least keep families together." She understood there was a divide, but she'd thought it only meant that they couldn't leave where they rested. "Did you die at different times?"

Maybe that was it; maybe whoever separated beings had made a mistake.

"Maybe I can talk to someone and fix this," Ellea added.

"Oh, sweet child," the woman said, and Ellea glared at her for the insult. They looked like they were almost the same age. "We died in a car accident at the same time. My son is considered a beast by this place even when he carries half of me. All you can do is leave me be so I may try and find them."

Ellea pressed her lips together, frustrated with herself and how things worked. A mother separated from her son only because his father was a wolven. Did he even carry the ability to shift? She shook her head and reached down her arm. The woman eyed it curiously.

"Take it," Ellea said, reaching for her. "Let me help you."

Mhairi carried them easily and Jocelyn, the woman clinging to her waist, was still getting used to the ride.

"Why are you helping me?" she asked.

"Why wouldn't I?"

"You'd be surprised how little help we get."

"I don't know, I've only read about this place," Ellea admitted. "Please tell me how it is. Are you miserable? Do they torture you for all your wrongs?"

"No, it's not all bad," she grumbled behind her. "I miss them. But every day is pretty easy. It's like living but...not? There is no time or worry, only peace. At first, I didn't realize anything was wrong. Then I started getting my memories back and I realized what was missing all along. I've tried a number of times over the years to escape and find them, but I'm always caught."

"I'm sorry," she said, storing that information for later. "Does anyone else try and escape?"

There had to be more; the world was full of mortals and supernaturals, Jocelyn couldn't be the only one.

"There are others, but they finally gave up," she said sadly. "From what I can tell, I'm the only one who tries to escape."

"That can't be true," Ellea said. "You two aren't the only interspecies couple to pass away."

"Maybe I'm the only one who remembers."

Ellea didn't think that was it either. She would have words with Azzy when she got back tonight, but first, she was going to get Jocelyn to her family. She smiled to herself, feeling like she was actually doing something besides training, reading, and eating. The sound of hooves stampeding behind them shook Ellea from her triumphant thoughts. Both women turned their heads to see two guards galloping after them.

"Fuck," they said together.

Ellea kicked Mhairi but she was already moving into a gallop, ready to outrun the chase.

They weaved and bobbed around rocks and trees, but the two trailing them were slowly gaining ground.

"Come on, old lady," Ellea whispered to the mare. "Show them what retirement really is."

Mhairi pinned her ears back and found another gear. Ellea worried it wouldn't be enough, and then an idea hit her.

"Princess!" one of the guards called. "Please, you'll get hurt."

"Princess?" Jocelyn hissed behind her. "You're one of them?"

"I'm not," Ellea huffed out. "I'm a witch, it's only a nickname. But I have an idea. Grab the reins."

She reluctantly grabbed them and leaned around Ellea to give her room. Pulling at her magic, Ellea summoned a rope with two balls on either end. It felt heavy in her hands. Leaning off of the mare, she turned around the best she could and whirled one end in a rapid circle before letting it fly behind her.

It was enough to spook one of the horses, and the guard slipped unceremoniously off, stopping the second horse in its tracks. Jocelyn whooped loudly and handed the reins back to Ellea. They galloped further up before Ellea pulled back and stopped the mare. She hopped off and helped Jocelyn slide into the saddle.

"What are you doing?" she hissed down at her. "They'll get us!"

"They'll get me," she said. "Now hold on and get to your family. Be safe, and when you are, send Mhairi back. I think she knows what to do."

Ellea didn't give her time to protest. She gave Mhairi a loving pat and then a loud smack on her rear.

Give them Hel, old girl.

"You lost a prized war horse, took down two guards, stole both their horses, and freed a woman from the mortal lands," Duhne said, pacing back and forth in his uncle's study. He kept glaring at her with every pass.

"All before dinner," Ellea said, leaning back in the leather chair across from Azzy's massive desk.

"My uncle is going to murder me," he said, sitting down next to her.

He quickly stood when the king strode through the door.

Ellea slowly stood, eyeing his demeanor. The situation she'd found herself in suddenly seemed much less fun. When Duhne swiftly bowed, the king gave her a wink, and she bowed in answer.

"Someone has been quite busy today," Azzy said, sitting behind his desk as if it were a throne.

"Uncle, my king…" Duhne began to sweat. "The guards are resting after seeing the healer. Ellea managed to not do extensive damage and their horses are safe, but…"

He swallowed hard. His mouth opened a few times like a fish fighting for air—or water—before his uncle rolled his eyes and cut in.

"Mhairi and the woman are still missing," Azzy said sternly.

"So it worked?" Ellea said, leaning forward with a grin spreading across her face. She looked back and forth from Duhne's abashed face and Azzy's blank one.

"They could be injured—or worse," Duhne scolded.

"How could someone who is already dead be in worse condition?" Ellea asked, but they both ignored her.

"Those lands have been quiet," Azzy said, worrying his lip. "They could be laying low."

"Why'd I put you on the devil of a horse?" Duhne grumbled. "I should have listened to my gut."

Ellea couldn't help but laugh. She caught a twinkle in Azzy's eye.

"So, what's for dinner?" Ellea asked, leaning back in her chair.

"You shouldn't have dinner!" Duhne said roughly. "You should spend a night in the dungeon for all the gray hair you're causing me. How am I supposed to seduce anyone when you're causing me stress wrinkles? Where is Rosier? Did you cause this much trouble topside?"

Duhne was standing over her and breathing heavily. Ellea smirked at him but didn't get the chance to speak before the king cut in.

"Nephew," Azzy said calmly, "I'm sure Ellea feels awful for all the trouble she has caused you of late. And as for my son—"

"Find a new babysitter!" Duhne stormed toward the door. He quickly bowed before swinging the door open and stalking out.

When Ellea looked back at Azzy, he had a warm smile spread across his face.

"Let's have dinner in the gardens tonight," he said, standing and walking toward her. He held his elbow out and she stood, looping her arm with his. "We can watch Mhairi come back, and you can give her all the treats I'm sure you bribed her with."

15

Ellea

Nine Days in Hel

The next day, Ellea trained with Azzy. He acted as though she hadn't sent two guards to a healer. Sitting on the floor with him, he guided her through shifting her appearance. His voice was kind, and he was patient as ever. She wondered if he'd known what would happen when he told her to go exploring. Mhairi had come back, like Azzy said she would; she'd pranced up to them in the garden, barely tired and hounding her for treats. She couldn't wait to see the beast again and see what else they could get into.

"Focus," Azzy reminded her.

She breathed out and went back to imagining her bones and muscles changing. Her skin formed into something new. It was wild to watch her hand go from pale, freckled skin to the same scales and claws as Kas had.

"Good. Now shift into another form. Don't go back to yours."

Sweat began to bead along her forehead as she concentrated and reminded herself to breathe and let her power move through her. There was a faint shimmer of age spots and wrinkled skin before her smoother skin reformed.

"Shit."

It was so much harder than the other things she had been doing with her magic, even creating objects and breaking wards. Shifting herself was such a challenge.

"You're getting it, don't get frustrated." Azzy stood and held out a hand for her to grasp. "Soon you will be able to turn yourself into any manner of creature."

"I never knew shifting was an ability witches had."

Elemental control, changing objects, and some illusions could be done in any bloodline. Shifting was only heard of in wolven and other beasts.

"That's because you're not a regular witch, like I keep reminding you."

"Yes, but you haven't told me what that means."

She'd questioned him on where tricksters came from, where she came from, but he kept pushing it off.

"I'm saving that lesson for once you've mastered the history and politics of this realm. I need you to focus on that, then we can speak of...other things."

He cocked his head, and his hazel eyes bore into hers. With a nod of his chin, she realized he was trying to tell her something. Something that couldn't be said out loud.

What was it?

Could her lineage not be spoken out loud?

"Speaking of this realm," she said, pushing that scary thought aside, "what's it like for the souls? Their day to day life."

"Why don't you go visit them and see?"

Ellea's eyes widened. "Visit them? But we can't disturb those that are at peace."

That was what he had told her during their first dinner. Even though rescuing Jocelyn yesterday would definitely be considered disturbing the peace. But she wasn't truly at peace without those she loved. Ellea pressed her lips together.

Fuck.

Had she done something wrong?

Was Jocelyn suffering now?

"You can visit them; sometimes people of the court, the guards, or others will go there. They visit the taverns or shops the souls have built in their time here."

"But they are from this realm. What if I run into someone I may have known when they were alive? Isn't that going against the rules? You said so about Esmeray." A pained look flashed across Azzy's face. "I'm sorry, I didn't mean to—"

"You can ask about her. I'm glad you do." He cleared his throat before raising his chin. Ellea could see the pain and love battling across his handsome features. "No one talks about her and it's time more did. But you can visit the souls without disturbing them."

He guided her to their usual table by a window with a magnificent view of the valleys and mountains. It was cloudy today, and Ellea reminded herself to ask about the weather after they got through this conversation.

"If you happen to see someone you knew, they won't recognize you. They will see you as a living member of this realm, as they see me, the guards, or anyone else. They know they are dead, where they are, and that they have lived a happy life." He paused, searching her face, which was painfully scrunched. "Are you following so far?"

She was but she wasn't. It sounded so simple but so complicated. Still, she nodded, and he continued.

"Their state of peace will not change until they are connected with someone in the afterlife who had touched them on such a deep level that death could not keep them apart. Then they will join in the afterlife as they did before."

"So if I were to see my grandfather, who I never knew since he died before I was born..." She chewed on her lip for a moment, thinking. "He would not recognize me now or after I die?"

He shook his head. "That depends. If your grandmother passed away"—he knocked three times on the wooden table, and Ellea did the same—"and reconnected with him, then you passed away and reconnected with her, he would know. Your grandmother would not rest peacefully if she did not have you in the afterlife."

It seemed like this was where the dead lived a new life. Now she was very eager to go see how they spent their days. She realized something. "So you visiting Esmeray won't disturb her peace, but yours? It would cause you too much pain."

He gave her a sad smile. "Why do you think the living are not allowed here?" Ellea frowned and shrugged. "Because they would see how peaceful their loved ones were and would want to join them."

"And there would be mass suicides everywhere." It would be chaos.

"The dead do not dwell on the living. It is up to those who still have time to remember those who have found peace. It is up to them to spend the years they have left to make the world a better place."

"And those who don't deserve peace?"

Azzy leaned back in his chair.

"That is for Beelzebub and his court to deal with."

164

Once again, her head hurt. She placed her face in her hands as more questions formed. Azzy never acted annoyed by her questions, but he had to have a limit. "What about the demons that go to my realm, why don't they show them?"

"Only those in the royal family, or close to it, can bring the living here. Like my son's hound, Garm."

Ellea turned away from him. The mention of Ros made her question everything. Where was he? Had he just left her here? Azzy reached for her hand, and she recoiled, leaning back in her chair. She didn't want his pity, so she pulled from the many questions in her mind.

"How do the souls arrive?"

He paused as they looked at each other. "It's like a light falling from the sky."

"You would think I would see something like that."

She couldn't remember ever seeing anything falling from the sky, but before her gallop across the land, the only time she'd looked outside was through windows.

"It's faint, and you wouldn't know what to look for. Only when we have multiple souls coming at one time is it easier to see."

Multiple souls? The question must have been clear on her face.

"If there was a mass exodus, like during a war, there would be so many souls coming to Hel that the sky would blaze with light. When that happens, we investigate to make sure it wasn't something supernatural or unplanned."

She needed coffee if they were going to continue. As though the demon could read her mind, Reaver appeared.

"You're becoming my favorite person," Ellea said sweetly as he placed a coffee in front of her and a tea in front of the king. He didn't say anything, but Ellea could have sworn a small smile spread across his face as he backed out of the room.

"Now that I have sustenance..." She sipped the delicious drink. "The supernatural war was supernatural, though."

"I mean a supernatural being using their abilities to cause a disaster. Wars are inevitable; a thousand souls being sacrificed because a God got angry is usually unplanned."

Ellea blinked a few times. "But the Gods are sleeping."

"Kind of. There hasn't been any mass casualties caused by the Gods since way before your time and early on in mine. There were two, actually, and they're why the Gods retired and the kings fully took over."

Azzy probably would have continued if a flushed Florence hadn't barreled into his study. She bowed quickly as they both stared at her.

"My king, Ellea"—she took a deep breath—"the other kings are demanding a meeting with you, and they want Ellea. It's about the soul. Duhne tried to hold it off, but—"

"It's okay, Florence," Azzy said. "Drinks to go, darling."

Ellea rolled her head and glanced to the ceiling.

Fine.

It was only a matter of time.

"Florence, if you could intercept Beelzebub, we can handle the rest."

She bowed once to him and then mouthed *I'm sorry* to Ellea before leaving the room.

"Are we both in trouble?" Ellea asked as they headed to the hall, coffee and tea in hand.

"We are far too powerful to ever be in trouble." His eyes glinted, and she couldn't help but laugh.

"If only I could have used that when I was younger."

The confidence Ellea had gathered on their walk to the meeting chambers was quickly turning into a temper tantrum. The room was full of the kings and their advisors. This made Ellea, Sonneillon, and Cara the only women in a room of twenty or so males. The other two ladies were no help, and Ellea felt like she was fighting this all on her own, even with Azzy's comforting presence. She refused to look back at him as another lord continued his rant about how one soul had led to several asking to be moved, how unrest was sprouting across the territory, and how something needed to be done. She needed to fight this on her own, even if one word from Azzy would quiet the group.

"So what if more souls want to be moved so they can live in peace with those they love?" Ellea's voice rang over the lord, and he turned toward her with a bored look.

"Child..." He shook his head. "You do not yet understand the ways of this realm, how it has been and always will be. Each soul brings power to the territory it finds peace in. To move them after they arrive goes against the laws of magic, of tradition."

Don't blow up the entire room. Don't turn this into a bloodbath.

She took a steadying breath and told her powers to chill. This was what she and Azzy had been working on.

"The living no longer separate themselves, they shouldn't be separate here."

The lord waved his hand. "They're fine."

"Clearly, they aren't!" She swallowed and shifted her shoulders. With a much calmer voice, she continued, "Jocelyn was unhappy, and from the sound of it, you have a lot of unhappy souls to deal with."

"Who's Jocelyn?" asked a reedy-looking demon in a black suit.

A few lords shrugged their shoulders.

"The soul I *rescued*." She said it through gritted teeth.

"Regardless, child—"

Ellea's powers crackled visibly across her skin. "Call me child. One. More. Time."

Azzy cleared his throat from behind her, and she refocused, but relished the scared look now on the lord's face. She didn't need him to be scared, she needed him to understand that this old way of doing things would not work.

"Regardless, this will not happen again, and we need a plan to calm the current unrest."

"How about you solve the unrest by moving the souls where they want to be?"

The lord shook his head and looked away from her.

"Are you upset because it's tradition or because you lose power if a territory gets more souls than you?"

That got his attention back.

"And what's the big deal? We are talking about two territories."

"How would it even be managed?"

So they wouldn't say why it was such a big deal.

"How is it managed now?"

"See, you know nothing and you are going around trying to change something that has been in place before you were even thought of."

Don't kill him.

Kill them all and let's start fresh.

She inwardly glared at her powers. It felt like a different being pacing in the darkest part of her mind, desperate to be unleashed on the demons around her.

The lord began speaking as Ellea leashed her powers. "The Gods' magic is what chooses where souls go. They came from a world where each species had their own realm and that is how it is here."

Murmurs of agreement rang around the room, but only from the lords; all three kings looked solemn. Thankfully, Beelzebub and

Belias were still being subdued by Florence.

"Magic can be altered."

"Says the child witch." He wheezed a laugh, and Ellea thought of a new stabbing maneuver Florence had taught her two nights ago. With the right angle, you could thrust up and stab someone through a couple organs and then sever their spine. "Only the Gods can choose. Only the Gods can change things."

"Wake them up! Things are different now."

Finally, a king stepped in, and Ellea resisted the urge to sag with relief. That feeling quickly died as Levithan spoke. "That's enough. We have heard both sides, and there will be no change. If a soul becomes restless, we will simply start over with them. Everything will be fine."

Fine? Fine!

Duhne looked at her from behind his father, and fear shone in his green eyes. Ellea felt it, tasted it, as a wicked smirk danced across her lips. "Fine."

"El—" Duhne started to say, but stopped as her magic pulsed around her.

Everyone stepped away from her as though they could read the wicked thoughts dancing through her mind. An idea formed as she turned on her heel and left the lords and kings behind.

It took her ten minutes to calm her magic and to be able to utter the name, "Reaver."

The demon stepped out of a wall and matched her storming gait.

"I need you to go ahead to the stables and have Mhairi readied for me, please."

"Princess." She shot him a look, and he visibly swallowed before shimmering into shadows.

Ellea's face was hot from her anger and the whipping wind. Mhairi had matched her energy and gotten her to the mortal territory at a deadly speed. Her adrenaline was pumping with so much rage and power, but she didn't have time to be scared. She didn't even have the energy to marvel at the beautiful surroundings. Worn cobblestones paved the streets, and the surrounding buildings had been built into the cliff that met a magnificent ocean. She breathed in the salty air before ripping open the wooden door of what looked like a tavern.

The mortal souls scattered around the small bar all stopped what they were doing, and the silence was deafening. A woman paused in the middle of cleaning a tanker, and everyone sitting at the dozen tables stared at her.

Ellea tried to look less scary, less frazzled by her encounter with asshole men set in their old, stupid ways as she shouted, "So, who needs saving?"

✦˙TRICKY PRINCESS˙✦

16

Ellea

Eleven Days in Hel

Two days later, Ellea was enjoying a coffee at a quaint little bakery in the supernatural souls' territory. The owner, Farren, was a witch who had passed away over a century ago. She was an adorable, young thing who had perfected her coffee making over the years. She prided herself in learning from everyone, the oldest of souls and the ones who came in after her, and Ellea was determined to try every manner of drink she had to offer. She sipped her usual latte while Duhne sat next to her, reading one of her shifter romance books. He looked cute as his eyes quickly ran across the pages, and she knew he would soon be asking her for another book.

Ellea was thankful she had gotten used to demons popping in and out of shadows; otherwise, she would have spilled her delicious drink and all its sugary, creamy glory when Cara's head popped out of a black hole. Her freckled face framed with fiery red hair was bright against the darkness, and Ellea wondered if she was headless in a study somewhere. The thought made her snort, and the demon rolled her eyes.

"You're going to owe me a favor," she whispered after glaring at Duhne, who didn't even bother looking at his cousin.

Ellea cocked an eyebrow and sipped her drink. She wouldn't owe the demon anything. They weren't exactly friends, but when Ellea had stormed out of the meeting with the kings and lords, Cara had wanted to help. The heir to the supernatural territory wouldn't tell her why, but over the past three days, she had joined in on transporting souls in the cover of night and shadows.

"Guards are on their way right now to try and catch you."

"Catch me drinking coffee?"

Cara's lips thinned. "Catch you doing you-know-what."

Ellea paused long enough to make Cara shift uncomfortably, and Duhne peeked over his book to stare. "So you will, in fact, owe me a favor when I don't tell your guards that you have been helping me do you-know-what."

Duhne knew what they were talking about since he was also in on it. He had finally given up on trying to get Ellea to follow the rules.

If you can't stop them, join them.

"I swear you're part demon sometimes."

A slow smile crossed her face. "Thanks for the compliment. I'll see you tonight." Ellea could see herself liking the demon; she was so different when her brother wasn't shadowing her every move.

Cara nodded her head and disappeared right before two of her guards barreled into the small shop. Farren greeted them as though they didn't look like hostile beasts looking for a fight.

"Good morning, gentlemen, what can I get started for you?" the witch asked sweetly. One of the guards blushed and opened his mouth to speak before his companion hit him on his armored chest, silencing him.

They both zeroed in on Ellea. She smiled at them and waited for the accusations and the threats to drag her back to the castle.

"May I suggest hot chocolate?" Duhne said, not bothering to look away from his book.

"Cut the crap," the meaner-looking guard said.

Ellea gave him a deadpan look. "What crap? I'm here to enjoy coffee and delicious muffins."

"Muffins?" The other guard looked toward Farren, who waved her hand to direct them toward the muffins coated in crunchy sugar. They were delicious.

The other guard growled and stepped toward them, but Ellea magicked a stool right in front of his feet, causing him to trip. He growled as he righted himself and pointed a menacing finger toward her. "We know you're still smuggling souls to the other territories."

"Do you, now? Do you have any proof?"

They wouldn't; Ellea had talked to those in the mortal territory first, and word quickly spread to not bring attention to yourself. If you wanted out, they had specific meeting times that were on an ever-changing rotation. It would take time, but until Ellea couldn't find a better way to make things work, sneaking around at night would have to do. It had only been two nights, but they had been able to move eight mortals and four supernaturals. It wasn't easy to figure out who should go where, but they were figuring it out as they went. If only they could combine the lands or not have some scary territory between them.

It was also cutting into her spying and training time. She and Florence had rotated these past nights, keeping an eye on Belias and his ilk. Cara and Duhne were helpful; they would rotate between using a portal to move souls from one location to the other. Just this morning, they had found older souls who had agreed to help the newcomers find their families or those they were looking for.

Both guards stared at her, and Ellea smiled. No, they could do nothing, not until they caught her in the act. Two men came in behind the guards, and they didn't acknowledge the uncomfortable silence that seeped throughout the small shop. Farren cleared her throat and took their orders. Her delicate cough broke the nicer of the two out of the stare-down, and he dragged his partner out of the shop before he could say anything else.

Duhne let out a heavy sigh. "It's only been two days and they are getting restless."

Ellea hummed in agreement, but an idea was beginning to form. "Do you think we could convert some of the guards?"

He took a steadying breath, one she was beginning to identify as an "Ellea has a crazy idea and I'm going to have a heart attack" kind of breath. "It will be hard; most of the guards are funded by the lords more than the kings."

"But the kings are, well, the rulers of this land."

His nose crinkled. "Yes, but they have a direct line to the lords. They are there to protect and to prepare for war, but their day-to-day life is mostly spent in the lords' lands."

Ellea thought for a moment. The way the one guard had looked at the shopkeeper had her wondering if any others were friendly with the souls and wanted to see them happy just as much as she did. Did any of them want to do something more than simply serve those who fed them? She tucked the idea away. They had an old wolven to meet with before her afternoon training with Azzy.

"I don't think Ellea's learned much since she's been here," Florence said to Azzy, who watched their training. She parried Ellea's attack, and the reverberation of the block vibrated to her tired hands. Florence easily redirected her weapon, pointing it at Ellea's chest.

"I've learned plenty," Ellea said through gritted teeth, taking a step back and readying her sword. Each lunge with her legs or swipe with her sword ached. Her whole body ached. She wasn't getting enough sleep, but she had been learning, and she felt stronger. Right now, she felt taken off guard; never had she trained with both of them. It was either fighting with Florence or magic with Azzy.

"Why aren't you using magic?" Azzy demanded as he circled them again.

Why wasn't she using her magic?

The thought made her pause long enough for Florence to swipe her feet from under her. She landed with a pained thud on the floor; the demon's sword was again pointing at her chest.

"You're never this bad in training."

She wasn't. Even after a long night of spying, she would be ready in the morning to take her on. They fought, using daggers, swords, or even their bodies. Where Florence was light and graceful, Ellea was strong and fierce.

"I'm tired," she said from the floor.

"Liar. You're holding back." The demon didn't even bother helping her up, only looked to Azzy and added, "She isn't strong enough."

"Strong enough for what?"

Both of them ignored her as she stood.

"Why are you here, Ellea?" Azzy asked as if he wasn't the one to drag her here in the first place. "What are you doing?"

"Filling your time until your sweet little prince gets here to save you from the evil demons," Florence said in a voice Ellea hadn't heard before.

Her power crackled under her skin. "No."

"Filling the souls' heads with promises, getting them thinking you're actually going to do something. But when your prince comes home, will you leave them?"

Azzy stepped closer. He didn't even react to Florence's harsh words. "Why are you here, Ellea? What are you doing?"

The faces of those she'd smuggled to different territories flashed through her mind. The happy and free looks on their faces. Their smiles. Their relief at knowing that they were one step closer to peace, to being reunited with those they loved. They weren't scared, they didn't hesitate; they stepped into a new place, ready to take on the next step of their afterlife.

Her heart raced as her power became alive. Electric currents ran across her skin, through her soul, and down the sword she still held. She swung a vicious slash at the demon's right side, and when she blocked it, Ellea let her power flow through her sword and up Florence's arm. The pained look on her face was so rewarding.

Azzy asked again, "What are you doing here?"

"I want to be here." She did. She couldn't think of anywhere else she wanted to be; the only thing missing was Ros and their friends.

"You don't belong here," Florence goaded, and Ellea kicked her square in the chest.

"I belong here!" Ellea slashed a mighty blow, and Florence barely dodged it. It left her open, and Ellea punched her in the jaw. "I have done nothing my whole life." She pivoted, sweeping Florence off her feet. "I have done nothing good or right, but this—what I'm doing—it's a start."

Florence smiled up at her, but when her eyes glanced over her shoulder, Ellea moved, swiping her blade and blocking an attack from the king. The power from his attack was deadly in a way she had never felt before, and it awoke something in her powers.

Finally, something we can fight, her magic hissed. Ellea's eyes widened, but she didn't balk, didn't shy away; she unleashed herself. Azzy's answering smile was wild.

"Are you strong enough to go against me? Against all of Hel?"

She didn't answer as he blocked her attack, but she was ready, slashing at him with a clawed hand.

No longer did her body ache; no longer did she feel weak or tired. She felt alive, and her magic danced through her body to the tip of the sword. She threw every move at him, and when her sword would fail, she would pelt him with furniture, books, anything in her reach. Her powers became a second entity, doing their own work as she used the sword. Asmodeus was strong and graceful for a man his size. Not once did he lose his smile; he seemed giddy to have a fair opponent... until she turned his sword into a snake. He shrieked, throwing the poor thing against the wall and rubbing his hands aggressively against his sweat-soaked shirt.

"I will be strong enough," she said, resting her sword on her shoulder. "We'll make sure of it."

If only Ros could be here to see this, see her. Would he want her to be here, in his home? She shook the thought and focused on what was next.

17

Rosier

Twelve Days without Ellea

R os didn't bother taking in his home. It was exactly as he
remembered; the only thing that was different was the group
of Beelzebub's guards trying to cut him down as he moved
through the castle. He'd known there would be a fight, but he had
thought it would be them trying to take him in. These guards were
out for blood, and he would have questions once they got to Ellea and
his father.

"Where would she be?" Sam asked, slicing through armor with his
half-shifted claws.

The five of them moved in perfect unison. Where Ros would blind
with his shadows, Billy would be there with claws and teeth, ripping

at muscle and bone. On and on it went until they made it up another floor. Kill, move, and kill again. There wouldn't be a demon left if he let his magic free.

"We need to get to my—" Ros couldn't answer as the hair lifted on the back of his neck. He turned quickly and released a dagger. It landed directly in the forehead of a guard who was ready to cut down Garm. "—my father. She would be near him, maybe with him?"

"You haven't been here in forever," Billy said, choking a guard.

It didn't matter how long he'd been away; he knew this castle, had run through its halls as a child, fighting with wooden swords with his cousin Duhne.

Duhne!

Where was the bastard? Maybe this place hadn't ruined him and he could help. Maybe he had been protecting Ellea. He shook his head and thrust his sword behind him, cutting a guard who was trying to sneak around the corner. All he knew was that getting to his father was the answer. His heart thudded with each step, each parry; he was here and he would get to Ellea. He would kill everyone in the process if it meant reaching her.

As Ros rounded the corner of the next floor, an axe was hurled down the wide hallway. His shadows swallowed up the glint of steel, and as it disappeared, he opened another portal. The weapon careened through it and embedded itself in the back of its owner. Blood sprayed, and they moved, climbed, and killed.

Ros and his friends blocked an onslaught of attacks. He tried to ignore the memories. That portrait of beasts and flowers had been picked out by his mother. She'd demanded it be hung in these exact halls. No one could tell her no. A vase, now covered in blood, had been broken over a dozen times from him and his cousins running through the halls. He shoved the memories down, down, down. He had to focus.

The guards continued to be reckless, throwing move after move that left them open to be cut down easily. One managed to get a little too close for comfort, almost slitting Garm's throat, but Billy was there. Her feral snarl had the guard shaking when he went to defend himself. She caught his arm as he lunged with a dagger. She whispered something so vile in his ear that he wet himself before she tore through his bicep with her claws, severing an artery and letting him bleed out on the floor. They made it to another level, and Sam screamed.

"Devon!"

A guard who looked as though he'd crawled out of the pits of Hel was about to gut Devon with claws that would make even Billy jealous. But Sam's large wolven body forced Devon away, pushing him across the floor. He hit the wall with a loud crack. Sam was fast to snap at the guard, but the demon was relentless and slashed with his vicious claws.

"Sam, no!" Ros was too late. His friend snapped at the demon's throat, but before he made his mark, before he could kill it, the creature dug his claws into his face.

With Sam's first whimper of pain, Devon broke. Blue and white flames raged around them, burning their attackers alive. Devon didn't even acknowledge the power he had let loose, only ran to Sam, cradling his big head in his lap. Sam panted, swiping at his face as something electric green seeped into his skin.

Though there were no guards left after Devon's outburst and they had a moment of peace, Billy and Ros readied their stances as Garm rushed to Devon.

"We need to stabilize him," Garm said, holding Sam's paws down to stop his relentless rubbing of his face. "Water, Devon, summon water and then a mora spell to stop the poison from spreading."

Devon shook his head as though to clear it.

"Dev, you got this." Ros left Billy's side to stand by him. "Deep breaths."

He held Devon's wrists, steadying him as he formed water. He let go to help rub away the blood and leftover poison.

"I'm sorry," Ros said to Sam as he panted and winced from his touch.

Once clean, Devon began mumbling the words to halt the poison. His hand glowed, and slowly, Sam's chest stopped heaving and he no longer flinched in pain.

"We've got to move." Ros wrapped him in a tendril of shadows, steadying the wolven on all four feet. "I've got you."

Sam blinked slowly and huffed a breath. They moved.

"How many more floors?" Devon yelled after embedding two obsidian daggers into a guard that was more beast than man. They had traveled twelve floors and had one to go; he mouthed the number to Devon, even though the guards probably knew his goal. He let himself feel guilty for a moment as he slashed through his attacker's knees with his stolen sword. He didn't feel bad for the guards; he felt bad for those who would have to clean up this bloody mess.

Ros flicked his wrist, expelling some tensions and reminding his magic to wait. He still had enough energy to keep his powers at bay—for now.

"We only want Ellea," he tried telling a guard who ran to him with his sword stretched over head. "Really? Who is training you idiots?"

He easily blocked the move and then spun, kicking him square in the chest and forcing him back several feet.

"Give us Ellea and we will end this!" he yelled for anyone to hear.

Why were they so vicious? Why were the guards so helbent on trying to hurt them? No one wanted to talk, no one answered their questions; they just kept coming. He glanced back at Sam, making sure he was still moving, still alive, and caught a guard glaring after them.

"You won't get to the witch bitch," he said to Ros, spitting up blood as he slid down the wall. "You and your father are so power-hungry, but I hear she likes to share—"

Devon stabbed him through the chin, cutting off his insult. Standing, he looked at Ros. He almost flinched at the deadly look on Devon's face. He hoped that this was only a façade, a mask he wore to get through this, to get to Ellea and be strong for Sam. Ros knew that the hags and this was the first time he had killed. He would kick himself for this later, but they were so close. This would be fixed, all of it would be. So they moved up to the last floor.

The light flutter in his chest was hopeful as the soldiers began to thin, most running now as they neared his father's wing. None of his father's men had shown up, and he began to wonder if this was all Belias or Beelzebub's doing.

"Rosier?" a general called as they went around the corner. It was Mythis, a general he had trained himself. A group of his father's soldiers stood behind him. He was clad in black and gold armor, the same armor that Ros had worn. He drew the sword that Ros had gifted him when he was promoted to general and pointed it at him. "Don't do this."

Ros readied his own weapon. "I've only been defending myself. Where is he, Mythis?"

"You cannot go to your father this enraged; let's put down our weapons and talk like civilized beasts."

Why weren't they standing down? Where was Ellea? If she was

hurt... "It's too late for civil," he said, throwing his shadows at a lunging soldier. "You took what is mine, and I want her back."

⁎ TRICKY PRINCESS ⁎

18

Ellea

Twelve Days in Hel

E llea turned another page of her book before shaking her hand. Her magic had been erratic the past two days and had begun changing or manifesting on its own. She'd had to ask Azzy what could be done. She felt as though she was overflowing with power. It wasn't like before when it had felt as though it would explode; now it was as though it was seeping from her pores. She needed to expel it somehow.

Fine, she could do that. Electric air hummed around her as she slowly let go of the book, making it float in front of her. Now that her hands were free, she could work on forming and deforming her favorite dagger while she continued to read. There, energy expelled.

Her powers seemed to sigh now that they could do something. She almost didn't notice a few women who scurried past her with their tails between their legs. Scrunching her brows, she shrugged and went back to what she was doing.

"'Man the dead,'" she scoffed at the words she was reading. "More like separate and ignore."

Another soldier barreled past her, causing her to whirl around, her skirts billowing around her.

"Hey!" Ellea called after him. "Watch it, ass-hat!"

A beautiful woman kicked him backwards. Her thick black hair swayed gracefully as she whipped around him, grasping him around the neck and choking him until he slumped to the floor. The woman ran off, not looking back.

"What the fuck?"

Ellea ran toward the hall, now noticing thuds and armor clanging. She reached the unconscious guard and peeked around the corner. A demon barreled toward her, running from the fight with shadows clinging to its eyes and mouth. A wolven followed, shadows wrapped around his body as he bit at the demon's heels.

Wolven?

Shadows?

Peeking around again, she saw a glimpse of fangs and fire as another demon slammed into the wall, forcing her to move her head back.

Rosier.

He was here and he was mad with fury. His eyes glowed red, and faint lines of fire and shadow she had never seen before ran under his skin. A demon slid toward Ros, trying to thrust a dagger upward, but Ros grabbed his wrist, twisting and roaring in his face. The dagger fell into Ros' waiting hand. Breaking his hold, Ros forced him down and pivoted left, bringing the demon with him.

Ros was using him as a shield, and Ellea found herself eager to learn that move as he blocked an attack with the demon's body and threw a dagger at another. Ros pulled roughly, and a snap rang through the hall as he dislocated the demon's shoulder. He kicked him toward someone she recognized, Mythis. Ros pulled back, a new dagger glinting in his hand, poised to strike.

"No!" Ellea yelled. "Not him, he owes me money."

Ros' ethereal eyes slowly turned toward her. He looked deadly and oh so hot. He let out a long breath, seeming to let go of the darkness that was driving him. Hazel replaced red, and he dropped the dagger.

"Ellea?"

"Thank fuck," Mythis groaned, laying back down.

Ros' long legs ate up the distance to where Ellea stood. Shock burned in her chest. The sight of him was damning. He was so beautiful—even covered in blood.

"Took you long enough," she said breathlessly as he wrapped his strong arm around her back and tangled his other hand at the base of her neck. He tugged on her hair, and a whimper escaped her mouth. She forced her eyes open; they wanted to close and stop the tears that were threatening to fall. The cool caress of his shadows ran across her neck and up her cheek before they toyed with her loose hair and the fabric of her dress. She found strength to move, reaching to rub her palm across his beard and his blood-splattered face. A shiver wracked through her, one of need and want. Would she ever not need him?

"Ellea," he said for the second time, his voice hoarse.

Words tried to escape his perfect lips, but she quieted them with her own. Pressing her lips to his roughly, she forced his mouth to open for her so she could taste him. There was no tenderness to their joining; it was all tongue and teeth, and she made the most absurd moan when he caught her bottom lip with one of his fangs.

191

A thud sounded behind her. Someone cleared their throat, and Ros broke free, turning to glare at whoever it was. His face quickly softened and he stood, steadying Ellea. She peeked over his shoulder, and warm brown skin and watery blue eyes stared back at her. Ellea sobbed and ran to Devon, jumping over bodies and crashing into his open arms. He breathed her in and let out a sob of his own.

"You shouldn't be here," Ellea whispered to him.

"And you should be in worse shape," he said, prying her face from the crook of his neck. He grasped her cheeks, searching every inch. "You look good. Too good."

"Thanks, ass." She swatted his chest. "And Sam?"

A wolven surrounded by shadows flashed into her mind, and she looked back to see a heap of fur on the floor near the beautiful woman she'd seen before. She stroked the wolven and looked to Ros, then Devon. "He's okay, but we need a healer."

Ellea ran to them, to Sam and the woman she knew but didn't.

Sam nudged her once before closing his eyes.

"Not worried about me, then?" the woman said, petting an unconscious Sam as she looked at Ellea.

Ellea's eyes danced between the two. Her voice was so familiar, but Ellea didn't recognize her warm skin and black hair. But those eyes...

Billy!

Me, Billy said telepathically.

Ellea couldn't move, could barely breathe, as Billy strode to her gracefully.

"I love your beast form," Ellea said, wrapping her arms around her oldest friend as silent tears ran down her face. "But this is hot."

"I know," Billy said into her neck, squeezing her enough to hurt.

A giant of a man scooted past them and hefted Sam into his arms. Ellea was about to protest, but when she met his stare and took in his height, she couldn't speak.

"I know," Billy said again. "You're drooling, Ellea."

Something was clicking—or melting—in her mind as she took in the ridiculous amount of muscle, the dark curls, and wild eyes that looked back at her.

"Garm?" He nodded, and before he could answer, Ellea elbowed Billy. "Lucky bitch."

"Mythis," Ros growled. "Where is my father?"

"He's in his study; it's almost time for tea," Ellea answered. "But that doesn't matter, we need a healer."

She pushed Garm toward her quarters as Ros turned toward her with a questioning look.

Yeah, I'm besties with your dad.

"Reaver," Ellea called as she led them all down the hall, leaving the bodies of guards behind. The demon stepped out of a wall and almost stepped right back in when he saw the group surrounding her. "Don't you dare. We need a healer, send them to my—er—our room."

The happiness radiating from Ros seemed to slip away, and a shadowed look covered his face.

Shit.

Ellea threw the large black doors open, and Azzy turned from where he was pacing.

"Darling, I was about to send a guard—"

"Cut the shit, Azzy," she scolded. "I know you know your son arrived, killing everyone on his way. I don't know how you expect him to rule anything; he's so dramatic."

Sam was settled in her—their—bed, and a healer was tending to everyone's wounds. Everyone except Ros; he had barreled in behind her, going straight for his father. Instead of a sappy embrace, he grasped his father by the throat, eyes raging and red. Then his brow furrowed.

"Did you call him…Azzy?"

"Asmodeus is such a mouth full," she answered, throwing herself down in her usual chair.

Ros looked horrified and loosened his grip on his father's throat. Azzy tried hiding his excitement that his son was here, but Ellea saw his tell-tale signs.

"I'm definitely not calling him my king," she said, making a face. "That's like calling you prince all the time. Gross."

Ellea picked at a small scone on the table beside her chair.

"Are you fucking kidding me?" Ros bellowed.

"I have been fighting to get here and you two have been, what, having tea and reading love stories all day? *Sam almost died!*"

"Son," Azzy cut in.

"Don't fucking 'son' me." He pointed finger at his father. "You kidnapped her and then blocked me from Hel even though you wanted me back so badly! One of the reasons I stayed away from this place was your stupid games, and you dragged me right back in. Now you have Ellea eating out of your hand!"

"Hey!" she yelled from her chair.

"I'll deal with you in a minute." He barely looked at her before he whipped his head back to his father.

Ellea snapped. He had no right. Grabbing the closest thing to her, she hurled it at him. It hit the side of his head. The scone crumbled to the floor. Ros was so shocked that he didn't notice how quickly she moved. Grasping his wrist, she twisted and yanked it behind his back. She kicked the back of his knee, and he buckled to the floor with a grunt. She used the momentum to slam his face into a plate of small sandwiches. He tried standing, but she sent a rod of electricity up his arm and he yelped in pain.

"Listen here, you fucking brute," she seethed in his ear. "I missed you more than coffee, and you come in here being a total jerk? I don't think so. I have not had it easy. You have once again underestimated me."

She sent another surge of her magic up his arm when he tried standing, and he quickly submitted, growling into the cucumber and bread. "I have been fighting off attacks left and right—"

"He should have protected you!"

"Don't fucking interrupt me." Her voice rang through the room with so much power that she paused and looked up at Azzy. He gave her a nod.

"You have no idea what I've been through and we don't know what you've been through," she said, a little calmer. "I've had enough male ego and drama to last a lifetime. So I'm going to let you go and we are going to talk like adults."

Ros pursed his lips but nodded. Ellea looked at Azzy one more time, expecting his jovial wink, but she couldn't read his features. Was he horrified? Proud?

Reluctantly, she let Ros go; she wouldn't admit to him how much she liked man-handling him. Maybe she would when he got his head out of his ass. He stood quickly and stepped away from both of them.

"Glad to see you've been training between tea time and reading," he said, rubbing his shoulder.

"Son," Azzy said once again, "I'm glad you're home, and I'm sorry about your friends. I had no idea what was happening. I'm going to look into it right away. But please know that I wasn't the one keeping you out. I thought at first you needed time, but then I knew that was stupid of me to think. I've been searching for reasons why—"

"You should have brought her back," Ros interrupted.

"Now that would have ruined my plan to get you home, wouldn't it? How about you clean up, and we will have dinner and discuss what has been going on?"

Ros huffed an exasperated breath, looking between the both of them. He stormed out of the room.

Sam almost died.

It was like her parents all over again. Ellea released a sob she didn't realize she was holding, and Azzy quickly gathered her in his arms.

Part Two

"But real witches, of course, are the kind of women who can make their own fate; they do not need men and they are wild with new feelings and ideas and spells. They may or may not have real magic, but they are the kind of women who can howl at the moon."
- Roxanne Gay

19

Ellea

Ellea wrung her hands once before remembering she needed to hide her anxiety. Even though Azzy's personal dining room was quiet and empty, she didn't trust this place. Secrets could be carried on any beast, unseen and tiny. Putting up a wall of shadows around them after Ros stormed off, he'd held her while she let out the past eleven days of anxiety, fear for her friends, and the uncertainty about her parents and her future. Once she'd stood tall, he'd called Florence to fix her up and lead her to the dining room. Her breath shook as she tried to settle her racing heart. Ros was here and he was furious—some of that was at her.

The sound of his long strides coming down the hallway had her anxiety battling with fervent desire. She knew those angry steps, but they were different—louder and clipped. It wasn't the booted sound she was used to or his bare feet padding along cabin floors.

His shadows came first. She found them darker than the black stone walls of the castle and more solid than any shadows she'd encountered here in Hel. They swept across the floor, slinking around the ornate furniture and darkening every corner of the room. They reached for her, swirling around her bare leg under the billowy skirt she still wore. Pressure built as they coiled around her waist, her neck, and twisted through her hair. She couldn't help the whimper that escaped or how her mouth seemed to go dry as their wielder stepped out of the darkness.

Ellea's powers crackled with lust as she feasted on the sight before her. Ros was clad in all black, except for the gold ring that glinted from his pointer finger as he clenched and unclenched his hand. His face wore a snarl until he took in Ellea. She couldn't believe it. He'd cleaned the blood from his hair and pulled his curls back in a bun. Some strands escaped and dangled across his forehead while others were tucked behind his ears. Her eyes traveled down his body to his feet. The leather of his black dress shoes shone in the low candle light. His slacks were snug and clung to his strong legs, showing off way more than his jeans usually did. Then his shirt—Gods, his shirt. It was a black button-down he let hang mostly open, exposing his bare chest. It was tucked in, which was so out of character, but then she noticed his rolled-up sleeves. There, that was Ros.

The way his eyes warmed to her almost made her forget how much of an ass he was earlier. Almost. Her lady bits didn't care, they actually reveled in the way he'd treated her, but they weren't in the bedroom.

"I'm sorry," she said first, hating the short distance between them.

"No, princess," he said, shaking his head. He rushed to her, gathering her in his arms. "I'm sorry."

"I'll never do it again," she said, closing her eyes as he caressed her jaw with his warm, rough fingers.

"What if I want you to?" he whispered above her lips.

Her eyes snapped open, and his were wholly dark. He smiled at her as she stared back in amazement, a smile that showed both fangs and dimples. It instantly sent a pool of heat low in her belly. Grasping him by the back of the neck, she pulled him and pressed her lips roughly to his. The kiss was quick as Ros' father loudly shut the doors behind him.

"Glad to see you two made up," Azzy said sweetly, heading to the table that was already set with food and wine.

Ros let out a loud sigh and untangled himself from Ellea. He held her hand and guided her to the table. She may have squeezed a bit tightly; the feel of any inch of his skin was like coming home.

"Ellea looks good in Hel," Azzy said. "Wouldn't you agree?"

She groaned inwardly.

Let the fun begin.

"No, she looks good anywhere," Ros growled. "But you don't have to worry about her looking good here, since she isn't staying."

Azzy ignored his comment as they all got seated.

"I would say she's flourishing here; she practically took your arm off." He sipped his wine, looking thoughtful and devilish. "A fifteen hundred-year-old demon prince, son of one of the most powerful witches—"

"Don't talk about her," Ros cut in.

"Why not?" He leaned forward, staring at his son. "She was my queen, my only love—"

"And you couldn't save her!" Ros interrupted again. "The same won't happen for Ellea."

Ellea leaned back, cradling her glass of wine as they dove right into the family drama part of dinner. Azzy didn't back down, and she felt grateful for their discussions of Esmeray.

"Reaver," she whispered as Ros and Azzy continued to bicker.

"Yes, my prin—Ellea," he said, clearing his throat.

"I know Duhne is partially mad at me." He may have been helping her, but he didn't like it. "But did he sneak in some tequila?"

"Actually, he did," he whispered back, pulling at his collar uncomfortably.

"I would like some tequila, please, with something citrusy," she requested, handing him her goblet of wine.

"Right away," he said before disappearing.

She regretted giving him her glass; she didn't have anything to hide behind as their bickering became more aggressive. They should fight it out; someone should get them some clubs and her some popcorn. She bet the others would enjoy it too—except maybe Garm.

Sam.

She sent up a silent plea to anyone listening that her puppy of a friend would be okay. The healer had mentioned possible scarring and permanent damage from the poison. The little wine she'd had soured in her stomach, and it all but came up when Azzy began shouting.

"I think you should let her decide for herself."

"I think we should eat before the food gets cold," Ellea added.

Both men glared at each other. Did they forget she was here?

"How's Sam?" Ellea asked Ros. Billy and Garm being in Hel wasn't hard to see, but Sam and Devon? She wanted them on the next train out of here.

"He's sleeping in a new room, and Devon is by his side. I checked on him before I came here, and he'll be excited to see you when he's more lucid. Then we can get you home."

Ellea chewed her lip and looked down at her empty plate. How was she supposed to tell him she wanted to stay, that she finally felt she was doing something good, something right? A nagging feeling reminded her she had her parents to deal with on top of the messed up rules of Hel.

"Good," she said, grabbing some food for her plate to do something with her shaking hands. "My parents?"

She hated to ask, having buried them in some dark part of her mind. Reaver appeared with a tall drink.

"Thank the Gods," she said, quickly taking it from him and taking a tentative sip. "Oh, thank you, thank you!"

She gripped his small arm, and his big green eyes widened to saucers. He quickly pulled away, and Ros let out a growl across from her. Reaver stood tall and took a step back.

"If you need anything else, my prince, my, er, Ellea, my king…" He bowed and shimmered away.

Azzy shook his head and huffed a laugh. "Stop scaring the poor demon."

"I didn't do anything," Ellea whined.

She'd thought they were finally getting past his initial fear of her. Her powers manifesting on their own weren't helping. It was fun in the beginning, but now she wanted the demon to trust her, especially now that he had access to her favorite drink.

Ros cleared his throat. "There have been some disturbances. Minor accounts that we can't quite place on them. Your grandmother and uncle are worried about you, but they are safe."

"What kind of disturbances?" She kept her voice steady and forced her powers to stop turning Azzy's pocket square from green to purple to neon green. He didn't even acknowledge that it was happening.

Ros' hazel eyes bounced across her face, mirroring her own uneasiness. She thought he would try to keep it from her, but he answered. "Minor vampire attacks, people saying they were being controlled while committing acts of violence. You know, weird things. Outside of the vampire attacks, no one has been harmed."

"Good," Ellea said even though guilt washed over her. Toying with the little food she'd put on her plate, she let her mind wander, trying to think of what her parents were trying to accomplish. Nothing came but destruction and their goal to get her back.

"You need to eat more," Azzy scolded, plating some more meat and bread for her. "After yesterday's training—"

"Don't tell her what to do, Father!"

"Oh my Gods, calm down!" Ellea yelled.

"Don't raise your voice at me," Ros growled at her so viciously his sharp teeth poked out from his soft lips. "I will lay you across this table and turn your ass raw."

Ellea's eyes widened and her face heated; other things heated, and she began to question her hate for underwear. She forced herself not to glance sideways at his father.

He wouldn't dare.

"Yes, in front of my father."

"Enough," Azzy said, slapping the table hard enough to rattle their plates. "If I wanted to have a horrible dinner, I would have eaten with the rest of the kings and their brats. I will not have you two ruin the happiest day of my life—outside of you two finally joining in marriage and giving me grandchildren, of course."

Ellea wanted to melt under the table.

"Jokes on you, Father," Ros said, sipping his wine with a smirk, "Ellea can't have children."

Ellea gaped at him. This was not the place or time, but...was he actually happy about that? They had never talked about it, but why would they? They hadn't been together long enough.

Azzy waved his hand. "Please. We can fix that, or you can adopt."

Ellea and Ros both gawked at Azzy, lost for words as he happily cut into his steak. What did he mean "fix that?" Ellea had thought about adoption, but it came randomly and she considered it an intrusive thought. She looked across to Ros, wondering what it would be like to raise a child with him. Grabbing her glass, she forced the cold liquid past the lump in her throat as the two men began bickering about something else.

Surprisingly, she ate. No matter how awkward the meal was or the ideas she continued to force into that dark closet in the back of her mind, she was famished. Florence and Azzy had combined their training after that first day. They took turns fighting, Florence with fists and weapons, Azzy with magic. The pride of taking on the King of the Gods was not enough to wash away all the anxiety that this meal was bringing. Azzy had helped her tremendously, having her push deeper into that dark place in the pit of her stomach, pulling out more and more.

Unlike her mother, who had her throwing out as much as she could, Azzy had her connecting with it and directing it precisely. Not only that, but he'd continued teaching her other languages and about Hel's politics. What would Ros think about it? She knew his father's goal, even though he didn't openly speak about it. He wanted her here as much as she did, maybe more. The souls she'd saved recently cemented that. She smiled at the memory of their elation, how they'd whooped with happiness when they were reunited with their families, their loved ones. She cleared her throat, realizing that the conversation had stopped around her. Looking up, she caught Ros' gaze from across the table.

"Are you done?" he asked in a sweet tone that didn't hide the heaviness between them. There was so much they needed to discuss.

She chugged the rest of her drink; the ice clinked sadly against her lips. "Done."

"Don't think that our training stops because my son has finally returned," Azzy added before she could stand.

"Yes, I know."

They all stood, and Azzy grasped Ellea's hand, kissing the back of it before turning to his son and patting him on the arm once.

"I know you're angry, but I'm glad you're home," he said, searching his son's face. "We can talk more after you've rested."

20

Rosier

The bedroom door slowly closed behind him, and Ellea paused in the middle of the sitting room. They were finally alone, and he couldn't figure out if he wanted to worship her or turn her ass raw, edging her until tears ran down her perfect face. That perfect face was still turned away from him, and she shook her head. Was she nervous?

"I'm not eager to leave," Ellea said.

Okay, not nervous—she was delirious. As soon as Sam was healed, they would head right back to Glenover. The curse that took his mother would not take her. "Excuse me?"

"I know you have your reasons—"

"Look at me." That decided it: she wouldn't be able to walk tomorrow. She squared her shoulders and turned to face him. Ros almost lost his breath as she stood there on strong legs, her dark dress hugging her curves. With her chin held high and her eyes alight with determination, it was enough to undo him. She did look good in Hel, and it made him want to punch his father in the face for giving her a crown to wear. How had he missed it at dinner? What else was he missing? He swallowed. First, he needed to feel her, touch her, anything to calm the roaring beast inside of him.

"We have a lot to discuss," he said calmly. "I'm not silencing you, but if I don't take that dress off of you this instant...I may burn this place to the ground."

"I know." She looked relieved by his confession. "I've been burning since I saw you in the hall, covered in blood, eyes glowing..." She paused, her throat bobbing as he stalked toward her, unable to have any distance between them.

"Did you, now?"

She nodded and arched into him as he leaned toward her.

"Would you have fucked me in that hall, surrounded by the dead and injured?"

Her eyes grew dark, and she inhaled sharply.

One nod and the hardness that was already growing became painful. He ran his nose up the column of her neck, breathing her in before whispering in her ear. "Would it have been hard and fast? Or would we have taken our time, still wrapped around each other while they carried the bodies away?"

"Oh Gods," she whimpered, closing her eyes. "Both, definitely both."

"Two times?"

She leaned away from him and looked into his eyes before nodding.

He growled, practically feeling it as heat and need radiated from her. "Don't magic anything off, I need to destroy something."

"Not the shoes," she hissed as he caressed her peaked nipples through the thin fabric. "Florence will kill me."

He didn't care who Florence was as he grasped the delicate fabric at the arch of her back and tugged. It made the most wonderful ripping sound, and Ellea let out a shaking breath as the cold air touched her flushed skin. He traced the blush that crept up her neck, inhaling her in again. He felt starved for her—her smell.

"No bra?" he asked, twisting the dress in his hands, trying to not rip into her with his claws or teeth. He tore more fabric and groaned. "No underwear? I don't know if I'm happy or if I want to spank you for leaving your pussy bare while you walked the halls of this depraved place."

"Both?" The blush ran from her neck up to her beautiful face. Her freckles contrasted starkly to the pink of her skin.

He would count every freckle, map them in his mind and think about them for the rest of his life.

"Have you been touching yourself while I was trying to get to you?" She shook her head. "No point."

He couldn't help the grin that spread across his face. "You haven't come in how long?" The question was rhetorical, and he hated himself for how happy he was that he owned all of her orgasms now. "Let me fix that for you, princess."

Her knees gave out, and Ros was there to catch her. She wrapped her arms around his neck as he carried her to the bed. Sitting down, he cradled her against his chest for a moment, breathing her in once again as she nuzzled his neck, kissing and biting him. Her hands felt desperate as she clawed to be closer.

"I need you," she whined.

He pried her off, setting both her legs on either side of him so he could look at her. She was breathtaking. Brushing her hair away from her chest and running his hand up her neck, she looked down at him with a heated stare. She still wore the crown, and he wouldn't admit how it bothered him in the best way possible.

"You have me," he said, and she seemed to melt into that answer. He gripped her neck harder, and she answered with a smile, grinding into his lap. "Now, let me watch you ride my hand."

He made feather-light touches along her back to her round ass, slowly working to where she was soaked against his pants. Where his grip was rough, his other hand searched, reminding himself of every inch of her.

"Gods, you're wet."

She leaned back, only anchored by his hand wrapped around her throat; she bared herself to him, and he couldn't help but stare, greedy at the sight of her wet and wanting.

"Ros," she whispered around the collar that was his hand.

"You're so beautiful." He breathed out the words and swiped a finger through her heated center, trailing it up to her swollen clit. "So beautiful—and all mine."

She nodded fervently in his grasp and rolled her hips again, searching out his hand. "I was promised finger fucking."

"That's not how I worded it."

Her mean glare was replaced with desire as he inserted a finger, then two, and Gods, she was already shaking. Her eyes darkened as she held his wrist, looking down to where they were joined. "I believe I said 'let me watch you ride my hand.'" He crooked his fingers, burying them deeper. "Now move, Ellea."

Her gaze shot up to him. He couldn't help the demanding tone, but when she looked at him like nothing in the world mattered but them joining together, it was enough to ruin him. And when she began to move, circling and grinding, dripping onto his palm, he almost spilled into his pants.

"That's right, fuck my hand."

The wet sound of her was as obscene as it was glorious, and he couldn't wait to be buried in her, balls slapping against her thick thighs, against her release that was making her slick. She was close, so fucking close, as she widened her shaking legs, searching for more as he ground his thumb right where she needed it. There was no matching her erratic rhythm; he could only watch as she came undone on his hand, could only listen as she panted and pleaded.

"Oh, Gods."

"No Gods, princess; only me and you making a mess of my pants." She whimpered at his words, but it was there, he felt it at the first clench of her walls. "Come for me, I need to be inside you."

He marveled at her as she clawed at his wrist, moaning as he controlled how much breath she could take. She came, hard and infinite as she tried to curl in on herself, moaning obscenities. When she pulsed around his fingers, his cock bobbed, ready. Another orgasm only for him.

He didn't give her time as he ripped at his pants, his dick hard and throbbing, and buried himself in her. She moaned as he grasped her by the shoulders, pressing her down, down, down until there was no way to tell who started where. Her orgasm was still falling, milking him, pulsing around him as he stretched her. He would be quick, and there was no room to be embarrassed, not when he was being wrapped in the perfect wet heat that was Ellea.

His balls tightened at the first stroke as he wrapped an arm around her waist to lift her so only his tip was inside of her. Then he grasped her shoulder, slamming her on his cock. She threw her head back, cursing to the ceiling as he continued the rough pace.

"Look," he hissed. "Look how you swallow me up, how wet you are." She followed his glance and groaned with him as he disappeared inside of her only to come out glistening.

"I want to taste you."

He choked on a moan, staring at her in wonder.

She licked her lips, staring back. "Please."

He smirked. "Since you asked nicely."

She kissed him swiftly, then pulled away to kneel on the floor in front of him.

Fuck.

She was kneeling, naked, with a crown still on her head.

Fuck.

Her mouth popped open, and it took every ounce of strength not to make a mess on her face. He waited a moment, letting the air cool his skin, and took his thumb and pointer, stroking himself and gathering up his pre-cum and her release. Then he placed his fingers on her waiting tongue. He didn't have to ask her to suck, she did, and did it while staring up at him with a heated look and a moan that sent shivers down his spine.

All he could think about was replacing his fingers with his cock, watching her swallow him down while on her knees, a submissive, wicked princess with her crown.

He had to yank his fingers free. "Are you making a mess on the carpet now?"

She nodded as he gripped her by the face and rubbed his leaking tip against her swollen lip. "You said you wanted to taste me. Open up."

There was no gentleness as she opened, sucking him down swiftly, then grazing his heated skin with her teeth as she released him. He couldn't stop himself from bucking back into her, hitting the back of her throat. But she took it, reveled in each thrust with moans and hungry looks through her lashes.

He couldn't stop the orgasm that came, spilling into her throat like it was his first time getting sucked off by a beautiful woman. He could only roar, gripping her by the hair as she swallowed all she could, but some still slipped out around her stretched lips.

After catching his breath, after she finished licking her fingers, making him harden again, he grasped her by the chin, making her stand. He kissed her roughly. "On your stomach," he growled.

She blinked once, a slow taunt, but moved, settling her stomach on the bed.

"You know the rules." He caressed her round ass gently before giving her a smack, her pale, freckled skin quickly turning pink. "Say stop if it's too much."

She nodded into the bed, and the anger he'd had upon arriving at the gates of Hel began to slip. She was here, she was whole, and she was in a bed they would share. He grasped her hips, raising her to position her on her knees. Instead of welting her, he tasted her, slowly sliding his tongue through her wet center. She moaned into the bed, widening her legs to open for him.

Such a good girl.

His cock bobbed, already eager for another chance to be buried inside of her. He wanted to be naked, to have every inch of her against him. He cursed the uniform he wore to play prince. Twelve days without her warm skin bare to him, without hearing her moans or tasting her flesh. He would hold off for as long as he could; he had missed her so much. In this moment, he knew he would do everything in his power to hold on to her for as long as possible.

"Gods, I've missed your sweet taste," he said before licking from her clit to her ass. "I can see everything from this angle."

Her pleas were muffled by the thick blanket she clung to, and he groaned at the sight of her. Slowly, he teased her with his finger, stroking. "What do you want, princess?

"More," she said, finally freeing herself from the blankets. "I need to come again, please."

"Don't worry," he said, inserting a finger and going for that magical spot that had her flattening against the bed. "You'll get what you want. You always do."

He teased and stroked, bringing her to the edge, and when she fluttered, he replaced his fingers with his tongue, causing her to curse and buck. She would get what she wanted, but when he decided it was time. When he did it again, she let out a feral growl, and he worried she would curse his cock if he didn't let her come.

He turned her over, chuckling at her face, blushed with frustration. He stripped off the rest of his clothes. He was still leaking and oh so ready to finish inside of her, to watch himself spill from her. He took a moment, greedily taking her in: flushed, sweaty, and dripping.

"Needy little witch," he said. "Needy for my demon dick to be buried inside you again."

Ellea nodded fervently, and he slowly crawled up her body, trailing kisses and bites across her skin. His sharp teeth left tiny red lines that only made her squirm more. Her skin tasted like power, electric and soft. She mumbled curses, telling him he was taking too long, but he quickly covered her mouth with his and slid into her.

He tasted his own blood as she bit at his lip, and she smiled at the shock on his face. Gripping her shoulders, he drove into her, pressing her so hard into the mattress he wondered if it would be dented with the shape of her body.

"Fuck." The word vibrated through him.

"Yes," she sighed back, glowing sparks dancing behind her eyes.

He held her gaze through each slow thrust. Before was hard and fast; this would take time. He would make her beg, make her power come out and play a little. He wanted to feel every inch, every touch.

He wanted to be consumed by her so he didn't know his name, didn't remember all he did to get here. Get to her. His Ellea, his powerful and fiery witch. Realizing how much she meant to him, how it had snuck up, had his balls tightening again, that shiver of release crawling up his thighs.

Ellea dug her heels into his ass, urging him deeper, harder. She was so close, and when he felt her power, a zap from her whole body, he came harder than he had ever come before.

Roaring into her neck as his release shot from him, he couldn't help but bury his teeth in her. When her sweet blood splashed in his mouth, he felt her clench around him, finding her own release from the sting of his bite. He would ponder that later, how much she could take. He knew, deep in his gut, that she was made for him. His pumps slowed and then stopped as panting replaced their moans. Their bodies were slick and heated, in desperate need of a shower and sleep. Ros wrapped Ellea's limp arms around his neck. Still buried inside her, he walked them both to the bathroom, needing to clean the beautiful mess they both made.

Ros watched Ellea from the bathroom door as she toyed with her wet hair, eyes sated and sleepy as she looked out the window. He never wanted to be apart from her ever again, but he couldn't make that promise to himself or her. The world was too wicked, and it punished men like him. So he would enjoy this, enjoy her, as much as he could.

They would talk tomorrow about all that happened these two weeks, about what was to come and what needed to be done. He walked to the bed and yanked her to a supine position by her ankles. She giggled sleepily, but her eyes turned shocked as he crawled up her body, kissing her softly on the lips before laying his head on her chest and wrapping his arm under her. He fell asleep wrapped around her, listening to her heart as she toyed with his wet hair.

21

Ellea

Two doors slammed open in the distance, jerking Ellea awake. It was light out, which meant she'd actually slept through the night—and missed training with Florence. She attempted to scramble out of bed, but was quickly stopped by two large and warm arms.

Rosier.

She melted back into him, turning to breathe in his scent. *Earthy embers and bergamot.* His strong body was hot and hard under her hands. She stroked every inch available to her until his cock stirred against her bare thigh. It would be so easy to wake him with her mouth wrapped around him, to repay him for all the torture the night before. He had made it up to her with gentle kisses and caresses as he cleaned her in the shower. She'd tried talking to him before sleep took them both, but she didn't know which one of them had fallen asleep first. Talking would come, but first she could play—

"None of that," a gruff voice called from the edge of the bed.

Ellea yelped as Ros was yanked roughly from her, sliding off the bed. Sleepily, he scrambled to grab anything, the blanket, a pillow, even Ellea's ankle. Nothing saved him, and he thudded to the floor, a pained grunt escaping his mouth. She hadn't noticed Duhne entering their room.

"What the fuck?" Ros yelled with a voice hoarse with sleep. Duhne didn't even acknowledge him, only continued to drag him out of the room, past her torn clothing, and through the open doors, still naked.

Ellea couldn't help but giggle as Ros' angry face disappeared. He looked adorable with his hair a mess and face puffy with sleep. She couldn't believe he had a tattoo, let alone two. That was another story that needed to be discussed. In the shower, she had traced the intricate lines with her fingers, her mouth. He had shivered under the touch. And she'd laughed so hard at the wolf one that Ros had blushed. Florence entered the room, her head turned away to watch the hilarious encounter. She leaned against the door and smirked wickedly at Ellea, who was naked in bed, looking as disheveled as Ros.

"I was ordered by the king to let you two sleep in," she said, eyeing the ripped dress. "I really liked that one."

"I saved the shoes," Ellea offered. Florence only shrugged and walked to the end of the bed. "I'm sorry I missed last night; hope you weren't too bored without my amazing company."

They mostly made ridiculous faces at each other instead of talking.

"It worked out; Belias was being detained, anyway."

Ellea perked up at this bit of information. "Oh really?"

So there would be repercussions for his guards attacking Ros and their friends.

"He hasn't admitted to anything yet, but why else would the guards go after them?"

Maybe making funny faces at each other for hours was paying off. It was beginning to feel like she was rooting around her thoughts like Billy did.

"Fucking Belias."

"I know. Get dressed," Florence said. "We aren't training today, we're going to be spying."

"But you're in your pretty dress. And Belias?" Ellea slowly got out of bed, stretching.

"Sometimes we spy in the open," she said, heading to the dresser and grabbing a pale blue dress that was far too bright for Ellea's taste.

"I'm not sure I like where this is going."

"Let's go see if our favorite cock-sucker has anything to say since our creepy prince is still locked up."

They both made a face at each other.

The breeze was gentle and the noon sun was warm on Ellea's bare arms as they walked toward the north gardens. Hel seemed to be the perfect autumn temperature no matter where she explored; brisk in the mornings, warm in the afternoons, and brisk again at night. She wondered if the southern part of the realm was this perfect. Mhairi would never take her that far on their travels, and she worried if she left on foot, she would have to walk the entire way back. Ellea liked the beast well enough, but wouldn't put it past her to leave her if she went against her best judgment.

Ellea sighed, tugging on Florence's arm that was looped through hers. "I've been to all three sides of the damned place, but I haven't been to the south."

Florence scoffed, turning them down a row of hedges.

"There is no need to go to that part," she answered. "He Who Must Not Be Named doesn't go there even though his father rules over it. There is nothing but evil beasts and wasted land."

"I still want to see it," she whispered. "If Azzy is so interested in me staying and joining his son to rule—ow!"

Florence had jabbed her hard in the ribs, silencing her. The sound of female voices became clear as they turned around another hedge. Florence quickly opened her book to a random page, prompting Ellea to do the same.

"Did you see him?" one hissed, a female with elegant green horns.

"No one has," another said.

"I saw him this morning," a pompous female said. Ellea recognized her instantly. "Prince Duhne dragged him to training late this morning—naked."

All three of them giggled hysterically, and Ellea gagged, earning another jab from Florence.

"Do you think he will come tonight?" the first one asked. "We used to have so much fun with him."

"You used to have fun watching him," the pompous one scolded. "I've been able to taste the crown prince."

Her powers crackled before Florence squeezed their joined arms, reminding her they were there for a reason. There was also no reason for her to be jealous. She wasn't jealous of Sam. But that was different; she loved Sam and the friendship he and Ros had. But that female... Ellea wanted to shake her, tell her she could do better than Belias and to not talk about her boyfriend's dick.

"Like any male would say no to someone putting their favorite part in your mouth," one said. "No wonder Belias keeps you around."

Ellea glimpsed the blush on the woman's neck, but she feigned ignorance. "You're just jealous."

"Maybe we can catch them still training," the one with the horns said to the other girl.

Florence spun Ellea, shadowing them through a hedge and out of the gardens. "I should have known there would be no point watching her now that the famous crown prince is back."

Ellea pressed her lips together, trying not to smirk like an idiot. That was her famous crown prince.

"Well, let's go check on them anyway. Maybe we can catch something."

Florence gave her a sideways glance. "Or...you want to make sure she catches something." Ellea rolled her eyes, and Florence scolded, "That was like a billion years ago. Literally."

Ellea snapped her mouth shut hard enough she felt her teeth crash. "Still," she grumbled. "I'd like to see her try."

Florence rolled her eyes and picked up the pace.

The sound of clashing swords came before the thuds of fists on bodies. It seemed the entire court had come to watch two of the princes battle it out in the outside training area. It was large and open, nestled between a thicket of trees and the castle. There were about a dozen separate sparring rings. A few soldiers were there, practicing with swords, shields, and what looked like an axe. It was quite a sight.

Ros had managed to find pants and shoes, but he was shirtless, and his hair was pulled back in a bun again. She was really liking this look—a little too much. She felt her skin heat at the sight of him landing a blow against Duhne's ribs. They were both covered in dirt and sweat, but there was no blood. And the tattoos, Gods, how they moved with him. The black ink along his spine flowed from the crescent moon on his neck. And the two wolven ears poking above his pants shone bright in the sun.

"Where was this strength when you were bent over the table by your woman like some kind of submissive brat?"

Ellea couldn't help the curl of her lips, smiling wickedly as the surrounding males "oohed" with mock hurt. She wondered how that news had gotten out as she began fanning herself with her book. The women from the gardens showed up, standing right next to her.

"Oh good," the pompous one said. "He's still here."

The female had a name, of course, and Ellea knew it well. She had been trailing her for four days since she was so wrapped in Belias. But calling her "the pompous one" was fitting, especially as she dramatically waved at Duhne and Ros. Neither of them noticed.

Ros hadn't answered his insult, only smirked and signaled him to continue. They traded blow for blow for another twenty minutes. Duhne kept throwing insults and Ros kept knocking him down.

"Speaking of the troublemaker herself," Duhne said a bit loudly, staring at Ellea from across the ring.

Ros had dropped his hands, following the direction of Duhne's stare and leaving the perfect opening for Duhne to punch him square in the jaw, knocking him on his ass.

"That's for taking so fucking long and leaving me with your annoying little trickster," Duhne teased, standing over him as Ellea ran up to inspect how bad the hit was.

Ros was on his elbows instantly, glaring at Duhne, then running his eyes up and down Ellea.

"Hi, Ellea," Duhne said, wiping sweat from his brow.

Ellea wound her leg between his, easily knocking him on his ass next to Ros.

"That's for stealing Ros this morning," Ellea scolded.

Florence groaned in the distance. "Don't ruin the dress!"

Too late.

Ros hooked her behind the knee, forcing her to fall on top of him. She giggled like a ridiculous girl, feeling his sweat seep through the thin fabric.

"Good morning, princess," he said over her lips.

He kissed her soundly as catcalls and whistles sounded around them.

"Good afternoon, handsome," she answered, kissing him again.

Duhne got up, and spat a "fuck off" before storming off.

They both ignored him as he made his way past Florence and disappeared around the castle.

"It wasn't the type of *first morning back together* I had hoped for," Ros said, caressing her back as they continued to lay there.

Looking into his eyes in the bright noon sunshine, she remembered how easy it was to get lost in the hazel depths. The green reminded her so much of the trees around his cabin, and the gold seemed to glint stronger here. The colors swarmed with mischief, and in case the hardness pressing against her leg didn't tell her enough, they darkened with need.

"Rosier," she scolded, but then melted as he ran his nose up her neck. Like he did the night before, like he couldn't get enough of her. The feeling was the same. She couldn't get enough of the feel of him, his hot skin; she wanted to latch onto him, make him carry her around, and never let go.

Okay, creep, calm down.

"Mmmm," he hummed against her neck.

"Are you happy to see me, or are you trying to lay claim in front of every male in the castle?"

"Both?"

"Someone is a lot happier than I expected." She suppressed a moan as his teeth grazed her skin. She wanted to rip her dress off when he did that. She wanted to show everyone the marks he left on her skin the night before. They would know whom they came from, whose mark was buried deeper than her skin. Turning her head, she saw the woman with horns smirking as her friend whispered to her. The pompous one stormed off.

"Neither of us has eaten," she reminded him. "And we should go check on our friends."

He pulled away, looking up at her with flushed skin and glassy eyes. "Since when did you become the responsible one?"

"Since I have a reputation I need to protect."

He leaned into the other side of her neck, pressing a light kiss on her pulse point before mumbling against her skin, "Stealing horses and injuring guards?"

"That." She shivered as he nipped at her ear. "I would be a horrible friend if I fucked you in the middle of the training ring while Sam was still injured in bed."

"Not if we gave him explicit details," Ros answered.

"Ros…" She pushed off his chest. "What has gotten into you?"

He was practically being boyish and devilish as he looked up at her with that glint in his eyes. They should talk, not dry hump in the dirt.

"You in this damned dress—and the damned dress last night," he said, pulling at the fabric.

"So you like me in dresses?"

"I like you in anything," he whispered in her ear, "but knowing you don't wear underwear, knowing you still don't wear it when you have a dress on…" One of his shadows snaked beneath her dress, toying down her ass and through her sex. Her eyes widened in shock and he pulled back, smirking at her.

"But right now, I like this dress."

She had always wondered if he could feel what his shadows were doing like how she could sometimes feel what her illusions felt. Her legs squeezed his thighs as a shadow dove into her once before quickly retreating, leaving her feeling empty.

"Fine," he said, pecking her quickly on the lips with an evil smirk. "Let's go see our friends."

He stood swiftly, bringing her with him and taking an extra long time with his hands running up her ass before he turned and walked them out of the training area. Was that swagger he walked with as they left the training ring? His arm draped over her shoulder like he was some high school jock.

They walked over to Florence, who slowly curtsied. "Your Highness."

"Please don't," Ellea said. "He's already walking around like a damned peacock."

"Are you letting your demon show, prince?" Florence smirked at him.

He swallowed hard and glanced at Ellea. He seemed to shake his head, trying to rid a feeling that no one could see. Ellea shot Florence a look and pushed Ros to the side.

"What's wrong?" she whispered, searching his face.

"I hadn't noticed," he said, twitching his shoulders.

"Noticed what?"

He glanced over his shoulder slightly, and Ellea followed his gaze. His shadows twirled around them, taking forms she couldn't quite make out.

"Hey," she said, placing a hand over his racing heart, pressing him further into the shadows of the castle. "You don't need to hide anything from me. I like you, even the demon bits."

Ros looked down at her, and she smiled wickedly at him.

"I've always wondered what you were hiding from me," she said softly, caressing his neck. His skin was hot under her hand, more than his usual heat.

"I've got it under control," he said through clenched teeth.

"What if I don't want you to have it under control?" He glowered at her, and she reached up to tug the hair at the nape of his neck. "How you bit me last night, I wanted more. I'm not fragile, and I won't shy away from what you are. We're in Hel, for fuck's sake. I'm in Hel with you, and I'm not going anywhere."

He said nothing, but he didn't need to. She would be patient and let him decide when he was ready. She slowly released him, tracing his jaw with her fingers. He kissed her on the forehead and led her to a waiting Florence.

22

Rosier

Ellea could say she wanted him to lose control, but she didn't know what she was actually asking for. She and Florence bickered the entire way to Devon and Sam's room. They would check in and then go clean up. Ros still needed to have a talk with her about everything that had happened while she was gone. Then, as soon as Sam was healed, they would make their way back home, regardless of what she said the night before.

How could she want to stay here for another day? This place was horrible; she deserved to be free, topside, away from all the beasts and monsters.

But she's thriving here.

Ros shook his head at the meddlesome thought. Of course, she was thriving here—she would thrive anywhere. She was Ellea, and she was brilliant. That didn't mean she should be here.

Florence said her goodbyes as Ros and Ellea stood outside of two black doors that led to Devon and Sam's suite. He went to say something as they looked at each other but the opening doors cut him off.

"Thank the Gods," Devon said. "He's out of control. He tried leaving."

"You can't lock me in this room forever. I want to see..." Sam said. His words trailed off right before something thudded to the ground.

He had fallen out of bed. Ellea ran to him.

"What are you doing?" she scolded and helped him stand. "You should be resting."

"I was worried about you." He groaned, getting back into bed. "I was pretty delirious yesterday; I thought I imagined you. Did you give me a sponge bath? Please tell me it was you or Billy. Gods, did you see her?"

He kept speeding through question after question, and Ellea shook her head. She glanced back at him lingering in the doorway with Devon. He couldn't step into the room.

The healer had said there would be scarring, but he didn't believe it. After everything they had been through—wars, hunting, dumb fights—not one thing had left a mark on him. His wolven blood wouldn't allow it. But now, Ros' chest heaved as he took in the jagged pink line that ran from the side of his head, across his temple, and barely missed the corner of his eye. A straighter line covered the bridge of his nose. His wolven blood may heal quickly, but that also meant it scarred quickly.

Fucking demons.

"Hey," Devon said with mock hurt as Sam began rambling about Ellea's dress and how good she looked.

"Oh, hush. I'm injured, let me be." He shooed him away, scooping Ellea up to lie with him in bed. He folded his hands under his chin and said, "Tell me everything."

Devon nudged him lightly, and Ros shook his head.

Sam's fine; it's only a scar.

Ellea's fine.

Everyone survived.

He plastered a smile on his face. "Tell him how you stole a horse and sent two guards to the healers."

Sam *ooh*ed, his face bright against the darkness of Ros' feelings.

"Not about my time gambling with the kitchen demons?" Ellea asked with a raised brow. Ros felt his face pale.

"I'm going to kill Duhne," he grumbled.

Devon pushed him toward the sitting area, one that was much smaller than his. Sam's laugh was loud as Ellea filled him in on her great Hel adventures.

"So she's truly okay?" Devon asked as they sat near an open window.

A calming breeze caressed his skin. He hated this place, but it was still home. He breathed in the woodsy, clean smell that tangled with the crisp smell of apples. He bet the kitchen staff were working hard on whatever celebration his father would throw to mark his prodigal's return.

"I wouldn't be so sure," Ros said. "Yeah, she is unharmed, but I'm not sure what she has been up to or through."

"You didn't talk to her last night?"

Ros gave him a look, and he chuckled. "Right."

"How's Sam?"

"Good; the healers say he will need another two days for the poison to be out of his system. He could finally shift this morning, and they want to make sure there was no other damage."

"And his mind?" Ros asked. They all had been through a lot. Sam may be laughing and flirting, but they were all good at wearing masks.

"We talked this morning, and that will take time. The forest really brought up something he's been suppressing," Devon said, looking over his shoulder to where Ellea was telling the grand story of her adventures with Mhairi. "He's carrying a lot of guilt he shouldn't. Failing the wolven, not producing pups, his time in the war, and not being able to protect me." He paused, his eyes bouncing between the two on the bed. "Did she really steal a horse?"

Poor Sam. If he only realized all he had done, all he continued to do. The wolven adored him, and even with his goofy nature, they respected him.

"Technically, she stole three," Ros said. "I hadn't heard about the gambling, though. And you can adopt like Ellea and I."

"You've talked kids with E?" Devon asked, shocked.

"Of course not, but my father dropped the idea at dinner last night."

"This is weird," Devon added.

"What?"

"We're in Hel, where you are the prince and your father is king," he said. "We are in a freaking castle in Hel, Ros."

Yeah, he could see how it was different for him and Sam. Not for him, he was bound to be back here eventually, but he never would've thought his friends would be here with him.

"You didn't see many castles on your many travels?" Ros joked.

"I saw plenty, but none this bloody or with so many beasts."

Ros worried his lip with a fang. This was hard. Devon had looked less drawn today, but they needed to discuss what happened yesterday. It seemed Ros had a lot of discussions that needed to happen.

"Devon…how are you?"

"Fine?"

"You killed a lot of demons yesterday," Ros pointed out. "You're fine?"

"I'm not fine, but I'm okay," he said, looking more serious. "Knowing

Ellea is safe, that she has been safe…things feel less heavy. I'm sure it will hit me, but Sam has been distracting—the fact that I'm in Hel has also been distracting. Maybe when this is all over I can have a breakdown."

"Devon—"

"Ros, I know, but we have enough to deal with right now. The demons were attacking me, you, all of us. What was I supposed to do? Cower in a corner and wait for it to be over? I'm a witch, the world is full of evil things, and the people I love are involved in this cruel part of our supernatural world. It's time I became a badass like the rest of you, don't you think?"

"You've always been badass," Ros said, leaning toward him to grip the back of his neck, looking into his pale eyes. "Please talk to me, though, or Ellea."

"Did you press Ellea this much when she killed her first demon?"

Ros furrowed his brow and then remembered exactly what he'd done after Ellea killed her first demon.

"Would you prefer—"

"I think Sam would lose it if I got to play with your shadows when you didn't use them on him," Devon laughed.

It was a true Devon laugh, one Ros hadn't heard since before this all started. He laughed too; he could picture the look on Sam's face if Devon got a chance with some shadow play instead of him. Ellea came into the room, pushing Sam in a…wheelchair?

"What's so funny?" she asked, wheeling Sam to sit between him and Devon. She kissed Devon on the cheek before crawling into Ros' lap.

"You can summon a wheelchair for me with your magic but not a chair for yourself?" Sam asked her.

"I could summon a whole sectional if I wanted, but I prefer demon chairs." She looked up at Ros sweetly, and he wrapped his arms around

239

her. "So, what's so funny?"

"Wondering how Sam would feel if I got to *play* with Ros' shadows when he never got the chance." Devon looked at Sam and laughed again. "Something like that."

Sam looked horrified and then crossed his arms. The dramatic pout must have pulled at his partially healed wound; he winced, and the expression vanished. Ros winced with him as guilt weighed heavy in his stomach.

"Oh, you poor thing," Ellea consoled him. "To have a demon boyfriend and to not get to play with his shadows...that's pretty cruel of you, Ros. At least you have matching tattoos."

She gave an eyebrow waggle that reminded him so much of Sam's, and Ros looked between all of them. "How did this become my fault?"

"You are the one with the shadows," Devon said, grinning.

Ros groaned, hitting his head on the back of his chair.

Ellea chuckled. "I never got to hear the breakup story. I would think two pretty men like yourselves would try to tie it down."

"I'm so glad that's what you base your ideals on," Ros said. "And that was it, two pretty men, one summer at war."

"I was sticking my dick in anything." Sam patted Devon's thigh. "Sorry, love."

Devon only shook his head. "You were asking Ellea to give you a sponge bath and you think I'm worried about where your dick was almost a hundred years ago? We have bigger problems."

Ros couldn't help but smile. It was grossly cute how they stared at each other as though they were the only two in the room.

"Aweee," Ellea squealed, and Ros almost threw her off of him at the high-pitched noise. They both looked at her and blushed.

"That was all; I was going through some shit, Sam was fucking everything, and we wanted each other happy. It was a spark for a very annoying friendship, nothing else."

"Oh please." Sam threw his hands up. "You love me and you know it."

He did, but he wouldn't say it. He didn't have time to; Garm and Billy strode into the room.

"We've been summoned," she said. "The king wants us to join him for dinner…all of us."

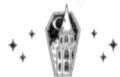

Ros twitched in his chair as Ellea and his father laughed at an inside joke to his left. Ellea sat to his father's right; apparently, the seat she'd had since her arrival. Billy sat to his left with Garm by her side. Sam and Devon were at the end, but never forgotten. Asmodeus had dragged them into any conversation going around the table or asked them about their lives, their fears, their wishes… Ros grimaced. This was not the father he remembered.

Maybe Ellea has rubbed off on him, Garm noted.

Ros glared at him over his glass. No amount of time with Ellea could change his father.

You don't think she has changed you? Garm remarked with an arched brow.

He could hear the *tsk* in his voice. Yes, she had changed him, but he was… Ros let out a breath.

He was being an ass and underestimating Ellea. Again.

"Did they ever find the soul Ellea freed?" Devon asked.

Ellea and his father's mouths both thinned as they passed amused glances at each other.

What was this?

His father was helping Ellea free souls? There was no way.

Maybe he was always like this, underneath all the politics and old ways,

Garm said.

"Enough, mutt," Ros growled, and everyone looked at him. He gave them a bored look and quickly changed the subject. "What I want to know is why Billy was here so often."

"Besides sneaking around with Garm?" Sam joked.

"Wilhelmina was a great and feared warrior before she became a familiar," Asmodeus said. "She was actually one of the first familiars after the Gods retired. She was changed by Loki himself."

"We don't talk about that, my king," Billy said with tight lips.

"Things are bound to come out," he added with a knowing look.

Billy didn't respond, only chugged her wine and looked sideways at Garm.

Great and feared warrior before the Gods retired?

Ros remembered bedtime stories from his mother of a legion of warriors that had gone to Hel with the Gods, a legion of female warriors. Only a handful had come to this realm.

"Loki?" Devon piped up. "*The* Loki?"

Devon's warm skin had paled to the color of cardboard, and his food loudly fell off of his fork. Ros was confused as Devon looked between Billy and Ellea several times with his mouth gaping like a fish. It was just Loki, the God of Chaos and…

Gods, he was an idiot.

"It makes sense why you were so invested in tricksters," Ellea said to Billy from across the table.

Where her tone could be seen as accusatory, it was filled with wonder and understanding.

"We don't have to talk about this now." Billy's eyes held the same openness as her witch's.

"Please talk about this now," Devon whispered.

Always the one to want to learn, no matter the circumstances. Ros was happy to see that glint of Devon he loved so much.

"I've learned a lot while I've been here," Ellea added. "I want to hear your side—when you're ready."

"Want to go for a walk soon?" Billy asked with a warm smile. Ellea nodded and went back to eating, acting like they weren't discussing her being a descendant from the God that started it all.

"You can come too, Devon," Ellea said, and he melted into his chair.

Ros had to go to the library first thing tomorrow and pull up everything on Loki. It had been too long since the history of the God had passed his mind. He glared at Garm from across the table.

What have you been hiding?

Garm raised his chin and glanced at Billy. This went deeper than Ros could have ever imagined.

23

Ellea

Light iron blades clashed in the fighting pit as sand sprayed, glinting in the early morning sun. Ellea wiped her face with her forearm. The dirt and morning humidity clung to her. It felt strange to train with Ros again after working with Azzy and Florence, but in a good way. If nothing else, she was glad to have some alone time with him.

"I saw Viatrix before I came down here," Ros said, swinging his blade in a wide arc as Ellea dropped to a crouch, holding hers above her head and blocking his strike. "I was trying to find a few books, but she said that you have them, along with another number of volumes on the history, politics, and geography of Hel."

"You know I like to read," Ellea answered, hooking his leg and forcing him to the ground with a loud thud.

She placed her sword under his chin, pressing it into his skin. They were blunt tools, only used for practice but solid enough to bruise.

"You don't enjoy reading things like that," he said, grabbing the sword and yanking so that she fell on his lap.

"And I didn't know you were interested in tattoos," she teased, kissing him swiftly. "Florence was easier to train with. She never flirted or tried getting me on top of her."

"Florence is missing out, but she's been training you well," he said, nuzzling her neck. "And my father?"

Ellea leaned back, searching his face to see if he truly wanted the answer. Ros didn't like to share outside of their group, even if it wasn't romantic or sexual. But she hadn't really had a choice, and she had learned so much; she was grateful for all of it. She didn't want their relationship to be jeopardized any more than it had been; they were both too stubborn and too jealous.

Ellea dropped her sword. Instead of saying how tirelessly Azzy had been training her, she would show him. She shed the fear of Ros judging her as she shifted her hand in front of him, turning it slowly as she grew claws and scales. Her long black nails tapered into vicious points, and the blue and purple colors of her scales were mesmerizing. Turning it again, it shifted to a gnarled hand with age spots and wrinkles. Ros jumped and cursed as someone stepped behind him, caressing his face and stroking his hair. He leaned into the feeling after a moment, and Ellea looked up into her own eyes, feeling Ros' beard and warmed skin as the echo of herself felt them.

That trick had possibilities outside of fighting, and she smirked as some ideas came to mind. The second Ellea disappeared with a wink at Ros, and he turned back to her with a face full of wonder.

He was breathless as he asked, "What else?"

"Everything," she answered.

"It's been less than two weeks." His searching eyes held so much awe, and she hated herself for thinking he would ever judge her.

"You have a lot more time when you aren't trying to undress a demon prince any chance you can get."

"Are you saying I was holding you back?" He sounded a little hurt, and that wasn't what Ellea wanted at all.

"Of course not. But I was determined, and I wanted you to be proud of what I've accomplished."

"I've always known you could do anything." He grasped her hips and pulled her closer. "I will always worry, I will always want to protect you, and I will forever be in awe of you. I'm sorry for how much of an ass I was when I got here. My fears aren't yours, and I should have known better."

He toyed with her braid. She could see the thoughts churning in his mind and wanted to give him the time to say what he needed to say.

"I see now that you were fine. I could say I shouldn't have worried, but even if I had your seer abilities and saw what you were doing, I would have still worried."

"I was worried too, and it hasn't been easy. My parents...sleeping alone with the sounds of the castle—"

"It was warded against sounds," Ros cut in, searching her face.

"I snuck out at night. I saw and heard a lot of things that kept me from sleeping, which pushed me to continue exploring..." She paused. "It's a vicious cycle."

"You're horrible. Stop distracting me; I was trying to say something." Ellea kissed him quickly.

"No matter how much I worry about you, I can't take my fears out on you. They aren't yours."

"But they are my fears," she said, picking at his pants. "I wished you were here with me, training me—"

"We wouldn't have been in Hel, first off—"

"Ros," she scolded. "There is more at play here and you know it. We are fighting fate and history; we can't be so blind anymore."

"I'm sorry I wanted to stay hidden in the woods for a bit longer," he grumbled.

"I wanted that too. I still want that," she said, caressing his face and lifting it toward her. "But we have things to fix and bad people to catch. Maybe when we're done."

She didn't think so, though. Something was telling her she was where she was meant to be.

"Your parents…"

"And others," she added, and he cocked a brow at her.

This wasn't the place to discuss what else she had been up to, and she could hear the castle slowly waking up. Their time alone was coming to an end, and they had a ball to get ready for.

"Is your prince less of an ass now?" Florence asked as she pinned another star into the braid that crowned her head.

Ellea had asked to go without a crown tonight; Florence tried fighting it, but eventually gave in. Instead, Florence adorned her brown locks in diamond-studded moons and stars. Gold and silver glittered across her head, matching the gold and silver chains that crossed the back of her emerald gown. It was almost modest with the long velvet sleeves and cut that stopped at her collarbone, but the long slits up the sides showed off her powerful legs beautifully.

"He is always one hundred percent ass," Ellea said. "But he's coming around."

"We've worked so hard, and there is still more to do," she said sternly.

They had. The spying, the training, all of her research, and those she had saved had all been the hardest, most rewarding things she had ever done. For most of the afternoon, she'd felt the inevitable pause in her plans. Something was coming, and she didn't like it. If she could, she would spend her days fighting Hel and getting the souls to where they needed to be. But with her friends here… She tried to fight the guilt of what they'd gone through to get to her and how she felt as though they were stopping her from what she'd started.

No, it wasn't their fault. The clock had always been ticking; she had to decide what to do with the time she had now. Saving the souls would be a lifelong mission, one she was ready for. And her parents needed to be dealt with swiftly and painfully—for them.

Ellea fought her powers that suddenly coiled, ready to attack at the thought of her parents. She damped them down, but a few sparks danced around the two girls.

Dammit.

Azzy had told her this would happen, but it was still annoying. She was overflowing with magic, and it needed someplace to go. She was thankful it wasn't explosive, but now she needed to find a way to set it free to play instead of destroy things.

"You've been at this longer than me," Ellea continued as though nothing had happened. "Give him a little time; he's still adjusting and thought you all had me in a dungeon somewhere, strung up by my fingernails."

Florence huffed, swatting one last spark out.

"We save that for week three," Duhne said, strolling in unannounced.

He looked handsome in his dark suit, the green of his tie setting off his eyes and freckles perfectly.

"Well, good thing he came when he did," Ellea said, rolling her eyes.

"Pretty sure it would be the other way, though," he said, throwing himself into a chair. "We would have been strung up by our fingernails if he didn't get here in time."

"I would have never tortured you…physically," she said with a smirk.

Florence smirked with her as she adjusted her own dress.

"No, you like to torture with anxiety and heart attacks," he said.

"Now that my keeper has come to rescue me, maybe we can get back to that friendship we were working on."

"That lasted about two days," he said. "I don't even remember why I liked you in the first place."

"Ouch." She clutched at her chest from the insult. "I remember you said I reminded you of a bauchan—"

"Horrible small creatures." Duhne shivered. "And I was one hundred percent right in my assessment."

Ellea glared at him; Duhne liked her and he knew it. So what if she had made his life a little difficult while she was getting her footing?

"Are you two about ready? Ros is pacing outside," Duhne said gruffly.

The doors opened on a swirl of midnight shadows, and Ros stood in the hallway. He looked nothing like a prince as he stood in the doorway. The universe and their friends melted away as she took in the shadows restlessly churning around him. Clad in all black, his suit hugged every span of hard muscle, making him look more like a god of death than a prince of Hel. The top three buttons on his shirt were undone, displaying his tanned skin, and his hazel eyes were feral as they took her in. Her poor demon couldn't even handle an hour away without needing to inspect her. Ellea sauntered up to him, placing her hand over his racing heart.

"Don't worry, big guy," she said, smirking up at him and seeing him relax slightly. "I'll protect you from the beasts and animals tonight."

Ros didn't answer, only melted into her, kissing the top of her head. He guided them to meet with their other friends before getting to the ballroom.

Sam and Devon waited for them outside of their suite, and they looked beautiful. She was curious where Sam had gotten his rust-colored suit; he stood in stark contrast to the darkness of Hel. Leaning in, she kissed him on the cheek, and then did the same to Devon, who wore a deep burgundy suit. It was so dark it seemed black, but it still held enough red to match perfectly with his boyfriend.

I have such pretty friends.

She smiled, and they all headed to the ballroom where Billy and Garm would meet them. They were staying in a different part of the castle that Ellea hadn't had a chance to ask about.

Two guards opened the doors for them when they arrived, letting Ros and Ellea enter before the others, Florence and Duhne included. The entire castle seemed to be in the massive room that glittered in gold and black. They all turned toward the door as a booming voice called out to the crowd.

"Rosier Danier, the shadowborn crowned prince and commander of Hel's four armies, has returned!"

Ellea hid her shock at hearing his title as whoops and shouts sounded through the room. Ros stood even taller at the attention, and she knew that even though he hated this place for what it had taken from him—his mother, his freedom—he belonged here. Ellea could feel the growl in his chest as he stared at Belias and his father. Belias had been let go from his house arrest when they couldn't prove he was the one to command his guards to attack her friends. Those that surrounded the two men didn't follow the jovial shouts that continued as Ros guided Ellea toward his father, who had the proudest look on his face.

"That was hot," Sam whispered, and Ellea couldn't agree more

24

Rosier

ucking Belias.

Ros glared again at his cousin. He should be buried in the pits of his own father's territory, not smirking back at him and not openly eyeing Ellea. Ros forced himself not to cover her, not to step in and be a total ass. She talked and mingled with those in his court like she was born for it, but he still wanted to hide her from all of it. "I'm going to kill him," Ros hissed to Sam.

Sam was almost fully recovered, enough to be here and thriving. It seemed like the whole situation entertained him immensely.

"Can I watch?" Florence asked, and Ros stared at the female. He didn't know much about her, but he was starting to like her. The way she glared at his cousin made him like her even more.

"Why does his father keep looking at Ellea like that?" Devon asked.

Beelzebub was glaring too; it was his typical look, but he eyed Ellea a little too much for Ros' comfort.

"Probably because Ellea insinuated she would share Ros and Asmodeus during her first dinner at court." Duhne ate a piece of meat off a stick like he hadn't just said what he'd said.

Everyone but Florence looked at him with wide eyes.

"She was joking." Duhne smiled wide around the food in his mouth, a truly unkind grin. "Enjoy the tiny taste of what I've had to deal with while you've been struggling to save your princess."

"She isn't that bad," Florence offered.

Duhne hissed. "To you. You two have been tramping around the castle at all hours of the night like a couple of spies."

"Shut your big dumb mouth," she hissed back.

Ros groaned. Yet another thing he would have to talk to Ellea about... He took a breath and closed his eyes for a moment.

She's alive, she's unharmed, and she's stronger than ever.

When he opened his eyes, Ellea was staring at him, her gray eyes dark and wicked. She wouldn't stop checking him out. He was pulled toward her, not caring that he stepped into the middle of a conversation she was having with his other evil cousin, Cara. He grasped the back of her neck and pulled her in for a searing kiss.

"Princess." He used his nickname for her like a caress, hovering above her lips and unable to pull away.

"Shadowborn?" she questioned with a nip at his bottom lip, melding her body with his as he shuffled them to a quieter part of the ballroom.

"Isn't that obvious?" He was sure she didn't know that he was born on the longest night of the year under a total lunar eclipse. If it hadn't been prophesied, he wouldn't have put his brilliant mother past planning it herself.

"Don't all demons have shadows?"

"Yes and no." He kissed her cheek and moved to whisper in her ear. "I'm the only one who can wield them in the wicked ways you love."

He felt her shiver against him.

"I've missed you and your shadows." She smirked, running her hands inside the opening at his chest. "But I do like this suit."

He hated wearing these types of clothes, but they were all here to put on a show. And when she looked at him like that, with want radiating across her blushed skin, he just might add them to his regular wardrobe. He also wanted her to add more dresses to hers. There was nothing quite like ripping an expensive piece off of her body.

"Dance with me." He blurted it out, trying to press down on the dark thoughts that were creeping up about the time he had left and all of his regrets.

She arched a brow up at him. "You don't dance."

"When I'm playing crowned prince, I do," he said, pulling her gently toward the few people dancing to an elegant song.

He twirled her once, the panels of her velvet gown glinting in the low light of the ballroom. Would he ever tire of how beautiful she was?

"Can you always play crowned prince?" she asked sweetly as he finished another spin. He grasped her low back and hugged her close.

"Maybe." He made it sound coy, but she held him in her hand; he would do anything she commanded. "What do I get in return?"

"You and your bargains." She caressed the back of his neck, and he didn't hide the shiver that ran down his spine. "I'll think of something."

Of course, he would always dance with her; the dances he'd refused early on in their relationship was one of his many regrets. He wouldn't take anything for granted anymore. He continued to turn them around the ballroom he used to watch his parents dance across when he was young. Young, naïve, and with no ideas on how dark life would get or where he would end up.

The night had been uneventful for the first ball Ros had been to. He'd hoped for more stabbing than getting hounded by the creepy cousins, glaring at Belias, and hearing Duhne complain about how Ellea ruined his love life. He couldn't help but watch her watching everyone else. She made her rounds like she was picking out targets. He knew she was up to something. She feigned watching Garm and Billy dance across the black marble, but he saw her eyes drift, watching some of Belias' court and even Belias at times.

"What are you up to?" Ros whispered, covering it with a sip of his drink.

"A lot of things." She didn't even look back, but began running her hand up his thigh, grazing his cock.

He leaned back in his chair and marveled that the woman he cared about was trying to get handsy at his father's table. Never in his fifteen-hundred years did he think this would happen. He glanced up to her, but noticed she was staring at Florence. The young demon gave Ellea a shallow nod and what looked like a hand signal, but he was quickly distracted as Ellea turned to him and began kissing along his neck.

"I think we need to call it a night," she whispered in his ear.

"Do we?" he groaned.

She pulled back, smirking at him, and rubbed her palm across his cheek possessively.

"Yes. I'm feeling so very, very tired," she crooned, tugging his hair at the base of his neck, cranking it back roughly to trail kisses up his heated skin. "I think we should head in for the night."

Ellea bit into his throat, and he couldn't help the growl that escaped. His cock twitching in his tight pants, he grasped her, fitting her on his lap so she would know exactly how she was affecting him.

"I'm happy to see you are getting along so well," his father said behind him. "I may be a demon of lust, but please take this someplace else. I don't trust you to not damage something or horrify someone."

Ellea chuckled into Ros' shoulder before sliding off of him. She kissed his father on the cheek and dragged Ros out of the room through one of the side doors. There was no hesitation as she attacked him, her mouth on his and her hands tugging at his clothes.

What had gotten into her?

She was pushing them in the opposite direction of their room as she ripped at the buttons on his vest and then his shirt.

"Ellea," he growled, breaking away from her. "What are you doing?"

She didn't answer, only dragged him into a shadowy alcove. He was trying to figure out how deep into the castle they'd fumbled, but Ellea slipped her hand into his pants, grasping his hardening cock. She scraped her nails along his sensitive skin, and Ros instantly bucked, red threatening the edge of his vision.

Ellea half yelped, half moaned as he pressed her up against the wall. Her legs instinctively wrapped around his hips, refusing to let him go as she stroked him roughly. Her braid crown had fallen loose, and Ros wrapped the thick plait around his wrist, tugging her head to the side and dragging his sharp teeth along her skin.

"Someone is being a little—"

"Shush." It was a hiss as she cranked her ear closer to the edge of their hiding place.

He looked at her in annoyed wonder. "Shush?" A growl left his throat as he pulled at her hair, yanking her head back.

Ellea didn't budge; she listened to something as she slowly stroked him. Ros took a moment to come down from his lustful rage to listen, his hearing picking up what she had to struggle for.

"Are you prepared for the influx?" a snake-like voice asked someone he couldn't see.

Belias.

Ros tried stepping out of the shadows to confront his cousin, but Ellea stared daggers at him, grasping him so hard it hurt. The pain and pleasure almost made his knees buckle.

"We're ready for them. There will be no problems and the result will be—"

"Belias! I've been looking for you," came a whiny female voice. From the pained *oof* that left his cousin, Ros bet she threw herself at him. Ellea cursed under her breath.

"Pompous fucking idiot."

Ros stared down at her as it all clicked into place. She was using him to spy on his cousin. This was all a ploy to get closer to him, but for what? He dragged her further into the shadows as Belias and the female strode past them.

"Who else is coming to our little get-together?" the female sounded whiney. "Maybe your cousin?"

Belias scoffed and headed further away from their hiding spot.

"You wicked little..." He didn't have words as he stared at her. A slow smile spread across her lips.

"Oh please, you seem so put off by it." She gave him another rough squeeze, resting her head against the wall.

"Of course, I'm not deterred from you using me," he growled against her lips. "I feel inspired by it. Inspired on how to punish you for thinking you can use me for your little spy games."

"They aren't games," she growled, and Ros tried to think of a time she'd seemed so determined. She almost seemed offended. "And I wasn't using you...it was perfect timing, kill two birds with one stone."

"I'm about to kill your ability to walk tomorrow."

"Do your worst," she crooned.

Ros planned on it. It would be short and rough, and if she was lucky, she would come fast. He moved the front panel of her dress out of the way, thankful for the long slits and her endless refusal to wear underwear. Gripping under her ass, she groaned as he dug into her soft skin.

"Put your hands around my neck, princess." There would be no teasing, no working her up to it. He barked a moan as he slammed into her wet center. She instantly clenched, and instead of giving her pussy a moment to accept him, he lifted her and did it over and over again.

Ellea rested her head on her arms that were anchored around his neck. She moaned loud enough for someone to hear, but he didn't bother hiding it. He wished she were naked so he could see her breasts bounce with his rough thrusts. A light flush crept up her neck, and she was already shaking around him. Lifting her the slightest, he drove into her at a new angle.

Ellea was breathless as she lolled her head back up, staring at him as she continued to hold on the best she could.

"Are you going to spill into me?" she groaned, her gray eyes dark. "Make me walk back to our room while you drip down my thighs?"

Ros' balls tightened at the thought and the vision. She was goading him, trying to take back some control with her dirty mouth.

"The goal is to make you not walk." He said it with a snarl, snapping his hips hard enough to bruise, but she didn't flinch, didn't balk. She smirked.

"Then I would go harder."

What a brat.

Ros slammed her into the wall, forcing her closer and grinding into her so her clit rubbed against his abs.

"Fuck, yes. That, right there." She was incoherent, breathing hard and cursing.

Now that the wall was holding her up, she gripped at his back. He wondered if she'd grown claws as she teared at his shirt. The tang of blood scented the air, and the pain that followed sent a shock right to his balls.

Too soon.

He reached between them, pinching her clit hard enough to make her howl and come so hard around him that he couldn't move, only thrust shallowly as her orgasm relented. She muffled her cries into his neck and then bit him hard enough to break skin above his collarbone. He came with a growl loud enough to be heard in the pits. He spilled into her so aggressively, he could feel it seeping out onto her and onto his balls, and he loved it.

Ros gently brought her head back, moving the strands that had escaped her braid off of her sweat-slicked face. She gave him a weak smirk, knowing this was all her doing. He wouldn't let anyone see her like this, thoroughly fucked; it was enough to make a succubus blush. He shrouded them in darkness and they stumbled into their bathroom. He commanded his shadows to start a hot bath as he began pulling out the pins in her hair. She slumped against his chest, and Ros couldn't help but chuckle.

25

Ellea

Mhairi shook her head impatiently while Ellea held her at a stop, allowing Ros to catch up. The weather was crisper than usual, and Ellea wore her new favorite sweater. She'd created it on her own. Azzy had tested her, telling her to form something more than plain clothing. She wasn't an artist, but she was able to easily recreate Ros' crest in gold on the deep green sweater. He'd given her a brilliant smile when they got dressed this morning. "I feel like a kid whose girlfriend is wearing his sports jersey." Ellea had melted at the comment and almost felt bad for the abuse she inflicted shortly after.

Ros had gone for Mhairi as soon as they'd entered the stables, but Ellea refused to ride the ancient stallion the other stablehand held. She'd ridden him once after Ros came home and insisted Mhairi was his. She lunged forward, tripping Ros by scooping her booted foot through his legs. He staggered into an empty stall, and Ellea slammed the door shut. The stablehand couldn't hide the laugh as Ellea took the reins and urged the mare as fast as she could go. Ros cursed loudly, but the beast's hooves ate up the sound.

"I'm going to have to warn some people at home that you've started stealing horses in your free time," Ros said, bringing his mount to stand next to hers. It had taken him almost ten minutes to catch up.

Back home.

It was time. They had to discuss what their plan was. No more interruptions or exhaustion taking them after having sex. They could no longer ignore words that were not being said, plans that did not include the other.

"Ros," she whispered, worrying her lip.

"I know, princess." He leaned over, giving her a quick kiss before Mhairi nipped at the stallion. "Let's ride."

"You keep saying home, that I need to leave…" She wanted to see her nana and her uncle. But that was all. There was no pull to go home besides stopping whatever her parents were up to.

"You do need to leave. You have family, friends, a life that isn't here. I knew I would have to come back eventually, but I ignored it for too long, enjoyed it too much."

He paused, looking out at the lands they walked as though he couldn't look at her.

Wait…

"When did you plan to end things with me?" She couldn't believe it.

"I never planned that." He turned to her with wide eyes.

"So what are you saying? You are going to shove me back into my world and we'll, what, owl each other? Send magical messages?"

This isn't how this was supposed to go.

"Look," she said, stopping her horse to look at him. "Maybe... maybe if I never came here, maybe if I hadn't spent time with your father, your people, I could see where you were coming from. Things have changed; I have seen things, done things, and I'm not ready to leave—"

"You cannot stay here." He said it with so much finality, but she wouldn't bend to it. She couldn't.

"Why?"

"Because you have a life back—"

"I need a better excuse than that," she cut in. "Am I too weak? Not demon enough? Do you not care about me enough to want me to stay?"

Was that it? Did he not feel the same way?

This was it. He saw them as too different. She wasn't enough. Her eyes burned, ready for the rejection.

"Of course, I want you, and I would want you to stay," he retorted. "This whole situation is killing me, but I need a universe between you and my fucked-up family. From Belias' father, from the creepy twins—how you made friends with Cara is beyond me."

"I have survived this long!" Mhairi shook her head in agreement as Ellea's yell disrupted some demon birds from a nearby tree.

"And so did my mother! Look where that got her!"

Ellea flinched back. Ros always avoided the subject, but she knew.

"Things have changed, and I'm not your mother." Changing her tactic, she said the words softly. It was such a hard subject for him. "We are more than curses and dark premonitions."

The pained look that crossed his face made her want to hold him.

"Life here will always be too dangerous. Someone will always try to cut down my father and I, and they'll use those we love to do it."

So he wouldn't admit to the curse. She wondered if he knew how much she had learned. How much would he continue to keep from her?

"I know she was fierce, I know she was powerful…but her fate is not mine."

"Things will never change."

Stubborn fucking demon boys…

"Open your eyes, Ros; they are already changing. You have been too focused on me, on my parents, you haven't seen it. It may be small, but one tiny pull of the thread can unravel so much."

He looked away from her, scanning the rising sun. They only had so much time before she needed to meet Devon and Billy, so she continued.

"You have seen your title as a curse, a tainted legacy you are being forced into. Maybe you need to embrace it, mold it into something you will be proud of."

He turned back to her, and a sad smile crept across his face.

"When did you turn into the wise one?"

"When I was kidnapped by a king of Hel and brought to a place that needed more saving than me." She wanted to say more, needed to, but he looked so hurt, so determined to not hear what she was trying to say.

"You never needed saving."

Ellea's head cocked so fast she thought something snapped.

"Excuse me? I'm sorry, I think I blacked out for a moment. Can you repeat that?"

"Don't be a brat. Now control your beast so I can kiss you." He walked his horse next to hers, and Mhairi barely contained her anger.

"I'm so proud of how far you've come." Ros cupped her face so gently, but his kiss was fierce. She kissed him with the same fever, pouring as much emotion as she could into their joining.

"I'm proud of how far you've come too," she added. "I would have thought you would try to kill your father at least once, or burn the castle down."

Ros laughed and kissed her again. Their conversation wasn't over and she'd been dumb to think something so massive would be settled during a morning ride around Hel, but it felt like a start.

"We should go back before Devon wanders off and tries to pull an Ellea," Ros said, rubbing his thumb across her puffy lips.

"I wouldn't put it past him." She turned her mount back the way they came.

"I heard they never found the mortal, even my father won't say," Ros said.

"Which one?" Elle asked.

"The only one?"

They had been keeping it a secret, refusing to speak of it in the halls or near the castle.

"There have been ten mortals and four supernaturals," Ellea said with a proud smile. Even her beast seemed to prance under her.

"You...ten mortals?" He gaped at her and fumbled with his words.

"Ten mortals and four half mortals-half supernaturals."

"You can't take people from their homes and put them in another territory, Ellea."

Not you too.

"But it's not their home; they aren't with their family, their friends."

"And yet you don't want me to send you back to your family and friends?"

"You know it's not the same." She couldn't help but glare at him. He didn't understand, hadn't seen what it was like. Maybe she could convince him to go, just once.

"Sounds pretty similar to me," he said.

It wasn't the same; they both knew it. Even the king knew it. The dead should not be separated from their family and friends because of their species. They should choose, or someone should be there to help make better decisions on where the dead rested. Ellea felt as though the kings were being lazy, hanging around and letting the dead be plopped in their respective territories. What if a half-breed had spent their life with mortals? What if a mortal had spent their life with supernaturals? It wasn't right, and it needed to be stopped.

They crested one of the last hills, stopping to take in the castle and surrounding lands. Ellea could see the gardens and noticed two familiar figures walking toward them, Billy and Devon. She couldn't wait to tell Devon all she had learned about Loki, her magic—Hel, even a bit about their world.

"You never said how beautiful it was," Ellea said.

"I forgot." His furrowed brow was replaced with a calm smile as he breathed in fresh scents around them, turning his beautiful face up toward Hel's sun.

Mhairi's head snapped up, looking to her left with her ears pinned straight forward. The mare vibrated with worry, and Ellea stroked her tense neck, shushing her, trying to calm her.

Ros followed her line of sight toward the southern territory, a place Ellea hadn't traveled yet. A bright column appeared from the sky, red and vicious-looking. Ellea had seen the same thing throughout her time here, but it was always one here or there. They were so faint she only saw them after she knew what to look for. "A soul coming home," Azzy had explained as they watched it one night.

But this was a lot more than one soul.

"How is that possible?" Ellea asked.

"Why were you spying on Belias last night?"

"To see what he's been up to," she answered. "After him being with my parents, I didn't trust him, and Florence has been on his tail longer than that. He's been having private meetings throughout the castle;

last night was the first time he said something that wasn't coded or worded weird..."

"'Are you prepared for the influx,' he said," Ros growled. "He knew about this. I bet he planned it."

"But how can so many evil people die at once?" Ellea asked, trying to steady her erratic horse.

She'd learned that, aside from the Gods throwing tantrums, the biggest influxes were during the Elimination wars when mortals rose against supernaturals. But even those that died during the wars weren't all evil. They were caught in an awful place, fighting for what they thought they believed in. Ellea had visited with some of those souls, some of the oldest ones here, and they regretted their actions. It made her wonder if those souls could live amongst the supernatural some day.

"Let's go find out." Ros urged his horse on, and Ellea followed.

26

Ellea

Ros stormed into the meeting room, Ellea keeping pace at his side. All four kings were seated in their high-back chairs, taking up their own sides of the large square table. Everyone but Azzy turned toward them; he alone faced the doors.

"Son, you called this meeting," he said.

Ros pointed his finger at Beelzebub. "Where is your son?"

The demon king gave him a bored look before glancing down at his nails, dismissing him.

"I don't need to keep track of my heirs, unlike your father," he sneered, looking at Azzy.

"So he isn't topside, killing over a thousand people and sending the influx of souls to your territory?"

"No, I only woke twenty minutes ago when my servant told me

about a meeting," Belias said behind them, slithering in through the doors Ros had left open.

"What did you do?" Ros demanded.

"Why would you think it was me?" Bel answered with a surprised look in his dark eyes. He walked to his father, placing his hands on the back of his chair. "I've been here all night."

Ros scoffed and turned toward his father.

"How many souls have been added to your territory, Beelzebub?" Sonneillon asked. Her bright red hair was loose and wild and so different from the crisp look the twins usually wore.

"How is it any of your concern?" he sneered. "We don't call meetings any time someone enters our territory."

"It is warranted if it was done deceptively by the territory's king or their heir," Leviathan said gruffly. Duhne's father leaned back in his chair, surveying Beelzebub and his son. "Tell us the number."

"How am I supposed to know the number off the top of my head?" he said with a roll of his eyes. "I have better things to do than count souls."

Belias gave Ellea a small smirk and an unapproved appraisal of her outfit.

"Not looking very royal today, Ellea," he teased.

Ellea rolled her eyes and looked back to Ros' father.

"Macaria," Azzy bellowed.

Beelzebub raised his chin, stretching taller and rolling his shoulders back.

A beautiful woman stepped out of the shadows. Her movements were graceful but predatory as her long legs stopped next to the king. When her black eyes flicked up to Ros, Ellea stepped in front of him. A wicked smirk spread across her sharp face.

"Welcome home, Shadowborn," she purred. "Why haven't

you visited—"

"Macaria, I called you for a reason," Azzy growled. "Your territory had a mass amount of souls enter."

Beelzebub's glare at *your territory* quickly paled when the creature slid her eyes to him. They were quickly back on Ros, and Ellea's magic burned under her skin. Her step forward was stopped when Ros placed a possessive hand on the back of her neck, holding her in place.

"One thousand, eight hundred and ninety-two souls have entered the southern territory this morning, my king," Macaria hissed, her predatory eyes never leaving Ros', never blinking.

"We get more than that every day," Beelzebub said, waving off the number off.

"Not in thirty-two minutes," Macaria said, still looking at Ros.

Ellea glared at the creature, and her powers roared at her to stop the woman from looking at Ros as though she wanted to eat him or steal him away. Her clawed hands curled by the sides of her pale legs as Ellea let out a hiss.

"The average mass-casualty influx of over a thousand souls can happen at any given time," Ellea cut in and Macaria slid her gaze to her. Ellea held it. "But never are all the souls considered evil or unworthy. Depending on the location, the numbers are split between the western and eastern territories during those events. The last influx to the southern territory was during the Great Elimination when over three hundred mortals deemed it pertinent to kill about two thousand supernaturals at once. They did not survive, and the eastern territory only saw an influx of a hundred souls—the supernaturals who risked their lives on the front line of that battle."

Ros squeezed her neck, and she forced herself to continue staring at the creature. She desperately wanted to see the look on his face, but not desperately enough to let Macaria look back at him.

"Isn't that correct, Macaria?" Ellea crooned.

"You are correct, princess," she hissed.

"Thank you, Macaria," the king said, and she bowed. "You are dismissed."

The creature looked to Ellea under her lashes before shimmering into nothing. She let out a breath and melted into Ros. Everyone seemed to relax.

"Someone has been reading more than I thought," he whispered into her ear before kissing the side of her head.

Ellea crashed into her armchair in Azzy's study, the one she usually sat in during their training or when they spent time together. It was plush and meant for someone much larger than her compact frame, which made it perfect for curling up and reading. Ros paced near the windows, glaring at his father and Florence.

The meeting quickly ended after Macaria left. Azzy made the excuse that he had to do his own research and they would reconvene the next day. Sonneillon and Levi both tried to fight the delay, but when the King of the Gods puts his foot down, you must listen regardless of your title.

"What now?" Ellea asked.

Ros only growled.

"Now we plan," Azzy said. "Florence?"

"I got word from one of our sources that those who died were under some sort of compulsion. None of them were meant to die at this time, and all were mortal," she said, speaking fast.

"Compulsion?" Ros asked. "Vampires?"

Florence shook her head.

"We still need to look into where the incident happened, but this was a different type of compulsion."

"My mother," Ellea said quietly.

All eyes turned to her.

"My mother can plant visions, make you feel you're someplace else. Feel things you couldn't imagine. Pain, fear, and even hate."

"It's not your father's power? That sounds more like an illusion than a seer gift," Ros asked.

"No, I got that from her, and it's very rare. We have never met another family that can do that; we used to use it to show the future of someone we were working with. Cerce learned to turn it, wield it for hate."

"And Belias?" Florence asked. "How does he play into this?"

"I'm not sure it's him or his father," Ros added.

"Could it be both of them working with my parents?" Ellea asked.

"I'm not sure," Azzy said. "Something isn't right in all of this, but I can't figure it out. I know they are hungry for power, to shift the way we rule. But that many souls means more work for him, and he is the laziest demon I know."

"We heard Belias last night," Ellea said. "He told someone to prepare for the influx."

"I saw the report."

It was on the tip of her tongue. What was Belias up to? Then it clicked. "What if he's nesting?"

"Like some omega?" Ros asked. She loved and hated that he was reading her books.

She rolled her eyes. "Not like that. Nesting is the wrong word." She thought for a moment. "What if he is preparing? Gathering as many souls as he can so that when he overthrows his father, he gets all the power?"

"But we don't gain that much power from the souls that cross into our realm, not like the Gods once did," Azzy said. "More souls means more land, that's what holds the power. We are not Gods, so the power doesn't go directly to the ruler."

"But that many souls? At once?" she added, and Azzy seemed to mull it over.

"It's a reach, but why would your mother help Belias? That is the big question. He isn't powerful right now."

"Because she is an evil bitch." Ellea's chest ached as she grasped to stay in the present. Each mention of Cerce was starting make her mind wander to dark and damp cellars. Her magic raging and ripping her in two as her mother's cackle rang through their "training" area. She tried catching her breath as the edges of the room grew fuzzier. Then warm hands grasped hers and Ros was kneeling on the floor in front of her. He warmed her shaking hands with his own powers. "She's trying to get my attention." Her voice sounded so small. "All of those people…"

Ellea couldn't finish. What if it was anyone from Glenover, from Halifax? They didn't deserve this.

"It's not your fault," Ros said, gripping her hands tighter. "There is more at play here than fucked up parents."

"What if you looked into it?" Florence asked.

"She is not going near them!" Ros roared over his shoulder.

He turned back to her, and red eyes met hers. Ros closed them and took a steadying breath. She could feel him holding back, holding on to the beast that was so desperate to be free. When would he learn she wouldn't care, that she would take him even with scales and claws?

Did he have scales?

She wanted to know, she also considered if his demon appearance affected…other locations. It was an easy distraction, demon dick.

Big demon dick. She couldn't help but smirk before she let go of a shaking breath.

"You are not going near them," he said more quietly, looking up at her with hazel eyes.

"I only meant 'to look.' She's a seer, after all, and we've been focusing on her other powers. What do the cards have to say?"

When was the last time she looked into the cards or the stars? Things were so different in this realm, and it never crossed her mind to use that side of her magic.

Was too much demon dick making her neglect her seer side?

There was never too much of that.

"You don't have to do anything you don't want to," Ros said, kissing her knuckles before glaring over his shoulder again.

"I know," she said, bringing his attention back to her. Poor Florence had been glared at plenty since he arrived. "But I hadn't even thought it was possible."

Ellea did her best to keep her eyes on him, even if she wanted to look toward his father. Ros was here now, and he had her; they were partners.

"Any seer here is dead," he said. "But it wouldn't hurt to try. Where would you like to start?"

"Maybe we should get Billy?" Ellea asked.

Ros thought for a moment before looking to his father for an answer. Azzy nodded.

"Should I be in my fluffy mutt form?" Billy asked as Ellea magicked a circle of salt, candles, and crystals.

The salt would protect her, the crystals guide her, and the candles would light her way back. Ellea repeated the steps, doing her best to distract herself from the tightening feeling in her chest and the fear of looking into her parents' current whereabouts. The goal was to not look too far, only to see a hint of a plan.

"Gods, no," Ellea said. "Except if Ros keeps snoring, then I may need you to turn into my fluffy cuddle buddy."

Billy snorted as she stepped into the large salt circle. "A bit of déjà vu?"

"Yeah, except we are in Hel, we both have demon boyfriends, and I'm insanely jealous of your legs," Ellea joked, joining her in the circle.

"I'm a helhound," Garm corrected from the chair he barely fit in.

Ros and Garm had joined them in a small room, both of them refusing to leave the girls alone. Florence and Duhne were keeping watch outside, and Azzy was off distracting the other kings with his findings.

"Don't bother us," Billy scolded.

She sat down, folding her legs under her and patting her lap for Ellea to lay her head on. Her chest ached, the motion reminding her of her uncle. It was the same position he would take when he would jump through her mind. She took a breath and a quick look at Ros before she lowered to the ground, turning and placing her head in Billy's lap.

The carpet was soft under Ellea's back as she stretched her legs and arms out with her palms to the ceiling. Her head fit comfortably in Billy's lap, and her familiar stroked her forehead, moving hair off of her face before gently placing her warm hands on each of her cheeks.

"Ready, Bug?" Billy asked softly.

Ellea looked up into her warm amber eyes, finding strength in their depths. It had always been them, her and Billy, ever since she was little. With her, she could do anything; and with her new family, she was unstoppable.

"Yes."

Ellea closed her eyes and cleared her mind, feeling anchored to Billy, to Ros, and even to Garm. She hadn't had a chance to explore her connection to Garm yet, but her magic knew him as much as it did Billy. She was anchored by her magic too—her trickster magic. It held her close, embraced her power, and protected her as her mind drifted.

Show me. Show me them.

The words rang through her head; they were angry, not curious and searching as they used to be. Her parents were causing destruction and needed to be stopped. She thought about the events of the day, the ones that Ros had told her about, and the time she saw them at the party.

What are they doing in our time? What are they planning?

A tether pulled at her stomach, lurching her from the room, through worlds, and into the woods. Woods she didn't recognize that were lit with artificial light. Tall floodlights were scattered throughout her path, their massive domes facing a clearing that held figures.

Ellea looked around her, unable to see through the darkness at her back.

"Well, there's only one way to go." Her voice was eerie as it echoed around her.

As she walked toward the distant figures, the feeling of being watched kept following her. Any time she looked over her shoulder, there was nothing there. Her surroundings flickered into flames and chaos and quickly turned back to the clearing. She kept moving, focusing on the meeting taking place and not the smell of death and smoke. A smell that still haunted her.

"The world we are destined to live in is nearly upon us," her mother's evil voice said to the audience. "We are superior, and we deserve to run free."

Ellea rolled her eyes as she remembered her mother's ramblings.

Things shifted again, and she could feel the weight of her mother's hand on her shoulder. She tried shrugging it off and stepped into the light, bringing herself back to the meeting. Her old vision was nagging her, and she needed to focus on the present.

"With the help of my daughter," Cerce said loudly, and Ellea looked up. Her mother was looking directly at her. "We will bring in a new world and right the wrongs of our subservient ancestors."

Ellea's heart raced. She shouldn't be seen. Was this a future vision?

"No," her mother's voice rang. "I see you, daughter. Don't you see all I have accomplished?"

Her mother directed her to look at the group. It was a mix of vampires and demons, none she recognized. Movement snagged her attention. It was a large male, a vampire, and he didn't seem to agree with what her mother was saying. He turned and walked away.

"You are all that's left," Cerce said. "Your powers will be what frees us all."

The world turned, and she was back in the clearing with fire and destruction laid before her. She tried shaking her head; she'd seen enough. She pulled on the tether, ready to go home.

Ellea blinked, and her mother was directly in front of her. She jumped and stepped back, but her mother grabbed her by the throat, hauling her close to her face.

"Where do you think you're going?" she hissed.

Ellea could smell her—stale sage and sour wine.

"No, this isn't real." Her voice wobbled as she gasped for air.

Her mother squeezed harder. Her voice was venomous as she said, "This is very real, and you aren't going anywhere."

Ellea clawed at her wrists, trying to pry her mother's bony fingers from her throat, but her mother only cackled as she scratched hard enough to make her bleed.

"Poor little birdy, too scared to fly," she seethed. "I should have pushed you out the window when I had the chance.

A tear escaped her eye as she was brought back to the threats her mother used to say to her when she was little. She remembered being kicked down the cellar stairs when she refused to use her magic. Her mother's grip loosened, and Ellea felt warm hands on the side of her face. *Come back.*

"I'm trying," she gasped.

Ellea dug deep, pulling at her magic.

Think, think; come on, think.

Spots and embers danced before her eyes. Embers—Ros—get back to Ros, to Billy. Warm phantom hands held her face, and the cool caress of a shadow circled her waist, pulling her from her mother.

"No!" Cerce screeched, clawing at the air as Ellea was tugged back through worlds, through time.

Ellea sucked in air and immediately choked. Rolling over, gasping, she reached for her throat and gagged on the pain as she felt the raw skin.

"Ellea!" Ros shouted, crashing to the floor to kneel next to her.

Billy was rubbing her back, and she could feel Garm pacing next to her.

"I'm here," she croaked. It hurt to speak. "I'm here."

Ros scooped her up, cradling her in his arms. Gently, he grasped the back of her head, baring her neck. All three of them gasped at what they saw.

"How?" Billy snarled.

Ros growled through pressed lips. "Who did this to you?" he asked harshly.

"My mother."

"How?" Garm asked from over Ros' shoulder. "That shouldn't be possible."

"I'm not sure I saw the future," Ellea said hoarsely. "I think I was brought to the present. But it felt like a vision?"

"You were here the whole time," Billy said. "Then you began kicking and bruises started forming around your neck. We couldn't get to you; it felt impossible to pull you back."

Ellea curled into Ros, remembering her mother's smell, her hands, all of it. She breathed him in, letting his warmth and scent wash over her.

"You got me back in the end," Ellea said quietly.

"Not soon enough," Ros growled, holding her tighter.

"I saw something, though."

"Shush, we can talk tomorrow," Ros said. "You need rest and a healer."

"No," she said, shaking her head, but the pain made her stop. "There was a vampire there, not like the others. He seemed older? Not crazed and hungry. But he walked away; he didn't want to be there…I could feel it."

"Was there anything else?" Garm asked, and Ros shot him a look.

"It felt wrong," she answered. "How I got there was off. I don't know how to explain it, but I also felt watched, like I was interrupting something. My old vision kept trying to take hold, like I couldn't get the right signal. Was that because I'm in Hel and not where she is?"

Ellea swallowed hard, suppressing a whimper. She knew Ros would haul her away any minute, but she needed to get all of it out.

"My father wasn't there; it was only her and a crowd of vampires and demons, none I recognized. Something is off, but I can't put my finger on it."

Ellea shuddered at the feeling of being watched. When you were in a vision, you were the one doing the watching. It must have been her mother's magic.

"That's enough," Ros said, standing and holding her. He turned toward Garm. "I want a healer in our room before we get there."

Ros stormed out of the room, and Ellea curled into him more, gripping his shirt and hiding from the world.

27

Rosier

Ros lay awake with Ellea's head in his lap. She clung to him in her sleep, one arm wrapped around his leg and her other hand resting on her neck. He brushed her hair back, watching the bruises slowly fading as the healer's potions took effect. Her mother was a dead woman, and each time Ellea shook in her sleep from a nightmare, he thought of a more creative way to kill her.

Ellea told him everything after the healer left, and it took every ounce of strength he had to not haul her away and hide her forever. He'd known things were bad, but he'd never heard the details of her training or how her mother threatened and abused her. He wished he'd known sooner so he could have killed her in her jail cell.

Even though it had given them a lead, he regretted sending her in like that. Ellea had described the vampire she saw, and Ros knew who it was. He would talk to his father tomorrow, and he'd make a plan to leave Hel to confront his *old friend*.

There was a soft knock at the door before Garm poked his head through. Ros raised a brow at the hound, who was still wearing his human form. He silently walked to the edge of the bed, looking over Ellea's curled-up form.

How is she? Garm asked.

I don't know; her voice should be back to normal in the morning, Ros answered. *Where is Billy?*

Ros wondered why she wasn't with him; he'd half expected her to call for the rights to comforting Ellea.

Billy is…calming down. Garm looked to the ceiling. *She went and hunted Belias down after you left; killed two guards and injured four.*

Fuck, Ros cursed, banging his head against the headboard quietly. *Is she safe? We can't keep killing his guards or his court.*

She is with Devon and Sam. We have a few witnesses who said they started it and she was only trying to defend herself. Garm's voice sounded amused.

Ros was not opposed to killing, but it was only a matter of time before the numbers got too high for someone to turn a blind eye.

I didn't think it would be best for her to see Ellea hurt; I didn't want her to get triggered again, Garm said.

You're probably right.

Her weight on him was the only reason he wasn't out there right now, hunting her parents. That, and Ellea would threaten his manhood if she woke up alone in bed.

She learned that from Billy, Garm chuckled, listening to his train of thoughts. *What do we do next?*

We talk to my father, Ros said. *The both of us, if you don't mind.*

When we were heading here, I heard word of you burning his kingdom to the ground. Garm cocked a brow at him.

Well, things seem to enjoy changing around here. I'm not sure what that means or what happens after we get her parents, but I would like to focus on one thing at a time before I make the world burn, Ros said, stroking Ellea's back.

We wouldn't let that happen. None of us will, Garm said sternly.

If there were no Ellea in the world, he might.

You've come a long way from that first night she made your powers think she needed to be killed, Garm said.

Yeah. They were actually telling me I needed her, Ros said.

Does she know that?

She can't read minds like you and Billy.

Ellea mumbled in her sleep, and both Garm and Ros looked down at her. When it quickly turned into a scream, Ros saw Garm reaching toward her, agony in his eyes.

"What does she need?" Garm asked, clearly pained.

Ellea was stuck in her nightmare, clawing at her throat. She couldn't seem to hear Ros as he tried to pull her out of it.

Billy...

But Billy wasn't here.

"Shift, get into bed," Ros said, pulling the blankets back.

Garm didn't hesitate. Skin turned to fur and hands and feet turned into large paws. He jumped into the massive bed and laid next to Ellea. Ros pressed her into his hound and continued talking to her as he stroked her face. Her stammers slowly faded as her small hands clung to Garm's large warm body.

Ros fought off waking up and pulled Ellea closer to him, but someone pulled back. He lifted his head, hearing one too many snoring bodies, and saw more than two lumps in his bed. A bed that seemed a lot larger than when they'd gone to sleep. Ros tried moving his feet, but they wouldn't budge, and a growl greeted him. Using his shadows, he pulled back one curtain slowly.

Billy was in their bed, holding Ellea's hands. Devon was also in their bed, wrapped around Ellea's middle. He lifted his head higher to see Garm, still in his hound form, laying on top of Billy's legs, his large nose pointed toward the door. Looking down, Sam was in his wolf form and snoring with his head in Devon's lap and his legs on top of Ros.

"What the fuck?" Ros cursed quietly.

"Oh, this looks like a fun orgy," Duhne said from the open bedroom doors. "Did they stay in their wolf forms the whole time?"

His cousin really had to stop walking into places he didn't belong.

"What the fuck, Duhne?" Ros cursed.

"I'm not judging; remember that one time with Macaria and the—"

"Do not finish that sentence."

"I would love for you to finish that sentence," Ellea said groggily, stretching and waking Devon, who was blushing as he glanced at Ros.

"No," Ros said to Ellea. "And when did this happen?"

He looked to Devon, the only one who could have magicked the bed to be almost two times larger.

"When Garm didn't come back last night, we came looking for him, and the three of you were sound asleep." He gave a small smile. "So I enlarged the bed and we all joined."

"Right," Duhne said dryly. "If you are done cuddling with your puppies, your father is ready to meet with you."

He turned on his heel and left the room. Ros flopped back into the bed "Don't get used to this," he growled. "Any of you."

Ellea gave him a small pout, and Sam seemed to be pressing more weight into Ros' legs. He turned on his side the best he could, reaching for her to come closer.

"How are you feeling?" he asked, brushing her hair behind her ear.

"Better," she said, closing her eyes and leaning into his touch. "Let's go see your father."

"Actually, it will just be Garm and I first." He sighed as she gave him a look. "It's father-son business; I'm not hiding anything."

"Right," she mocked, sounding like Duhne.

"You need to rest, maybe go for a walk with the rest of our harem."

Ellea choked on a laugh. "You don't even know what a harem is, old man."

"Hey, I read some of your books while you were busy wooing my father and fucking up his kingdom."

"It's not only his kingdom," Ellea said. "There are others...hey! What books did you read?"

"I got up to the fifth book of the series I bought you." Ros thought for a moment, trying to remember the name. "The one with the cock pocket?"

A pretty blush crept across her cheeks, and her gray eyes got wide.

"The one with the guy and girl shifters and the..." She paused, glancing down at Sam, who had his head turned away.

"The wolf with two cocks for both his lovers?" Ros said loudly, and Sam jerked his head up.

"*Dual Force, A Wolf and His Mates*," Ellea whispered.

"That's the one." He kissed her on the forehead. "I especially liked when—"

"Don't say it," she said, covering his mouth with her hand.

"Are you embarrassed of your books, princess?"

Billy coughed, trying to hide her laugh, and he could feel Garm slowly inching toward the end of the bed.

"Never. But when we are in a bed full of our friends, I would rather not talk about how the character used both of his dicks...at the same time."

"I can't say it didn't give me ideas," he growled, leaning in to kiss her more.

"That's enough of that," Devon said, sliding out of bed and dragging Sam with him.

Sam's tongue lolled out of his mouth as he looked back at them, and Ros could only imagine what was running through his mind. Billy followed, and Garm bolted from the room.

I'll see you in twenty minutes, Garm said telepathically before he closed the bedroom door.

"You're the worst," she said, hitting his chest.

"I am." He kissed the top of her head. "Come shower with me before I have to head out."

Ellea gave him a coy smile and stretched lazily. He would give anything to have her so relaxed and happy, especially after such a rough night. He would never admit it, but he was grateful for their friends coming in...even if he wasn't one for sharing their bed.

Ros and Garm strolled into his father's study, and Asmodeus was staring out the window lit by the bright morning sun. Ros had loved his office as a boy, pulling down the many volumes and reading what he could. Now he wasn't so sure. He knew that one day he would be in the same position, but no matter his father's faults, Ros could not imagine a world where he was not king.

"Father," Ros said, and he turned toward him.

Garm bowed low, and his father nodded his head at the hound.

"Rosier, how is our princess?"

Ros clenched his jaw so tight he thought a fang would crack.

Our princess!

"Ellea only belongs to herself," Ros growled, and Garm smirked beside him.

"Don't we call the Gods, *our* Gods? We worship and revere them… how is she any different?"

"Are you saying Ellea is a god?"

Garm turned his head completely to Ros, but he didn't want to see the look on Garm's face.

"As good as one; she is better than all of us, stronger than you and me." A sharp intake of breath sounded next to him, and his father stepped forward, holding his son's angry stare.

Ros stood taller, towering above his father. What would Ellea think if she heard this conversation? Stronger than the both of them… She had spent so long fearing her own power, and now his father was putting her in the same category as a god.

"I think you've spent too much time with her; she seems to have won you over too much," Ros growled.

"Don't be jealous. I was only doing what any future father-in-law would do while his son could not get to her."

"Keep talking like that and you will scare her off for good." Ros stepped toward his father, feeling his power burn under his skin. Ellea didn't need any more stress; she carried too much. "She has feared her powers for so long, don't you dare add this to the list of things she has to worry about. Speaking of being unable to get to her, have you figured out why that is, Father? Because you are my first guess. Maybe you wanted her all to yourself, King of the Gods."

A slow smile spread across his face at Ros' accusations.

Smug bastard.

"That's why I called you here. But first. How. Is. Our. Princess. Doing?"

Ros stepped forward, ready to punch the smug look off his father's face, but Garm cut in, grasping him by the arm.

"You are doing a wonderful job at hiding your demon, son." His father walked around his desk and turned back to the two of them. He threw an ancient leather-bound book, so small it could fit in the palm of his hand. "I found that on Belias when my guards searched him after your attack. He is the reason you two couldn't get to her, using an ancient spell from the Gods. I'm not sure how he got it, and we are still looking into the soul situation, but he has been banned from leaving for the next year or until he can show he wasn't involved. You should go topside and check in with the council. I'm sure Ellea's family will be happy to see her in one piece. I wish I could see the look on their faces when she comes back as the powerful creature she is now."

He looked thoughtful and so young as a devilish grin spread across his face.

"You're letting me leave?" Ros had a hard time believing it. He was happy about Belias; that was one less thing to worry about.

"Why wouldn't I let you leave?" His father looked confused, and it made Ros want to punch him even more.

"You fucking kidnapped Ellea to get me here, now you are sending us on our way?"

"You said it yourself, there is more at play here." He stood taller and looked more serious. "But you will be back, both of you. I'm not done with you and Ellea isn't done with us. She has started something, and there is no turning back now."

"I don't want her involved in our kingdom's business," he said

292

through his teeth.

"I'm pleased you're calling it our kingdom, but maybe you should ask Ellea what she wants to be involved in."

28
Ellea

E llea stood in the garden she and Azzy had used for most of their dinners. It had to be her favorite spot in this whole place, especially at night. The stars were spectacular and so different from the stars she was used to. Today, she would leave, but it didn't feel like leaving for good. Florence and Duhne stood off in the distance, talking with her friends as they prepared to help them leave. Ros, Ellea, Garm, and Billy would meet with the council in the city. Duhne and Florence would head to Glenover with Sam and Devon and wait for them there. Then they would plan to stop her parents once and for all.

Ellea turned as she felt Azzy walk out on the veranda. It was as though her magic recognized him and knew when he was near. It was so much stronger with Ros.

"Azzy, I can't believe you are letting us leave."

"Don't lie," he scolded. "You knew you weren't being kept here, like I know you will be back once you finish up business with them."

He didn't enjoy calling her parents by their names. Ellea smirked at him, then eyed the wrapped object tucked under his arm.

"You need your own, and I can't think of anyone more deserving than you, darling."

"Please don't be a crown," she said, rolling her eyes.

"I don't think you need a crown where you're going." He held the long object in both hands and brought it toward her. "But you may need an obsidian and gold sword forged by the Gods."

Ellea gasped as she pulled away the black fabric. The sword was smaller than she expected, and it was sheathed in a leather scabbard. The straps were longer too, too long to go around her waist.

"It's called a baldric scabbard," Azzy said, picking up on her thoughts. "You wear it on your back. I thought it would be easier to conceal there until you learn that part of your magic."

Ellea groaned. She still hadn't figured out how to store things in pockets like Ros and Azzy could. Dragging the sword from the sheath, she gasped again. Even though she could remake and create objects, this sword could not be replicated.

"It looks like the one Ros has in our room." She traced the intricate gold lines that flowed down the middle. "But a whole lot smaller."

Azzy chuckled. "It's a short sword and the sister to Rosier's sword. It used to be his mother's."

Ellea staggered back, leaving the sword in his hands. She couldn't; there was no way she would carry a sword that belonged to his mother. She wasn't worthy.

"I can't…" She shook her head.

"You will," he said sternly. "Don't disobey a king."

Ellea laughed as his façade quickly crumbled; he would never say that to her.

"Ellea, it was meant for you even before it was meant for Esmeray." He stepped toward her, holding the straps out, waiting for her to loop her arms through them.

"I guess I can at least try it on. And it goes with my dress," she mumbled, turning to help him fit the straps to her. It fit similarly to a backpack but a bit higher, and damn, did it feel right.

The sword sat at an angle, poking over her right shoulder and next to her left side. It would take some getting used to, but the weight was a surprising comfort at her back. It was as if it was always meant to be there.

"She had always complained how the sword at her side wasn't comfortable, especially when riding," Azzy said with a distant look in his eyes.

"Thank you." She fought the burn in her eyes and forced herself to look in Azzy's watery gaze. "I will look after it."

"It's yours, forever." He clasped her by each shoulder and kissed her on her cheek. "Now go show that council what you're made of. Remember all you have learned and done while you were here."

Ellea smirked up at Azzy, thinking of all the horrible things the council would faint at.

Ellea stared up at the massive white building as she stepped out of Ros' shadows. He shivered next to her. It had been too long for him to go without being able to use that part of his magic, and he seemed more relaxed now that he was free of the spell Belias had used. She felt her braid tug as Ros pulled it free from her harness and wrapped it around his hand. He tugged her head back and planted a chaste kiss on her parted lips.

"I'm never walking again," he said before deepening the kiss.

Garm and Billy brushed past them in their beast forms, both nudging them as they continued toward the building that housed the council's meetings. Ros glanced at the sword at her back and gave her a small smile before releasing his hold on her hair and grabbing her hand instead.

Before they left, Ros said he was happy for her to have the sword, that it was meant for her. But she still felt...undeserving. Ellea shook off the feeling, replacing it with the mask she'd worn most of her life, the bored and quiet heir to an ancient and prominent seer family. One that had complete control of her magic and who wasn't on the path that her parents had laid for her, a path shrouded in hate and destruction.

Her heart hurt knowing that her nana wouldn't greet her with love and affection; she would have her mask on as well. She only hoped that Ros would see the roles they were playing. But as they stepped into the meeting room where the most important people on their side of the continent looked down at them, she felt his magic, felt the anger and need to protect her. At that moment, he looked more demon than prince.

The fifteen council members sat high behind a mass of white marble in a crescent shape. In the center were three human mortals, and to their left were three wolven and three demons. To their right were three witches and three vampires.

She let her eyes pause on her nana for a moment, trying to show as much affection as she could with just her eyes. In response, her nana touched her nose once, their signal that she was there for her.

"Someone looks whole and well for being kidnapped and dragged to

Hel," one vampire said.

Ellea recognized him, but not really. He looked similar to the vampire in her vision, but he had bright auburn hair where the one she had witnessed was all dark hair and bright eyes. She squeezed Ros' hand.

"Who says she was kidnapped?" one witch said. Isaac's father. "I wouldn't put it past her to go there on her own."

Ellea leaned slightly to take a step, to open her mouth and say she would in fact go there on her own, especially after all she had learned. Her nana gave the slightest shake of her head, forcing Ellea to bite her tongue and stay in her spot.

"Showing up here with two beasts from Hel and a sword on your back like some barbarian... What a shame." He clicked his tongue.

Garm snarled beside Ros. Her nana spoke up before things could go too far south.

"Are we here to discuss my granddaughter or my daughter?" she said with a raised voice.

"I'm not sure you should be here at all," the red-haired vampire said.

"And I'm sure you're the only one of the fifteen who thinks that," her nana snapped back.

The three demons to the left let out a collective sigh, leaning back in their chairs and rolling their eyes.

"We don't have time for this," the centered human said. Ellea wasn't sure of his name, but he was young for a council member. "We have lost too many of our own and wasted enough time."

"Maybe if Rosier wasn't busy chasing his new toy and doing his job, we wouldn't have had such a catastrophe," the vile vampire said.

"I am not the only hunter, Vladdy, and you know it." Ros gave him an evil smirk. "And who said I haven't been working on things? I killed over thirty of your ilk before I was able to connect with Ellea."

"You mean saved her," her nana corrected.

"I'm sure you know your granddaughter never needed saving, Jadis."
Jadis barely held back her smile.

"Do we have a plan?" the young man said.

"You don't have one?" Ellea asked. "My parents have been free for
weeks and you have nothing? You waited for us to crawl back from
Hel before you did anything?"

"We have been dealing with the families of the dead, setting up
evacuation routes, setting up more watches, and bringing in more
hunters," one of the wolven said.

"But you haven't figured out how to capture them?" Ros asked.

"You've seen the reports," a demon said.

They had. They had pored over them every day while they were in
Hel. There was no pattern, no way to tell their next step. All they
knew was that her parents were working with vampires, demons, and
Belias. He had claimed he wasn't helping them, that his only part in
their scheme had been getting Ellea to them.

"I have, but it seems you need the witch you have so much fun
insulting." Ros eyed Isaac's father and then paused on the vampire.
"We have our first lead. Your brother appeared in a vision Ellea had
about her mother."

Jadis' sharp intake of breath could not be hidden, and Ellea
raised her chin.

"You are not to look into the future of your family," Isaac's father
scolded. "It is forbidden."

"I do not consider the woman who birthed me to be family," Ellea
said, staring at the man that reminded her so much of her ex—not
that she would call him that. "I also feel it was warranted with the
circumstances."

"We will add that to the list of your other grievances that have yet

300

to be dealt with," he said harshly, and Ellea couldn't help her flinch.

"My granddaughter is not on trial, Simon," her nana said.

"Maybe she should be—"

"That's enough!" two or more people shouted. Ellea thought that one of them had been the demon who was now standing.

The human in the middle stood as well and glared at every one of the council members before looking at Ros and Ellea.

"You have the full support of the council to move forward in any way you see fit. Any resources you may need can be requested from the heads, but it is my understanding that all of Hel is already ready to support you."

Ros and the three demons nodded.

"Whatever you need or need to do, Rosier, do it."

Jadis stood as Ros dragged Ellea out of the council chambers. She looked over her shoulder one last time and gave her nana a nod.

I'll check in with her, Bug, Billy said telepathically.

Ellea shivered as they stepped out into the evening, more from the stress than the chill. She was thankful her dress had longer sleeves, but the slit up the side had her second-guessing her choice of clothes.

Billy and I will talk with Jadis. Why don't the two of you eat and we will meet up tonight? Garm suggested.

"Yes, I'm starved," Ellea said, snuggling closer to Ros for warmth. "I know our princeling is now opposed to walking, but it will only take a moment."

Billy chuffed a laugh, and the two beasts walked back into the building.

"Come on, princess. Show me what you city folk like to eat."

29

Ellea

uck.

F Ellea stopped before they reached the restaurant that had one small group of people standing near the hostess stand.

"They look busy," she said, trying to tug Ros away. "Let's try a different place."

"What? There are plenty of tables," he said, cocking his brow as she tried to continue to move his large body.

An excited voice called from the restaurant. "Ellea?"

Fuck, fuck, fuck.

Ros stiffened next to her and turned to glare at the tan and tattooed witch that broke away from the crowd.

"Please don't kill him," Ellea grumbled up at Ros. "Luke!"

It came out like more of a screech than she'd hoped. She continued to hold on to Ros' arm as Luke stepped in to kiss her on the cheek.

"Ellea, oh my Gods, I heard you got kidnapped by demons or something." He grasped her by the shoulders and took in every inch before realizing she was connected to a very large and angry demon.

"Silly rumors." She batted him away. "But this is Rosier. Ros, this is Luke."

She gestured to the both of them, but Ros stood still, glaring at Luke. Ellea could have sworn there were embers behind his dark eyes.

Luke's mouth had popped open as he was openly taking in Ros. He glanced over his shoulder quickly before whispering, "Is there a sign-up form?"

"What?" both Ros and Ellea asked together.

"To get kidnapped by demons." His smile was all warmth, spreading across his handsome face.

"Ha, funny." She tugged on Ros again. "Well, it was good seeing you, we will be going."

"Going?" Ros tugged her close to his side, placing a kiss on the top of her head. "Princess, I'm famished, let's go here."

Ellea glanced behind Luke to see Aiden gawking and Isaac with a glare harsh enough to match Ros'.

"Cool!" Luke said, oblivious to her suffering. "The guys will be happy to see you and meet your new beau."

Ros took a step toward Luke as he turned. His skin practically vibrated, and the tattoo poking above his collar seemed to darken menacingly, but Ellea held him back.

"Please don't kill them," she mumbled under her breath.

"Am I to guess that those three are the same three—"

She gave him a look that stopped his question. "I didn't ask about your sexcapades while we were in Hel. Now don't kill them. We have enough to deal with."

"No promises," he said as they headed toward the hostess.

Ellea pulled at her dress, a little sad that Ros had put her sword in a shadow pocket. It would have drawn attention, but she felt naked. She wondered if wearing it would have scared people off or made the restaurant owner refuse them service. She glanced at Ros as they neared the door, and his face was pure smugness with a hint of *I can kill you with a thought.*

The young hostess dropped her tablet as Ros neared, her mouth wide. Her eyes seemed to glaze over at the sight of him.

Yeah, yeah, he's hot.

Ellea glanced at Aiden, who had a look to match the hostesses.

Luke nudged him, waggling his eyebrows before saying, "Look who the cat dragged in."

"This is Rosier. Rosier, this is Isaac and Aiden."

Ros gave Aiden a small nod while the sweet man was trying to remember how to swallow. Ros did not return the favor to Isaac.

"I had the worst conversation with a man who looks like you less than an hour ago," Ros said, sizing up Isaac. "Gods, he was an ass."

"Simon, my father. He did say he was going to be meeting a few brutes today," Isaac said with a sneer.

"And you so happen to be at a restaurant around the corner, Zack?" Ros said to Isaac. Ellea knew he knew his name; he must have been using the wrong name on purpose. "What a crazy coincidence."

Ellea pressed her lips together. She and Isaac had run into each other at this restaurant several times after council meetings. Of course...

"It's Isaac," he hissed.

"Right." Ros turned to the hostess and gave her a winning grin. Ellea was certain panties were burning somewhere with a look like that.

"Five?" the hostess squeaked.

"No," Ros and Isaac said together.

⁖

She quickly gathered up the menus and opened the door for the three men.

"Have a sumptuous dinner. It was great meeting you, Luke and Aiden." He gave them the same grin, and Aiden blushed. "Zack, enjoy your evening."

Luke pushed Isaac through the doors before he could say anything, and Aiden gave her a small wave.

"Gods, you're horrible—"

Ellea was quickly cut off as Ros pressed a searing kiss to her lips. She melted, her anxiety quickly replaced with need. Forget dinner, she wanted to go home and have a big demon prince for dinner and dessert. He pulled away and nipped at her bottom lip.

"Yes, princess." He kissed her roughly again, grabbing her ass and pressing them together. "And remember how much you like it."

The hostess coughed behind them, and Ellea turned toward her. She could have sworn she mouthed "lucky bitch" as she fanned herself with the menu. Ellea gave her a small smirk as she found the strength to walk.

She wound them through the restaurant and gestured at a table in the middle. Ros shook his head and pointed to a dark booth in the back. The hostess obliged and guided them there.

"Enjoy your dinner," she said breathlessly.

"Prince of Shadows wants the dark booth?" Ellea asked after reading through the menu. She ignored the angry glances from Isaac. She could just see him in her peripherals.

"Yes, so he can play with his princess," he said, whispering in her ear. "You wouldn't."

"I would." He nipped at her ear and pulled away. "Are you going to stop me, Ellea?"

Ellea. So much wicked promise came when he used her name. She couldn't breathe, couldn't swallow, as heat crept up her neck. He knew all too well what he was doing, especially when he flashed another grin at the server who filled their glasses with water.

"Can we have five minutes to look over the menu, please?" Ros asked.

He nodded and walked away.

"You can't wait until dessert?"

Ros gripped her thigh under the table, bringing it to rest on top of his leg.

"No." One simple word had her dripping in the booth. And when he wrapped his arm around her, she was a goner. He was serious.

Anyone around them would think they were a young couple cuddling in their booth. Ellea watched Ros sip his water. With both hands in view, no one would know that his shadows were circling her ankles to keep her wide open.

"I want you to come in this booth before the server gets back, so those *males* over there have to sit through their entire meal knowing that I'm the one in control of your pleasure. That I alone get to coax those pretty little sounds from your lips."

"Ros," she whispered as he kissed her neck and caressed her face.

"Yes?"

Evil, evil demon boyfriend. She should have known to go home, but a petty part of her had wanted to parade him around the town that had given her so many mean glances her whole life.

"You're hori—" She couldn't finish the sentence as his shadows caressed her sex.

"Gods, you're wet." He kissed her lightly, groaning as he tugged on her bottom lip.

"You can feel what they feel?" She could barely get the words out as they teased and stroked. All the pent up energy from the council meeting and then running into her exes had turned into leg-shaking lust.

"Of course," he said sweetly. "I can feel how hot and drenched you are, how you're already pulsing around them."

Ellea tried curling in on herself, but Ros held her up with his arm still wrapped around her. One shadow circled her clit while another swept in and out of her center. A low moan escaped her, and the sound of silverware being dropped came from her left, where the boys sat.

"That's my good girl," he said, tugging her braid to stop her from ducking her face. "Let them hear you."

"Fuck," she hissed as the shadows sped up.

"You have about one minute," he said.

She craned her neck, following his gaze to where their server was clearing a nearby table.

"Ros," she groaned, looking up into his dark eyes before her eyes rolled as she stretched around the shadows, the pressure building as her legs shook.

"That's it, take all of it," he groaned against her lips, kissing her lightly. "I can feel your tight pussy; you're so close, so wet. I only wish I could have a taste."

She moaned again, and the sound of breaking glass came from the boys' table. Ellea glimpsed the server heading over to help clean up the mess from under her lashes.

"Looks like you bought yourself another minute." His husky laugh sent shivers down her body, and when he kissed her neck, she begged her powers not to make her a sparking mess in the middle of a restaurant.

She was so close. How was she going to do this? Glancing around, she saw no one was paying her any attention. Besides Ros, there were only three pairs of eyes on her. She chanced a peek to see Luke and Aiden were smirking. Isaac looked like he wanted to flip the table.

"Eyes on me," Ros said, gripping her chin. "I want to see the look on your face when you try to hide that pretty sound you make when you come."

She whimpered at his command but held his stare. Her ears rang as a sound of more breaking glass sounded from her left. Her orgasm crested and fell rapidly, and there was no way to suppress the moan that bubbled in her chest. Ros saved her and swallowed the sound with a rough kiss.

He held her up as she shook and whimpered, his shadows slowing their rhythm until they uncurled from her ankles and knees. She slumped back against the booth, a panting mess.

Ros kissed her hot cheek once and handed her a glass of water. "Good girl."

She glared at him and mouthed "you're a dead man" as the server walked up to their table.

30

Rosier

No matter her pleading, Ros had insisted they walk home. He wanted as many people as possible to see her while he held her hand. He thought it would be fun to show off Ellea and to meet her friends or neighbors. But he quickly grew angry—not that she noticed. She was too busy pointing out all of her favorite places, the best cafes, and even her favorite bookstore. Despite the late hour, the city was bustling with humans and supernaturals, mostly witches and a handful of supernaturals Ros was too distracted to identify. He was distracted by the witches that were openly gawking at her, not him. The looks weren't the awed ones she deserved, but indignation. Some of them even looked afraid. Ros didn't know how to handle it. He wanted to shout at them, growl, or even kick a few tables. Instead, he held her hand and smiled as she pointed at her favorite herb shop.

Finally, they arrived at her home, and before he could ask her about those nasty looks, her grandmother had thrown open the doors and run out to hug her and kiss every inch of her face. Ros looked over the two witches and met the stare of her uncle, Felix, who gave him a knowing look. "Rough walk?" he seemed to ask. Ros flexed his shoulders and put a small smile on his face as he grasped Jadis by her hand and kissed it once.

"Jadis," he said, forcing himself to look into her searching green eyes. Her face was stern for a split second, and then she smiled back at him. "Rosier."

They walked together to the front door. Ellea wrapped herself around her uncle's middle, seeming like a small child. It reminded him of how young she still was. He shook Felix's hand while she still clung to him.

"I missed you both so much," she mumbled into her uncle's chest.

"I'm not surprised to see you in one piece, Zaza," Felix said, pulling her off of him by her shoulders and searching her from head to toe with a smile. "I heard there was a sword?"

"There was, but we thought it would be best not to walk down the streets with it." Ellea looked at him, and he widened his smile. She saw right through it.

"I'm surprised you didn't show up to the council meeting with a crown on after all I heard about your trip to Hel," Jadis said, grabbing Ellea by the hand and leading her inside.

Ellea looked back over her shoulder, mouthing "sorry" as her grandmother dragged her to the couch. Jadis shooed away the napping Garm and Billy before plopping down next to Ellea on the plush velvet cushions.

"I'll give you a tour after my interrogation," Ellea called from the couch as Felix led him to a vast kitchen.

The house was so much bigger than her family's cabin. He felt like he could fit his whole home in the kitchen and living room alone.

Felix grabbed four mugs from the cabinets. He placed the cups near the espresso machine as the giant hunk of metal came to life on its own, grinding coffee and pouring milk into a pitcher. Ros tried to stop the plate of cookies that came flying toward him with an upturned hand; chips, a multi-layered sandwich, and an assortment of fruit followed quickly behind.

"I'm fine," he growled to the house, and Felix chuckled, turning toward him.

"So how'd you like the city?"

"Seems to be infested with a bunch of asshole witches," Ros grumbled, taking a seat at the island.

"They aren't all that bad, but they don't care that it was her parents that fucked with a bunch of mortals. They see the daughter of two monsters who murdered with no regret and who almost ruined things for our whole community. Then you mix her powers into that and... well, it was hard for her growing up, but she's learned to ignore it."

"She shouldn't have to ignore it." It came out like a hiss, and Felix arched a brow at him. He took a steadying breath. "She is more than her parents, more than her powers."

"I know that, my mother and you know that," Felix whispered. "But the council and our community may never see that. It doesn't help when she retaliates with her tricks and small backlashes."

"That is nothing. I wanted to burn the place to the ground after the tenth witch sneered at her."

Felix shook his head, and four mugs floated around him. One landed in Ros' hands as the other three flew into the living room to join Ellea and Jadis.

"You're being pretty decent when my father was the one to kidnap her and bring her to Hel for almost two weeks." Ros glanced between both of them, then eyed Ellea as a mug and the plate of cookies Ros had refused floated to her. She scooted over.

He could sit next to her.

"Thank you," she said, smiling up to the ceiling as though the house had a mind that lived in the attic.

As soon as she was settled, her mug in hand and a cookie in the other, she leaned into him. She wasn't at all acting like they were about to talk about her kidnapping, her parents killing over a thousand people, and probably several other uncomfortable things.

"So your father kidnapped my granddaughter," Jadis said blandly.

Ellea rolled her eyes and pressed into him like she wanted to guard him from her grandmother.

"Yeah, and it was fine," Ellea said.

Felix cocked his head at her. "It was not fine. We were worried."

Ellea waved her hand before taking a long sip of her drink, moaning around the rim of the mug. "You had nothing to worry about."

"None of us knew that," Ros added. "And I'm sorry you two had to worry. I never thought my father would do something like that."

"You told us it was to get you home, which seemed to work," Jadis said. "Now you're back, but only because of"—she paused as though words hurt her to say—"my daughter and her husband?"

"Speaking of those ass-hats," Ellea cut in. "What's the plan?"

Ros couldn't help it as his shadows curled possessively around Ellea's waist, ready to pull her away at the mention of her parents.

"We can't trust the vampires on the council, so besides Rosier's lead, I'm not sure."

"I want to head to Glenover tomorrow to talk with Sam," Ros said. "The west coast pack is still in the area, and they may have some insight on Vlad's brother."

Felix and Jadis both nodded in approval.

"Now, back to your father, Rosier," Jadis said pointedly, sitting taller. "What are his intentions with Ellea? Is he trying to force you two to marry? Is he holding her over your head for something—"

"Nana!" Ellea squeaked.

"No one is getting married," Ros said quickly, hearing both Billy and Garm chuff from their spots on the carpet.

It was true; no matter the pain Ellea's flinch caused him and the coldness she left as she leaned away, he would not subject her to the curse of the kings. She didn't deserve a life in Hel, looking over her shoulder and wondering when the time would come for her to die. He couldn't bear a life without her in it, but as long as she was alive, he would learn to live without her.

"Why didn't you tell me I'm a descendent of Loki?" Ellea said roughly, seeming to try and fill in the silence. "You, my tutors, and even Cato never mentioned it."

His shadows squeezed harder again. Her fucking father. Where was he in all of this?

"We're all descendants from some God or deity," Felix said. "It didn't seem important."

"Well, I find it important. Where I come from is important. I know being a trickster is scary for me and those around me, but I've learned so much from the library in Hel and from Azzy—"

"Azzy?" Jadis questioned with a furrowed brow. It was such a signature Ellea look.

"King Asmodeus," Ellea said, as though it was nothing.

"You call the King of the Gods 'Azzy?'" Jadis looked offended for his father as she placed a hand to her chest. "To his face?"

"For someone who never spoke of the man, you are very concerned about my nickname for him." Ellea placed the mug on the table and crossed her arms. "Are you hiding something from me, Nana?"

Jadis rolled her eyes and Ros instantly knew how Ellea had learned her signature bratty move.

"Don't be mad at me for not telling you about Hel, it wasn't—"

"Important? What other non-important things are you not telling me?" Ellea said, a bit harshly. "You've spent my whole life protecting me, training me, and for what? So I can learn there is so much more to our realms, to my magic, in the span of three months? I'm twenty-nine years old; there was plenty of time for you to explain a few more things to me."

"You're practically immortal, Zaza," Felix said. "There is plenty of time to learn about the cruel world we live in. You had a rough start, so please forgive us if we wanted you to live a simpler life for a bit longer."

Ros placed a hand on her shoulder, squeezing once, and she finally leaned into him.

"I'm a billion years old and I only learned about tricksters three months ago," Ros said jokingly, kissing her on the temple.

He wanted to tell her that there were going to be plenty of things for her to learn, for them to learn together, but it would be a lie. So he squeezed her shoulder again, and she looked up at him with a smirk.

"Regardless, can we please stop with the secrets?" she asked all of them.

"You know we can't promise that," Jadis said. "We are old and fickle...I've probably forgotten most of the important things. I only get reminded of them when something major happens, like you getting kidnapped or falling in love with a demon prince—"

"We aren't..." Ellea interrupted before shutting her mouth with a snap.

It was Ros' turn to flinch; he tried hiding it by looking down into his empty mug and ignoring the stares from the two beasts on the floor. Why would they be in love? They barely knew each other, and he'd been such an ass. This would end eventually, they might as well keep their feelings out of it.

But she's been calling you her boyfriend.

He shook the thought. This would end eventually.

Are you sure about that? Garm said in his head, reading his thoughts.

Ros stood at the edge of Ellea's giant bed as she washed up in the joined bathroom. She had given him a quick tour after her grandmother and uncle left, and they'd stopped here. It was nearly midnight, and they both seemed exhausted after the day's events. He'd had so many plans for after their little moment in the restaurant, but they were all burning in a trashcan somewhere.

"The bed doesn't bite." Ellea walked up next to him, and he tried to hide his snarl. Visions of her with other men wouldn't stop flashing through his mind.

"I don't think I can sleep in a bed knowing that any of those males…"

He let the statement trail away. What was he saying? Breathing out, he glanced at Ellea, who looked at him with her eyebrow cocked and her fists clenching and unclenching at her side.

Fuck.

"The only one who has ever stayed in this bed has been Billy." She crossed her arms over her chest. "*I'm sorry* I didn't hand you a list of every bed I've fucked someone else in. This one isn't on it."

She turned and stomped to her closet.

317

Fuck.

Gods, he was an ass. Ellea stomped right back into the room, wearing an oversized t-shirt. Angrily, she pulled back the blankets and got into bed. He closed his eyes, his lips thinning into a straight line.

She was mad enough to wear something to bed; she never wore anything to bed.

"Princess," he started. He stopped, unsure of what to say, unsure of which part she was mad at. Was it the bed comment? Or the awkward way the conversation went with her nana and uncle?

Probably both.

"I'm tired, Ros. If you don't want to sleep in here, you can sleep in any of the guest rooms, but know that they have been slept in before."

"Ellea, I am not going to bed with you mad," he said, sitting on her side of the bed, still fully clothed.

"I'm not." Her eyes were downcast, watching as her fingers toyed with the silky fabric of her comforter.

"I don't believe you." He grabbed her hand. "What's on your mind?"

She looked up at him with big gray eyes, and he felt his chest heave. "Today was a lot. Can we please go to bed?"

"I thought we weren't keeping secrets anymore."

"I could tell you the same thing." She pulled her hand away, and a chill ran up his arm. Without another word or look, she turned away from him and placed her beautiful head on the pillow.

He wasn't keeping secrets; he was keeping his feelings and fears from her. She didn't need to bear them on top of everything else weighing on her shoulders.

31

Rosier

os turned over, reaching for Ellea, but found her side of the bed empty. Scrambling out of bed, he summoned a dagger out of his shadows.

"Ellea!" he called.

Ros was about to leave the bedroom and search for her when he heard the shower running. In five long strides, he was in the bathroom and surrounded by steam. Ellea was in there, standing still under the scalding water. Already naked, he ripped the door open and stormed toward her. She didn't flinch, only glared at him under wet lashes. He wasn't having any of that. Grasping her by the throat, he pressed her against the heated tile, and stared at her. He didn't squeeze, only held her there as the panic slowly faded away. When her beautiful eyes opened, he saw her anger still simmering from the night before. They glared at each other.

"What?" she spat.

"You weren't there when I woke up," Ros grumbled. He leaned in close, towering over her. She let out a breath and wrapped her small hand around his wrist, not to pull away but to hold him. His head fell to hers, pressing their foreheads together. He breathed in her rose-scented soap.

"Isn't that something you need to get used to?" The look she gave him was so sharp compared to the way she held his wrist. It took him a second to understand where this was coming from, but then she continued. "Isn't that what last night was about? No one is getting married because you don't see a future for us? I'm not asking to get married, I'm asking for time, for you to not end things because of something you fear."

If only she knew all he dreamt of last night was a life with her, a wedding. Between his father and Jadis, it had been floating in the back of his mind. It would have been in that valley overlooking all of Glenover's lakes and forests. She would have worn anything but white, and it would have been only their friends and family. Then all of Glenover would be at the farm to celebrate, making her extremely uncomfortable, but she would endure it so that he could show her off, fully his.

His court would be equally excited; balls and parties would last weeks as they celebrated her, practically worshiping her like they had his mother. But the dreams quickly turned to nightmares. No longer was Ellea walking with souls or being chased by little demon children. She was brutalized and left for dead in the throne room. Like his mother. Like the curse promised.

"I will not take the chance." It was all he could get out; he had to hide her from his dreams as much as his nightmares.

She didn't answer; she shoved his hand away and went to leave. He grabbed her wrist roughly, stopping her, but her magic reacted with sparks crackling across her skin.

"You're being a child." He didn't mean it as the words left his stupid mouth. He didn't know how to fix this.

"And you're being a stubborn old man." She pulled her hand away with more strength than he remembered her having. "We talked about this; I'm not going anywhere."

"I remember what you said." He did; she hadn't planned on leaving, but she was not in Hel anymore. Maybe now that she was out, she would realize that she needed to stay away. "Regardless of what you said, I still don't want you there."

"You don't want me there, you don't want me...is there anything else you don't want?"

"I don't want you to be like this! Can we enjoy our time?"

"Our time? What fucking time, Rosier? That got derailed by my parents and your father. I thought you wanted us to date, to try the relationship thing. We have done none of that, and it's clear to me now that you never planned on this going anywhere."

She tried storming out of the shower, but Ros caught her by the arm. She let out a sob. His heart clamped hard enough that he lost his breath; this isn't how it was supposed to go, he was supposed to be taking every moment he had and enjoying all of it with her. Of course, he wanted all of that, but that wasn't how things worked out.

"Ellea," he said, pulling on her. "I wanted all of that. I still want all of that. But being home, seeing what you went through while you were there...I don't want that life for you."

"It sounds like you don't want a life with me." She wouldn't turn to look at him. "I thought we talked about this, but I was wrong, and you were only entertaining my ideas."

He searched the side of her face, her tears mixing with the steam.

"No, I was entertaining my own dreams and hurt you instead."

"You forget, Ros." She turned toward him. "Every time you underestimate me, I prove you wrong."

"What does that mean?" he asked, furrowing his brow.

"I don't give up as easily as you do."

By the time Ros left the shower and got dressed, Ellea had dried her hair, dressed, and made them coffee. Or the house had. A mug waited for him on the island, and Ellea was sitting on the back porch with Billy's head in her lap.

"Well," Garm said, walking into the kitchen in his human form. "You're an idiot."

"Tell me something I don't know." He sipped his coffee, one he didn't deserve, and watched Ellea idly stroke Billy's head. "What am I supposed to do? You've lived in Hel longer than I've been alive. You know how it is there, what everyone is like. The curse...no ruler of Hel will have someone rule beside them."

"I think you should talk to your father," Garm said, also watching Billy and Ellea. "And stop trying to make decisions for El; it's clear where she wants to be, and that's with you in Hel."

"Really? Because yesterday and this morning are telling me something different."

No matter how much her words hurt the night before, it gave him a bit of horrible hope that maybe she didn't care for him enough. Enough that she could walk away.

"You dumb boy." Garm growled and turned toward him. "Because she said she wasn't in love? After you said no one was getting married and days after you told her you didn't want her in Hel? Both of you are blind and extremely tiring. There is too much going on for you both to be so hung up on ignoring your feelings and desires."

"My desires aren't possible, and you know it."

Garm shook his head, letting out a sigh.

"I know how possible your desires are, how possible it is for the both of you to get what you truly want. You're the one who doesn't see it."

"Ellea doesn't belong in Hel, I do, and—"

"I swear to the Gods, boy," Garm said, slamming the hard marble countertop they leaned against. "If you finish that sentence, I'm going to slice your cock off and shove it down your throat. Enough. Go talk to your father; I'm done with you, we all are."

Garm glared at him for a moment as he towered over him, making Ros feel like the small child he was when they first met.

"All four of us are going to portal to Sam's." Garm's voice was stern, commanding, and Ros couldn't help but dip his chin. "Then you are going to go to your father, tell him the plan, and talk to him about your future. Figure your shit out and don't come back until you know what you want."

"I know what—"

"You don't get to speak," he seethed in his face. "Figure out what you want and know you can have it. Don't come back until you have a plan. Ellea deserves more than half promises and your grumpy ass."

Ros snapped his gaping mouth closed as Garm walked out to the back porch. He watched him tug on Billy's ear and then touch Ellea's cheek lightly. He said something Ros couldn't make out, and Ellea smiled sadly at him.

He knew he was an ass, but he didn't know how his father would give him insight on the issue. He had clearly lost his mind in his old age if he was entreating the idea of Ros and Ellea being together. The king, of all people, knew how cruel the curse was.

Maybe he knows something you don't.

Ros shook his head. Things were the way they were, and that was how they had been since the Gods left.

Ros didn't like leaving Ellea behind, but as they shadowed onto Sam's farm, their friends greeted them. Duhne and Florence were there too. She was safe here, and he knew nothing would happen to her. He would make it quick, and he told her as much. She only stared up at him, looking sad and tired.

She leaned into his touch before he disappeared into shadow, stepping out into his father's study. Looking down at his hand, a drop of Ellea's tears clung to his skin. He gripped his fist and looked up to his father, who wore a knowing look on his face.

Part Three

"Hearts are wild creatures, that's
why our ribs are cages."
- Elalusz

32

Rosier

It was bright in his father's study as Hel's morning sun crested the mountain outside of the large window. The king wore a simple black linen shirt tucked into his black pants; Ros couldn't remember a time he hadn't worn a suit.

"Father," Ros said.

"Rosier."

"Is it a dress-down day?"

"I finished training twenty minutes ago and felt your need to come home." He nodded toward the door that would lead them toward the small hall. "I didn't think a suit was needed for the conversation we're about to have."

"And how do you know what I came here to talk about?"

"I don't need Ellea's powers to know why you're coming home, without her, after being gone a day."

"What if I'm only here to tell you about our plan to get her parents?" Ros cocked a brow at him as they stopped in front of his suite's doors. His father shook his head and led them to two armchairs in front of a roaring fire.

"You could have sent Duhne or Florence, and I doubt you have a grand plan this soon."

Ros grunted; his father had always been too intuitive. He could never get away with anything as a child.

"Do you still blame me? Do you still hate me so much that you can't bring yourself to confide in me on what troubles you?"

"What troubles me?" Ros hissed. "All of it is because of you!"

"I do not control the strings of fate." He said it so calmly, but Ros couldn't miss the glimmer of sadness in his eyes.

"No," Ros growled, searching for the right words. "You're the reason I was born, why I'm destined to rule after you, and why I cannot be with the woman I love." Ros choked on the last word, and his eyes were wide as his father grinned at him.

"And why can't you be with the woman you love, son?" The smug bastard didn't even try to hide how happy he was.

"You know why!"

"Do I?"

"Have you gone mad in your old age?" Ros seethed. "The curse! The reason my mother is dead, why no other ruler has someone ruling beside them."

His father stared at him coolly, waiting for him to calm down.

"Do you remember the day I told you about the curse?"

Ros nodded his head; of course he did. He was about ten, sneaking looks into his father's many volumes in his office.

"You were so small then," he said with a distant look in his hazel eyes. "So young. I remember you on the floor with one of my giant journals in your lap. You asked me about the saying—"

"'The binding of the Gods' chosen and their promised will amend the lapse of the realms. The chosen must seek the Creator Of Chaos and Bringer Of Shadows. Until they are forged, there will only be death,'" Ros recited word for word. "You also told me then that it was about you and mother."

Ros looked down at his hands; the memory was still fresh in his mind from his journey through the Gods' woods and his nightmares last night.

"And at that time, I thought it was true," Asmodeus said with a sigh. "You know I never chose her because of the prophecy. It was fate, and I loved her more than old words and curses."

"That doesn't change anything with Ellea." His words were bitter.

The curse was still alive, and she needed to stay far away from it.

"You were never meant to rule alone," he said, and Ros whipped his head to him. "You remember the destruction that followed your mother's death, all those I killed, all those I interrogated. It wasn't only to find her killer."

They had never found her murderer, but Ros had always blamed Beelzebub. He was always jealous of them, of how his father was more powerful thanks to the Gods' blessings.

"I stormed the Gods' territory, furious and crazed with loss," his father said with a sad smile. "I rode for days, hunting for their resting spot and leaving damage in my path. Loki was actually the one who found me."

"You never told me that." He knew his father had been with the Gods before they retired, but to hear about them being awake, able to be hunted down...

"You'd left by the time I came back," his father said, cutting into his train of thought. "Loki stopped me before I could reach all of them, and he told me the truth. The prophecy was never about me; it was about you and his chosen."

"His chosen? You were his chosen, you were all the Gods' chosen." Ros was confused.

"I was, but only because I was a fair ruler and destined to have you. You were always meant to find his chosen…his descendent."

His descendent?

Ros felt the color drain from his face.

"No," he whispered.

"Why?" his father asked with a cock of his head. "Why not her? She thrives here, she is stronger than any of us, and she can learn to rule. She was already putting the work in and she didn't even know she was destined for it."

"No," Ros said again.

"You can't stop it." He said it with so much certainty, Ros almost believed him. "I'm not asking you to start tomorrow; you have time. You both have a lot to learn and a lot to do."

Ros shook his head. It couldn't be. This was too much.

"What are you afraid of?"

"Her getting hurt, this place corrupting her." He breathed out a shuddering breath as horrible visions flashed through his mind. "Her dying."

"There is only so much we can protect her from, but don't let your fear get in the way of loving her, of her knowing and feeling your love. You both deserve to be happy, and if what I've learned from the Gods and from history is true, you are both on a path to turn worlds upside down."

Ros searched his father's face before he crumbled into his hands.

"I don't know how to do this," he groaned.

He was an idiot and had fucked up so much. Ellea was furious with him, and she had every right to be.

"I don't know if she feels the same way," he whispered into his hands. "How could she care for someone like me? She is so much better than us, better than demons."

"Loki, give me strength," his father grumbled. "You are too old to be this naïve. She could not care less about what you are; she cares about who you are and how honest you are with her. I will bet my favorite sword you have told her none of your feelings."

"It's been months…" He trailed off.

"I don't know why the Gods planned for two of the most powerful beings to be so stubborn and blind *and* to have them be destined for each other. It feels like a curse for anyone they care about."

The king shook his head, and Ros rolled his eyes.

Destined for each other.

Was that what he had always felt? That pull to her? Maybe he could kill everyone in the courts and start over? He shook his head like his father, who was smirking at him.

"You aren't helping," Ros said, banging his head against the chair. "I still don't like it, but I love her."

"Focus on that; the rest will come when it's time."

"Gods, I fucked up," Ros grumbled.

"And you will probably do it a lot more." His father laughed. "You are immortal."

"Wait." Ros sat up as another issue arose. "Ellea isn't immortal, not really, and an heir…"

That had to be something.

"She is a descendent of a God; she is more immortal than a mere witch who gave up a part of her."

"But—"

"Focus on now, son," his father said sternly. "Love her, tell her how you feel, get her parents, and then love her some more. We have a long time before you need to worry about anything else."

It couldn't be that simple. They had been so up and down since day one, how was he going to move forward? What if she didn't have any interest in forever?

Forever.

That had never been an option for him; but as visions of them together flooded him, he felt lighter.

"I need to apologize," he said, thinking. "Viatrix?"

His father gave him a knowing smile as she appeared between their chairs with a bow.

"Yes, my prince?" she said with a bored tone.

"I need a book," Ros said, and she rolled her eyes.

"Of course you do."

33

Ellea

The sun had set over an hour ago, and Ros still wasn't back. Ellea tried to not worry; no matter how mad she was, she still cared if he was in one piece. What if Belias got to him? What if his father didn't let him leave? What if several things happened while she wasn't there to keep him safe? She sighed and shivered against the chilly night air. Sam had lit the bonfire without Ros, and she was thankful. She felt so cold without him. She stepped closer to the warmth of the flames dancing before her. It was smaller than a celebratory bonfire, and all the wolven could manage in a short time. Tonight was a full moon and the perfect time to celebrate the alpha coming home. It was also a great way to give thanks to all the wolven who had stepped in to help while they were all gone.

There were only minor attacks while they were in Hel. A water demon trying to drag a child to its cold depths, a minor vampire attack, then a minor scuffle between the packs. All events were quickly taken care of, and even the child was unharmed. Ellea had met the boy earlier with the rest of the town's children. He told her of his battle, making it sound like an epic fairy tale. Ellea listened intently as he told his tale and then showed him a few simple defense moves. With him being so small, it would be best to go for the eyes or scratch as much as he could.

Ellea actually spent her night with the children, turning her nose and eyes different shapes and colors, and creating miniature versions of their favorite creatures. She even helped some kids make crowns out of wildflowers and fall leaves. But she didn't understand how they kept them on the entire night; they itched something horrible. She wouldn't admit she was hiding from her friend's sad looks, but she was.

Where the fuck is Ros?

Maybe they needed to fight it out; maybe she should tell him how she felt. Maybe he could stop being such a stubborn old bastard. Yes, Hel was cut-throat, vicious, and dangerous. You couldn't walk down a dark hallway without wondering if some demon from Belias' court was going to snatch you up. But she had managed, she'd learned, and she was stronger than ever. Then there were the politics, the rules, and the separation. If she wasn't there to help drive Hel to a new path, who would? Azzy helped her, but he was only one king. In order for change to happen, it has to be constant moves along the chessboard. It would take time, meaning she needed to be there often. Ellea scoffed out loud; this was stupid. Ros wasn't here. Maybe she could steal a horse or car and go back to her cabin. She glared at the fire, thinking how she could sneak out before her friends could stop her. Turning quickly, she went to stomp away, but ran right into a hard body.

"Fuck," she said, falling back. Powerful hands caught her.

Ros.

Ellea looked up into his handsome face, and his eyes were wide with wonder.

"I think I prefer the flowers over the shiny crowns my father made you wear."

Her breath caught at the sight of dimples and fangs. He was too handsome—and too happy after their horrible night and morning.

Did Azzy kick his ass when he went home?

Ellea hoped so.

"I don't know." She scratched her head. "The kids picked the flowers and leaves, and I'm pretty sure I have bugs in my hair now."

"Bugs and all, you look like a queen." Compared to what she'd worn in Hel, her outfit was hardly worthy of royalty. It was just her beloved boots, leggings, her new favorite sweater, and the jacket he'd given her for motorcycle rides. But she was glad he liked this too; it was way easier.

He ran his thumb across her cheek, and she leaned in to the touch, swallowing her bratty retort.

He shouldn't say things like that when he didn't see a future for them. She wasn't striving to be a queen, but she wanted to be with him, to help him with Hel, anything to be in his life for as long as she could.

"I was about to go home." She sounded breathless as he kept stroking her face.

"Can you wait for me? I wanted to make the rounds and then I'll take you home. We need to finish what happened this morning." She huffed a breath, and he must have taken that as a yes; he grabbed her hand and led her toward a group of wolven.

"What took you so long to get here?" *And why are you so happy?* "I was worried."

He gave her another smile and kissed her hand. "I'm sorry, but I think it will be worth it later."

"More secrets?"

"No." He laughed as she grumbled. He seemed so calm, almost content. "A present you will have to wait for until I show my face to the wolven who have been taking care of things while we were gone."

"I don't need presents." She stomped her foot and stopped him before he could keep dragging her. "I need—"

"I know what you need," he interrupted. "Be patient, we have time."

Ellea pressed her lips into a thin line, but he only smiled at her. Maybe his father really had kicked his ass.

Ros seemed to have left his grumpy pants in Hel as he graciously met with every small group and talked with each of them for a few minutes. All the wolven greeted him with smiles and hard punches to the shoulder. One even put him in a headlock and gave him a rough rubbing on his head before he growled and twisted the man's arm behind his back. The encounter ended in laughs, and Ellea had to walk away to find some semblance of sanity.

She found Florence and Billy spread out on a blanket near the fire, both looking up at the full moon. Ellea dramatically threw herself down next to them.

"I see our prince has arrived in one piece," Florence said with a wave of her hand.

"I'm not so sure it's him." It came out as a grumble, and she didn't have the energy or desire to reel in her attitude. "Do you have shapeshifters in Hel?"

"Only you and Loki, from what I remember," she answered, and

Billy chuffed in agreement. "Maybe it's your father? We haven't had word of his whereabouts in a while."

"No, I don't think it's him."

It was definitely Ros, but she wasn't ready to admit he wasn't as stubborn as her. How could he change his mood so quickly after being such a jerk? This wasn't the plan. After the restaurant, she'd had so many dirty ideas, and then she'd gotten cockblocked by her nana and uncle and then again by Ros' stupid mood. Now she didn't know where they were in their fight or their relationship.

Devon flopped down with them, using Ellea's thighs as a pillow.

"I see Ros is back," he said in greeting.

"Mhmm."

"Did you get tired of the hand shaking too?"

"Yeah, what is with that? Ros hates people."

"Nah, he doesn't hate everyone. Some of the wolven and him go way back."

Ellea mumbled something incoherent.

"Kind of like not everyone hates you?" Devon poked her in the stomach, and she swatted him on the head.

"Come with me to Halifax and then tell me that. I thought Ros was going to eat some of them."

Ellea was a pro at ignoring the looks and glares, but with Ros vibrating next to her, it had been a battle to stop her powers from answering his. They always came alive when he was around, when they fought or fucked. It should scare her, but she only felt excitement.

Devon huffed a laugh. "I'll come if Ros comes. I want to watch him eat some bitchy witches."

Ellea sat up on her elbows to look down at Devon, who had a wicked smirk on his face.

"When did you become so bloodthirsty?"

"Who said I wasn't always like this?"

Ellea looked toward Florence, who only shrugged, and to Billy, who was snoring.

"Am I in a different realm?" Ellea asked, bouncing looks between all three of them. "Did I get off on the wrong exit when we came back from Hel?"

"No," Florence said. "You are surrounded by a bunch of touchy beasts and we all have masks; you'll get used to them. I'm slowly getting used to yours."

"And how many masks do I have?" she asked with mock sweetness.

"Five," both Devon and Ros said at the same time.

She hadn't noticed Ros walking over.

"Five?" she questioned.

"One, when you're fighting and act as though you aren't tired or worried," Ros answered.

Devon added, "Two, when you're pretending you are present but you're actually stuck in an old memory."

"Three, when you are in front of the kings or council members. You look bored, but your magic is screaming to tear them apart." Ros said it with so much fire in his eyes.

"Four, when you meet a new person, you act standoffish or mean because you are protecting yourself," Devon said.

"And five," Ros added finally, "when your magic is burning up inside of you and you play it off as if you don't feel a thing."

"Well," Ellea said, standing up quickly and not giving Devon a chance to move. "I'm glad you both have so much fun trying to figure me out."

"It's because we care." Ros stopped her before she could storm off. "We aren't asking you to take them off. We're here for you, and we understand."

Ellea didn't know what to say as she looked between Ros and Devon, who seemed to be trying to say the same thing.

"Are you done?" she asked. "Can we go home now?"

She loved her friends who were now her family, but today was too much. The whole year had been too much.

"Yes, princess," he said, grabbing her by the back of the neck and kissing her on the forehead. "I have a book I want to give you at my place."

Ellea blinked up at him. She couldn't stop the smile that spread across her face.

"If you want me to suck your cock again, you don't need to use a fake book as an excuse," she said as her friends groaned and covered their ears.

His smile was all dimples and fangs, making her quickly forget why they were fighting in the first place.

34

Rosier

R os watched the ice crack throughout Ellea. Slowly, she was thawing after all he'd put her through. He would learn to be patient. All day, he'd planned the first step for the rest of their lives. Viatrix had helped him scour the library for a particular book, then his father had helped him search the human territory for its author. Ros smirked as he stormed up his stairs, Ellea shuffling behind him. The book had been in his jacket pocket the whole time, but he wanted to recreate their first night together.

"Seriously, Ros," she huffed behind him.

He only smiled wider and rushed to his room. He turned in place, pulling the book out of his pocket as she entered the room.

"Oh, you actually—actually have a book." Her eyes danced between him and the book, and he continued to try to be patient.

"Yes, princess." He stepped toward her, feeling that pull that he never gave much mind to. "It's why it took me so long to get here."

She took it from him, and he saw how her hand trembled a little. She looked at the spine, and her eyes shot up to him.

"How?" He barely heard her say it.

"I had a mean librarian help me." His heart beat erratically in his chest as he watched her, still holding the book closed. "She had a hard time letting it go. Apparently, *Coming in a Crypt* is one of her favorites."

"Viatrix reads C. Clair!" Ellea exclaimed, almost dropping the book. *Please open it.*

"She knows C. Clair."

Ellea's gaze whipped up to him. "What?" she screeched, practically vibrating.

"Next time we go to Hel, I'll introduce you." His voice broke, and he coughed to clear it.

Ellea gasped, clutching the still-closed book to her chest, and he couldn't take it.

"Calm down and open the fucking book," he growled.

Ellea gave him a confused look but slowly opened the first page.

"OMG, the details of these papers… Is this gold?" she said, holding it to the light. "How she keeps them in such good condition—"

"The next page," he growled again, and she rolled her eyes.

"Who was talking about patience earlier?" she scolded.

Slowly, she turned to the title page, where he'd had the author scribble a note for Ellea before signing her name. Ellea let out a sob, and the book shook in her hand.

My dearest Ellea,

Please come back to Hel to help Ros make things right. I would very much love to meet you and be able to meet all the wonderful beasts I spent my living life writing about. I would also love to share some stories I've written in my afterlife with you.

C. Clair

"What..." Her eyes glistened as she looked up at him, searching his face. "Wait."

"I was a jerk, and I said the wrong things. I will always want to protect you, want you safe; but where you are, where you want to be, that isn't my decision to make." He walked to her; he needed to hold her and have her understand all he was trying to convey.

"Ros, what are you saying?"

"When all of this is done with your parents, I want to know if you will help me in Hel, help my father, my family. They—no, *we*—need you."

He wanted to say so much more. He'd almost asked the author to write "rule beside me," but he needed to take small steps. He needed to know how she felt.

Her mouth opened once, twice, and finally, she found her words. "You don't want to end things with me?"

"Gods no, I never wanted that. I didn't know what I was saying," he said, but that wasn't right and she knew it. "Hel's history is cursed, and after talking with my father, I realized I have the wrong information. Regardless, it should have always been your choice where you go. I won't stop you from being in Hel. I want you wherever I am."

"Will you stop hiding your demon from me?" Her small hand fell to his chest, and that one touch almost had him crumbling. He was sure she could feel his heart racing.

"Can we take small steps, please?" he asked quietly. "I want to move forward, not back or sideways."

"Okay, big man." She bit her lip. "Small steps."

She grasped him behind the neck with her free hand and pulled him down to her lips. The kiss was searing, and he wrapped his arms around her to press her body against his.

He finally took a steadying breath as she relaxed in his hold. There had been a chance she would have thrown the book at him and cursed his dick for how stupid he was. He breathed her in and relished her sweet scent, one that was becoming laced with arousal.

"Wait," she said, pulling away. She placed the book gently on his desk.

He reached for her, ready to pick the kiss back up, but she stopped him with a hand on his chest.

"No." She *tsk*ed. He was lost, lost in her and how far they'd come, and then she pushed him so hard he fell onto his bed—naked.

Ellea hadn't even blinked, hadn't even flinched, and she could make his clothes disappear. He pressed onto his elbows and sucked in a breath at the sight of her. Her leggings and sweater had been replaced with black lace things he had never seen on her. Her top was cut high, a silk bow wrapped around her neck, but the base had a scoop, revealing the bottom of her small breasts. It barely hid her peaked nipples. A garter belt hugged her stomach, and its straps criss-crossed her thick hips. The tight straps stopped mid-thigh, where three small obsidian daggers were tucked away on each leg.

"Fucking Gods." He swallowed hard, groaning. "Where were you hiding that?"

"I created it," she said slyly, caressing the frilly lace bottoms.

"So you're still mad?" He hoped so. The thought had him hardening. And those daggers...

Fucking Hel.

"Oh yes, I am still furious." She slowly kneeled to the ground in front of him.

Ros didn't have words for how fucking sexy—how dangerous—she looked. Dangerous for her powers and the sharp objects decorating her perfect thighs. Also dangerous for how much of his soul she held in those hands that grasped the back of his calves, yanking him closer to the edge of the bed. He shuffled back to his elbows, not wanting to miss anything. She stared up at him under her lashes, a wicked smirk spread across her face as her newly grown claws slowly walked up his thighs. Gripping him hard, she sent waves of electricity through him, and he let out a strangled yelp as the pain shot straight to his dick.

"Mmmm," she hummed, licking her lips as she eyed the pre-cum escaping his already too-hard erection.

"Fuck," he cursed, long and low.

Her devilish eyes were fixed on his as she leaned in, licking him from base to tip, swirling her tongue around the wetness before opening her mouth to swallow him whole. Pleasure shot up his spine, followed by pain as she shocked him again, forcing him to buck down her throat. She gagged around him, and he was going to pull away, but she only gripped him tighter. Releasing him with a *pop*, she caught her breath before cleaning him with her tongue.

Again and again, she shocked him and swallowed him so hard he could see stars. He couldn't help the embarrassing panting noises that escaped his mouth, the whimpering after she released him. He was so caught up in her torture, he didn't realize he was slipping further into himself. Red and black veins spread across his skin; instead of staring in shock, Ellea ran her tongue along them, humming appreciatively.

"Small steps," she cooed, nipping at his skin that was so hot with lust and dark power.

Ros let out a growl, trying to press his demon back down, but the air was full of her magic, her arousal, even her love. He could taste it, making his mouth water with the need to feast on the power in her blood and the wetness he knew was sticking to her thighs. She seemed to sense his want, that her tormenting had to end before the world exploded around them. Ros grabbed her as she stood, not giving her a chance to make the next move. She was under him in an instant, smirking up at his flustered glare. Pinning her legs under his, he welcomed the small stab of her daggers, letting the pain ground him.

"Small steps," he echoed, letting his own claws show.

Tracing them across her skin, a blush followed the trail of their sharp line. It was time for her to pant, to beg. He made quick work of the lace fabric, and with each tear, she whimpered and shifted under him. Her back arched as her breasts were freed to the cold air.

"Ros," she pleaded.

"You had your fun," he growled, tracing her nipple with the sharp tip of his claws.

She sucked in a breath, and when Ros glanced at her, there was barely any gray left; her eyes were blown wide with hunger. Leaning in, he kissed her hard, moving her so her legs could wrap around him. He pressed his hard cock into her, the feeling was foreign with her wearing underwear. He only spent a moment here, grinding her into him, making her suffer through the fabric until she tried reaching for them.

"No," he said, moving away from her so he could rest between her thighs.

One taste, he promised himself as he ran a clawed finger down the fabric, tearing it easily. He groaned at the sight of her, soaked, pink, and desperate to be filled. When he pressed his nose against her clit, inhaling her perfect scent, he almost came against the blanket. When he licked her fully, consuming her from ass to stomach, her legs shuddered, gripping his head hard. He begged to one day die this way.

"Fuck," she growled as he crawled up her body.

She clung to him, fighting to get her center over his throbbing cock, and he obliged, sheathing himself in one hard thrust. They both moaned; she was so hot, so tight, and already pulsing around him.

"Please," she whimpered, nipping at his jaw, his neck, and clawing at his back. "Please fuck me, I need..."

"I know what you need," he grunted, then answered by dragging out to the tip and thrusting into her.

He grabbed her by the back of the neck, stopping her head from rolling back. Her eyes were unfocused, and she mumbled obscenities as he drove into her, hard and slow, feeling every inch of her and rubbing against her clit, driving her to the edge.

"Look at me." It was a demand, but she answered.

It took her a moment, blinking away the lust, and his shadows brushed away the hair sticking to her already sweaty face.

"I see you," she said, grabbing him by the face and clawing at his beard.

He felt seen, cut open and raw. The red light in his demonic eyes glimmered across her pale skin. She brushed a shaking finger across his brow, looking at him with so much wonder. He didn't know what to do other than angle his hips and drive into her harder. He hit that spot that had her crying out and zapping him so hard that a feral growl escaped his lips.

A smirk flashed across her face before pure ecstasy replaced it. She was so close, and with that first clench, her magic came to life. Her sparks danced wildly across her skin, and his shadows greeted them, swaying to their rhythm.

"Ros," she said breathlessly, trying to keep her eyes trained on him. "I need this, always."

Always.

One word held so much promise as their smells mixed, their magic danced, and their powers roared to spend every day side by side.

"Forever," he answered, kissing her roughly.

Their kiss was broken by her guttural cry as she pulled tight before crashing around him. The grip she had, the relentless pulse around his cock, dragged his own release out of him, and they both cried out as he spilled into her. Their breaths were heavy as they stared into each other's eyes, both flayed raw. His embers and her sparks danced and lit their path to something eternal.

35

Ellea

A prince of Hel was drying her hair. He was drying her hair after he'd thoroughly fucked—no. That was not fucking. After that beyond-special *bedding*, after they caught their breaths and whispered promises to each other, he carried her to the shower and cleaned every inch of her. She returned the favor and stopped herself from playing with her favorite thing, not wanting to break whatever spell they had cast.

Now she sat on the floor between his legs, reading a book that shouldn't exist while the all-powerful demon witch dried her hair with his magic.

She'd gotten almost halfway through the book by the time he finished with a kiss on top of her head.

"How's your father?" Closing the book, she crawled into his lap.

"Fine; misses you, of course," he said with his powerful arms wrapped around her. "Did you learn anything new today?"

"Only that all wolven seem to be the same and none seemed against Sam and Devon being a couple."

She had worried there would be family politics, fights to be in charge, and several other things.

"Most of the wolven here are from Sam's generation and don't share the same ideals as their elders." He yawned the last few words and then laid down with her, tucking her to his side.

She magicked a blanket on top of them and shimmied closer to his heat. It was getting so cold at night; she missed the warmth of the castle with its roaring fires in every room. He pulled her in tight, grabbing one of her breasts in his large hand, and she smiled.

"Goodnight, Ros."

"Goodnight, Ellea."

Ellea's heart raced as the cold, wet ground chilled her naked skin. She beat against the walls in her mind to wake up. She needed to take in her surroundings and figure out how she got here. Her arms twitched, then her legs, and finally, she could roll over and stand on two shaking legs. She ran to the closest tree, pressing her back against the rough trunk. Blinking rapidly, she was thankful for the clear moon that lit the surrounding woods. She was still in Glenover, and from the rough boulders that peppered the forest floor, she was in the northern part of the town. It was where she and Ros would travel on his bike to picnic or train with Sam.

Ellea shivered as a breeze blew through the trees, carrying the cackle of two men.

Fuck, fuck, fuck.

How did she get here? Why was she here? The voices grew louder, and Ellea scrambled as quietly as she could, searching for a spot to hide so she could conjure clothes and a weapon. She cursed not having the same magic as Ros; she wanted to portal back to bed. There was a boulder about fifty feet in front of her, if she could just—Ellea froze as the two men came into view.

"Fucking wolven... They're finally gone, and we can move in tomorrow night," a man said, walking in her line of sight but not noticing her.

She stood there, trying to conjure anything to cover herself, but her magic didn't answer.

What the fuck?

"Want to make sure they're far enough away that they can't be called back," the other man added.

Ellea ducked around a tree as the two men walked past.

Vampires.

She could see their pale skin, elongated doubled fangs, and their thin stature. Could they not see her? Was this a dream? She pulled at her magic again, but nothing answered, which was beyond weird with her magic being stronger after her time with Ros. This had to be a dream.

Fuck it.

Ellea jumped out from her hiding spot, but neither vampire noticed.

"It's going to be a bloodbath," the first one said, licking his lips.

"I can't wait to see the looks on their faces," the second one replied, rubbing his hands together.

Ellea trailed after them, waving her hands and throwing rocks, but nothing got their attention. She suddenly heard the wicked snap and crackle of burning trees behind her and whipped around.

The world was burning at her feet. It was her old dream. When she turned around again, she could see the two vampires walking on the same path.

No, no, no.

Ellea ran as hard as she could after the vampires. The world slowed around her as she gained no ground, practically running in place, until everything tipped and she landed on her back. Her mother loomed above her, and Ellea screamed.

Her screams continued as she shot straight up in bed, Ros by her side with a dagger in his hand.

"Ellea!" he called, grasping her face, searching for her for injuries.

She panted, resting her hand on his chest. His heart beat as hard as hers.

"Dream," she breathed. "It was a dream."

She shivered, still feeling the coldness of the night.

"Are you sure?" The dagger disappeared, and he pulled her closer.

His skin lit up as his veins ran red, and she melted into his heat.

"M-maybe," she stuttered.

He squeezed her tighter.

"So much for hoping we would have a restful sleep after our evening." He smirked against her head, kissing her hair.

"I'm okay. It felt quick," she said, thinking back to what she saw. "Did the other wolven leave yet?"

"Not till tomorrow, after they sleep off their hangovers. Why?"

"I saw two vampires, and now I'm wondering if my magic pulled me into a vision," she said lightly, trying to chase away the flicker of fear that had come with the second part of her dream. "They mentioned the wolven had left and said it was the perfect time to attack. They were also in Glenover, near the valley we usually go to."

"Fuck," Ros growled. "We need clothes."

Ellea quickly conjured them both clothes, and Ros instantly portaled them to Sam's bedroom. Ellea smacked his chest as soon as the sounds of what her friends were doing in the darkness reached her ears.

"Playing bottom, Sam?" Ros called from the shadows.

Ellea covered her eyes as Devon and Sam cursed. She heard someone fall to the floor, and Ros laughed beside her.

"You're a fuck nugget," Sam yelled.

Ellea peeked through her fingers to see Sam in bed with a pillow clutched against his crotch and Devon on the floor wrapped around a blanket. She couldn't stop her stomach from dropping every time she saw Sam's scar, a jagged cut from his temple to his beautiful amber eye. And the one across his perfect nose... She wanted to find the demon responsible for them, bring it back to life, and flay it alive.

"Emergency meeting," Ros said, bringing her out of her thoughts. He cocked his head as though he was listening. "Garm is here with Billy."

"At least they had the decency to arrive in the living room," Sam growled. "You're going to pay for this."

"You have five minutes to finish and get dressed." Ros began pushing Ellea out of the bedroom.

She threw an apologetic grimace over her shoulder before Ros led her through the old farmhouse toward the kitchen.

"Does Devon look bigger to you?" Ellea asked.

"Not sure, he was covering his dick up," Ros answered blandly.

"Gods, you suck sometimes." She huffed. "His muscles."

"He's been training harder since your...trip," he said.

More guilt washed over her. Devon had been through so much because they'd "needed" to rescue her from Hel. She wanted to make sure that Devon never needed to worry again. She was glad he was training, but still hated the reasoning.

All of her friends had been through too much because of her, and she cursed how magic could be wonderful and useless at the same time.

Why weren't inter-realm cell phones a thing?

"Maybe Devon can join our training," Ellea said. "Florence, too, when she's here?"

"Maybe," he said thoughtfully. "I've been meaning to brush him up on a few things when we had time. But with your latest vision, that will have to be put on hold."

"What vision?" Billy asked, sidling up beside Ellea to wrap her arm around her waist and kiss her temple.

"We'll talk when Sam and Devon get down here."

"This couldn't have waited?" Garm asked, annoyed.

"No."

Ellea wondered if Ros had also interrupted something between Garm and Billy. She began to feel really sorry for getting in the way of her friends' fun. Not only had their worlds been turned sideways by her parents, they'd gone to Hel for her. And now she was interrupting one of their few free nights.

"Next time, I'm going to call an emergency meeting while you and E are going at it like beasts," Devon grumbled, coming into the kitchen. He gave Ellea an angry peck on the cheek before heading to the fridge.

"Agreed," Sam said, coming in to lean against the wall, glaring at Ros.

"Okay, let's make this quick so we can all get back to what we were doing." Ellea gave Ros a stern look. "I had a dream that may have been a vision."

"It was a vision," Ros added.

"Were you there?" Ellea cocked a brow at the brute.

"We need to contact the other wolven before they head out." Ros ignored her look and question, turning into his commanding self.

"Ellea saw two vampires in her vision. They're waiting to attack until the western pack is too far to be called back. I'm guessing we cannot avoid an attack, but we can rally our numbers to give us the best chances. I want to set up a decoy so that the vampires still think the pack has left us. We'll have to create a protected place for them to stay or illusion their current whereabouts until it's time to fight."

"I'll call Williams now." Sam stood taller, and his alpha look replaced the whiny frustration Ros had caused. "Have him meet us here in the morning. We can solidify our plans then."

"Do we get the council involved?" Ellea asked.

"No, I don't want Vlad getting a jump on us."

"I want to call Duhne and Florence back," Ellea added. "We could use their strengths and powers."

"Agreed. Garm, Billy, interested in a trip to Hel?"

"Now that we can go there the easy way, yes," Billy said. "We can go sleep there tonight and be back by mid-morning, maybe noon."

"Anything else? Okay, good." Ellea was quick with her words, not giving *Commander Ros* time to add more tasks. "I'll see you all in the morning, how about nine?"

"Dawn," Ros growled.

Ellea widened her stance and crossed her arms. With her chin high, she stated, "Nine o'clock." He pressed his lips together, and she added, "Ros will buy us coffees and muffins."

He went to retort, but Ellea kept her glare, and he backed down.

"Get some rest," he said, holding his hand out for Ellea.

"And?" Ellea asked, staying put.

"Sorry for the intrusion," he grumbled.

Devon tried to hide his smirk behind his glass of OJ, and Sam openly chuckled.

"Playing bottom, Ros?" Sam asked with a wicked grin.

Billy laughed too, then gave Ellea a big hug before stepping into Garm so they could portal to Hel.

"We will phone next time," Ellea said, walking toward her grumpy demon.

"They were too busy to answer," Ros added.

"Who's the seer in this relationship?"

Sam quickly kissed her on the cheek before Ros shadowed them back to their own room.

"How did you know they were doing the dirty?" Ellea asked.

Ros didn't have that type of power; half the time, he was too aloof or grumpy to realize what was right in front of his nose.

"I didn't," he said with a smirk. "But a demon can hope."

"You're horrible," she said, heading to the bathroom to wash away the dream and new fears.

She felt Ros come in and stand at the open door while she splashed cold water on her face.

"Are you okay, princess?" he asked with such a soft voice.

Was she okay?

She looked at him from his bathroom mirror while she wiped the water from her face. Turning, she leaned against the sink and sighed.

"I was hoping for a longer break between kidnappings, parents' murdering sprees, and vampire attacks." She looked down at his black tiled floor.

Ros' bare feet walked into her view, and he gripped her chin, making her look at him.

"None of this is your fault."

She couldn't help but pout. "It sure as shit feels like it."

"That feeling will never stop." He pulled her bottom lip from her teeth, and her skin instantly heated regardless of their conversation. "And outside of your parents, I feel like all the work you're going to do will not be easy."

"Fuck," she breathed. Her parents were an instant mood killer.

"Let's go to bed."

"I'm not feeling tired anymore," she said as he grasped her hand and pulled her out of the bathroom. "I think if you read to me, maybe it would help me sleep."

She batted her lashes at him as he turned to her with a face she couldn't quite read.

"Anything for you," he said.

And damn, if that didn't make her melt.

36

Rosier

They were fucked. There was no getting around how unbelievably fucked they were. The past two days of planning were burning in a trashcan somewhere, and he was ready to burn with it. Everyone was injured and running low on magic and energy, and the vampires kept coming. Ellea's vision had been correct, but they'd missed something in their scouting. He wasn't sure how they'd miscounted the mass number of volatile fuckers. The addition of the west coast pack hadn't even mattered.

As the second hour of battle turned into the third, Ros began questioning how they would get through this. Going to Hel for help wasn't an option; he didn't have the time or magic. The same was true for Florence and Duhne. His cousin was soaked in blood, but it didn't seem like it was his. And he looked like he enjoyed it. A feral roar rang around the massive demon as he tore a vampire in half, holding the severed ribcage in the air. Several vampires began running from him, and he laughed at their retreating forms. Florence paused her fighting to glare at Duhne. He guessed his cousin missed their time on the battlefield and was using this catastrophe to sate his bloodlust.

Ellea's magic had held out longer than all of theirs. She continued to shield with illusions or power and then cut down any threat with his mother's sword—*her sword*. She swung a graceful arc, its dark design swallowing the light. The same design marked his spine. He wished he had time to watch the beauty of her fighting, the rawness and unrelenting strength she showed with each parry, each counter attack. He could look at the feral glee on her face all day. Ellea roared, and Ros turned to see yet another vampire bite her. The bite wouldn't turn her, it only turned non-supernaturals, but he still had to fight the urge to go to her. He had his own group of fifty or so to kill. Her pale skin was peppered with bite marks and blood, but she kept pushing through. They all kept pushing through.

Sam and Billy were working with two other wolven. They would dance around the outskirts of the battle, picking off vampires as they tried to enter the main fight. Devon and Ellea had worked side by side, one always there to help the other. Devon's magic had dwindled first, but the recent training he'd done was paying off as he fought with knives and force. He would hold off as many as he could and Ellea would go in for the kill.

Ros kicked in the chest of an oncoming attacker as Garm swooped in to bite off his head.

I don't know what to do, Garm yelled, mind to mind.

"I don't know what to fucking do either," Ros yelled.

Can we retreat?

"I don't know how." Ros grunted, ripping out the throat of a female vampire. She clawed at his arms until death took her.

The only retreat was for the injured. Some omegas and those who could not fight were on standby to swoop in and drag them to safety. The vampires didn't care for them; they only seemed to go after Ros and Ellea. It was the only thing he was grateful for in this fucked-up situation. Maybe he could give up. Would they take him and leave his friends?

Doubtful, Garm answered his thoughts.

"Any other bright ideas?" Ros growled.

"Nooo!" Ellea's scream rang through the entire forest.

Ros and Garm turned to see five vampires ripping at Devon's skin as they dragged him from Ellea. She ran for him, not seeing the trap. She blasted them with magic he didn't know she possessed, but it didn't matter; more immediately replaced them, pulling Devon further and further away. He screamed with pain, and Ellea lost it.

Her body was alight with lightning, and time seemed to slow as she barreled for Devon. Every vampire that ran toward her thrashed and screamed when they came close to her magic. She was unstoppable, and when she neared Devon, the three holding him were thrown hundreds of feet into the woods. Ellea fell to her knees, looking over his wounds. She sobbed as she tried to stop the gush of blood coming out of his neck.

No, no, no.

Ros scrambled for her; she was helpless, and her guard was down. He saw all the vampires closing in, and his heart stopped. They would take her, they would do horrible things to her, and he wouldn't make it in time. He pulled for the shreds of his magic, but nothing came. Actually, nothing happened. He was frozen in place, and the world was silent and still around him. A figure crested a hill in front of Ros, his eyes glowing with the same light Ellea's power had. The figure radiated raw magic as that glowing gaze looked upon her huddled form. The air vibrated around him, and Ros' skin tingled with the power he held.

Cato.

He thought it like a curse. Ellea's father was here, and for the first time in his life, he felt truly scared. His magic answered as visions of the world burning around him flashed through his mind. If he took her, nothing would stand in Ros' way to get her back.

Yesss, his powers hissed. That demon lurking at the surface would guzzle the blood of her parents and bathe in the blood of those that dared to think of touching her. He felt the veins of power slowly crack open as time continued to stand still, then a *swoosh* sounded around them. A scream was stuck in his throat, a plea to leave her, take him instead. But Ros knew no matter his begging, they only had one goal: to get Ellea.

A blur of pale skin and dark hair passed Cato and moved between the frozen bodies. Snarling and slicing took up the silence, and time slowly crept back to normal. Ros' heart hurt in his chest with each desperate beat.

Could he get to her?

Ros fell to the ground but jumped up quickly, ready to dive toward Ellea. He froze as the sound of squelching and heavy thuds rang around them all at once. In the blink of an eye, every vampire had been decapitated; the only ones standing were the wolven, his friends, and two figures at the top of the hill. Ros pulled at his magic and shadowed to the hill. As soon as he was solid, he went to punch Cato, but a powerful grip caught his wrist. Snarling, Ros tore his eyes away from the trickster and looked to his partner.

"Hello, princeling," the ancient vampire said. It was Sebastian, Vlad's brother.

"Hello, Seb. We've been looking for you," Ros growled.

Ellea dumped potions and packs onto Devon's neck and kept glancing over her shoulder to where Billy and Garm held her father.

"Let a healer do that," Ros said softly. He had been pleading with her for too many minutes, desperate to whisk her away from here.

"They're busy; I got this." Ellea looked back at her friend.

Devon was awake and very pale, but well enough to glare daggers at the vampire beside Ros.

"Well, aren't you a pretty one?" Sebastian said to Devon.

"Even when you've caught me on a bad day and your ilk tried ripping my arm off," Devon responded.

"Shush," Ellea hissed. "You need to rest."

"They aren't mine, pretty," Sebastian said.

Devon ignored him and looked back to Ellea. "Don't heal all of them." Ellea's eyes went wide and her hands shook; Ros practically shook with her. His knees almost buckled when he heard Devon whisper, "I'll look badass, and—and Sam won't be the only one with a scar."

Even Sebastian paused his horrendous bedroom eyes and flirting at Devon's words. A silent tear escaped Ellea's eye, running through the blood coating her face, but she nodded and continued working on his neck.

Sebastian went to speak again, but Ros stepped on his foot. The sound of crunching bones rang around them. The only reason the vampire wasn't in irons was because he'd saved all of them. Her father, on the other hand...

"Ellea, you need to rest," Ros said as she looked over her shoulder again. She was vibrating with fear, and Ros wanted to get her and his friends as far away as possible.

"I'm fine. What's happening with C-Cato?"

"I was going to wait to ask what you wanted to do." Ros kneeled down to take the gauze from her shaking hand.

Ellea pressed her blood-soaked hands against her eyes. "Can we send him somewhere?"

Ros looked up to Billy and Garm, giving them a nod. They would take him to Hel while Ros finished here. Devon grasped Ellea with his good arm, holding her hand as she shook. Sebastian walked away to toe a dead corpse nearby, giving them some privacy.

"Sam?" Ellea asked, looking between the both of them. "Duhne and Florence?"

"Talking with the wolven and making rounds." He didn't want to tell her how many they'd lost today. "Florence and Duhne are back in Hel, ready for our word and letting my father know what happened here."

"Good...good," she said to herself. "I should help the healers and others."

She tried standing, but Devon held her hand, forcing her to stop.

"You need to see a healer yourself," he scolded.

"It's only a few bites; I have more potions at the cabin."

"Ros," Devon pleaded.

"How about I take you and Devon back to the cabin to shower and grab some food?" Ros said, trying to compromise. "Then after we have a talk with Sebastian, we can come and see what's left to help with?"

"I'm starved," Sebastian said with a wicked grin.

Ros rolled his eyes and begged the Gods for patience and a little more strength to whisk them to the cabin in one piece.

37

Ellea

Ellea leaned against the shower wall as the water continued to run red. Ros had stayed downstairs to keep an eye on Sebastian, leaving her to her thoughts. So many vampires, so much killing, and so many people hurt and dead…

Devon is alive, he is downstairs, and he is alive.

All of her friends had survived, but Ellea knew that wasn't true for the wolven packs. The battle had been nothing like any of the vampire attacks she was involved in before. How were they going to get her parents—no, her mother—if they couldn't handle a hoard of blood suckers? Her father had been there; he and Sebastian had saved them. Today was not what she'd expected, and she was left a confused mess in a shallow puddle of watery blood.

"Step one, don't crumble. Step two, get clean. Step three, figure out what the fuck happened today." She breathed out after the last statement. She could do this.

"Talking to yourself, princess?" Ros said, standing outside of the shower.

"I thought you were downstairs." She peeked up from where her head was lowered under the spray.

"Sam is back, he's watching our *visitor.*" Ros began taking his bloodied clothes off.

Yay, more blood.

"We have so many tricks and spells, why don't we have one to get rid of blood?" Ellea grumbled.

"I think the Gods wanted to make sure we can't wash away something like that too easily."

He turned on the second shower head, and she was thankful he'd been such a diva when remodeling his old cabin. Not caring how dirty he was, she took a step toward him and wrapped her arms around his muscular torso.

"The Gods suck." It came out muffled as she smothered her face into his chest.

"That they do." He kissed the top of her head and began washing her.

Ellea eyed the vampire lounging on Ros' couch, reading one of her romance books and acting as if he didn't just kill over a hundred of his own kind.

"What's your deal?" she asked, leaning against the doorframe.

Ros and Sam were helping Devon shower, and since Ellea was the only one left with fully functioning magic, she was babysitting.

"No deal, sweetness," he said, turning the page of the book.

"Why do all you boys like to give me a nickname?" She rolled her eyes. Fucking supernatural males. "My name is Ellea."

"Oh, I know your name." Bright blue eyes peeked at her over the book.

Ellea chewed her lip, mulling over the best way to approach him. The big vampire had long brilliant black hair that made her feel jealous of its perfect waves. He was a lot less pale than other vampires, and he seemed so relaxed. Vlad, his brother, was a stuck up ass-hat and would never be caught slouching or reading a shifter romance.

"Getting along?" Ros asked, coming up beside her.

"His fangs are bigger than yours." Ellea nodded to Sebastian.

The vampire's bright eyes glimmered, and he put down the book to turn toward them.

"Amongst other things," Sebastian added.

Ros straightened, and Ellea suppressed an annoyed huff.

Whatever it takes.

"He has a nice accent too," she added, which he did. She often wondered why Ros didn't have one. "Why don't you have an accent? You're a billion years old, and I'm surprised you don't say things like 'wench' or 'ye ol' something or other."

Ros gaped at her like a fish.

Keep playing into my plan, big guy; you're so good at it.

"I don't have an accent because I'm a billion years old and I've lived everywhere." Ros growled as Sebastian's smile grew. "This fucker is a pretentious prick who likes to be dramatic and play big bad vampire."

"I don't know; compared to Vlad, he seems cool."

Dimples appeared on Sebastian's perfect face, and she knew she had him.

"I doubt *Vlad* would have been able to kill as many vampires as Sebastian," Ellea said. "How did you know to come, anyway?"

"Oh, easy. Your father and I stuck around your crazy mother long enough to know what her next plan was." He snapped his mouth shut and glared at her. "You sneaky little—"

"Don't bother. Keep going. And I do think you have a nice accent," she said, walking over to sit on the couch with him. "Continue what you were saying."

"What about my fangs?" Sebastian said, batting his eyelashes and grinning at her.

"Definitely bigger," Sam said, coming into the room to sit across from the vampire.

Ros threw his hands in the air and plopped himself in another chair.

"Now that's covered…" Ros growled, and Ellea noticed the tip of his tongue toying with one of his sharp teeth.

"I have a hard time believing my fa—Cato is going against Cerce," Ellea said, clearing her throat.

"You'll have to ask him about that, but believe it, sweetness," Sebastian said.

"Why didn't you come sooner?" Ros asked.

"Something to do with Cato only being able to be gone for so long," Sebastian said.

Ellea didn't know what that meant, but now Cato was in Hel, so he wouldn't be getting back any time soon.

"If he doesn't want to leave her, then why come and help us?" Ellea questioned.

"You're getting it wrong." He paused. "Let me start from the beginning. Belias came to me—"

"Fucking Belias," Ellea and Ros said together.

"Yeah, fuck that guy." Sebastian shook his head. "Anyway, he came to me with a proposition, and after I said no for the fifth time, I threatened to eat his balls and he finally gave up. But some of my vampires went missing. Being the amazing leader I am, I went to investigate." Ellea couldn't help but roll her eyes. "And what did I find? Belias was recruiting under my nose and poaching from other clans. Since he's such an idiot, I told him I changed my mind and wanted in on his big scheme. That was about a month ago, and soon I realized he wasn't pulling the strings at all. It was Cerce. That bitch is crazy. Last week, she had this rally that gave me some old-world creeps, and I couldn't handle my double-agent games anymore. I got my vampires and got out of there as quickly as I could. That's when Cato approached me."

"What do you mean approached you?" Sam asked.

"Fucker tiptoed through the campsite like some prisoner and jumped me when I was almost out of there. Asked if I would help him go against Cerce. He knew I wasn't interested in what she was spewing, and he was looking for an ally."

Ellea blinked a few times, shaking her head, trying to rid herself of the memories that were threatening to creep in.

"So we kept in contact, and he said he needed help. Cerce had claimed that this was the battle that they would finally get you. Their numbers were so much higher than yours. So Cato contacted me, and we got here as quickly as we could."

"Just like that?" Ros said skeptically.

"Just like that," Sebastian answered with his arms wide.

It was getting harder and harder to suppress the memories, the thoughts of both her parents. "I don't believe you."

"You don't have to believe me," he said. "It's the story."

Ros and Sam began grilling him on logistics while Ellea's mind wandered back to a time when her father stood by while her mother gave her no mercy. He would come after her torture sessions, sliding food under the door of the basement or leaving healing supplies so she could fix her own wounds. He never stopped her then, so why would he stop her now?

"I'm going to check on Devon." It was an excuse to get out of there.

She stumbled toward Ros' front door, desperate for air as the cabin began to close in on her. Her powers raged as she took each unsteady step out of the too-stuffy home.

Never again.

"Hey," Devon greeted as she threw herself out onto the porch, stumbling to grip the railing.

Devon was next to her in an instant, dragging her toward the wicker couch he was sitting on. He swung his newly healed arm over her shoulder and tucked her into him. The crescent shapes that peppered up his neck to the side of his chin caught her attention right away. He'd asked her to leave the wounds, but guilt swirled with her panic. Another friend was scarred thanks to her. Thanks to her parents and their never-ending goal for destruction and reclaiming her.

After a few minutes of Devon rubbing her shoulder, she didn't know if she would get out of this spiral. "You know what I never understood?" he said suddenly.

She couldn't answer, only looked at him with wide eyes.

"Why 'Mione never ended up with Draco," he said, searching her expression with a soft smile on his face. "I mean, sure, her signs were compatible with Ron's, but—"

"No," Ellea whispered. Clearing her throat, she added, "They were not compatible and you know it."

"Right, but Draco was a scorpio," he said thoughtfully.

"No, his son was named Scorpios." She shook her head. "He's a gemini and she's a virgo…they were perfect for each other."

"So you keep telling me," he said with a laugh.

She rested her head on his chest, listening to the steady rhythm of his heart along with the bickering inside the cabin.

They were all right. They were whole.

"We'll get there," he said. "We have to."

38

Ellea

The dungeons of Hel were straight out of someone's nightmares—not hers, though. Ellea's worst nightmare was losing control of her powers and causing mass destruction. Her father was sitting in a cell across from where she stood in the darkness. A whisper of Ros' shadows curled around a piece of hair that had escaped her braid, tucking it behind her ear. He waited behind her; he would reveal her when she was ready.

She let out a quiet breath as she took in her father. Cato's freckles and big gray eyes mirrored her own. Even his scowl was hers. People thought she got her frown from her mother, but she'd gotten most of her traits from her father. He looked bored in his cell. His long legs stretched out in front of him. His arms were hugged tight around his chest as he stared up at the tiny window.

"Daughter," he drawled, turning to look at where she was hidden. "No matter what you think, I'm not here to harm you."

Ellea stepped out of the shadows, noting the tick in his jaw as he took her in. She had hoped he would look worse after spending two nights in a cell.

"That's not why I'm taking my time," she said, not hiding her accusing tone. "Forgive me for contemplating whether or not I want to confront my neglectful sire."

Cato flinched.

"Does that bother you, Cato?" Ellea slowly walked to his cell, stopping a few feet from his reach. "I would bet you and Cerce play my torture sessions on repeat, reminiscing on your favorite pastime and then cursing your failed heir—"

"I'm the one that failed you." He stood quickly, towering over her and interrupting part of the speech she'd worked so hard on.

He stood half a foot above her, and his gray eyes glimmered.

Were those tears?

She pressed the thought back. Her father's eyes had always glowed bright. Their ethereal shine sometimes haunted her dreams, always watching, never reaching a hand to help her.

"I have failed you since the day you were born," he whispered. "No, I failed you the day I fell for your mother's tricks."

She scoffed. "Says one of the tricksters."

"It's one of our curses." He huffed a harsh laugh. "We're too gullible sometimes, and someone always seems to slide in when we aren't looking. How could someone out-trick one of the most powerful beings?"

He let out another harsh laugh and sat back on the hard bench, the only thing in the cell.

"What are you getting at?"

"You mother—"

"That bitch is not my mother," Ellea hissed, leaning into the bars.

"Cerce," he corrected, "was lying the whole time; about her love, how we met...and as soon as you were born, as soon as she had something to hold over my head, she came out and told me the truth. Proud of all she had accomplished, she didn't leave a single detail out."

Cato threw up his hands dramatically, and Ellea couldn't help but flinch. His jaw ticked again.

"I'm sorry. I did what I could, but she had something else to hold against me besides you." He hit his head on the wall. "Cerce had a vision when she was in her teens of meeting a great trickster who would change the world. So she began hunting me down; it took her years since I was so reclusive, so afraid after a lifetime of torment. Once my parents were murdered, I hid my powers and lived among mortals. I often wondered if her constant hunt, constant visions of her own future, drove her mad. She was such a talented actress, knew all the right things to say, to do, and I was such a fool. I lived a miserable and lonely life until her. It was so wonderful to have someone accept me for who I was and care for me."

What was this bullshit? Her powers churned, full of uncertainty. She felt the shadows churn with it, ready to pull her back.

Her father cleared his throat. "I was so starved for love, starved enough to make a stupid vow without realizing what I had done. One would never go against the other, we would love and support one another no matter the circumstance. Fucking bitch cursed our wedding ceremony. The vows we spoke were a blood vow, and I didn't know what I was agreeing to."

He was lying.

But it sounds so like Cerce.

Ellea tried swallowing, but her mouth had gone dry. What did any of this mean? What did it matter?

"I kept telling myself 'As long as you were alive, as long as you were whole—'"

"Whole! I was anything but whole." She swallowed a sob, turning away from him. "I was a scared child, fraying along the edges, and I would have rather died than go through what I went through."

She stumbled back as the words left her mouth, and the surrounding cells grew dark as Ros' shadows crept in further, curling around her legs. She took their strength and turned toward her father, standing taller.

"You may have been dragged into a false marriage, but I had to live through her torture, her ruthless hunger for power, and I will never, ever forgive you or her."

Ellea turned away, ready to leave him behind.

"I know how to stop her."

"Yeah, by capturing her and bringing her here so you can live happily ever after in the pits of Hel," Ellea said over her shoulder.

"She's too strong, no one will get near her. But if you stopped time…I could show you how I did it with the vampires," he offered.

Ellea closed her eyes, finding the strength to continue to be anywhere near him.

"If you hate her so much, do it yourself."

"That's the thing about blood vows," he said. "If I tried to stop her from doing what she wanted to do, if I tried killing her, I would die. Even now, I grow weaker after escaping her."

"Looks like you're going to die here anyway." She smiled wickedly at him.

Cato stood. If she didn't know any better, she'd say he looked sad. He strolled toward the bars, then stepped through them. Ros was at her side in an instant, pulling her away from him.

"I'm only here because I want to be, daughter," Cato said before Ros' shadows circled his neck and held him in place.

Ellea knew he could fight them off, but he didn't; he only stared at them with that sad look in his eyes.

"Let me show you how to stop her. You alone have the power to kill her," he whispered.

"I would rather die," she hissed in his face.

"I'm sorry. I am so very sorry for all of it," he said as tears streaked his face.

Then he was gone.

The moment Cato vanished, a deafening noise surrounded her. Shadows, guards, and chaos all tore through the place; two guards sandwiched Ellea against a wall as Ros stood in front of them, shouting orders and snarling. Next thing she knew, Garm appeared and shadowed her directly to Azzy's office without giving her a chance to think. Billy was there in a moment, and now the two of them sat in the king's office. Seven guards kept watch over the past few hours; three lining the large window, three standing near the doors, and Mythis standing beside her. Their gold armor glinted in the afternoon sun streaming in through the windows.

"This is a bit dramatic," Ellea drawled. She sat sideways in the massive armchair as her crossed foot bobbed.

Billy grabbed it and gave her a look.

Stop being a brat and talk to me, she said telepathically.

Ellea rolled her eyes and pried her foot from her familiar's clawed grasp. There was nothing to talk about, nothing had changed. No matter what her father said, they were in the same position. They had zero leads and no way to capture him or Cerce.

My father spewed some pretty lies and then he escaped. I'm not sure what you want from me, Ellea thought, not wanting the guards to know.

I can get those details from Ros, Bug. Stop blocking your emotions from me. Ellea practically felt the pleading in her voice.

She would not; there was no time for how she was feeling, it didn't matter. That's what she kept telling herself as a door slammed open. Azzy strode in, and all the guards stood at attention. His long horns glinted, and a snarl spread across his mouth.

"Leave us," he spat, and all the guards moved out on stiff legs. Mythis was the last to go, giving Ellea a nod bowing to the king. "You too, Billy."

Billy looked as if she would refuse for a moment, but even she wouldn't argue with his request. It seemed only Ellea was immune to his knee-wobbling command. Billy kissed the top of her head before bowing to the king. Ellea swiveled her chair to stand, and Azzy reached for her hand, holding it tight. She held her chin high as he searched her face.

"Ros?" she asked when he finished his assessment.

"Talking with the generals," he said, sitting on the edge of his desk in front of her.

"And he told you what my—what Cato claimed?"

"He did." Azzy took a deep breath, and she couldn't help but feel more settled in his presence.

"We've never covered stopping time in our studies and training."

"And I've never heard of it," he added. "Rosier described it to me; I've never witnessed a witch, demon, or God doing something like that. It doesn't mean it isn't possible."

It took her a moment to say the words that had been circling her mind. "He claimed it was the only way."

"I know what he claimed," he snapped.

Azzy crossed his arms over his chest and pinched the bridge of his nose. He looked tired, and she would bet her favorite book he'd been searching the castle and grounds with the guards.

"I should have killed him when he arrived," he added.

"You promised that to me," Ellea said sweetly.

"That I did, darling," he said, reaching to hold her by the shoulder. "Your magic seems strong, and after only two days' rest?"

"I feel fine," she said, grasping his warm hand.

"I'm sure you keep telling yourself that, along with everyone else," he said, giving her a small smile before stepping away to sit behind his desk. "I spoke with Rosier, and if you're up for it, you two are going to work on some training I suggested. I'm going to do my own research on what we've discovered."

"I'm up for it if he is."

"Yeah, I don't mind telling you that my son is a little upset you held out longer than him." Azzy smirked.

Ellea pressed her lips together, toying with a small black book on Azzy's desk. He pulled it away and it tucked it into his drawer.

"I'll see you for dinner," he said, dismissing her.

"No guards?"

"Oh, there will be guards, and don't bother pouting about it," he said, leaning back in his chair and shooing her away with a flick of his wrist. "I won't have the future of my kingdom being jeopardized because she likes to walk and read."

"There weren't guards before."

"That was before one of *them* could escape out of Hel." He cocked a brow at her. "Don't be late for dinner."

He flicked his wrist toward the door again. She wanted to stick her tongue out at him, but as she left the safety of his study, she couldn't help but feel a little shaken. Pushing it down, she went to hunt down her demon, two guards trailing behind her.

39

Rosier

Ellea glared at him as she hung upside down. Her face was flushed, and the cutest little vein began showing at her temple. He was glad his father had suggested trying to keep her restrained, unable to move or fight. It wasn't something they had worked on before. Until they figured out what Cato had done to stop time, his shadows were the closest way to replicate it.

Anger quickly replaced the humor on his tiny princess' face. She glared at him as she turned slowly away. He'd felt so close to losing her again a few days ago, so close to seeing the world burn if anything harmed her. They needed to do better, plan better. He was almost tempted to be her backup instead of Devon, but he worried about his manhood if he even thought about suggesting that. He didn't want to interfere with the relationship they were building, the bond they had.

So he would keep training her.

"Are you even trying?" Ros asked.

"No, I'm trying to figure out if this is some sick demon game or if we are actually working toward something," she grumbled.

He breathed a little better, hearing her bratty remark. His cock stirred at the thought of sick demon games and tying her up.

"The longer you think about it, the more blood is going to rush to your head. You're going to pass out," he scolded, scolding himself too as his mind wandered to thinking of her flushed skin. "I told you, we need to see if—"

"I know," she hissed. "Fine, I'll play your stupid game. I thought there would be swords and a fighting ring. Not some non-fun bondage in our bedroom."

She continued to grumble as she tried moving her arms. A wave of electricity danced across her skin, but Ros had grown used to it and continued a firm hold. They had actually added that to his training, learning how to hold off Cato. Never again would the man stop him from protecting Ellea.

"Ros," she breathed. "I'm getting dizzy."

"Then try harder."

He really hated this, especially after hearing her confession this morning. She rolled her eyes before taking a breath and continuing to try to free herself. Her magic crackled around them, not only across her skin, and his shadows loosened. He reinforced them, gritting his teeth a little, and they held strong again.

"Good, keep doing that," he encouraged.

Again, the air became heavy with her magic, and his own threatened to loosen as a smirk spread across her face. Ros braced his feet, forcing his shadows to hold tight. Her hair floated around her as electricity ran along her skin, around his shadows, and connected with him.

He accepted the pain and pulled deep from his magic. She could last another minute; he had to fight.

"Harder," he gritted out.

She obeyed, and her eyes glowed like her father's for a moment. Ros roared at her to hold steady. Then Ellea blinked, and her eyes were back to normal. She tried turning her head to get a better look at him.

"Whoah," she whispered.

"Keep going." His voice came out harsh, and it shook him.

Ros didn't recognize the tone. It was one of a beast buried deep within, and it shouldn't be surfacing at a time like this. Looking down at his hands, his arms glowed with fire, and veins of ash cracked across his skin. Ellea took his distraction and easily freed herself from his shadows hold, floating gracefully to her feet. He tried to take calm breaths, but they came out in feral pants.

No, no, no.

Yes, yes, yes.

He couldn't lose control, but the beast was excited, eyeing Ellea like she was a delicacy it couldn't wait to taste. He couldn't scare her after everything she'd been through the past few days. Ellea stepped toward him, and he turned away, trying to press it down.

So stupid, he scolded himself. How could he not realize the strength he would need, the side he would tap into, after she'd become so strong? His father had probably known this would happen.

"Ros..." She circled him, trying to get him in front of her. "Look at me."

"No." He turned away. "Give me a minute; I'll make it go away."

"I don't want you to." She lunged and grabbed him by the forearm.

His mind raced as he felt her skin on his burning flesh. He would have to call for a healer, they could heal the burns if they got there quick—

Burns?

He looked down at her hand. It was unmarked. She reached for him again, placing it over his heart. Her eyes flicked over his body, his bare chest; his power had burned away his clothes. When her eyes met his, they flashed with white-hot electricity as if her magic was answering his own. A wicked smirk spread across her beautiful face as she took in his horns.

"I wondered how big these would be." She reached for him, pausing when he shied away. But she waited, looking at him again with so much wonder and acceptance in her eyes.

He couldn't speak, couldn't breathe, as his soul was ripped open to her. Leaning down to her height, he held still as she wrapped a small hand around one of his horns. He shuddered; no one had ever touched them before. Slowly, she traced each ridge. Instead of disgust, her face held fascination and a bit of mischief. She grasped both of them by the base and dragged him to her for a searing kiss. It caught him so off guard, he almost didn't realize he'd started to slip back into himself.

"Don't make these disappear," she said, holding on to them harder. "And don't think for an instant I didn't see that tail."

He kissed her again, harder this time, needing her to not push this. There was only so much he could lay out there.

Small steps.

Ros ripped at her clothes, shredding them instantly as she kicked off her boots. With all her weight and strength, Ellea leaned down, her hands still gripping his horns, and threw him over her shoulder. Her small body tucked and rolled with him, and she landed with both legs on either side of his chest.

"Déjà vu?" she said with a smirk.

Ros gripped her hips as her scent wafted across his nose. He inhaled sharply, closing his eyes and remembering their first time in the woods.

"Yes," he growled. "But now I get to do what I want with your sweet little pussy."

"Is that right?" She gripped his horns tighter. "I think I'm the one with the reins."

She had a direct line to his dick that bobbed in answer to her rough grasp. Curling in, she kissed him swiftly and then slid onto his face. He groaned at the first taste of her as she hovered above his mouth, but he wasn't having any of that. He wanted to fight for air as he drowned in her. She let out the most delicious squeak as he gripped her ass with clawed hands and pressed her fully onto his face.

This was the way he wanted to die.

Strong thighs squeezed his head as he devoured every wet inch of her. They squeezed harder as his teeth lightly scraped at her clit. When he dove his tongue into her center, her legs spread beautifully, letting him in deeper. It was filthy and divine as her wetness flowed down his chin. His cock begged to be buried inside her heat as she softened around him. Her clit was swollen and needy as it rubbed against his nose. As though she could read his mind, she strengthened her hold and ground down on his face, chasing her sweet release.

Her magic was sentient as it crackled across her skin, sending delicious shocks through his body. It took all his strength to not spurt across his stomach. His hand twitched to rub at his length. He fought it off, focusing on his tongue, his teeth, everything to drive her orgasm from her. Her legs widened more as her moans became incoherent pleas.

"More, please, Gods," she cried.

She clenched around his tongue before her beautiful body arched and bucked above him. She cried out his name, begging him to never stop—*like that was possible*. Stars shot across his vision as she was pushed off the precipice. The exquisite sound of her release could be heard in the pits, and he was both proud and possessive of that noise.

Every beast and demon would know she was his. He stroked her slowly as she rode out the waves. His claws scraped across her stomach that was still fluttering with her release. Like the beast he was, no longer able to hold it back, he pitched her forward. She was dazed as she landed on her hands and knees, but he was on her instantly, lining up his aching cock to dive into her pussy that was so desperate to be filled. And oh, did he oblige.

40

Ellea

Ellea glanced back as Ros gripped her hip while trailing sharp claws down her back. The sight could only be described as glorious. She added it to the list of fantasies she never knew she had.

Those horns...

They would be her undoing. Their blackness reminded her of his shadows, curling elegantly toward the ceiling. And with his eyes alight and glowing a harsh red, how could she not need him—now and forever? He licked his lips, moaning as he tasted her release that coated his face. She knew that any female or male would know that he was hers. She wanted to coat him in her smell, wear his marks, and make him scream her name so loud that every creature in all the realms knew that this godly beast was hers and no one else's.

Ellea was imagining the things he could do with his tail when he stopped every coherent thought. As he impaled her on his cock, she screamed, and her mind went fuzzy at the feel of him, hot, hard, and relentless.

"Mine," he growled.

Her magic reacted on its own again, flickering across her skin and dancing with the power radiating from her demon prince.

"Yours," she whimpered, meeting him for each delicious, harsh thrust.

Her pussy was quivering around him, still reeling from coming on his tongue. Ros growled her name, and she knew he was close. She would not taunt him for his quickness; she begged for it only so they could go again and again...

"Fuck," he hissed, slowing his pace, but she arched into him, allowing him deeper and forcing him over the edge.

"Are you going to spill into this pussy, Ros?" She breathed out the words as her body shuddered, and when his look turned feral, she couldn't help but clench around him. "Make a mess of me, mark me, show everyone who I belong to?"

It was a question and a demand, causing Ros to pause, eyes wide. When she shifted, moving him, he snapped, and it was transcendental. He wrapped his hand around her braid, pulling her toward him, and he latched onto her shoulder. With his fangs buried in her skin and his hot release pouring into her, she came again, and she thought the world shook under them.

Ellea stroked his arm that was wrapped around her middle as he slowly licked at the mark, shallowly thrusting into her as their releases dripped onto the floor beneath them.

"You're so perfect," he said, kissing her shoulder. "And so very wicked."

She felt his smirk against her skin.

"I don't know about that." She didn't feel wicked—she felt insatiable. She clamped around him, and he groaned against her skin.

"Princess..."

"You're still hard," she murmured. "We should fix that."

A whirl of night and shadows engulfed them as Ros magicked them to their soft bed. She landed on her back with a giggle, and he began to slowly kiss his way up her body. Her eyes fluttered closed as the feeling of being worshiped consumed every inch of her. He nipped hard at her nipple, causing her to gasp and snap her eyes open. No longer was he a Helish being as his hazel eyes glimmered with so much emotion.

Ellea reached for him, caressing his cheek and guiding him to her waiting lips. Their kiss was soft, a whisper of the roughness from moments ago. He slid into her slowly, and Ellea sighed at the perfect feel of him.

"I'll always need this," she said between kisses.

She continued to pour as much into them as possible, whispering her praise and thanking him for trusting her with something he fought so hard to hide. He shouldn't hide anything from her—Rosier was hers.

"Mine," she stated above his lips, causing him to moan and thrust into her harder, deeper.

"Always," he answered.

Ros gripped her tighter, their skin slick with sweat as they clung to each other through each push, each stroke, chasing yet another orgasm. The only sounds were their breathless moans and feral kisses. So much emotion and wild magic surrounded them. Ellea wanted to say everything, all that she felt, but as her legs tingled and Ros' cocked throbbed once again inside her, she had only curses for the Gods and his perfect dick that would make it impossible to think of anything else.

Ellea cried out, and he smothered the sound with his lips, tasting her words and burning with her. They burned and burned as their releases snapped out of them, white-hot and endless. Her orgasm felt never-ending, and she wondered if Ros felt the same way as he trembled above her. He rolled them over so she could rest her head on his chest. He was still buried inside of her.

"Ros?" Ellea asked.

"No more, you sex-crazed demon," he said, kissing the top of her head with a tired sigh.

She laughed, and the movement caused them both to groan. He slowly stroked her back with dull fingers, no longer clawed. If she had the energy to look, she was sure she'd see that his horns were gone too.

Good. She didn't trust her pussy if they were still out.

She sighed, drawing small circles on his chest.

"We should shower and nap," she mumbled. "Maybe get an ice pack for my bits."

"Your bits?" he grumbled. "How about mine? You practically cut off the circulation with your tight—"

She clenched around him, cutting off his words, and he hissed.

"You were saying?"

"Evil dick demon," he grumbled.

His shadows curled away from him, heading toward the bathroom, and the sound of water running made her groan with relief and a bit of sadness. She would make him run around coated in her scent another day.

41

Ellea

Warmth spread through Ellea's body as she watched a mortal embrace her supernatural husband. They had been apart for Gods know how long, but now one more thing was righted, and she felt an immense amount of joy—even with the creepy red-headed demon next to her.

"Thank you for helping me," she said to Cara, nudging the icy heir in the ribs with her elbow. "I was worried this would all stop with everything going on."

Cara chewed her lip, and Ellea couldn't remember another time she'd looked so human.

"Well…" Cara paused, swallowing hard. "I've continued it without you."

Ellea's eyes went wide, and when she pressed her hand to her chest, feigning a heart attack, Cara grimaced. Turning on her heel, she stormed away.

"Wait!" Ellea's short legs chased after her long strides. "I'm sorry. I just didn't expect you to be so invested."

Cara stopped, tapping her foot against the hard dirt. "Well, I am."

"Why?" Ellea tried to sound open, not wanting to poke the very unstable princess. "Is it an exchange of power thing?"

She had been told a few times that the number of souls in a territory barely tipped the scales, but it made her wonder if there was something she didn't know, something she had missed in all of her research.

"No, it's just something to do." Cara picked at an invisible piece of fuzz on her impeccable cream-colored dress. Ellea cocked a brow at her, knowing that wasn't all. "It's something to do that is truly my decision and doesn't involve my brother."

"Oh." She could understand that. "It is strange, but I get it," she said, raising her palms before Cara began hissing like a cat. "Does he know? You're always so glued to each other."

"He suspects something, but I don't think he knows."

"Gods, you two are creepy."

Cara smiled at her deviously. "You enjoy my creep. Especially when I used it to scare Sam."

Ellea smiled right back and nodded, then they continued back to the castle. Ellea had purposefully lost Sam in a confusing set of hallways. Little did the poor man know that she had turned herself into Cara so the two of them could scare him at every wrong turn. When they finally joined up and the real Cara stood next to her duplicate, they'd slowly walked toward him, reciting lines they had practiced. He'd turned, screaming, and ran into Ros' waiting arms. She still wasn't sure how he'd found them, and she was a little annoyed she couldn't play more.

"Poor Sam," Ellea said with a laugh. "Oh, speaking of jokes, let me grab some muffins to drop off to the stables."

They were nearing Farren's shop, and she felt particularly bad for getting Sam to ride a winged beast. The spanking she'd gotten that night from Ros was delicious, but it left her raw for a whole day.

Cara dropped Ellea off near Azzy's office after their pastry delivery. Before she could head off to find Azzy or Ros and let them know she'd made amends, she heard a gaggle of old men stating requests and ridiculous demands. She poked her head around a corner to see Ros, clad in a crisp black shirt, pants, and—Gods—a wicked-looking black crown. She loved when he played prince, even though he spent hours afterwards complaining about how itchy the clothes were and how his shoes were too tight.

Fucking backwoods lumberjack.

She smiled as she watched him glare at a few of the lords and dukes. One broke from the fray and began whining about her in particular.

"Your woman has been running amuck—"

He wasn't able to finish his grievance against her as Ros wrapped a large hand around his throat, easily slamming him into a nearby wall. Everyone else took two steps back.

"My woman has a name, you sniveling bastard." Ros got closer to his face, and his shadows crept down his hands to circle the lord's throat. A delicious squeak left his lips that were quickly going blue. "I may be able to crush your spine right here in front of the other sniveling bastards, but I won't. Instead, I will drag your ass to the dungeons and leave you to *my woman.* She's brilliant and beautiful and she'll do far worse to you. She can do whatever the fuck she wants."

The demon shook in his hold, and Ellea couldn't help but bite her fist and moan. Panties were burning everywhere from the sight of him, at the sound of his words, and the way her powers reveled in it. She took a steadying breath, ignored the gathering wetness, and headed toward the crowd. They all took another step back, and the demon still in Ros' grasp squeaked more.

"Is this a very late Samhain gift, Rosier?" She stalked toward them, and Ros gave her a shit-eating grin.

"Or a very early Yule gift."

Ellea smirked and walked her fingers up the chest of the lord before patting his pale face. "Though I would love to play, your father is waiting for us, and I'm hungry for food, not the cries of those who annoy me."

Ros let go without warning, and the male crumbled to the ground, sobbing.

"Anything you want, princess."

Their kiss was wild, and those around them stared in horror.

Ros would not wake, not that Ellea blamed him. After she'd found him in the hall, the rest of the day was a whirlwind of him prancing around, being all princely, glaring at his father over a late lunch, and then training her in the evening. But as the sun continued to rise, Ellea felt restless. Even after her training the day before, creating multiple versions of herself, she was not tired. In fact, she was wired, her powers churning under her skin. Even reading wouldn't calm her or the magic begging to be shed. She stared down at Ros; the glow of the morning light softened his features but could not erase how massive he was, how much space his presence took up. Yanking the blankets away, he didn't even flinch, only lay there on his back, one knee bent and cock already partially hard.

She could…play.

No, she should let him sleep.

It would be fun.

Her powers were evil but oh so creative. Training was giving her so many interesting ideas of ways to wake Ros. It was always him and his shadows that got to have all the fun. Why couldn't it be her and her magic? A wide and wicked smile spread across her face.

"I don't think you would mind if I had a little taste…"

No, he probably wouldn't; he had said so once, after Duhne had impeded her waking him with her mouth. Later that day, he said he would've loved it. But what about more than one of her? A huff sounded, and when she looked up, two sets of electric gray eyes met her own. No pang of jealousy rang through her. How could she be jealous of herself?

"Gods, we're hot." She scanned her echoes from head to toe. They were perfect copies, down to each freckle and curve. "Get to work, ladies. Let's see if I have a voyeur kink."

"Let's see if we have a voyeur kink," they said together.

"Don't make this creepy."

All three of them smirked before Ellea leaned back on the pillows, ready for a show, and the echoes crawled up to their demon.

She could feel the brush of their skin against his, the soft blankets under knees and hands. Each touch was heightened two-fold, and she shivered in anticipation. Ros' cock twitched with each touch, each inch they traveled, peppering his legs with bites and kisses. He shifted slightly, moaning low in his sleep. Their excitement escalated, and she had a hard time separating the two; all three of them were greedy for a taste of his silken skin. Ellea focused on the echo to her left, directing her to swirl her tongue around his wide tip. She made the other lick straight up his balls. When they did, Ellea moaned at the taste of him and the feel of his hard erection against her echoes' skin.

"Yeah, definitely into this." She shivered; watching them had her feeling all types of hot and bothered, her thighs becoming slick with her arousal.

Instincts took over, and they mimicked movements she had done so many times before. Gripping him hard, twisting, sucking, and when they both used their tongues to toy with the sensitive underside, Ros woke.

"Yes," he sighed, eyes still shut.

She ran her hand across his hard chest and leaned in to kiss his sleep-lined cheek. "Do you like that, handsome?"

"Fuck, yes—what?" His eyes snapped open and he looked at her for a moment, then down at the woman. One had him so far down her throat that Ellea felt like she couldn't breathe. That echo smirked around his length, and Ros cursed something obscene. The other was lapping up his balls.

"Fuck. Ellea. Gods."

He was a blubbering mess, and Ellea was enjoying every moment.

42

Rosier

This wasn't a dream. This was a new type of blissful Hel, and he was about to embarrass himself. It took every ounce of strength to not shoot in the back of her throat when she ran her teeth along his sensitive skin. Her—the copy of Ellea. The other was doing something wicked to his balls and—oh, Gods.

"This. You." He couldn't think, couldn't speak. The room was suffocating with arousal; Ellea's sweet scent was telling him she was enjoying this, enjoying watching herself suck on his cock.

Fucking Hel.

He was going to come. "Too soon," he couldn't help but blurt out.

"I don't know," Ellea said. He knew it was the real Ellea by scent and feeling alone. "They were working for a bit before you woke up."

"You. Naughty. Little. Witch!" He couldn't help but thrust into the hot mouth that was moaning around him.

"Are you going to come?" she breathed against his throat. "Are you going to make a mess of my echoes?"

Ros glanced down again, and two Elleas were looking up at him from under their lashes. Their tongues circled around him, circling around each other. And when they smirked, his head went wholly blank. He came with a feral roar, arching and spilling into someone's throat. It was never-ending, mind-numbing, and when he stopped shuddering, one Ellea released herself from him with a *pop*, then the other took over to clean up whatever mess was left.

"Oh, Gods. I'm going to come again."

Ellea laughed huskily, and he knew then that she would pay in the best way for waking him like this.

43

Rosier

It had been a week since Ellea's father disappeared. A week with no sign of attack. Ellea was still being kept in Hel, but she enjoyed being there. He was working hard on getting used to that. Since they were now stationed here, everyone visited when they could, which meant every day. Ros could admit to himself that he may have spent all of his years grumbling in the woods for no reason. That grumpy asshole never imagined his friends gathered around a table in Hel, eating lunch with his father. Devon sat to his father's left today, and they were in a heated discussion about something Ros had lost track of, while Sam and Ellea were snickering like a couple of children. He looked toward Garm for help, but the hound was too busy making heart eyes at Billy.

Fucking Hel.

Ros was slightly afraid of whatever Sam and Ellea were cooking up. Sam had officially been banned from the library, the stables, and the kitchens. Everyone was too scared of Ellea to ban her, which meant that Sam wasn't actually banned at all. First, he'd hunted Viatrix through the library in his wolven form while Ellea stole a few romance novels and documents pertaining to the history of the Gods. Another day, he'd insulted the cooks and kitchen staff on their inability to cook some of Ellea's favorite meals correctly. Lastly, Ellea had talked him into taking one of the winged demon horses for a ride. She had lied, of course, telling him she did it all the time. That got him called into Asmodeus' study for a scolding, but Ros was pretty sure he hadn't heard a bit of it and had spent the time checking him out instead.

Kill me now.

Sam and Ellea had started calling his father "*Daddy Azzy,*" and Ros was regularly looking for ways to magic his ears.

"So what you're saying is we have the full support of Hel, but not the full support?" Devon asked his father, which piqued Ros' interest.

"Hel supports Rosier and Ellea on their mission and we will aid them in any way we can. But we cannot send an army with them."

"Why not?" Sam asked. "It seems like the easiest solution."

"You all may feel adjusted and find it easy to be both here and in your realm"—he leaned back in his chair—"but our soldiers have lived here their whole lives. They have not stepped foot outside of this realm for a millennium. If they did, it would do more harm than good."

"But you've aided the humans before?" Ellea asked.

"Yes, but that was a very, very long time ago."

"Would you go to our realm?" Devon asked.

Ros' eyes widened. He couldn't remember a time his father had visited or even spoke of visiting. His cousins had traveled topside often, but the kings never left Hel.

His father looked pointedly at Ros, then his eyes moved to Ellea. "I would, for the right reasons."

"What reasons?" Devon pried.

Did he not realize what his father was implying? Or was he actually trying to get him to say it? He glared at Devon, but then Sam cut in.

"Leave Daddy Azzy alone. You've been hounding him our entire meal."

Stab me in the head, please.

"I'm sorry." The tips of Devon's ears turned red, and Ros knew he was only hunting for knowledge. "I get carried away."

"It's good to be curious," his father said. "At least you aren't stealing horses and horrifying shades."

Sam smirked and looked down at his empty plate. Ros couldn't believe how open his father was, how he entertained Ellea and his friends. This was nothing like growing up during stuffy parties or private dinners. He cleared his throat, trying to stop his mind from wandering to a darker time. Things could change for the better. It was something else he kept reminding himself.

"We should get Devon back," Sam said.

"Are you running from your latest prank?" Ros asked, turning his attention away from bad memories.

"No." He laughed. "I have to check in with my betas and Ags. We'll be back in the morning so you can whoop Devon's ass and I can whoop El's."

Ros raised a brow at his friend. They had begun training together after her father disappeared. Ellea was actually training Sam, not that they would tell him. She would create beasts to fight him while Mythis battled her with a sword. He was the only guard Ros trusted to not accidentally try and stab her. Never mind that she could take care of herself.

Ros had focused on Devon's shadow magic since he was fairly strong at all the other elements. It forced him to tap deeper into his well of power, and they were slowly digging further, strengthening his powers. If he took the plunge for immortality, he would be a force to reckon with after more years of training.

Ros and Ellea had been training in the evenings. She would come at him with claws and teeth, and he would be in a partial demon form. It was the only way she could fight something close to her strength. They didn't admit she was stronger, and he didn't know if that was for his ego or her fear of accepting how powerful she was.

They had also formed a new plan. Since her parents were so eager to get her in particular, Ellea had been focusing on making duplicates of herself. Plan B was to disguise herself as Cato. If she couldn't get near enough to her mother to apprehend her, maybe he could.

Ros cleared his throat and shifted in his seat as memories from the morning she'd used her echoes for evil instead of good clogged his mind. Getting his cock sucked by two Elleas while a third watched was a fantasy he hadn't known he possessed. It made him wonder what else they could do. She had said her feelings were intensified when she made more of herself. The thought of his princess sitting back and watching, enjoying every second of it, made his cock grow hard. Sam kicked him under the table, breaking him from his new favorite memory.

"Can you make your boner go away long enough to take us home?" he said with a wicked grin.

Ros grumbled under his breath while adjusting himself. He heard Ellea snicker next to him before he gave her a scathing look. She only blinked at him, sipping her water.

"It's your fault," he said, grabbing her by the chin to kiss her soundly. "I'll see you when I get back, princess."

Both Devon and Sam kissed her on the top of her head before bowing awkwardly to his father. Ros led them out of the dining room.

The three of them stepped out into warm autumn sunlight on Sam's property. Sam's shit-eating grin quickly disappeared, and he took a fighting stance. Ros and Devon followed suit, looking for an attacker.

On Sam's porch stood two snarling vampires. Sitting in a wicker chair like it was a throne was Cerce.

"Get out of my fucking chair," Ros growled. His shadows uncoiled around him, ready to strike.

"Where is my daughter?" she asked, stroking the wicker arm. Ros realized she looked nothing like Ellea. Ellea was all curves and muscles, bright smiles and sparks in her eyes. Cerce was a dull husk of a woman, too thin and bony. Her eyes were dead when they looked up to Ros, and he wondered how she had the power to take down anyone.

"She is not your daughter," Devon snarled next to him.

Ros put up a wall of shadow in front of Devon, blocking Cerce's ability to burrow into his mind. It was something he and Ellea had been working on. The witch didn't seem angry at being blocked; she gave him an evil smirk and appraised him. It felt violating.

"I know my husband went looking for her but sadly came back empty-handed," she said, standing and wiping her hands together.

So she didn't know Cato had gone to Hel. He hadn't given away their location.

Interesting.

"You have two days," she said from the porch. "Or I will begin what I started, where I started it. It's time to finish this."

The vampires grabbed her hands and sped away before Ros could attack.

42

Ellea

Ellea paced the small room at the inn they were staying at. It had been two days since Ros went back to Hel with a murderous glare and fire curling in his restless shadows. Two days of anxiety, training, and scouting the small town of Portsmouth where it all started.

That day, over twenty years ago, Cerce had locked Ellea in the basement. She had been too young to realize what her parents were doing, only that she feared her manic happiness far more than the crazed, torturous teacher. That day, her mother had buzzed with excitement. Her circling conversations with herself had risen to another level of insane, and Ellea remembered shivering at the wild look in her mother's eyes as she closed the basement door. "If you work harder, next time it can be you that I use to bring a new order to our world," she'd said. Ellea had been found two days later when a task force came to their home.

She swallowed past the dryness in her throat and paused to take in the town outside her window.

The small city sat on the coast three hours north of Halifax. Mostly mortals inhabited the tourist spot, and it was the perfect spot for Cerce to lay down destruction once again. With its small cottage homes, the smell of the sea, and what had been bustling streets before all of this, Ellea felt comfortable, like she could live or vacation here. If only she were visiting for other reasons.

Ellea often wondered why her mother and father chose this spot to start their reign of devastation. She didn't think this town was mostly human for any reason that went against supernaturals. But her mother was probably too evil to see past that. The council had been able to evacuate most of the town the day before; she could hear the final cars rolling out. This was it. No matter the outcome, this ended today.

Ellea had been waiting her whole life for this moment. Before her parents had escaped jail, she was barely living, barely reaching for more. Then she met Rosier and her friends, and that all changed. The friends she now called family seemed to be growing with the additions of Duhne, Florence, and even Sebastian. The vampire had been reading one of her books from a chair in the corner.

Azzy was more than a friend; he was the father she never had. He wanted to be here with them. He had grumbled about it for an hour. But Hel couldn't be left without one of the only trustworthy rulers. Duhne and Florence had joined them instead. It was a blessing to have them. What would it have been like if they'd been there on her birthday, the day Sam had been hurt? She would find out soon. She watched Cerce stroll down the small town's road with a group of demons and vampires spread out behind her.

Cato was in the midst of bodies, not beside his wife.

That's odd.

He seemed to be on the edge, glaring at the wild demons beside him. Ros had told her that her father hadn't revealed their meeting to Cerce, but she didn't have time to think about the story he'd told. She didn't want to; it was already chipping away at her hate for him.

"She's here," Billy said as she came to stand with her by the window.

"I know." Ellea glared down with her familiar. She glanced sideways at her, grasping her clawed hand in her own. The night before, they stayed up late talking plans, Dean Winchester, and ways they would torture Cerce. When they both refused to part, Garm ended up joining them in bed. Then Sam and Devon did the same. Ros didn't have the balls to protest, only demanded that Devon make the bed bigger than last time.

Billy brought their joined hands to her mouth, kissed it once, then went back to snarling at the evil bitch standing in the middle of the street.

"Remember the plan: it's Ros and I against the two psychopaths. You work on the vampires and demons. Don't let them get away; I don't trust that the whole town was evacuated, and I want the casualties to be kept to the supernaturals."

"Spoken like a true warrior queen," Devon said, leaning against the doorframe. The small room was getting too crowded. Ellea returned his small smile, grateful for his light in the sea of darkness.

"Thank you for being here, Sebastian." Ellea turned toward the vampire.

He gave her a fanged smile and a wink. "I'm only here for your books and blood."

Devon scowled, but Ros appeared before he could make a remark. Everyone left as Ros strode into the room. She could feel all the emotions he was pouring into the hard look he was giving her. It took everything not to say what she wanted to say as his eyes—flecked with more ember than usual—shone bright. As bright as all the love she felt for him.

After.

Once this was done, once she could breathe, she would tell him.

"Let's make this quick," he said, grasping the back of her neck. "No games and no mercy."

She closed her eyes, breathing out her anxiety and breathing in all that was him—his scent, his dark magic. She felt ready for anything with him beside her.

"No mercy," she said, opening her eyes to meet his fierce stare. "We capture them and bring them to Hel."

Azzy was ready for them; he'd put special spells on their prison cells. They weren't going to stay in this realm; they were no longer allowed to cause destruction here. And they were not allowed to ruin her life anymore.

"I—" She almost said everything, but Cerce's evil voice ruined the moment.

"Come out, daughter," she called. "Or I will set my army on this filthy mortal town."

Ellea took a moment to memorize the way Ros held her and his beautiful face.

"This is it," she said, turning toward the window.

Closing her eyes, she conjured an illusion.

"I'm here, now what?" Ellea sneered, stepping onto the sidewalk and walking a wide arc around Cerce. She noted her father's flinch in the small crowd, but she kept her eyes trained on the woman.

"Now, I teach you a lesson I should have taught you a long time ago."

"It didn't work then, and I don't think it will work now." She gave her a wicked grin.

Cerce's face contorted with concentration as she sent a fearful vision into Ellea's mind. She crumpled in pain, feeling the rocks and gravel bite into her palms and dig through her thick jeans.

"You dumb girl," Cerce hissed, leaning over her huddled form. "I thought you would have at least hidden from me. You loved doing it when you were an insolent child."

Ellea whined and writhed, begging her to stop. Cerce only cackled, so consumed by her torturing that she didn't see the illusion. Ellea's echo reached up, grasping the vile woman by the hair and yanking her to the ground.

The yelp from Cerce was so delicious. It took all her strength to stop her echo from trying to summon its own sharp object and tear more noises from her. "Sorry, *Mother*, I'm not the real Ellea. But that doesn't mean I don't want to seek my own vengeance."

Ellea reeled in her magic, and her echo pouted as she began to shimmer into nothing. Cerce let out a hiss, searching around them as the echo disappeared with a middle finger held in front of her. The vampires and demons clawed at the air, twitching as they waited for the call to attack.

As soon as the illusion disappeared, Ros let loose a ring of fire, cutting off the demons and vampires from Cerce and Cato. While Ellea was distracting her, Cerce didn't see the group of her friends taking their positions. They would kill any of the demons or vampires that didn't surrender.

Ellea reminded herself of the goal: quick and no games. Her powers screamed at her to go back to toying with Cerce. She was desperate to repay all of the torture she'd endured, to get revenge for all of the innocent mortals and supernaturals she'd killed. But she wouldn't—not now.

Quick, no mistakes. We'll get to play back in Hel.

That quelled her powers slightly, and Ellea walked up to stand beside Ros. Her powers crackled in her veins as her mother snarled.

"Tricky little child."

"I'm not a child anymore, and you don't control me."

Ellea let her powers radiate out, creating fifty Ellea and Ros illusions. They all descended on the evil witch, cursing her and everything she'd ever done.

"Cato! Do something, you imbecile!"

Cerce missed the eye roll her father gave as she was swallowed in a mass of bodies. He released a round of electricity, but it was barely a caress, and the illusions didn't falter. He was holding back. Ellea shook her head.

I don't have time to think about this.

A slither of Ros' shadows snaked around Cerce's ankle, yanking her to the ground. She threw her own magic at Ros, trying to blind him. She missed, hitting an illusion that dissolved in a glimmer of smoke. Cerce was quick to get up; she had so much power for an evil and frail witch. She threw her arms out, blanketing them with her attack. Ros struck, throwing up a wall of shadow to stop her blow. Cerce screamed in frustration, and Ellea snuck closer—so close.

Cato let out another false wave of electricity, appeasing Cerce as the witch bellowed again.

"Enough games," she yelled. "You can't hide behind your illusions forever. I will always come back; I will always be here."

Another attack crept out, sneaking into Ellea's mind. She screamed once, but it was enough to show the real her. A flash of flame and heat tore through her mind. She was burning, and the person administrating the torture was not her mother, but Ros.

Not real.

As quickly as it came, roaring with a newfound fear, it was gone. Ros, the man she loved and knew would never hurt her, sent a wave of shadow to smother Cerce. But it was too late. She stormed to the real Ellea.

Lightning cracked through her mind and all around her as a storm rolled in. Ros put up another wall of shadow and flame, giving Ellea a moment to shake off the vision and conjure another illusion. She managed to create two of herself and scattered as his shield fell. Cato hit him with stronger electricity this time, and Ros turned toward the man with a snarl.

It was only her and Cerce. That was fine. She could do this.

"You failed as a witch and you failed as a daughter," Cerce sang out, her eyes dark with hate and her skin flushed with anger. "We could have done so many great things, the three of us."

"You would have never had us," the three Elleas said together.

"Oh, I will have you, and you will submit—"

"Like your husband?" Ellea interrupted. "He did find me, you know. And he helped kill most of your precious little army."

Another crack of lightning lit up the darkening sky as a gust of cold wind picked up the strands of hairs escaping her braids. Her mother glanced back to where Cato and Ros were battling. Her demon prince blocked an onslaught of electricity with his great sword. Its dark center swallowed the light like it was hungry for it. Each block, each counter-move, got him closer and closer to capturing her father. "Lies," Cerce hissed, turning as the three Elleas closed in. "He cannot go against me."

"He told me the truth, how you caught him, tricked him."

Cerce threw her magic at one of the Elleas, but nothing happened.

"I tricked a great trickster, and soon I will have two in my command."

"Never." Ellea said it with so much certainty that she could feel it in her bones.

The three of them pounced, zigzagging and blocking Cerce's magic. Ellea was so close; she only needed to get the magical cuffs Azzy had given her around the witch's wrists.

Cerce turned, grasping Ellea by the throat—the real Ellea.

"Keep trying, dear daughter," she breathed, and her putrid scent washed over her, making her gag. "You should submit to the vision we've always had."

"There's a new vision, Cerce," Ellea hissed as her throat was crushed. "You're not involved in it."

"You are as dumb now as you were as a child. You cannot win this. I have seen it; I have worked so hard to accomplish total destruction. It is only a matter of time before us godly beings will rule this realm once again."

Ellea fought off the spots of black clouding her vision. Before she left, Azzy had told her about a prophecy given to him by Loki himself.

"You. Will. Never. Be. A. God." Ellea panted as her vision began to fade.

"I don't need you anymore," Cerce bellowed, shaking Ellea's body.

How did she become so strong?

"I should have killed you in the crib, you useless—"

She froze, her words sticking in her throat. She was frozen in time. When Ellea's breath came a little easier, she turned slightly, seeing Cato with his hand out and eyes glowing. He was panting, and Ros moved toward her slowly.

"Sometimes I wish you had, but not anymore," Ellea said, turning to look into her mother's eyes that grew wide with shock. There was no stopping her, no way to claim vengeance without the worry that her mother would try again. Something was pushing her to a new plan, one that meant not everyone was getting out of this alive. Grabbing the sword at her back, Ellea put as much hate and regret into her face as she could. She wanted it to be the last thing the evil woman would see—well, almost the last. She smirked, proving that she wasn't broken; she was whole and her mother was nothing. With a turn of her arm, she drove the sword through Cerce's heart.

Time righted itself as a short scream rang through the street. Ellea crashed to the ground as her mother's lifeless hand released her throat and grabbed at the sword buried in her chest.

Ellea gasped for air, scurrying back as death quickly stole Cerce away. Her eyes were as glassy and dark as they had been when she was alive. As Ellea looked upon the husk of a witch, she felt nothing but sweet relief. It was over. They could get her father and move on.

Movement caught her eye as she looked over at Ros.

No, no, don't—

She hurried to stand, but her legs gave out. She crawled to him. Every slide of her knee, every press of gravel into her palm forced her to wonder how much of this was Cerce pulling the strings. Her father reached for her with his hand that wasn't clutching at his chest, and Ellea couldn't stop the sob that wracked her as she reached for him too.

"No," she croaked, cradling his head in her lap. "She's dead; I killed her, not you. You get to live."

Gray met gray as they stared into each other's eyes. Nothing could give her back the years they'd lost, but they had time. She could learn to forgive him. Learn who he was without *her*.

"I don't," he breathed out. "I couldn't let her take you, and it was worth the cost."

His eyes closed for a moment, his body heaving as the blood vow took hold, tearing apart his body. Ellea shook him; she had read about the consequences, had even looked for a way out of them, but nothing could free him from such a curse, such a promise.

"Stay. I'll forgive you." She sobbed harder as he cried out in pain, and Ros rested his hands on her shoulders. "I'll try and forgive you."

Ellea cursed the Gods and begged for a way out. Tears fell down her face as her father's electric eyes opened to look at her. He reached a twitching hand for her, wiping at her tears as his body calmed. Her parents had never touched her so gently, so lovingly. Somehow, she didn't jerk away from him. She leaned into it, begging again for more time. The lightning in his eyes began to flicker.

"Find Loki," he said, taking a final breath as the magic in him died. "I have loved you since the beginning."

He stilled in her arms, and Ellea screamed, screamed for all the hate and years lost, screamed for the father she never had or would have. If she could kill her mother again, she would. She would travel to the pits of Hel and find Cerce's ravaged soul. She would teach that foul woman what torture really was.

Her body wracked with pain as she closed his eyes and brushed away his hair. Never again would a trickster suffer for what they were. It was a promise and a curse to whoever would stop her. The weight on her shoulders disappeared as a thud and a clink of armor sounded behind her. With her father still in her lap, she turned to see Ros being dragged away by two of Hel's guards.

43

Rosier

Ros didn't have time to register what was happening. He had his hands on Ellea, holding her as she grieved, and then he was on his ass, looking up at two of Beelzebub's guards.

"What the fuck?" he cursed, trying to get away.

That battle had gone by quickly, and he wondered how his friends were doing. He wondered if Ellea's parents were only a small part of this fucked-up situation. Maybe Cato's sacrifice had been enough to save him from the pits and Beelzebub's torture. Well, not his; his uncle was too lazy for that, but he employed the nastiest demons.

"Ros?" Ellea called, her voice thick with emotion.

Later; he would figure this all out later. His magic screamed and burned as he was dragged farther away from her. He threw shadows at the beasts, grabbing them by the ankles. They both fell to the ground with pained thuds.

I don't have time for this.

He jumped to his feet only to find soldiers with their swords drawn. They were surrounded by the destruction the little battle had left. Windows were shattered, cars overturned. The council would have to pay to fix things—and then some more things after Ros finished with these assholes.

Their cold dead eyes were pools of blackness as they glared at Ros. Their dark armor glinted with menace, and soon they would be covered with blood. They all readied into battle formation, slapping their breastplates once and then widening their stances, ready to attack.

"Fuck."

He turned to look at Ellea, catching her gently laying her father's head on the ground. He wanted to buy her more time, but life was cruel; she would not get the chance to grieve. That would have to wait. Turning back, Belias emerged from the group of soldiers.

"Fucking Belias," Ellea hissed, coming up behind him and wiping at her face.

"What do you want, cousin?" Ros sneered.

He could still hear the snarls of demons and vampires in the distance as their friends' battle still raged. He could portal to them quickly—it was a short distance—but curiosity kept him rooted to the spot.

"Peace, love, and Hel," Belias said with a smirk. "Not in that order."

Belias looked toward Ellea, and Ros wanted to carve his eyes out for the way he appraised her. He would carve his eyes out when this was over anyway. Belias was out of chances.

"Hello, Ellea," Belias said with a bow. He went to say something else, but a giant iridescent beast bolted from a nearby street and wrapped its massive maw around his body as if it were nothing. The beast bounded around a stop sign as the guards watched their "leader" get swept away, drool coating his pristine suit. They didn't move until Belias shouted, "Seize them!"

After a second of confused glances, they turned and attacked. He and Ellea groaned with exhaustion, and she looked toward her dead mother. Ros knew she wanted her sword, so he wrapped his shadows around the hilt and whipped it toward her waiting hand.

"Thanks, big man." She smiled weakly.

They were taking a long vacation when this was over. Somewhere sunny, where she could have endless margaritas and could fill her time with reading and fucking. He wanted to see her free of worry, skin flushed from the sun and all the ways he would worship her.

"Almost there," he promised, and then lunged to the right as she took the left.

They clashed and roared. Ellea's electricity made short work of a handful of soldiers. He would try and not kill them all to leave a few for questioning later. How did Belias get out of Hel, and what the fuck was he doing? He hadn't even blinked at the sight of Cerce and Cato's bodies. Ros thought he would've cared a little since they had been conniving for Gods knew how long.

Months ago, Belias had offered to partner with him, and Ros cursed himself for not looking into it more. What was the point? Why would he want alliances? The rulers of Hel all had their places, plenty of power, and time to live whatever life they wanted. Why search for more? And why involve Ellea's parents? Bel would have to be the biggest idiot if he'd thought that would work. Whatever his endgame, it wouldn't be worth it.

Ros shot a wave of helfire at ten soldiers, incinerating them where they stood. They didn't even have time to scream. Even though he wavered slightly from such an intense use of power, the beast inside him roared for more. It was ready to give its all to stop the attack, to make sure Ellea was safe. He hated himself for not listening to his beast, for ignoring the signs and smothering it under all the darkness and ash. They had the same goal: get Ellea, keep her safe, and love her forever. If only he had realized that sooner.

Two soldiers came for him with swords raised. Lunging back, his heart slowed as he readied to counter-attack. With his exhale, he landed a dagger in the thigh of one and turned to come down on the other with his sword. He breathed in, stepping back before burying his sword under their armor. As he pulled back, blood and innards fell to the ground. Ellea's roar had him turning, catching her shocking two men until they were unconscious, foam spilling from their mouths.

"Let's keep two alive, princess." He scooped her into his arms quickly, kissing her with so much passion before depositing her back on her feet for another attack.

"I'll do my best."

He sent a wave of razor-sharp shadows at another huddled group, slicing and cutting them as they ran toward them. Blood sprayed, mixing with his shadows. He had five left to Ellea's seven. They were close, so close.

He shouted out as a soldier caught him in the thigh with his sword. Pain shot through his knee as he crashed to the ground.

That one is dead.

Ros growled, impaling the soldier through the chin. Ellea cut down two more as she tried to get to him. She was almost caught by a soldier as she lunged for him, still on the ground.

"I'm okay. Focus," he called to her, finding the strength to stand.

Ellea faltered slightly, but shook her head and got another soldier in the gut with her sword without even turning. His cock pulsed, a weak attempt with how much pain he was in and how weak he was, but the sight of her so ruthless and powerful...he couldn't suppress the way his body reacted to it. She gave him a tired smirk, seeming to read his thoughts. She had used so much magic, and he was sure the beast she'd conjured was sucking her dry. He would ask her to do it again later just to watch it tear Belias' limbs from his body.

Ros stumbled back, limping as blood gushed from his leg. Four soldiers sneered at him as he took a steadying breath. With the last of his magic, he wrapped shadows around the gash, stopping the blood and supporting his weight. Ellea's war cry rang around him, and she was left with a few unmoving soldiers at her feet and three soldiers glaring at her.

Good girl.

"Come on, bastards," Ros jeered.

They lunged, and Ros decided he didn't need any of them alive. Slicing the throat of one, he reared back, kicking another. His bad leg buckled, allowing a soldier to hit him in the back of the head with the hilt of his sword. Ros crashed to his knees, and visions flashed before his eyes. Visions of Ellea, his love for her and all he wanted to give her. All he ever wanted was slipping through his grasp, and it left him feeling hollow and empty.

"Enough," Belias called out.

His black suit was shredded and soaked as he limped around the corner. He looked to be covered in slobber and black blood. Ros wanted to laugh. Belias wiped at his face and sneered at all of them.

The two guards left placed their swords on Ros' shoulder, sandwiching his head between the sharp blades. Ellea finished off the final male that had tried running from her. She zapped him and he fell face-first to the ground. She reached forward, ready to do the same to Belias.

"Enough, or he dies, Ellea."

"Fight me, you bastards!"

443

"Stop, and we will take him back to Hel instead of killing him in front of you."

"No."

"It's okay," Ros said as Belias conjured a portal behind him.

A soldier grasped him by the collar of the shirt, ready to drag him through the swirling darkness. He studied her face while cursing the Gods. How dare they dangle this perfect creature before him only to have it ripped away by his snake of a cousin? Under the dirt and tears, she was fierce, and her eyes began to glow as her magic reached for him.

"It will be okay, princess," Ros said as a tear escaped him.

He would go, and he wouldn't fight. Their friends would be there soon to help her while he—

"No," she breathed out. Her hair began to float, and he saw the power she would unleash.

"I love you," Ros said as he was dragged into the darkness.

The vision of Ellea burned into his mind. Her shock at his confession, the tendrils of magic that reached for him. Her power raged as the portal closed around them; it turned into a speck of light in the blackness and shadows. Then, blinding light blasted around him as he was plucked from darkness. A wicked grin floated before him, one that reminded him so much of Ellea.

✦∴TRICKY PRINCESS∴✦

44

Ellea

"I love you," Ros said as he was swallowed by darkness before her tendrils of light could reach him.

Her magic dug at the concrete as if it could burrow to Hel and get him back.

I love you.

His words repeated in her head as his devastated face flashed before her eyes. She knew they were still glowing with white-hot rage; the world around her was brighter, more intense. She felt full to the brim with power and endless possibilities, but her heart felt empty.

I love you.

She hadn't said it back. Not that she had the chance and she would hunt Belias down and rip out his heart for taking that from her. She needed to get to Hel; maybe she could save him before it was too late.

Garm!

Garm could get her to Hel. She went to race to her friends as two final snarls rang in the distance. Her eyes fell on her father in the distance, his still body. If Beelzebub had his soul, she would fight to get it back. She would travel to the off-limits part of Hel, torture Cerce for a bit, then get her father to his rightful place, back to the other trickster souls. She suppressed a sob; she would grieve later. Ellea stopped as her magic's blinding light reignited. But it wasn't her magic. A white-gold portal crackled to life where Ros had been ripped from her. Her heart raced, and she had to shield her eyes from the blinding light.

Gray horns tipped with gold materialized first, then wavy dark hair, a wicked grin, and freckles. Ethereal eyes took her in, and Ellea gasped at the magnificent male standing before her. It took her a moment to realize that he had someone grasped by the collar, dangling in front of him. Another crouched on the ground before his feet.

"Hello, princess," the stunning male said. "I am Loki."

"No!" the male in his grasp yelled, and Loki turned toward him with a sneer.

She blinked away tears caused by the light and power radiating around him to see that it was Belias.

Rosier.

Ellea looked down, ignoring the call in the back of her mind that a God was standing before her. She ran to him, to Ros, who was looking up at Loki.

"Ros!" Ellea yelled, cursing her feet for not moving faster.

Ros turned and ran, eating up the distance and crashing into her. She grasped him by the face as he lifted her.

He's here. He's whole.

Her magic sang as it was reunited with him; she felt it embrace his large body, all that was him. Ellea searched his face, his beautiful eyes and perfect lips. His beard scratched at the palm of her hand. She would chain him to her; never again would they be ripped from each other.

She went to tell him everything, but was cut off by another whine.

"I was promised Hel!" Belias screeched, turning in Loki's grasp to point at Ros. "All I needed was to get rid of you."

They both turned and looked at him, still dangling a foot above the ground. The snake was still going to die; she only hoped Loki would give her a chance to rip off some body parts before he laid into him. Or that's what Ellea thought he wanted to do as he glared at the demon.

"Tell me more," Loki said in a devilish voice that seemed to echo through her body. The baritone of it spoke of all things old and not of their world.

Belias gulped once before pressing his mouth closed, shaking his head with a whimper. The God rolled his eyes and threw the demon about twenty feet. Before he hit the ground, he screamed and was swallowed into another portal of white-gold light. Loki turned his eyes back to them, their glowing light dimmed to a grayish gold color that churned like the sea.

Gods, he was tall.

Not *giant* tall, but maybe seven feet. Was that giant size? Ellea cleared her thoughts, ready to go back to telling Ros all that she needed to, but as Loki opened his mouth to speak, she knew it would have to wait.

"We have some work to do, prin—" His commanding voice was cut off by Sam and Devon rushing toward them..

"We got them all," Sam said proudly, swiping his hands with a loud smack. "Duhney Bug and Florence are beginning cleanup, and Seb is calling their sires. We wanted to check. Billy and Garm are—who the fuck are these soldiers? Oh no, your parents are dead! Who the fuck are you?"

Sam's face contorted from pride to sadness to confusion so fast that Ellea felt like she was watching a cartoon character. He openly eyed the God before him, from his gold-tipped horns down to his emerald satin pants. The wolven shivered and stumbled, curling in his finger that had been pointing at a being who could wipe him off the face of the earth in a blink.

Ros set Ellea down. She swallowed past so much emotion clogging her throat. This was not something they could have predicted; it was beyond anything they had planned.

"Er...Sam, Devon..." She paused, wondering how to introduce them to a God. "Apparently, this is Loki."

The loudest silence she ever felt snaked around them like a fog. Then, Devon screamed—screamed so embarrassingly high-pitched— before fainting to the ground. His body was a pile of noodles, and Loki chuckled in a low grumble that caused Sam to blush profusely.

"As I was saying," Loki began, but Ellea wasn't having any of that.

"Nope," she said, holding up her hand to the giant of a God before her. "Before we get interrupted again and before you send us on yet another death mission, I would like to talk to my demon boyfriend who decided to say 'I love you' before he was dragged off to go die."

Loki's mouth shut with a snap. He squinted at her slowly, assessing her, then he bowed, allowing her to continue.

Ellea turned back to Ros, grasping him by the shirt to pull him close to her. His eyes were wide with wonder and shock.

"You said 'I love you,'" Ellea whispered as she ignored Sam's gushing *oh my Gods* over and over again.

"I did," he said, closing some of the distance between their lips.

"Say it again."

The sky cleared around them, and her restless magic calmed, waiting. How had they gotten to this point? How did one hiccup all those months ago in Halifax lead to this moment?

"I love you, Ellea," he said, both dimples showing as he smiled. "I have loved you for longer than I knew, and I wish I told you sooner."

A tear escaped Ellea's eye, running down through the rivulets of her earlier ones. Closing her eyes for a moment, she basked in Ros' warmth and scent.

"I love you, Rosier," she breathed, and when she opened her eyes, his shone with unshed tears. "I don't know when, but I'm pretty sure I loved you first."

She smirked at him before his mouth was on hers, consuming her and her confession as Sam continued to freak out about them, about Loki—it didn't matter. All that mattered was they were whole, they were alive, and they would continue on.

"This is going to be fun," Loki said.

EPILOGUE
Noema

"The binding of the Gods' chosen and its promised will amend the lapse of the realms. The chosen must seek out the Creator Of Chaos and Bringer Of Shadows. Until they are forged, there will only be death." Noema gagged out the words as she overlooked the embrace in the street below her. Her talons scraped along the windowpane, desperate to claw out the eyes of those two imbeciles. They had escaped her plan. Twenty-eight years of setup hadn't been enough. The room still smelled of *her*—electric, soft, and powerful—and the demon that was grossly grabbing her ass.

"Gods' chosen, my ass," Noema cursed.

They were her words, spoken eons ago when those weak Gods had entered her realm and taken over all she had created. Speaking the prophecy out loud was one of her biggest regrets. Her second biggest regret was the bodies in the street below, useless to her now. They'd been a waste of time; they couldn't bring the heir to her. She would not let the prophecy come true, even if she had been the one to speak it, damning herself from the worship and power she deserved.

The Goddess clawed three Xs into the window over the heads of those who would die. They would not outsmart her; she had created the very earth they were standing on. All she needed was to out-trick a trickster. She cackled, and then bright, ethereal eyes turned to her from the street below. She let out a snarl; only he could see and hear, no matter the distance. With a hateful wave of her fingers, Noema shimmered into a wisp of gray shadows, ready to set a new plan in motion.

⁕ TRICKY PRINCESS ⁕

EPILOGUE

Ellea

The leaves were changing in the supernatural territory as Hel's autumn fully took over. Ellea had begun wearing thicker clothing on her outings with the souls, mostly to appease Ros, who was as protective as ever. It had been a month since the fight. Loki kept appearing at the oddest times, never being seen outside of her immediate group. He had told her he wasn't ready to be fully present, but he was there to help clean up the mess.

There had been a cult involved, information they'd gathered from the vampires they'd left alive. They had been capturing women and children to fill the pews to worship a new Goddess. Except she wasn't new at all, but the oldest of all the Gods, even older than Loki and those that had rested with him. They'd dismantled the cult, and the council had given those affected a way to get back on their feet.

Loki also said that he believed the Goddess, Noema, was behind the actions of her parents—or at least her mother. Ellea wasn't sure that was fully true; she couldn't bring herself to believe that her torment and torture hadn't been her mother's fault. If that were true, then she would be in the supernatural territory with her father.

The Gods' magic had deemed him worthy, depositing him in the wooded lands, surrounded by his family. Ellea watched on from a distance as he talked animatedly with fellow witches and tricksters. She couldn't stop the tears that fell as Ros' strong arms wrapped around her. He always came with her when she checked on her father and walked with the souls. He'd even started to help her move them to their rightful places.

"That's your family too," he mumbled against her hair and brushed a kiss across her temple.

She couldn't respond as so much hate and love circled her chest. Her father was free from the clutches of his wife and a Goddess who had some part in it. He was with those he loved after spending his life alone and afraid. But she felt jealous, like she was missing out on what they could have had. And that made her feel guilty since her days were spent being loved and surrounded by those she loved.

"I hate this."

Ros squeezed her tighter. "I know, princess."

"I love it, but I hate it so much. I just want to see him and I want him to know me."

The only way for her father to know who she was to join him in the afterlife. She turned in Ros' arms, smothering her face into his warm chest that rumbled under her.

"We'll come back tomorrow and the next day." He squeezed her tight, kissing the top of her head. "But we have to go."

She groaned. They had a feast to attend, one to celebrate all the

Gods had done for this realm. Beelzebub's court weren't invited; they were banished from all meetings, events, and balls. Belias was still in the pits where Loki left him. That was yet another thing they were sorting out.

"You're lucky I love you." It was barely heard in the fabric of his shirt, then she smiled. Even though she was sad, she had love. They whispered it to each other every morning and night and when they were wrapped around each other so deeply that their magic became one.

Ros peeled her face from his chest, grasping her chin so he could give her a warm glare, "First, I love you more. Second, you're the one who wants to be here as much as fate does. Welcome to your new life in Hel, princess."

With one last teary look to her father, who was laughing so freely, she left. They had work to do.

THE END FOR NOW.
SEE YOU SOON, WITCHES!

Billy & Garm

Billy took in the surrounding grounds from her high perch on the balcony. The stone was cold under her palms as she breathed in the night air. She pulled the air deeply into her lungs, holding it until her lungs screamed, and released it on a shaky breath. It did little to quell the itch that was constant, the anxiety that ghosted across her skin. Even the sight of two of her favorite males leaving the thick trees in the distance didn't help the dread, the feeling. That all the heartache that had happened was nothing compared to what would come. She thought about catcalling them— her supernatural sight would let her watch Devon blush from his ears to his bare feet—but she didn't. She only let the love she felt for them splash against her anxious heart. A smile tugged her lips as they laughed at something she couldn't hear. They clung to one another on their way to the castle, not a hair of distance between their bodies.

Each day made it harder for her to be carefree, to flirt and joke with those she cared for. How could it not after everything they had been through? But she didn't need to fake her bravado from the safety of Garm's quarters. So she took another breath, begging it to ease the ache. Billy's eyes drifted to the low light of Ellea's room. It was enough to ruin any progress she'd made. Her little witch, her best friend, the girl she loved more than anything, had been through so much. Thinking of everything Ellea had to carry after losing her father and learning so much about herself had her chest yawning open in pain. Her claws came out on their own. Billy knew deep in her gut that this was why she was in a constant state of worry. Everything horrible that had happened until now was only the start.

Warm arms wrapped around her middle, shaking her from her thoughts. The kiss on her shoulder almost soothed her—almost.

"Come back to bed," Garm grumbled against her cooling skin.

Billy scoffed and then choked as a black fox left the treeline where Devon and Sam had come from. Was Loki watching her friends' little hunt and romp through the woods?

Probably.

"I can't get used to your father being back," she said, ignoring his request to leave her perch.

Garm rubbed his scruffy beard across her skin and nuzzled her neck. "We knew he would be back one day."

She huffed a breath, remembering the day Loki had left them, leaving behind an entire realm of responsibility. There was a small part of her that wished she'd retired with them. She may not be as old as Loki and Garm, but she was older than this place, and she was getting tired. Regret had her glancing to Ellea's window again.

No, she didn't want that.

She would never regret giving up being a valkyrie for protecting the Gods' children. She was still a warrior, but she had traded battlefields for claws and war cries for guiding young trickster witches.

Garm squeezed her, seeming to feel the vibrations of her inner battle, and gently tried to pry her back to the room. "Come back to bed."

"I won't be able to sleep."

"It's been weeks." He bit down on her shoulder, and the jolt it sent through her whole body had her mind blissfully blank for a moment. "We can't solve all the problems tonight. Our family is here, they are safe, and probably resting after tonight's festivities. You need to rest too."

He was probably right. They had spent hours dancing and feasting in Hel's grand ballroom. The night had been a whirl of autumn colors and smiles. It was the first time in weeks that they'd all acted and reveled as though Ellea hadn't lost a father and their lives weren't hanging in the balance. The courts and kings had partied as though war wasn't on the horizon—only three of the courts, though. Beelzebub's court was banished until Asmodeus could figure out what to do with them. He'd said he would after the feast, making tomorrow feel like the start to something horrible.

Billy would have never guessed she would be back in Hel celebrating what the Gods had done for both realms. They'd included her in those that were celebrated since she'd been in the group that had stepped through worlds to leave a warring race and start anew. Her mind was a constant storm of anxious thoughts of Gods, new challenges, and her grieving witch; she could accept that she needed a reprieve.

I won't be able to sleep unless…

Garm, ever aware of her moods and needs, growled against her skin. He turned her, grasping her thighs and seating her on the narrow ledge of the balcony. Her legs wrapped around him instinctively, pulling him close so she could steal his body heat, begging for a distraction.

"Do you need me to demand it of you? Tell you what you need and make sure you're taken care of?" His question had shivers running across her skin.

Billy rolled her hips, watching his eyes flash red in the darkness. It lit his handsome features, ones that made him look like he was stone carved by an ancient and brilliant artist. She would never tire of all that was him—ferocity, darkness, and ancient beauty. "Please."

"I should deny you. Maybe you would listen if I didn't give in to you so easily." He grasped her by the back of the neck, kissing her so roughly that it stole her breath. "I need you as much as you need me. As much as you need to be taken care of."

"What I need is for you to bury your face in my pussy and put me out of my misery. If that doesn't work, bend me over any surface of your choosing and force me to forget everything."

Claws formed quickly at the tips of his fingers, and her insides melted as he tore at her underwear. It left her in only the oversized shirt she'd stolen from his side of the bed. He tore that too, her breasts freeing to the cold air. Her nipples painfully peaked as he walked his fingers up the planes of her chest to grasp her throat.

He was rough but loving, but that didn't stop the rage ringing in her ears as he teased, "Look at you using your words like a big girl."

She hissed. He *tsk*ed, but the bastard dropped to his knees before she could snap back. His chuckle warmed her already wet skin, and instead of cursing him, she moaned. She moaned long and low as the flat of his tongue roved over her clit, sending jolts of pleasure through her. Her body reacted to him too quickly, recognizing him and giving him anything he asked of her. She cursed her traitorous lady parts that caused a shriek to wrench from her throat as his tongue drove in and out of her.

"I could taste you for eons and never tire of your sweetness." He nipped at her thigh and she melted. "Your soul might be hard and your words sharp, but this pussy sure as Hel knows how to soften and swell for me."

"Yes."

"Only me. This is mine. It's not even yours, is it?"

She refused to answer, but he chuckled as the clenching around his newly inserted fingers gave her denial away. He owned her body and soul, but it wouldn't escape her lips. Well, her lips that spoke were sealed against her admittance; the ones he was spreading with his large fingers gave her away every time. Always wet for him, always accepting how large he was, and that knot... It was mind-blowing how she could stretch around him.

The ache in her belly was drowning out her anxious thoughts. A hazy need for him twirled around her brain as he circled her bud with his rough tongue. Stretching her with his fingers, the obscene wet sounds mixed with the rustling of birds and beasts below. There was a heady rush from how high up she was, how she balanced on the ledge, anchored only by her hands and her legs thrown over his shoulders.

She ground into him, chasing her release, her breasts swaying with the frantic pumps of her hips.

"Garm," she moaned, and he answered by hollowing out his cheeks, sucking on her flesh, and meeting each of her desperate movements with a plunge of his fingers. She was so close. Her eyes wanted to close, but she forced them open—she wanted to watch him, watch his beautiful face framed by her tan legs as he continued to chase her anxious thoughts away. It was only him and the stars...unless someone gazed out of a window. The thought of being on display for anyone to see was enough to push her over the edge. Marble crumbled under her hands as she found purchase with claws and shaking hands.

Her hips bucked wildly as she cursed him and his perfect mouth. Her face tingled, and there were no thoughts as her orgasm wrung her dry. There was only the blood that rushed to every pulse point, pulsing in time with the flutter of her core.

She panted, her eyes blurring as she continued to gaze down at him, seeing her release coating her chin. She felt so much hate and love for him. Hate for how weak he made her, how she always ached for him, and how he would one day let her down again. She fought the thoughts and lost herself in him again, bringing him to bed. She rode him till her body was languid and sleep was the only other thing she could give in to.

Author's Note

Thank you so much for reading the second book in my first series. Sometimes it was hard but these characters made it so worth it. Rosier was a freaking pain at first and Ellea was a goddess the whole time lol. I hope you enjoy this book and I cannot wait to hear what you think. Unless it's bad, then feel free to put it on Goodreads 'cause I won't go there. Remember, reviews are for readers so be nice and don't tag authors in a bad review. Even if you think you're trying to help them, you aren't.

WANT MORE?

Facebook Group: L.L. Campbell's Smutling Society
Instagram: @authorllcampbell
TikTok: @authorllcampbell
Patreon: patreon.com/authorllcampbell
Sign up for my newsletter to get exclusive awesomeness!
Website: llcampbell.com

Acknowledgments

There have been so many people to make this second book possible. Even outside of everyone listed below. If you don't see your name, please know I see you and thank you for all you have done to support me. For all of those sending me messages about how they love these characters and the world I built, thank you! I thank you endlessly.

To Chris: You make everything possible and worth it. I love you more than anything and I don't know where I would be if you didn't walk into my life and ordered the sugariest drink all those years ago. Thank you for putting up with all of this and telling me I could do anything.

To Ash: Gods, you made this easier. Thank you for listening to my ramblings, not making me feel crazy, and just being singularly the best person ever. You get to touch these characters first and they are who they are because of you. I love you!

To RaeAnne: You have been an amazing editor and it has been a joy to work with you. I appreciate all you have done for this series and thanks to you, I'm proud of my work.

To Elizianna: You made my characters come to life. I will forever be grateful for you, for what you do, and for how amazing you are! Mon ami, je t'aime!

To Leez & Diamond: Thank you for being the first ones to read Tricky Princess when it was at its worst. And for not telling me it was crap lol, you helped make it so much more.

To Jess, Gabbie, and Britt: Thank you for always having my back and always supporting TMS even though you all are so busy doing amazing things. I adore and love you all so much!

The Street Team: Thank you all so much for being a fucking blast-and-a-half! You all have made it possible to exceed my goals and get this series out in the world. I swear, one day I will drink a bottle of wine for you and write that...one scene. I love you all and you're a blessing!

To my ARC Team and Patrons: THANK YOU! Thank you for the support, love, and always being there. Thank you for the reviews, shares, and accepting my craziness.

Everyone in my DMs: Gods, you make my days so much better. Please know I see you and sometimes I'm overwhelmed, but you have my love.

To Scarlett and Corrine: You both have been a dream to have in my life. All the guidance, support, and perspective made everything even more possible. Thank you, a thousand times thank you!

To all four of my parents: Thank you for the tequila, not pushing me off a cliff with my crankiness, saying you would go to bat for me, and just being amazing. I love you all so much and I can't believe you're supportive of your daughter writing demon smut, ha!

To you, my smutty readers: Thank you from the bottom of my dark and witchy heart. This was a story just for me, but knowing there are so many of you out there who love these characters as much as I do has been a gift from all the shadow daddies.

www.ingramcontent.com/pod-product-compliance
Lightning Source LLC
Chambersburg PA
CBHW030848030726
47495CB00005B/1427